Gwenda Bond is the *New Yo*
novels, including the first offic
Minds, as well as the Match
American series. She lives in a
Kentucky, with a veritable zoo
(including a border collie name
as Sunflower). She writes a regular newsletter, *Dear Reader*, at
gwendabond.substack.com.

gwendabond.com
Twitter: @Gwenda

Praise for *The Frame-Up*:

'Between a sheepdog escape artist, a monstrous painting,
a team of eccentric criminals, a finest art thief ever to
get her heart broken, *The Frame-Up* is tense, romantic, and
clever and makes grand larceny more fun than ever before.'
**Holly Black, *New York Times* bestselling
author of *Book of Night***

'*The Frame-Up* is Gwenda Bond at her absolute best:
magical, romantic, and fun as hell. Dani and her crew
will leave your pockets empty and your heart full.'
Alix E. Harrow, *New York Times* bestselling author

'A clever art heist, a smoldering old flame, an irresistible found
family tied together through magic, Gwenda Bond's *The
Frame-Up* is a twisty, riveting, and fantastically original story.'
**Elle Cosimano, *New York Times* bestselling
author of *Finlay Donovan Is Killing It***

'Magic, mystery, and a daring art heist set the stage for
Gwenda Bond's twisty, delightful read! Brimming with
secrets, danger, and intrigue, *The Frame Up* explores the lure
of power, the bonds of friendship, and the legacy of family.
Clever, suspenseful, and impossible to put down.'
**Megan Miranda, *New York Times* bestselling
author of *The Only Survivors***

Also by Gwenda Bond

THE DATE FROM HELL

MR. & MRS. WITCH

NOT YOUR AVERAGE GUY

SUSPICIOUS MINDS (An official Stranger Things novel)

THE
FRAME-UP

Gwenda Bond

WILDFIRE

First published in 2024 by
WILDFIRE
an imprint of HEADLINE PUBLISHING GROUP

First published in paperback in 2024 by
WILDFIR4
an imprint of HEADLINE PUBLISHING GROUP

1

Cataloguing in Publication Data is available from the British Library

ISBN 978 1 0354 1584 7

Offset in 9.98/13.3 pt New Caledonia LT Std by Jouve (UK), Milton Keynes

Printed and bound in Great Britain by Clays Ltd, Elcograf S.p.A.

Headline's policy is to use papers that are natural, renewable and recyclable
products and made from wood grown in well-managed forests and other
controlled sources. The logging and manufacturing processes are expected
to conform to the environmental regulations of the country of origin.

HEADLINE PUBLISHING GROUP
an Hachette UK Company
Carmelite House
50 Victoria Embankment
London
EC4Y 0DZ

www.headline.co.uk
www.hachette.co.uk

For Lisa Haneberg,

who would plan an impeccable heist

The name "con artist" really does capture it. They're artists, and I have admiration for all artists.

—Maria Konnikova

TEN DAYS OUT

CHAPTER ONE

DANI WAS SETTLED at a sticky back table in the empty dive bar, waiting, when the mark arrived.

Tad Russell, attorney-at-law and cheating shitheel, had someone who looked like a bodyguard with him, and Dani wondered if this meet was going to be more complicated than expected. She hadn't decided where to go after St. Louis yet, because of her more immediate cash-flow problem. She was broke, so this job needed to work out. Him bringing a gym rat along wasn't a good sign.

Dani's dog, Sunflower, growled without taking her head off Dani's foot, throat vibrating against her leather boot.

Sunflower's radar for the rotten rivaled Dani's own. Most people looked at the dog and saw a lean, smiling border collie. They missed how smart she was, how sharp her teeth were. They had that in common too.

"I hear you," Dani murmured and Sunflower subsided.

The mark spotted Dani and his chin ticked up. Bravado was an interesting choice, given the way he'd visibly sweated through his dress shirt. He could've hidden that by wearing his suit jacket, but he chose comfort instead. Just as he could have one less witness without his plus-one. You can tell a lot about people by the stupid decisions they make.

He'd made plenty to end up here. But then, so had Dani.

Dani nodded to indicate the chairs on the other side of the scarred table. The legs scraped the floor as the two men took them. The bodyguard type had a salt-and-pepper beard and didn't quite hide the wince as he sat. Bad knees. He also had a weak chin and a certain kind of meanness around the eyes. Dani sized him up immediately: former law enforcement.

The bartender was the only other person here with them. The Meet and Greet was a shoebox-sized establishment that probably hadn't been the site of an actual meet-cute in decades, if ever. Her brief encounter with the bartender told her that he'd never been a hero. Dani was on her own. Which . . . fine. Safer that way.

She believed that, most of the time.

"Tad, you rented yourself an ex-cop . . . Given why you're here, I'm surprised." She focused on the friend with the muscles. "Has he told you what he did?"

"He told me some little blond girl from out of town is trying to shake him down."

Dani was average-sized, not little. And, at twenty-seven, not a girl, but a woman—although she was fine with the term "girl" when it wasn't being used by a guy like this. She had no quibbles with the blond or the shaking-down or the out-of-town parts. Those were facts. But she wasn't *trying* anything.

"So," Dani said, "I'll take that as a no, then." She leaned in conspiratorially. "How do you two know each other?"

Tad's smile was vintage sleazy lawyer. "I helped him put some crooks away."

That was *really* how he was playing this? She took in the ex-cop again. "You and I may have more in common than I assumed. You liked making sure the bad guys got theirs?"

"I don't—" He squinted and then said, "Yes."

Tad frowned.

Dani reached down into her bag and extracted her folder on Tad without taking her eyes off either of them. She placed it on her side of the table. Tad's hands gripped each other; it took effort for him not to reach for it.

"Don't worry," she said. "These aren't the photos."

"I don't judge what goes on in people's personal lives," the ex-cop said.

Good for him, Dani supposed. She cared more than she should; she always had. An occupational hazard . . . to her.

But her line of work would be a lot trickier if men like Tad Russell weren't so predictably awful. She'd come to town and hunted down the courthouse, rummaged through court filings to look over current custody disputes to find a promising case. It didn't take long. It never did.

The juiciest stuff in family court is private, so she had paid a visit to the soon-to-be-divorced Mrs. Tad and offered to help her out for access. Mrs. Tad happily agreed. After all, her husband was attempting to take her kids and short her on alimony. His attorney was his business partner, and Facebook showed them both at a fundraiser with the judge assigned to the case. The wife's lawyer went to night school and had been practicing for only two years. None of Tad's colleagues wanted to piss him off, so she was going to get screwed.

Or she was before Dani showed up.

Tad's financial disclosures were on the light side, especially after a few days of following him. He picked up the girlfriend he denied having in a sensible car and took her to a cheap spot for lunch. The house was nice enough, but not a mansion. His wife said he turned cheap two years ago, and before that he spent money like he had an endless supply. Looking at the assets of his firm and weighing them against his sensible lifestyle, the math put itself together. He covered his tracks more carefully than most, but she had done this plenty of times before.

The photos of him and his next wife that Dani snuck into his office after hours and left on his desk were only to get his attention. She needed some account info she correctly figured he kept there.

When she called him, he blustered legal terms. She let him, and then told him to find the blonde with the dog at the Meet and Greet tonight at eight-thirty sharp. But the affair wasn't why he ended up here.

"How many other men has your partner coached to do this?" she asked. She was genuinely curious about that. She lifted a hand before he could answer. "Never mind. Let's get to it."

Her fingers tingled as she flipped open the folder. She could have used magic, falsified the records so he'd accept them as real no matter how off they looked, except she didn't let herself do that anymore. The community had iced her out after what she did. It didn't seem right to use her power.

Yes, she sometimes felt bad about doing this too. She passed the real bank statements she'd retrieved from his office safe across the table anyway.

He launched into a blustery pretense of confusion. "What is this—"

She held up her hand. "Can we not? I know you. You're used to always believing you're the smartest person in the room. But that's not a fixed state," she said. "The smartest person in the room one minute can turn into the biggest idiot you've ever met like that." She snapped her fingers. Sunflower shifted beside her but stayed put.

The mark's eyes narrowed. The cop friend was leaning forward, checking out the rows and columns. "That's not his name up there," he said.

She managed not to sigh. "No, but it's his money in the account. I didn't have time to look up the worst-case scenario for a lawyer caught falsifying assets in a divorce . . . But I know that skimming accounts and lying to the court about it will definitely mean disbarment."

Look at that. Maybe Tad wasn't as dumb as he seemed. He said, "What do you want?"

"Half the money." He grimaced, but she wasn't done. "The rest is your wife's and she gets custody." Behind every thieving man with a fat bank account, there was a woman who deserved more than she had. Dani could take all the money, but she didn't need to. She could make peace with herself and sleep at night this way. Sometimes. And when it ran out, there'd be another mark, and so on, ad infinitum.

"You can't make me give up my kids."

"Oh, buddy." She rustled the paper. "I could, but I won't have to. You just wanted to win, and that's no longer a possibility. I'm sure you'll be happy with overnights and weekends. Like I told you, Tad, I may not be from around here, but I know you."

He looked pleadingly at his ex-cop friend like he was about to suggest he rough up Dani or . . . honestly who knew what? She raised her brows and waited to see which direction this went. The bartender sensed a shift and disappeared into the back. She'd called that one.

The ex-cop pushed back from the table, and like that, he loomed over her. Sunflower growled. Tad grinned.

Shit, she was hoping it wouldn't come to violence. She wasn't expecting *two* of them either, and she didn't love the odds.

But she'd been doing this a long time. He had to transfer the funds or her work was for nothing.

"Go for it," she said, which they would think was for them, but was for Sunflower.

Dani reached beneath her leg to grab the Taser tucked there and lunged toward Tad, planting it between his thighs. Sunflower was growling and nipping at the ex-cop's ankles, darting in and out too fast for him to kick, herding him away from the table. Some border collies herd sheep. Hers herded assholes.

"Now, Tad, have you ever been tased in the balls?" She tried not to take pleasure in how pale his face had gone, how afraid to move he was. "The manual calls it extremely effective."

She glanced over. The ex-cop was still trying to land a blow on Sunflower, but he was an amateur. Her dog was a pro. The best muscle she'd ever met.

"What the fuck—" he said.

Tad blinked. "All right," he said. "All right."

"Tell your friend to sit down."

"Do it," he said, a shake in his voice.

The ex-cop was big mad at being outmaneuvered—literally—by some little blonde and her dog. He huffed, red-faced, but he did as he'd been told.

"Down," Dani said, and Sunflower returned to her side and sank to the floor. Dani reached into her bag and pulled out a tablet, back to business, but keeping the Taser close at hand. "I can help you do the two transfers and sign the custody agreement."

The door opened, interrupting her triumph, and admitting a tall, oddly dressed . . . gentleman. Yes, "gentleman" was the word.

He was slim, pale, with a tailored black coat that hit above his knees. The lines of him were expensive, from his aristocratic face and bearing to his bizarrely out-of-place wardrobe. The Meet and Greet was not a place for suits, let alone evening tails.

All three of them were momentarily stopped by his approach. And, yes, he was approaching.

The stranger had a walking stick with him, black and gleaming, with an ornately carved gold top. He could've stepped out of an old movie. His face was handsome, hair a dark mass of waves, cheekbones sharp, and a full mouth that almost certainly lied with ease. Beneath the long jacket, he wore a suit just as old-fashioned, the crisp white shirt open at the neck.

"I'd like to speak with you," he said to Dani.

"I'm busy right now." Dani didn't like interruptions. She had no idea who this man was. Something about him made her stomach clench and her instincts scream.

"Who are you?" Tad asked, his sexism showing, automatically giving this stranger respect Dani didn't merit until she threatened to electrify his precious manhood. "Are you her partner?"

She really didn't like this.

"I work alone," Dani said, focusing on Tad. "Now to the transfers."

The ex-cop was ready for this to end. "Yeah, Mr. Peanut, we're in the middle of something here."

Mr. Peanut wasn't bad as far as an insult went. The stranger lifted his walking stick and set it back down hard, with a thud that rattled Dani's spine. And Tad's and his friend's too. She saw it in their faces.

"I have business to discuss with this woman, and I don't like waiting," the man said.

At Dani's feet, Sunflower gave a low growl. She didn't like this any more than Dani. Who was this guy to waltz in here and interrupt her, demanding an audience?

The stranger met her eyes and waited.

This man was definitely more dangerous than either of the other two. She hoped she hadn't inadvertently encroached on his turf and pissed him off. None of her jobs from the past year seemed like anything he'd be involved with—but you couldn't always see the type of dirt on the surface. This wasn't the life she wanted, but it was the one she'd earned. She had plenty to pay for.

Her hands trembled and she put them below the table to hide it.

"Fine," Dani said, her voice level only because she had a lot of practice keeping it that way. To Tad she said, "Let's finish this." Before the stranger could protest, she added, "Then we can talk."

"Excellent," he said, and he smiled at her. A hungry, needful smile.

Every instinct told her to run, abandon this job, and race to the door as soon as he was far enough away for her and Sunflower to have a chance at making it. But maybe it was her turn to be the dumbest person in the room. She was too curious to leave.

Well, that, and she wanted her money.

CHAPTER TWO

ONCE THE TRANSFERS were concluded and the paperwork was signed, scum and scummier took off like the devil was on their heels. Dani should have felt better with some padding in her accounts, but she found it impossible to relax with the unpredictable stranger lingering at the bar.

"Buy me a drink?" he said, voice carrying across the space. The request was rich.

She got up with a wary "Why not?"

Though she could think of plenty of reasons.

Sunflower stayed right beside her as they crossed the warped floor to the battered wooden bar. The bartender had returned once it became obvious no cleanup would be required. His face was about as battered as the rest of the place, scored with the deep wrinkles of a life spent on worries. He had the look of someone who'd been in and out of jail.

"Whiskey," the man told the bartender as they sat on the stools. "Whatever's the best you have."

"Same," Dani said. She dropped a hand to Sunflower's head, an attempt to reassure them both.

The bartender poured the drinks, and though the stranger was so keen not to wait before, and his index finger ticked against the bar with a silent urgency that signaled his impatience, the stranger didn't say a word until their glasses were filled and set in front of them. He picked his up, and Dani sensed she was to do the same. She didn't like the subtle manipulation of it.

"You're Danielle Poissant," he said, saving her the need to pretend to introduce herself. He obviously knew something about who she was or he wouldn't be here. "I'm Archer. I was your mother's partner."

Her brain snagged on "Archer"—a name she'd heard only in whispers, long ago—but her heart fixed on the new information: *This* was her mother's former partner. The reason Dani made the decision that lost her everything.

She picked up the cheap whiskey and downed it in a single long drink. The burn sharpened her. "What are you doing here?" she managed with a slight cough.

"I have a job for you." His dark eyes found the bartender. "Excuse us. Leave the bottle."

Ah, so he wanted privacy for whatever ambush this was.

The bartender pushed the fifth of Jim Beam between them and again exited through a small door into the back. Dani wished she had *this* magical ability, to quietly order men to do things and have it happen wordlessly, without even needing blackmail or knowledge of their secrets.

"How did you find me?" Dani flew so far under the radar she might as well be a bat.

He raised an eyebrow and sipped his drink. Then, "Do you still paint?"

That one hurt. Sometimes old wounds were the freshest kind.

"Not in ten years," she said before she thought better of it.

"That's what I figured. Do you miss it?"

Did she miss painting copies of old and new masters that appeared indistinguishable from the originals and that her magic *made* so, even to the most educated eyes? Well, she missed the rush of creation. The weight of the paintbrush in her hand. She missed a lot of things.

But she gave them up for a reason. "Not particularly," she said, unsure if she was lying.

"You'll want this job," he said.

She didn't like him assuming he knew her. No one knew her, not anymore. "What is it?"

He sat back, swirling the brown liquid in his glass. "Are you familiar with the Hackworth Collection?"

Her mother's El Dorado fantasy in one big art score—the job she was always dreaming about and working toward. The one she'd been on the cusp of doing when Dani messed it all up. William Hackworth started as an oilman but eventually had a finger in several different billion-dollar pies. She remembered seeing the stories when he died five years back, noting that his will had created a stir among the family and prevented anyone from opening up or selling the collection—even them. Nicknamed the "Fortress of Art," there were rumors it was filled with gains both legal and ill-gotten.

Supposedly every famous artist of the last five hundred years was represented, but no one could say for sure. Hackworth had reportedly never let anyone except himself see the art assembled inside. An infamous prick with enough money to keep his treasures private, like a pissy dragon with a hoard.

Every criminal they knew who had tried to break in failed or got caught. Even one of her mother's chief rivals, Mica—Danish, with magic fingers that could get him into anyplace. Mica, at least, didn't end up doing time after he was apprehended. He released himself from jail and laid low until it made sense not to anymore. Last Dani heard he was somewhere in Europe, grifting the good life.

Archer was still waiting for an answer, as if putting this question to *her* wasn't an insult. "You mean the completely impenetrable one outside Louisville?" she said. "Tougher to get into than Fort Knox?"

"So you do know it." Archer put down his glass. "The family figured out how to work around the will, finally. They have legal clearance to proceed as of two days ago, so there's about to be an unveiling and an auction onsite. It's being sold off, and they can't do it fast enough."

"And?"

He inclined his head. Yes, there was more.

"There is a single piece, not particularly valuable monetarily, that I need. I would like you to get it for me."

"Why not just buy it?" The obvious question. He must have money.

Archer shook his head. "Let's just say that I cannot be the buyer, even through an intermediary. I greatly desire to own it, but there are others who will want the piece and attempt to purchase it. We must circumvent them."

She might have left that part of the game, but she knew more about the art world than most experts.

"Describe the piece." She shouldn't be intrigued. But she was. This was Archer, sitting across from her—an unwelcome link to the past, but flesh and blood.

Archer reached up and touched the back of his neck. He was uncomfortable talking about it. Interesting.

"Well?" she prodded.

He looked down at the bar. "It's a portrait of me."

"Ah," Dani said, as if she understood. She didn't, unless the portrait implicated him in a theft or was a forgery or . . . Well, it could be any number of things. So maybe she understood enough.

He settled the full weight of his attention back on her, heavy as a hand. "I'm prepared to get you access by putting a whisper in the right ear to bring you on as the family's special security consultant."

She nearly fell off the barstool.

"Me? A security consultant?" She scoffed. "That is almost genius."

"Only almost?" His lips quirked.

"You're insane. Why in the world would anyone with the resources of the Hackworths go for it?" Except, the way her mother

always acted, Archer *must* have powers. "Unless you plan to persuade them in some special way?"

You didn't just come out and ask what people's powers were in
the secret world. You waited until they revealed them because they
trusted you or you were working together and there was no choice.

Dani's mother had powers of persuasion too. Thing was, those
type of powers didn't work on Dani. Not that she was about to reveal that.

Archer didn't look at her as he responded. "The wealthy think
differently—you know that's true. They lost their previous security
manager recently. They'll see your background as a pedigree." He
shrugged one elegant shoulder as he continued with this lie, as if
she'd buy such a thin explanation. "I can ensure it will happen.
You'll be contacted to confirm the job, assuming we have a deal."

She didn't need him to be honest with her, but she wanted to
pierce his cool demeanor. "Admit that you're convincing them with
magic, and I'll continue this discussion."

"Fine." His eyes locked on her again. "It does not matter. I will
get you the access I promise."

He was serious, even though he couldn't be serious. Not about
this. "I don't have a crew," she said. "Even with the access, there's no
such thing as a one-person job like this. And I don't do art anymore."

He picked up the bottle and topped off her glass. "Not in ten
years?"

She was dying to ask about her mother. He must have been
aware of that and he had offered her nothing.

"Why come to me?"

"Your mother isn't available."

The ache inside her was a black hole. "I'll be going now."

He had his walking stick in his left hand in a heartbeat and
tapped it on the floor. Hard. Sunflower snarled and inserted herself
between Dani and Archer.

"Good girl," Dani said, without bothering to call her off. She
raised her voice, rummaging in her pocket for enough cash to cover

the drinks. She wouldn't sit there to be threatened. "We'll just be going."

She could leave. No matter how much it would cost her to walk away from the infamous Archer with nothing . . . except her take from the Tad job. That was all she had expected from today, and it was enough. It had to be.

Dani was excellent at lying to herself. She'd had a long time to practice.

"I can get your mother back for you. Your old life too." Archer considered her, then set the walking stick against the bar. He reached into his coat pocket and pulled out a document, placed it in front of her. "This is an advance."

Dani shouldn't look. She absolutely should turn and walk out of here with her payday and her dog. She shouldn't keep talking to Archer—the man who ruined their family, whether he meant to or not. But . . .

She caught a snatch of the address, and then she was lost. The paper on the bar was a deed. The deed to the stone house in Lexington, to be precise—the closest thing they ever had to an actual home. Brad Hackworth, who must be some relation of the old man, was the owner.

"How?" she asked.

"I convinced the older couple who bought it to relocate to Florida. It's yours if you do this. Brad will sign it over, no questions asked. You can stay in it for the time being. Make it your headquarters again."

The deed looked legit. She touched it, picked it up, held it to the light. If it was a forgery, she'd see the signs. A hesitation in the signatures, the ghosts of lines traced. The stop and start marks of someone checking their work.

Oh, she was tempted. This alone, the idea of walking through the front door, was almost enough. His other promise—that he could give her mother back to her, and something like their previous life . . . She couldn't see how. Not even if he'd gotten the stone house to tempt her with. Unless he intended to use his powers on her mother.

Same question, harder to ask this time. "*How?* She won't talk to me."

"What I'm offering you is as real as the house," he said and set a key on the bar. "That's to the door. I want the painting, and you must want your life back. Manage to steal from the Fortress of Art, and you'll be a legend. Offenses forgotten, lies forgiven. No one loses."

The deed did seem legitimate. She couldn't quite let herself believe the offer was, but the hell of it was she wanted to.

Dani's mother taught her well enough, that things that were too good to be true were always fakes, promises like this were fairy dust that dissolved when you flipped the lights on. Yet, in this dark bar, Dani felt hope in every beat of her heart.

She realized she wanted to say yes, for multiple reasons. Archer was a mystery, still, after all these years. This would give her a chance to pry, to solve it, to figure out who he was and what hold he had on her mother.

That wasn't the most enticing part of his offer. She could hardly allow herself to contemplate it. But suppose he *could* close the abyss between her and her mother?

Complicated as returning to that life would be . . . She was older now. Archer had told her what he wanted. This painting. It was a start to understanding him, and possibly why her mother made the choices she had, at long last. And he wasn't wrong—pulling this off would earn her back respect. But what she wanted most was another chance with her mother, no matter how it came.

"Just the portrait, nothing else?" she asked. "And you get me an introduction to the Hackworth family?"

"The job is yours, Dani. Working for me, and for them."

"What's the timeline?" she asked. He intimated soon, but preparing for something like this—even with access—wouldn't be straightforward.

"The preview is in two days, the sale a week later."

"You're *serious*?" she asked.

"I told you the family was in a rush. Just be glad for the opportunity. If anyone can do it, it's a Poissant." His smile was a seduction and she ignored that part of it. She had no interest in flirting with him. She had hated him for too long.

He seemed surprised by the lack of response and gave her a subtle reconsideration.

Dani worked hard to keep emotion off her face. Him not being aware of how much the timeline worried her or how she loathed him were advantages, and she was going to need all of those she could get. She picked up her glass and gestured for him to do the same. The terms weren't hers, but they weren't to be entirely his either. She clinked her glass against his.

"The first thing I'll need is to get my crew together."

Convincing them to talk to her would be the hardest part. That was another thing he didn't need to know.

She downed the whiskey, plucked the deed and key off the bar, and nodded to him. "If I need to be in touch . . ."

"I'll find you. The details will be waiting when you get to Lexington."

She'd rather do the contacting instead of him, but left it for the time being. It was a job even her mother was never able to do, and she had to pull it off in nine days.

She was on her mark, and now it was settled: *Go*.

NINE DAYS OUT

CHAPTER THREE

DANI CRASHED EARLY the night before leaving for Lexington, partly to mentally prepare herself for the homecoming journey. But she was up early, because tick-fucking-tock, and toss-and-turn. She had to cool her heels until her noon brunch meeting with the soon-to-be-ex Mrs. Tad, where she handed over the paperwork, confirmed they were good, and declined an offer of bottomless mimosas. Then, it was into the car and heading east on the interstate, making as good a time as she could without getting pulled over.

Driving made it impossible to avoid dwelling on the past. Each turn of the wheel on pavement was a siren song, calling up memories of the life she left behind ten years ago.

She never thought she'd come back here.

Admittedly, here was less a place than a world. There was the past and her present, and they didn't exist in the same space. The past was full of magic. And the secret world she would be reentering was one where specific gifts were used in very specific ways for profit—and always had been.

Take Vincenzo Peruggia, a humble worker who supposedly hid in a closet at the Louvre and walked out with the *Mona Lisa* wrapped in his jacket in 1911, seeking to repatriate it to Italy, only to be caught and have it returned two years later. In truth, a mysterious con man named Marquis de Valfierno hired Peruggia after having six copies of the painting made to sell to millionaires in America. His talent involved fraudulent deals; no one in his presence could say no to him. The deals proved binding. Lots of people doubted Valfierno's existence, believing him made up, questioning the story because the copies never surfaced. But that was simply part of Valfierno's power, as was erasing any trace of himself except the one printed by a newspaperman he forgot to swear to silence. The revelation caused a sensation when it appeared in *The Saturday Evening Post* in 1932 under the headline "Why and How the Mona Lisa Was Stolen." It later got debunked by "experts," despite being mostly true.

Or, in 1990, seven years before Dani was born, there was the Gardner Museum Heist in Boston, known to Dani as her mother's criminal origin story. An expert in art with the gift of a silver tongue, Dani's mother, Maria, convinced her friend Rabbit, who could bend electronics to her tinkering will, and a now-dead associate named Frankie, who could put anyone to sleep with a touch, to partner with her on the job.

They left with at least five hundred million dollars' worth of paintings that included irreplaceable pieces by Vermeer, Rembrandt, and Manet. Her mother used her ability to muddle the guards' memories of the night's events, and left breadcrumbs leading in many different directions besides theirs. It was this theft of the century that sealed her legendary reputation for untouchable brilliance in the community. She never tried to sell the pieces—too much heat. Even Dani wasn't sure where they resided, or if they even still existed. It was a question she was too afraid to ask.

The success brought Archer into Maria's orbit, and also inspired Maria's future modus operandi, when she saw how the press focused on the museum's security deficits. Glamorous Maria Poissant, nicknamed the Poison Angel, would steal a few paintings from this museum or that private collection and fence them to well-heeled scum, or occasionally put them up for ransom. The twist was that she then presented herself as the solution to the museum, a way to prevent future thefts. She was the world's best art thief *and* its most famous security consultant.

And Dani's mother. Until . . . she wasn't.

Dani never cared for what happened to the art or for most of the people her mother dealt with. At first, she loved having magic, delighting her mother with it. But like most things, it got more complicated.

When she was a little kid, still presumably powerless, she spent plenty of time looking for a hidden opening into the extraordinary. She was surrounded by people with magic, so it was logical to look. To press aside the smelly old coats in the wardrobe that might hide the entrance to frozen Narnia. To peer at the ground for the rabbit hole into the Red Queen's acid trip. To travel through a market with an eye out for the magic carpet that suddenly flew higher and higher, away from what you were to what you wanted to be. To think magic solved problems.

Those stories lied. So far as Dani's experience went, magic wasn't a blessing. It was a curse that made people do things they might not otherwise.

She should know. She was doing one of them now.

She turned the car onto the road heading out of Lexington, toward the stone house, and there was something almost sinister about how much it looked the same, like no time had passed at all. The shadows of trees dappled the two lanes of asphalt, the light at sunset dazzling. The pastures of the Thoroughbred horse farms were an unreal, verdant green.

Dani used to riff on the names on the fancy Thoroughbred farm signs to amuse her mother. Bloodstone Stud might be the property of a coven of witches with a giant, magical rock for sacrifices. Lucky Horseshoe could belong to an Irish family blessed by, and under the control of, leprechauns. Her mother even pitched in sometimes. Her stories were more savage, of the terrible things the rich Carmichaels and Dennisons and Angelos had done to wrangle their holdings, speculation on what pieces they might have worth stealing on the walls of their enormous mansions.

Well, not speculation. Her mom knew every last significant private art collection inside out. But she would never have risked stealing so close to home. Save for Maria's fixation on the Fortress of Art—her ultimate score, next on her list when she got caught. But now Dani wondered whether it was less general that it had seemed, and more about the painting of Archer she'd been hired to steal. Who was he and what hold did he have on her mother? She would find out. Finally.

Dani reached the stone house as evening settled in, but hesitated to pull into the driveway. She could park alongside the road, like a stranger, but the deed was in the glove box. She'd examined it under brighter light, with a loupe, in her hotel room. It was legitimate. Bradford Hackworth's name listed as owner. Her nerves thrummed, because this might well be some twisted sort of game.

But she turned in to the front circle drive and cut the engine.

The house looked eerily the same too, partially illuminated by a security light. The stone was a motley of browns, the roof slanted black. Inside, there should be three bedrooms, a working fireplace in the living room that heated the medium-sized kitchen in winter. The steps upstairs with their haunted creaks. Would the house's secrets be intact? The occasional hollow place in the wall or floor? The hidden studio out back?

The stone house wasn't a mansion. Just the closest thing Dani ever had to HOME, capital letters.

The wash of nostalgia made her feel ill. In her memories, the light streamed in through the kitchen windows on her mother's intense planning sessions with the regular crew, close as family, and sometimes the other strange, unsavory characters who populated their universe, forever dropping by or taking off. Then, the dark crept at the windows, once the people were gone. Her mother whispered in the shadows to the silent partner Dani had met only yesterday. Archer.

There was a risk in revisiting places this important in your personal mythology. Everything had a tendency to seem smaller, more ordinary. Once you stopped making new memories with people, they became like a book. You could revisit the story, but in the end, it turned out the same.

Archer had given her a shot at understanding the past. Possibly rewriting it. She was determined not to waste that.

Dani climbed out of the car. Sunflower hopped down and took off into the yard to relieve herself.

The first test would be to see if the key Archer gave Dani worked, so she headed for the front porch.

It slid into the lock.

Dani paused on the threshold with her forehead resting against the door. Whoever said you couldn't go home again was full of shit. Most people who made such sayings were.

She straightened, opened the door, and stepped inside, letting her eyes adjust to the darkness. The light switch was by the door where she remembered, and although she wasn't sure it would, it even worked. When she flipped it, the overhead light popped on.

The previous owners were fans of curtains—lots of them. The living room held some left-behind furniture. Not her style, too oversized, but it looked comfortable enough. The couch would give her somewhere to sleep. The built-in bookcases on the wall were empty, no longer filled with her mother's art reference library. There was a slightly airless atmosphere too—the stale smell of a house that had been closed up for weeks.

And then Dani spotted movement in the kitchen. A person.

Someone was here. Waiting for her in the lone chair at the table.

Archer had set her up. It had to be a trap.

Humiliation burned through her at having fallen for it. He would not get away with this.

Dani whistled, high and sharp.

In seconds, Sunflower rushed in past her and darted straight at the interloper. She barked up a storm, the sound echoing through the house.

A woman stood and stepped back from the table, and Dani's

breath caught in her throat. She was leveling a handgun. Not at Dani. At Sunflower.

Dani crossed the space without wasting a breath. "Who the fuck are you?"

"Call off your dog, please," the woman said coolly and waved the fingers of her free hand. She was wearing so much jewelry it glinted even in the low light.

Sunflower snapped at the motion but didn't bite. She wouldn't unless Dani said to. Dani didn't like being the one without a gun in this room. Her Taser was back in the car.

But she didn't have to be unarmed—maybe. Taking a risk, she lunged for a spot in the wall, shoving aside the false panel her mother installed years ago. She thrust her fingers in and there it was, among stray brushes and some of her old palettes. The silver of her X-Acto knife, thin and sharp at the end—a tool that had cut many paintings from frames and pieces of canvas down to size. The old couple who lived here must never have discovered the cache.

The woman continued to hold off a growling Sunflower as Dani advanced.

"Quiet," Dani said and Sunflower stopped. The dog's alert brown eyes didn't move from the woman. "Put the gun away unless you want real trouble. You hurt my dog, that's what we're going to have."

The woman waved the gun around. "You're bringing a . . . very small knife to a gunfight? Aren't you a security consultant? I'm not the one with an attack hound."

Dani's suspicions about who the hell this woman might be coalesced. Archer said the details would be waiting for her in Lexington. Was this one of the people she was going to have to work for? Because if so, the Hackworths and their retainers were plainly out of their minds.

"She's not a hound, she's a collie. And this is her house. Who are you and what are you doing here?"

The woman finally lowered the pistol, though Dani could tell by the ease she handled it with that she knew how to use it.

"Lower your tiny knife too, then." Again, she sounded annoyed at the fuss, as if she didn't cause it.

Dani located another light switch and hit it, brightening the kitchen to get a good look at the intruder. Not the kind of person she usually came into contact with these days, but familiar from the past.

"And it's not your house yet," the woman said with a sigh. She was in her mid-fifties. Flowing tunic and pants, chunky, artisan-made jewelry. Impeccably highlighted hair. Glasses dangling from a bejeweled lanyard around her neck. A phone lay on the table in front of where she'd sat before. "I was told the family is loaning it to you. That if you do the job, it's yours. For now, you are a guest here too. An employee."

"Tell me who *you* are," Dani said, putting herself in front of Sunflower.

The woman slid the chair back out and sat. Rude, since there was only the one. Ruder, because it should be Dani's mother's chair.

She smoothed one errant lock of hair off her face. "I'm here on behalf of your new employers, the Hackworths. But I've been waiting here for hours. I suppose I could have waited outside . . ." She shrugged.

Yes, you could have. "Where is your car? I didn't see one out front."

"I parked in back."

"And you just hung out in here in the dark? Why?"

"I promise you, I'm with the Hackworths."

She had the polished look of a longtime retainer and the quirk of an art dealer. It tracked. "Personal curator? Available for some light gunplay?"

"Good eye, though I've never killed anyone," the woman said, her thin lips stretching into a smile. "But I do know where some bodies are buried, so to speak. And yet, since William died, I've spent my time fighting the battle to honor his wishes. I lost to the family, and I guess now I'm just an exquisitely paid errand girl, forced to help sell off what I built." She picked up the phone on the table and extended it to Dani. "This is for you. So you can be reached. Day or night, keep it on and with you. I'm told you've been briefed on the broad strokes already."

"By who?"

"Brad. William's son. You'll meet him tomorrow."

"At the showing, I assume." Dani accepted the phone. She rarely had one with the same SIM for more than a week. She'd have to create a dummy phone so they wouldn't be able to track her movements, but that was no trouble. "You have an actual name, other than Knows-Where-the-Bodies-Are-Buried?"

The woman looked surprised to be asked. "Rose."

That fit. She was prickly as a fistful of thorns. Her name had turned up in Dani's glancing research into Hackworth and the nearly half decade of court battles over the estate. The legal cases started just two months after the man's death.

"As you obviously already know, I'm Danielle Poissant. Dani, for short." Dani offered her hand while trying not to feel ridiculous that they went from an armed standoff to awkward politesse. Rose's shake was brief. Sunflower took the hint and melted down to relax on the floor. "Must be a wild job buying for the Hackworths, if you're toting around a Glock in your handbag." Dani wanted to do more digging into this woman, and soon. Had she bought paintings that weren't strictly legal and how many? Leverage.

"It definitely was before William died." Rose frowned and hesitated. "And you think I'm beyond the pale? Get ready. I'm nothing compared to the wives. I guess it's good this happened. You'll be somewhat better prepared."

"Oh? Care to enlighten me?" This woman had no idea the kind of bizarre Dani had seen. She looked around. "I'd offer you something, but I just got here. As you know."

"Yes, sorry. Brad didn't tell me to have the place stocked."

"I can do my own shopping," Dani said.

"If you must," Rose countered and then got back up. "No one else I know can or does."

"The son—Brad—what's he like?"

"He could've inherited it all, was supposed to. That was William's wish. But he wants to sell. So I think he's a pleasant asshole. You can tell him I said that." The hint of a smile crossed Rose's face then.

Might as well push while Rose was talking. "Want to give me a preview of what's in the collection?"

"The NDAs and the will prevent me—and you—from seeing it early. Yes, even the new head of security. You'll see it with everyone else tomorrow. It took them a long time to win the litigation. Thus, the rush. They don't want to risk delays." She started for the door. "I should be going—you'll need to be at the main house at eleven A.M. The address is in the phone. Don't be late."

"You're not going to tell me what to expect when I get there?"

"I wish I had a clue, most days," Rose said. "You'll get a full packet on the goods and the existing security then." She paused. "I was against hiring you."

"I heard you lost the person in charge of security. What happened?"

"He had a heart attack. Might live. Hasn't been awake yet." Rose shrugged, as if she wasn't talking about someone she must have worked with for years. "See you soon. You should know I have my eye on a piece or two." Then she was gone.

Dani wondered if the former head of security's health emergency was Archer's work or natural causes. Working with people like Rose and the Hackworths could obviously be stressful. The curator would be tricky to navigate, with her open grudges about the auction and the family.

Dani was left alone in the house with Sunflower and a thousand metaphorical old ghosts. Not the first gun pulled in this house, but hopefully the last.

She'd gotten by with Sunflower as her main muscle for years.

Dani checked the phone to make sure it worked and decided against sitting down in her mother's chair. There was so much to do. Far more than groceries. Hard work. Research. People to track down, apologies to offer. Rabbit had to be the first visit on her list.

She was the only one who knew as much as her mother about planning to grab a piece of art—and who could be an entrée to the other people Dani needed on her crew. Then, yes, she had to check out the Fortress and identify its weaknesses. And she'd need to examine the piece she was meant to steal so she could start on a forgery. To make an unimpeachable copy, she needed a clear view of the piece. She could work from a reproduction, but for a job this high stakes, she wanted to look at the original as closely as possible. She'd also have to obtain the materials to make a close facsimile of the frame; her ability meant no one would dig beneath its surface appearance.

She walked the X-Acto back over to the stash spot she had pulled it from. She pushed her hand back inside to feel around for where to put it. There was comfort in finding one of the house's secrets intact.

Her fingers hit something else metal. She discarded the X-Acto and fumbled it loose. A small key with a number on it . . . A vague image flashed in her mind, her holding her mom's hand on the way into a bank . . .

A safe-deposit-box key. The feds probably raided it, but it might be worth a look.

She added visiting local banks until she figured out which one it came from to her list of Too Many Damn Priorities, Too Little Time. The saddest part was, she'd rather do that than go see someone she'd always considered family—someone else who cast her out anyway.

But she could get through some of her homework first. She needed to learn more about the Hackworths and whatever else she could find about the collection. More about Rose.

She collapsed on the left-behind couch for just a moment, putting a hand out to pet Sunflower's head. Truth was, she was waiting. She knew that if Elliott was still working with Rabbit, which she assumed that he was, he would sense her return—if he wanted to, if any part of him was waiting on her to come back. She'd be close enough.

So she'd wait here tonight and see if the door between them was truly closed.

Dani told herself that if he didn't come, catching Rabbit first thing tomorrow morning would be best anyway. Maybe she would even have the beginning of an approach from what she learned online by then.

Tick-tock.

The night passed long, and lonely.

EIGHT DAYS OUT

CHAPTER FOUR

EVEN THOUGH DANI was seventeen the last time she visited the so-called Rabbit Hutch, she had no problem navigating her way. Rabbit lived farther out in the country. While it'd be too early to call on most people, Rabbit always had a habit of collecting strays—both human and animal—along with a few goats and chickens.

Anyone who had a farm got up early, and Rabbit barely slept. She was like the human embodiment of amphetamines, her mind buzzing like the electronics she communed with, bending them to her will. That and a toe-tapping tic were the source of her nickname.

Dani took the turnout to the intentionally isolated property. There was no sneaking up on Rabbit.

Her tires crunched on the long gravel road that led to the rambling house and farm buildings. When they came into view, she wasn't surprised to see someone outside. But she was shocked at who it was.

Her childhood best friend Mia's silhouette was unmistakable. Rabbit's daughter. She sported threadbare overalls, her hair clipped short, a flock of chickens surrounding her.

Anger surged within Dani at the sight of her. Anger at Mia.

She hit the brakes, then parked in the drive. "What are you doing here?" she demanded of Mia as soon as she got out.

"Quite a question coming from Dani fucking Poissant. I live here. What are *you* doing here? Mom is gonna flip her lid." Mia had a sprinkling of freckles across her dark skin. She put her hands on her rounded hips. "You better go."

"She's not here?"

"Early meeting. Some angels are looking out for you."

As if that'd *ever been true.*

A rooster crowed and then launched itself at one of the chickens. "Damn it," Mia said. "Hold on. I don't know why Mom got this guy. He's a holy terror." She stepped toward him. "Come on, murderbird."

Dani stood, watching as Mia herded the black rooster toward the barn, the chickens following in their weaving, pecking way. She flapped her hands until the rooster was inside the old red barn, then shut him in. The many-colored chickens focused on their grit.

"You're welcome, my little dragons," Mia said to the chickens and dusted off her hands.

Dani's emotions were a mess of love and hate and moving on and holding tight. She had underestimated how hard this would be. Elliott hadn't come, and she felt like a fool for expecting him to. That and finding Mia still here . . .

"Now, you better go," Mia said.

"I'm here to talk to your mother." Dani needed to understand, though. "But . . . why didn't you leave here? You should've left."

Mia didn't have magic. She could've had a normal life. Dani had always imagined her living one. That was why it made her so angry that Mia stayed.

Mia frowned. "I can still help Mom. I don't have her gift, but I'm not bad at backing her up. And someone has to keep this place running when she's working. Not that it's your business."

She chose this. Of course. Dani was always the one who worried what they did was wrong.

"Are you back?" Mia's brows lifted. "Because that's not a good idea."

"Can we talk?" Dani asked. "Please?"

"Your mother would shit if she heard you add a please to anything." Mia hesitated, then said, "Talk. But we better stay out here."

The chickens surrounded them again. Not menacing, just being friendly or oblivious; Dani wasn't sure which. She was nervous. Seeing Rabbit was going to be hard enough. She wasn't prepared to talk to Mia.

"Good thing I didn't bring my dog; she's never met chickens," Dani said, playing at casual. "Her name's Sunflower."

Mia blinked. "Cute name. Is it because of . . . ?"

Dani nodded, and she knew they were both remembering that day. The first time her power expressed. They were eight years old. The two of them and Rabbit's latest stray, Elliott, were hanging out in the stone house. Rabbit set a book with a spread of Van Gogh in front of the two of them and told them to "make masterpieces, so we won't have to work so hard." Dani's crayon copy wasn't perfect, but when Rabbit glanced at it—then called her mother over to do the same—they thought it *was* a Van Gogh. Her mother asked her that day if she wanted to learn to paint. She said yes, of course. Maria had never looked happier.

"Cute dog?" Mia said—Dani assumed so they'd both stop remembering. They always were like sisters. Neither of them had fathers in the picture; they had each other and their mothers.

"Well-trained dog. She probably wouldn't chase your chickens. They are yours, aren't they?" When they were kids, the animals at the farm—two cows and chickens and a goat and a rotating cast of cats and dogs—were Rabbit's. They trotted around behind her like she was a mother duckling. The strays were all kids with magic, who usually disappeared again after a while. "You called them yours before."

"They're ours," Mia said. "Mine and Mom's."

Dani wasn't able to hide the envy from showing on her face apparently.

Mia kicked the dirt. "I didn't mean it that way. Wait. Why am I apologizing to you? You still haven't told me why you want to talk to Mom."

They'd all felt like one big dysfunctional semi-happy family back then, bonded together forever by crime. As thick a bond as blood, Rabbit had always said. One Dani had disregarded.

The rooster crowed loud from inside the barn. "Shh, bully," Mia called out.

"How is your mom?"

Mia gave her a big head shake: no. "She wouldn't want me to answer that. She's fine, and that's all you're getting from me."

Mia crossed her arms in front of her chest. The sun was getting hotter by the second, and beads of sweat trickled down her neck into her old blue shirt. Dani was in danger of dissolving into a puddle of sweat, but she didn't suggest going inside. Mia would only say no. Inside was for family or temporary allies.

"I'm here because I'm sorry, obviously. I've been sorry since it happened, you know that."

"Too late," Mia said.

"I was seventeen."

"Old enough to know better."

"Right." Dani's turn to kick at the dirt. "Okay, I'm here because I may have a way back. I'm working a job. I need a crew, and I could really use Rabbit's help."

Mia's eyes widened. "Dani . . ."

A pickup truck came flying along the road in the distance, throwing up dustbowl-sized clouds in its wake the way Rabbit always liked to.

"Shit," Mia said.

Mia turned to Dani and put her hands on Dani's arms. "I would hear you out, but . . . I'm not allowed and you know it. I'm not the one you need anyway. But it's not awful to see you."

That was something—a crumb—and Dani clung to it.

"It's good seeing you too." The words slipped out like a confession. "I just don't know who else to go to. There's . . . there's no one I can trust." The irony of ironies.

"Brace yourself," Mia said and shoved her hands into the deep pockets of her overalls.

The truck pulled up beside Dani's car, so at least she wasn't blocked in.

Rabbit jumped out. She was eccentric as ever: big crown of kinky hair, neon green gum boots *and* glasses frames, going full tilt at it as she aged. She looked across the yard at Dani and her eyes narrowed. The chickens started to make their way over to her.

Then the other door of the truck opened, and Elliott climbed out. Dani could barely breathe.

He hid whatever his reaction to seeing Dani was better than Rabbit did, but she could practically feel his presence in her bones. They always had that secret lightning between them. She thought they were forever once, but he chose this world instead.

Dani squared up and waited to take her medicine. She held her head high. "Rabbit, I want to talk," she called.

Rabbit angled her head as if she didn't hear right. Instead she stalked across the yard, lifted her hand, and slapped Dani across the face. Mia put her hand up to her own cheek, as if in sympathy.

"What are you doing here?" Rabbit pointed at the gravel road. "Get off my land."

"Rabbit," Dani said, "I need help. *Your* help. It's about Mom's partner, Archer. I met him—"

Rabbit shook her head. "I don't care. You're out and you know it. Those are the rules."

Dani looked at Rabbit, then Mia, and finally at Elliott. The two of them stood across from each other for a long moment. He was a few inches taller than when Dani had last seen him—a late growth spurt. He had more muscles too, and his face had more angles. Gawky kid Elliott had matured into the hot, quiet type. The three of them were inseparable as little kids—Mia, Dani, and Elliott. And then later, Elliott and Dani were inseparable in a different way. Her heart still wanted to sing at the sight of him. Foolish thing.

He could've come after her, found her, the way he could find anything. But he didn't.

"We—" he started.

"Get inside," Rabbit cut him off.

He also could have said no to Rabbit, offered *his* help, but after a brief hesitation he didn't say another word. Just turned and walked into the house, and that told her everything last night should have. That as far as he was concerned, they were over.

"Go on," Rabbit said to Dani then, like she was talking to an unwanted animal. Something that had never shown up at the Rabbit Hutch. Just Dani. "Get."

Dani walked to her car, climbed in, managed to start it and leave. Her hands shook on the steering wheel, her heart breaking all over again. But it would mend. It would. Scars were proof of life, in their way.

With no crew to back her up, Archer's hard-as-hell job just turned to damn-near-impossible. And she still had to figure out how to do it.

CHAPTER FIVE

Dani had her shit mostly back together by the time she arrived at the Hackworth estate. She stopped at the entry gate, hit the buzzer, and gave her name. The gate slowly opened and she drove through into the manicured grounds. At least her hands weren't shaking anymore.

Seeing them . . . all of them. Rabbit's slap. Mia's barely concealed pity. And Elliott. She hadn't been ready to see Elliott, period. Why couldn't he have turned out nerdy or schlubby? Not that it mattered. She should have boxed up any lingering feelings for him long ago.

So she'd have to assemble a crew out of strangers, which was never ideal—and, in fact, was usually the first step to getting busted. But none of her mother's former accomplices would work with her, that much was clear. Archer's name opened no doors with Rabbit, but he might know others . . .

Though asking him was humiliating to contemplate.

Additionally, Dani had thought the trigger-happy Rose might be exaggerating about the Hackworths, but the scene in front of the sprawling mansion begged to differ. Two women were screaming at each other on the tidy lawn, while a third trotted outside and dumped an armload of dark suits on top of a heap of the same. Rose stood nearby, conferring with a well-built man in a suit and a little girl in jeans with circles of face paint on her cheeks.

What else could Dani do? She added sunglasses for a layer of armor and joined the party.

"You absolute crazy bitch," said an older woman involved in the fighting, dressed to kill and face-lifted to live forever.

"I'm not crazy, but I *am* the B-word," a younger, willowy blonde with talon nails shrieked back.

"You can't even say it. 'The B-word,'" the other woman volleyed. "You are *such* a child."

"And you are an ancient crone!"

"Better a crone than a bitch baby."

The third woman emerged from inside again. She dressed more casually, but still looked expensive. She carried a heap of men's shoes, tossing them on the pile.

Rose flagged her down. "William is no longer here to appreciate these antics. Someone will have to pack this up."

The third woman raised her chin. "It's very satisfying. And the staff are well paid."

"Not well enough," Rose said under her breath.

The little girl ran over and jumped onto the pile of clothes. The man attempted to hide his laughter but couldn't.

"Emma," Rose called, "you're not helping."

That was when Rose noticed Dani. She shrugged. "Told you."

"Who're you?" the crone asked her.

"She's the new security consultant," Rose said. "Here for the Fortress viewing. We're all headed over shortly. If any of you bothered to look at the daily schedule, you'd know that. I assume you haven't forgotten the gala we're hosting as well?" Her gaze went to the pile of cast-off suits, but she was ignored.

The women stalked over to surround Dani, their arguments and gleeful clothing purge forgotten for the moment. This must have been what the threat of attack from the Greek Fates or maybe the Furies felt like.

"You're the art thief?" the so-called B-word baby asked, and trained eyes big enough for an anime character on Dani, assessing.

"Former," Dani said. "That was a long time ago."

The crone clapped her hands together. "This is too delicious. You're really Maria Poissant's daughter? The Poison Angel?"

"I'm afraid so," Dani said. At least in terms of DNA.

"And you're consulting for *us* now?" the more normal one, except for the clothes throwing, asked. "I don't think that's smart."

"And you do know everything," the crone said.

"Ladies," Rose said, "enough. I told you, but as usual, you didn't listen. This is how you voted. She was recommended by an associate of Brad's. Dani has the job. Let her do it."

The defense didn't merit comment from Dani, so she stayed quiet.

The normal-ish woman relented. "I'm Diana, also known as the second wife."

Neither of the others offered a name, and Dani couldn't decide if it was because they expected she already knew them—she did, from her research; the crone was Beverly, wife number one, and the baby, Sandi, the third and final wife—or because she was the help.

She'd gathered the man must be Brad, Hackworth's son. A broad-shouldered and strong-jawed type of handsome, polished as newly cleaned glass, he took the little girl by the hand and led her over. She couldn't help comparing him to Elliott, who was still scruffy around the edges, all untucked T-shirts and jeans that had been worn to work on the farm.

"Brad Hackworth," he said, "and this angel here is my daughter, Emma."

The little girl grinned up at her. "He's not married. He and my mom are divorced. They're friendly, but I live with Dad most of the time."

Dani blinked down at her. This might be the most shocking thing to happen yet.

Brad coughed, biting back a grin. Dani decided to take it in stride.

"Very informative," she said to the girl.

"She is that," Brad said. "Ems, you stay with your nona. She'll get you settled with the sitter."

Emma stage-whispered, "I'm not allowed to call Nona 'Grandma' because she says it hurts her prospects, but she is my grandma."

This revealed, Emma raced back over to the middle wife, Diana. Hackworth had only one child, which made sense of what Rose had said about the inheritance of the collection having been intended for him. It didn't explain why he'd fought to sell it off. Publicly, the legal team's arguments were focused on the family's right to dispose of the deceased patriarch's assets as they wished.

"She seems fun," Dani said carefully, meaning it.

"Best thing in my life," Brad said.

Dani liked him more by the second. Which was a liability in a situation like this, but she couldn't find it in her to mind—not when it helped ease the sting of Elliott's brush-off.

"Come on," he said. "I'll take you over and get you the security materials. We can talk on the way."

"Great," Dani said. Given that Archer was one of his "associates," she needed to—politely—grill him.

Brad waved to Rose. "We'll meet you there."

"I know you're abandoning them to me," she said. "I don't blame you." She raised her voice, "Everyone, five minutes until we get in the car. You have to make an appearance. The press will be there."

"Hurry," Brad said to Dani, and started walking. "Move quick. Or we'll end up with the others. They're like barnacles."

Dani snorted and did as he said. There was a well-kept pebbled path leading away from the house. "I take it the exes aren't close?"

Brad grinned. "Despite appearances, I suspect the three of them secretly love each other. They're the only ones in the world who know what it was like to be married to Dad . . . And they're not wrong to expect some kind of compensation for that."

Dani was surprised by his candor. "Not a daddy's boy, then?"

"Not for one second of one day. He was an unethical bastard—expected me to be the same. Imagine his disappointment." He cast her a sidelong glance. "I get having a complicated family history. That's one reason I wanted to hire you, and why selling the Fortress's contents is going to be so much fun. He'll be whirling in his overdecorated grave."

And Dani thought *her* family dynamics were messed up. She appreciated having something in common with the only sane person she seemed to have met here so far.

"Rose mentioned she fought you on the sale. I'm curious why you're allowing her to stick around?"

Brad hesitated, then said, "You are here to help with security, so I guess I shouldn't be surprised you have questions. She did a lot for my father, and even though she disagrees with my decision . . . She deserves to be involved. She should have the closure of that."

"Generous of you."

He paused and gave her a long look. She felt another stir of interest.

"I can afford to be," he said.

Dani turned away just in time to see another mansion—smaller than the family home, but not by too much—appear over a rolling hill. Two stories tall, white, with columns like some sort of temple. A small crowd was assembled outside it: the prospective buyers.

But it was the sculpture in front—a giant metal spider with spindly legs—that made Dani pause. "That's a Bourgeois?" Dani mentioned the name to impress, but also with a touch of wonder. She only knew the barest amount about sculptors, but Louise Bourgeois's spiders had always spoken to her.

"You'd know more than me. I just remember it took a crane to get it in place."

"Not an art fan, I take it—but I heard your recommendation got me this gig. How do you know Archer?"

He shrugged. "Does anyone really know Archer?"

The first time he'd been evasive. Interesting.

"Will he be here today?"

"Archer?" Brad sounded amused. "Not his scene, I don't think."

Considering his history with her mother, that was nowhere close to true. She wanted to ask if the security head who had the heart attack seemed healthy before, but too many questions like that might make Brad suspicious. She turned the conversation back to him—always a safe bet where men were concerned. "What do you do for work?"

"Try to keep everyone from killing each other and manage the family finances. The proceeds from the sale will go a long way to keeping the peace—which is, of course, why Dad tried to prevent it in the will. He thought he could force me to accept and maintain his pet project. I have zero interest in that."

Pebbles crunched underfoot. "Isn't it weird to do the auction here instead of at Sotheby's or Christie's?"

It would've made things a lot easier for her. The big houses always had security flaws, and the gaps were usually deceptively easy to figure out.

"Another part of the will—and the one thing we couldn't get around. The items can't be removed as long as they are owned by the family."

"He almost thought of everything," she said.

"Almost," Brad agreed. "We're all staying at the main house right now in case we have to go back to court. Sorry about the timeline, but the sooner the better. I think we're finally through those hurdles. Rose has promised that while she disagrees, she's done."

"She mentioned she has a couple of pieces she wants to buy."

Brad stopped. "That's the first I've heard of it."

Dani shrugged.

"Did she say which ones?" Brad asked.

"Considering making a gift?" Dani asked. "An olive branch in the form of a masterpiece?"

Brad shook his head. "The will—"

"—prevents it," Dani finished. "Of course."

What had Hackworth been playing at with all these restrictions?

As they got closer to the crowd, she saw the guards stationed by the door. "We have security personnel at all the entrances and exits, day and night," Brad said. "And rotating through the galleries. Dad handpicked them."

"Ah, good," Dani said. "What about cameras and motion detection?"

"Outside cameras are a rotating fleet of drones. You can download the app to see the footage on your phone. We also have a security station where copies are kept. And there are more cameras inside. Yes to motion detection. Dad used to turn it off so he could touch the art if he wanted."

Dani sighed. "No comment."

But mental note made.

"I've got a binder with the plans and security specifics we have in place. I truly appreciate you stepping in on such short notice. For the auction itself, we're expecting about fifty people to show up, plus some members of the FBI and the auction house reps. You'll have your work cut out for you."

No kidding. "To get to see the Fortress of Art? Worth it."

She wasn't lying. Excitement built in her. They were almost there.

"You'll all be the first," Brad said with a smile of acknowledgment. "Even when he acquired new stuff, he required the people mounting the art to wear blindfolds until they got to the appropriate gallery."

There was secretive, and then there was this. Why take such care? "You've got provenances and valuations, correct? I'll need all that too."

"Why?" He stopped and looked at her again.

She didn't hate the sensation. She wasn't used to that.

"To figure out what the highest value targets are," she said. And to figure out where Archer's painting came from.

"Of course. I'll text Rose and my business manager to get that for you."

He tapped into his phone as they reached the building.

Dani scanned the crowd. She recognized a famous collector

from New York, bald and wearing a seersucker suit. There was a tidy business-suited woman who had to be a museum curator. Another male curator in sedate navy. But lots more private collectors and buyers, dressed to show how well-heeled they were with flashes of personality—jeweled insect pins or hideous forty-thousand-dollar purses or custom Italian leather shoes. With the exception of one, a brunette in yoga pants and a T-shirt. What a flex; she was probably among the wealthiest here and half her money would be from gaming the crypto market. The journalists were easy to spot due to their jeans and notepads.

"No recording devices allowed inside, except ours. We already collected their cellphones," Brad said, and she realized he had explained the analogue note-taking.

Which meant he was sharp enough to be tracking her attention.

Still, Dani inadvertently put her hand to her chest and rubbed when she spotted the three figures standing off to one side.

They were from the secret world. Brenner she remembered. Roughly her mother's age, and he had a way with locks. The other two, a man and woman, ordinary enough no one would look twice, were known collectively as the Evil Twins. Jer and Jenn, who'd briefly attended her elementary school before moving away. She couldn't recall their exact gifts—she'd need to find out. She should've known it would be open season with Maria Poissant no longer in the game.

Brad caught her eye, a hint of concern in his expression. She managed to smile at him, and he relaxed and returned it.

A limo pulled up behind the towering spider, and Rose and her three ex-wifely charges emerged from it. She nodded to Brad and Dani, and Brad took Dani's hand—which, again, she was surprised to find she didn't mind—and led her up the steps of the portico behind Rose. The wives began smiling and working the crowd.

Rose turned to address those assembled and everyone quieted. "I'll skip the preludes, and just say behave yourselves. Our security consultant, Danielle Poissant—"

A few gasps and murmurs came from the crowd, and Dani

watched Brenner's silver eyebrows lift. The twins whispered to each other.

"—is right here"—Rose nodded to her—"and so don't get any ideas. All right, then, shall we? *Entrez-vous!*" She clapped her hands together.

Brad said hi to the security guys, who opened the heavy double doors. She'd learn more about the safeguards when she got the materials Brad mentioned. For now, she planned to pay close attention to which pieces the three with magic lingered at.

The inside was temple-like as well—a grand entry foyer, marble floors extending a path through the first floor, or to a grand staircase up to the second. It was also like walking into a net made of magic, a mesh held taut throughout the space. She'd never felt anything like this, a constant pressure, steady and strong, weaving around her.

When she scanned the walls, her knees weakened. She sucked in a breath. "Oh. My. God!"

She tried to absorb the unbelievable sights around her, struggling to get her bearings amid the wild tapestry of power. As if such a thing was possible.

Frida Kahlo in a jungle. Jackson Pollock's chaotic splotches across a giant canvas along one wall. A Rembrandt. A fucking Rembrandt! A Sargent portrait of a society matron. Georgia O'Keeffe's unmistakable blooms, some of Dani's favorite flowers in the history of art.

In appearance, master butted up against master in no coherent narrative. The closest story, in Dani's mind, was this was the storage space of a master thief. The message: *I own these, and I'll treat them however I want.* That is what he expected people to believe. It made sense now why he wouldn't have risked allowing anyone inside.

William Hackworth had been part of the secret world too.

Because there was a hidden rhyme to the way the pieces were displayed, a reason. She'd never heard of anything like this, and yet her senses told her she was right. All great art had a bit of magic in it for Dani; it's part of what she drew from when she painted a copy, the thing that made it appear real. And somehow, Hackworth had configured these pieces to maintain the magic pulsing within this structure. The collection was a sort of engine, each piece in its place to amplify the effect.

She realized standing there gawking wasn't, perhaps, the most professional response. She should be paying attention to the crowd. Brad was watching her with amusement as people parted around them. The majority of them clearly didn't sense the magic.

"Overwhelming?" he asked, brows raised.

She nodded. "You're going to make a fortune."

"Another fortune, you mean," Brad said. "That's the idea."

Good, she wanted to say. *Whatever he built this for, these works shouldn't be hidden away in here. They deserve to be seen.*

A subtle pull urged her to continue on, a nexus somewhere ahead. She kept track of the sensation as Brad led her through room after room transformed into galleries. Only one seating point in each—a brag, as if to make clear that William Hackworth was the only one allowed access to these pieces. The arrangements remained similar to the placement in the entryway: masterwork upon masterwork, nestled together, with no discernable coherence. Except that the magic built, continuing to tug her along as she moved through the building. De Kooning beside Basquiat, Goya jowl-to-cheek with Warhol, Rothko alongside Vermeer. Vermeer! There were supposed to be only thirty-six paintings by Vermeer in existence, and this, while clearly a Vermeer, wasn't on that list. Yet it didn't even have its own wall.

The second floor proved to be more of the same. One thing Dani did note was the abundance of portraits. She'd gathered already that Hackworth didn't truly *care* about any of these pieces. He was after the power they held in concert. What role did Archer's painting play? Where was it?

Rose was in her element, answering questions and preening, finally showing off what she'd built. Dani overheard her explaining that she had recommended against the haphazard placement, but that Hackworth did what he liked.

If Dani read her right—and Dani was an expert—Rose had no idea what this place was. Hackworth had wanted to pass it to Brad. Her new question was whether *he* knew.

Dani had lost track of the three from her world. They would definitely be aware. "Will there be security footage of this and can I get a copy?" she asked Brad.

"Anything you want," he said, leaning in close to her. "It's fun watching you enjoy the art. I almost get why people are so into it."

They entered another gallery and Dani was distracted by a glimpse of Archer's painting in the corner. The pull she'd been feeling since she entered intensified. Here was the place the power radiated from, emanating out, reflecting between paintings to create Hackworth's magic web. The smallest of the galleries, with far fewer pieces than the rest, yet a high-backed antique chair was placed directly in front of the portrait.

She walked toward it as if she were sleeping, wondering if the visual feast she'd just gorged on had dulled her ability to tell what period something was from. She didn't recognize the artist, but she recognized Archer. Tall, pale, in what looked to be the same outfit he wore at the bar. The long black coat, and the walking stick.

She also recognized the materials and the technique. Impressionist; classically so. Brushwork visible, even now. She approached, careful not to get so close she set off the motion sensors.

"Why are you so interested in this one?" Brad asked.

"I don't know," Dani said. "Something about it."

"Looks kind of like Archer, doesn't it?"

Does he not see it looked *exactly* like Archer? Or was that his point? But how in the hell could there be a hundred-plus-year-old portrait of her mother's partner, a man she'd just met?

Because this painting *must* be from the 1890s. She'd bet her life on it. The only person alive talented enough to forge a painting of this era so convincingly was her. And she hadn't painted this.

Also, there was magic and then there was . . . this. She almost expected Archer's eyes to start following her around the room. Could it be an ancestor of his? But no; he said it was a portrait of him. And of course she had no way to contact him.

She examined it more closely. If he wasn't lying, that meant Archer had to be more than a century old. Or in league with another master forger. She needed to know which.

Brad touched her elbow and she turned her head to see Brenner and the twins watching her. She was so interested in finding out what the thieves would be paying attention to, she forgot to be careful herself.

Brenner raised his hand to his brow and tipped an invisible hat her way. The Evil Twins smiled.

"Friends of yours?" Brad murmured.

"I don't know them." Dani didn't miss that he was waiting for more. "Probably fans of my mother. It happens."

He accepted that with a nod.

Rose stepped up beside her and linked her arm through Dani's familiarly. "Good eye," she said, nodding toward Archer's portrait. "This is one of the pieces I mentioned. I'm determined to get it."

Well, fuck. Like this wasn't going to be hard enough already.

CHAPTER SIX

By THE TIME Dani got back home, the stone house was shadowed, darkness sliding down from the sky, eating up the last scraps of sunset. She'd brought a bag of salt and grease and a fizzy, caffeinated fountain drink home, along with a thick portfolio of material and a laptop with an encrypted flash drive from Brad Hackworth. The drive-thru felt necessary, something low to rub off the day's high art—both the literal kind and the figurative pretension of it all. To remind her of where she started and where she belonged.

She carried the bag and portfolio toward the front door, dreaming of removing the heels she still had on. Impractical shoes for impractical people, but she wanted to dress the part for the first meet. As soon as she got inside, Sunflower's teeth gleamed as her dog smiled up at her.

"Yes, the fries are for you," she said and kicked off the stilts.

Sunflower scampered out past her, and Dani set up camp in the living room. She changed clothes and inhaled the burger, then she rummaged through the contents of the portfolio. The empty bookshelves reminded her this wasn't home anymore, and that was when she noticed she had set up the same footprint with her preliminaries that she would in an anonymous hotel.

She widened the circle into a sprawling oval. Set up a hot spot, since there was no internet yet. Sunflower trotted back in, banging the door shut with her butt—smart girl—and accepted a few fries. The kitchen was stocked with the necessities Dani had gone out for pre-dawn: coffee, protein bars, dog food.

Dani pulled the new laptop out of her bag and plugged the secure drive Brad Hackworth had given her into the port. She was hesitant to use the computer, *but* if the Hackworths were tracking her keystrokes (and she would, if she were in their place) she should show she was working. Still, she'd be a thousand times more comfortable if Rabbit were part of her crew and could scrub it first. As long as the Hackworths didn't see anything to spike an alert, they wouldn't let her *know* they were watching her. So she'd just be careful.

With the uber-rich, you never knew for sure, though. They could afford due diligence. Which meant they could also afford to be lax. Dani was a backup security consultant, after all. It was possible the heart attack guy wasn't that good, that they truly didn't have the protocols in place they should. Or, farther fetched, it could be that the Hackworths decided to trust her.

Thieves tended to be more mistrustful and thorough than the people they stole from. But there were always exceptions.

Dani had her own laptop, obviously, and once she had the files open, she could copy the relevant parts over manually. She might not have Rabbit's extra magic touch, but she had never been busted by sloppy electronics work either.

The paper Brad gave her was more interesting than she expected. She sorted it into a few stacks.

The building plans for the Fortress were included, along with an overlay showing the current security features as well as lights, fire exits, and safety provisions. There were a few concealed stairwells and spaces obviously meant for transporting paintings from the loading dock to various galleries without being seen, as well as hidden HVAC nooks and crannies.

Everything fit with the profile of Hackworth she was developing—aka that he was a paranoid magic hoarder who didn't want anyone else laying eyes on his art–slash–source of power—and any portion of it might come in handy. No secret tunnels, alas, or adjacent buildings. Though, in Dani's opinion, too many movies had been made from real-life cases that involved digging ways in and out for it to be an effective strategy at this point anyway.

The secure drive unlocked the laptop, and she quickly searched to see what else she had access to. She wanted to know all about Hackworth and his relationship to magic, but that wasn't likely to be documented. Instead she found deeper information on the contractors and specifics of the security system. Background checks on the security guards, along with employment data. She skimmed through those quickly—lots of ex-military, a few ex-cops, and none of them new hires.

She wondered when Hackworth usually visited the Fortress, and who'd have been on duty then. He didn't seem the type to leave anything to chance. Would any camera footage from before he died be available? Her instincts told her no, but she made a note to check anyway. She walked over to the kitchen table, removed a small piece of tape, and returned to put it over the laptop's built-in camera. Then she fetched her own machine and logged into it.

She ran down the checklist of information she needed to absorb to even begin preparing her plan to steal the painting, and her knees weakened. Sensing her mood, Sunflower crushed up against her. How was she possibly going to manage this without help? And the question she still couldn't answer: Who the hell *was* Archer? She hadn't wanted to spike Rose's interest by asking why she wanted that specific painting. She had a few days to figure that out.

Her phone buzzed. It had to be her new employers, since they were the only ones with the number. She picked up quickly. "Yes?" she said. Then, realizing they'd probably expect niceties, "Danielle Poissant speaking."

A warm chuckle came back. "Am I bothering you, Danielle Poissant?"

Brad. The way he said her name was flirtatious. An attraction might come in handy.

Besides, you like him.

"No, no," she said. "Hi, Brad." She sat down in the clear spot she left for herself on the floor between the computers. "Sorry. I was just digging into the files."

"That's why I'm calling."

Was *he* the one watching her keystrokes? Or was she just being paranoid to wonder?

"I just got the provenance and estimated valuation information for you. I'm adding it to the drive now. Along with the security footage from today."

Oh.

"That was fast."

"You don't have much time, so I figured the sooner the better." He laughed again, soft and friendly. She refused to let herself return it. "The information already existed. Prying it loose from Rose was the hard part."

A notification popped up on the screen for a new file share titled *The Collection*. So . . . why were they still on the phone together? "Great, I'll let you go, then."

"Don't you want to make sure it's all there? I want to make sure you have what you need."

No one had checked to see if Dani had what she needed in a long time. She didn't know if she liked it. She knew she couldn't trust it.

She grunted noncommittally and opened the first file. A spreadsheet, helpfully columned so she could reorganize the info however she wanted. She scrolled and scrolled and her mind nearly blanked. The sheer length of the list was just as overwhelming as seeing the pieces in person.

"I can tell you're in deep focus mode," Brad said—and not like he was offended. "I do the same thing. I'll let you go."

"Bye—and, Brad, thanks for checking in and, ah, making sure I've got everything I asked for." Not everything she needed, of course, but if she managed to pull this off . . .

"We'll talk soon," he said, and she noted the low promise in his voice. This could get messy.

Unfortunately, Dani excelled at that. Messy seemed to come as naturally to her as her magic. So why did the prospect create a hint of excitement this time?

Because it was better than dwelling on Elliott.

She set down the phone and opened the security video. Brenner and the twins hadn't stuck together initially. Brenner had paused in the second gallery—she'd have to cross-reference the map later since the angle didn't show what he stopped to look at. The twins made their way through, hesitating occasionally, and yes, they were definitely keeping an eye on her. Eventually, Brenner had joined them.

As she suspected, the trio spent a few minutes in front of Archer's portrait. She had competition. They'd moved away when she and Brad entered the room. What she couldn't tell yet was if the twins and Brenner were definitely working together.

There was no hint of Brad paying attention to them, which was another mark in the column that he didn't know the real truth of the collection—as was his selling it. Wouldn't he want the power his dad had amassed? The art was a symbol of his wealth, but Dani also assumed that the machine he'd built had helped him continue to enlarge it.

His history in business had been a rags-to-riches story, an upward trajectory without the usual hiccups. There were eventually investigations into human rights violations, calls for environmental fines and regulation. He had a finger in any corporate pie with a hint of lucrative corruption—oil, coal, fast fashion, plastics, you name it. He'd seemed immune to consequences for any shady business practices, something most people chalked up to political donations. Now she knew the likeliest real reason why, if not exactly how the collection worked to his benefit. Though he'd done well for many decades, the project of getting the Fortress of Art to where it was now must have taken continual acquisitions . . .

Digging back into the collection spreadsheet, she realized she had another problem. She didn't know the title of Archer's portrait or the artist. She'd roughly estimated when she thought it was painted, though that still didn't seem possible.

The phone buzzed again. Okay, Brad's calling had gone from intriguing to annoying like that. She had to work. She had a week. In no universe was it enough time. She paused for a slow breath so she wouldn't sound irritable and picked it up. "Forget something?" she answered, lighter this time.

The call had a tinny sound. A blasé woman's voice asked, "Is this Danielle Poissant?"

Her first inclination was to say no, but that would be foolish. The Hackworths were the only people with this number, so it had to be someone they'd put in touch with her.

"Yes." Dani propped the phone between her shoulder and ear and re-sorted the spreadsheet based on the age of the works.

"This is a call from the Federal Medical Center in Lexington," the woman on the other end said.

Dani straightened and the phone almost fell. She fumbled to catch it. "And?"

"Your mother has been transferred here."

The medical center was where sick or injured federal inmates in the region were usually sent. There were also some low-risk female prisoners at the camp next door. Back when, they'd had some associates end up there, from time to time. Dani had been toted along to one or two visiting days to distract the guards with her cuteness through well-timed crying fits or tripping over her own feet.

Her stomach clenched like a fist. What if her mother was sick . . . what if she was truly ill or hurt and with Dani so close and . . .

"Is she okay?" Dani asked. Sunflower laid her head in Dani's lap, big brown eyes staring up in concern.

The woman was emotionally vaccinated against her effect on the people she called. *Figures, given the notifications she must make, working where she does.* Her voice didn't change a note. "She was attacked, but her prognosis is good. She's added you to her visitors list. Hours are tomorrow morning starting at ten-thirty . . ." The woman continued to rattle off requirements, things Dani could and couldn't bring, and Dani absorbed none of it.

She hadn't seen or heard from her mother in ten years. Not since the trial. She'd tried to get in touch, obviously. Once she turned eighteen, every couple of years she put in a request to be added to the list, cleared to see her mother. She'd have driven anywhere.

The response was always no.

The fact she was summoning Dani *now,* and that she'd been transferred to Lexington just as Dani returned and was getting ready to hit the Fortress of Art . . . Well, that was something. There were no coincidences that big. She'd obviously schemed her way into Dani's new phone number, likely through Archer himself.

Dani imagined her childhood years, so often spent right here on this floor with Mia—and Elliott nearby, two years older and reading fat Stephen King novels in order to better ignore the girls. Rabbit would pace back and forth from the kitchen to the living room, unable to stay still for longer than a hot minute. Barefoot, because her mud boots weren't allowed in their house. And Dani's mother, Maria, tidy and ever in control, would be perched at the edge of her chair and leaning over the kitchen table, the occasional cigarette between her delicate fingers, usually a pair of building plans in front of her.

Their other associates came and went as required, but this was *them.* The crew, and the family.

Only it wasn't everyone, and never had been. Memory was a house that always seemed to win, rewriting history for either maximum escape or maximum pain. Look closer, and there was Archer, present but invisible, the whispering figure who showed up late at night and talked to Dani's mother alone. Dani had snuck to the top of the stairs so many times, waiting to catch a glimpse of him. She never had. Only the shadows of his presence.

Who is he? And what did he hold over her mother?

Tomorrow loomed, and it had been so long coming. She ran her fingers over Sunflower's head, stroking, drawing some comfort. She was going to need it . . .

And that's when she thought to check. She searched on her own name on the Hackworth machine. There was the paperwork for the house and the payment account with lots of zeroes for the job. That wasn't what she was looking for.

But then, yes, there it was.

The file on her.

She opened it and skimmed the background check, and of course, it was her life. There was nothing surprising. There was also nothing that couldn't have been gleaned from the public record, from any one of several true crime specials about her and—mostly—her mother. *Dateline, 20/20,* the *60 Minutes* on which the great Barbara Walters definitely did *not* make her mother cry, despite showing pictures of little Dani onscreen. (Tough luck, Babs; Dani could've told her that wasn't going to happen. Maria Poissant did not show weakness. She might not even have any. Her daughter certainly wasn't one.)

The lack of any true insight was a good thing, except if this was all they had . . . Dani still had no idea how Archer had found her.

She went back to the spreadsheet Brad had sent over and finished reordering the columns by age of artwork, and swallowed bile at the confirmation of just how much art history William Hackworth had been hoarding. Hundreds of years of it, paintings that would be called priceless. One of the articles she read quoted him as saying he'd found that "Nothing and no one is priceless. I can buy anything or anyone I want." The trite wisdom of someone soulless and wealthy, describing themselves more than the world.

Most people he was right about, but not all of them. *You have a price, Dani. Don't pretend you don't.*

Dani wished her inner compass would shut up. She'd been wishing that since she was a kid with skinned knees and a paintbrush. She'd be seeing her own price tomorrow. Much as the rest of the world might view it differently—as her mother might—Archer had known the truth. He'd never even met Dani, but he knew exactly how to get her to do what he wanted.

The list of paintings from the late 1800s was long, and she clicked through the linked files with photographs from the sellers he originally acquired from. These were all official catalogue photos taken under special lighting by museums, private owners, and auction houses. From what Dani could tell, he'd never sold a single piece once he owned it. That matched up with what Brad said about William Hackworth restricting the enjoyment of the Fortress's contents to himself. A mystery was certainly worth a lot in the world he traveled in, but the typical move would've been to flaunt his possessions, not hide them. It must have galled him to not get to show off what he'd made. He'd been smart enough to know what had to be the biggest secret of his wealth was worth keeping. But smart enough not to tell *anyone*? She had to figure out how much Brad understood.

Archer's portrait didn't come up. Well, obviously, it *couldn't* be that old, could it?

Another thought occurred to her. She scrolled to the end, and as expected, there was a grouping of undated artwork. She dismissed a few based on the descriptions, and hesitated before choosing the most likely option: *Untitled Gentleman, portrait. Artist: Unknown. Era: 1890–1900.*

As far as she could tell, there was no original catalogue photograph for this piece, alone of all of them.

There's a rule among thieves. The good ones anyway. Always know what you're stealing.

Dani switched computers and looked up the visitation guidelines for the morning. She wouldn't sleep, but she had to try.

The Poison Angel ate up Barbara Walters's baiting questions like a tasty snack. There was no telling what she meant to do to Dani.

SEVEN DAYS OUT

CHAPTER SEVEN

THE FIRST BANK Dani decided to try the safe-deposit key at was the second oldest in town, but it had the benefit of being more or less on the way to the Federal Medical Center.

She had managed to toss and turn for a few feverish hours—Van Gogh sunflowers like orange-yellow-gold explosions behind her fevered eyelids, the walls of the Fortress tumbling down on her in a fun house of portrait faces, Archer cool and serene and pale, laughing silently, Brad's easy smile, and then Elliott's face. His appearance disturbed her enough to wake her. There was no point in making an attempt to go back to sleep once she started dreaming about Elliott.

Dani had a while to kill and her focus was shit. She could sort through more information, but she'd only have to do it again. Sunflower was happy to go on a long, dewy, sunrise walk through grass so green that if you tried to capture the hue in paint it always managed to look neon, fake, impossible. The difficulty of that green was at least half the reason so many painters from Kentucky did thin, cheap-looking work. The rest was the reliance on an endless boring monotony of horse scenes. It took no skill to make a boring-ass painting of a horse, and real talent to make a good one. Why bother to split the difference if it sold? Lots of people preferred mediocre art, with its ease, the lack of challenge it presented.

Dani parked at a bank that might be in any town—a square box of reflective windows. She rotated the safe-deposit-box key in her fingers, palming it on her way inside.

They never did bank jobs, but she found herself casing the place anyway. Second nature. If she got lucky, she'd walk in to see her mother with a card tucked in her back pocket. There was no way this key got hidden in the wall by accident.

Three security guards were on duty. Two on the door, who both smiled pleasantly at her. Another stood by a large reception desk with two tellers at it. The rest of the lobby was bland and white and modern, Ikea style, redone within the last five years. The art was a series of shockingly bad abstracts, but probably expensive. They should've stuck with horses that looked exactly like horses, running across too-green fields.

Dani approached the desk and the man on duty gave her a tired nod. The woman beside him had a line of small porcelain collectible dolls on her side of the shelf, propped to face her. One of them was a clown. She must be a delight to work with.

"Can I help you, miss?" he asked.

Dani wasn't sure if she was relieved or insulted she wasn't yet in "ma'am" territory. She felt about a hundred years old—as old as that painting of Archer apparently was. She smiled her safe smile, the "don't worry about me, I'm as normal as it gets" smile she mastered from watching her mother, and opened her palm to produce the key.

"I'm, ah, closing up a family estate and found this. One of yours?"

The man bent closer to look at the key. The woman beside him stared at Dani. A true stare, like she was watching a hit-and-run and needed to get Dani's license plate. Or like she was trying to place her.

The man squinted and finally shook his head. "Not ours. You might try Trust Bluegrass. I hope you find it."

Dani should nod, keep smiling, and go. Instead she pocketed the key and stared back at the woman. "Yes?"

"You're her." The woman lifted a finger to point and caught herself. She hissed to the man. "That's her."

The man started to apologize and Dani interrupted, "You're right, I am her." She leaned over the countertop. Lexington was too big to be a small town, but she had forgotten how it managed to be so despite that. For better and worse. "You a true crime fan?"

The woman nodded.

Of course. The local interest angle of some special hour or another probably grabbed her attention.

Dani truly should leave. That was another of her magic acts. Let people talk about you, just don't let them see you react to what they say. Leave before they know they've drawn blood. That it was even possible to. Not that a woman like this could manage that, but Dani was on her way to see her mother, who could and would, without even meaning to.

"Thanks," Dani said to the man and then she reached over and plucked the clown from the row of dolls. She looked at the woman with a dare for her to do anything, then to the security guards. She made it all the way to the door on their frozen shock and tossed the doll into the trash can there.

"Don't worry," she said to the security guards. "I won't be back."

Fuck, what was she thinking? She wasn't. The result was she'd be lucky if they didn't warn every other bank in town she had a safe-deposit-box key and was incoming.

She grinned in the seat of her car—a real smile. She'd defended herself, and she didn't regret it. She might have a little of her mother left in her, after all.

No, that was a foolish thought. Her mother was never impulsive.

Which meant Dani was probably still the same person she was as a kid when she exploded their life.

The open sweep of a city park alerted Dani she was close to the detention center drive, so she didn't miss her turn despite forgoing GPS. She provided her name and showed ID at a guard booth, and proceeded up a pockmarked asphalt lane toward a long parking lot and the complex beyond. The Federal Medical Center itself looked less like a prison or a hospital than a high school in bad need of an update.

Dani checked in at the front desk and was told to take a hard plastic seat and wait until the inmate count was finished. She let her mind wander and it settled on the first job her mother ever brought her along on. It wasn't the first time Dani did work for her; her paintings began to pass muster when she was twelve. She'd be provided with the closest to the original materials or simulations as her mother could manage through her network, because she always cautioned against relying only on Dani's magic. "Magic can fail you at the worst of times," her mother would say, and Dani would wonder *why* she said it, what she meant, when her mother's ever had . . . At least that her mother knew about.

She might have even asked once—though her mother wouldn't have answered.

The job was a private home collection, lower stakes than some others, because if anything went wrong, the owners would be less likely to advertise they'd been a target. The rich often purchase art for its financial value, and writing off the loss is just as good as the work on the wall. Even if the person happens to love it, the chagrin at revealing that their security wasn't up to snuff often kept such incidents quiet. And the FBI Art Crime Team tended to honor the wishes of the owners, because if they didn't, fewer people would report thefts. So despite the splashy headlines, and the cachet in the criminal world, museum thefts were far less common than those from private home collections.

That was the night Dani received her first ski mask. Probably not something a lot of kids found significant. Or, if they did, it was to go along with the memory of a snowy day. Sledding down a hill in bright hats, screeching with glee and bombing snowballs at the rest of the neighborhood. But for her, accepting the black mask from her mother had been a sacred rite. She had pulled the scratchy cot-

ton over her face with the feeling of standing on the cusp of everything she longed for. She was certain she would emerge from the
night as sure of herself as her mother was, and closer to her mother
than ever.

But the night had begun and proceeded with a continual series
of cautions followed by corrections. Dani was no natural cat bur-
glar, based on her mother's reactions. She was a cob horse, plod-
ding, no good for fieldwork. It was only when they finally reached
the gallery and had swapped out a small Renoir for Dani's copy
wrapped in cloth in her backpack, that her mother had put an arm
around Dani, squeezed her shoulder, and tucked her into her side.
She said, "Remember this moment."

Obviously, Dani did. She'd soaked in the command, every second available for her to revisit. But what she remembered most?
The feeling she didn't belong there. That she and her mother were
two entirely different people. That Dani would mess things up.
Somehow. Eventually.

She remembered she'd been right.

The heavy door to the waiting room cracked and a woman in
khaki scrubs called, "Miss Poissant?"

This time, the "miss" made her feel even younger. Dani rose to
her feet.

"This way," the woman at the door said. And after she closed it
behind them, "Your mother is . . . something. But you must know
that."

"Mm." Dani focused on preparing her game face.

Her mother's charm, her ability to manipulate, wouldn't have
gone away just because she was behind bars. As it was, she'd been
so notorious about swaying people to her side that by the time of
her trial, she always had two guards assigned to her. They might not
know about magic, but they'd figured out she could win people over
if she got them alone.

Dani often wondered what her mother might have gotten by
with if her power had a few less limits. If she could use it on multi-

ple people at a time, if the effects didn't wane eventually . . . And she imagined the possible range of reactions if Maria ever found out it didn't work on Dani.

The woman led her far beyond the regular visitors' lounge, on a winding path through halls with the smell of bleach barely covering the stench of illness. And then, at last, they slowed at a line of patient rooms.

A guard was posted at the door they stopped at, and Dani spotted a second just inside the threshold. The protocol hadn't changed. She wasn't surprised to find it a single either, not since they'd mentioned an attack. They'd want to keep her isolated, in case it was gang or grudge related, making a repeat attempt more likely.

Dani still couldn't imagine anyone having the guts to come at her mother.

The bare-bones décor continued the run-down prison non-chic. If it was possible for sheets to have a negative thread count, the white set on the bed looked scratchy enough to manage it. A cuff bound her mother to the bed's side rail by her left wrist.

She sat up, her posture erect as any queen's. Someone had challenged her rule, though. A deep gouge with stitches marred her perfect cheek, a healing black eye above. But those alone wouldn't be enough to get her sent here.

"How are you?" Dani asked.

Maria ignored Dani and looked to the escort. "I was hoping we could go out to that cute patio next door. I heard sometimes you let people visit out there, since Covid."

The escort eyeballed the guard, who shrugged. "She asked."

The woman turned to her mother. "You took a knife to the stomach that could've killed you. You're on bed rest. When you are feeling better, you'll be going back to your own camp. Now, you have twenty minutes with your daughter. You will take it here."

"Can we have privacy?" her mother asked, but it didn't sound like a question.

"You okay with that?" the woman asked Dani.

Dani nodded, still trying to find words.

The guard said, "We'll be right outside. Just let us know if you're ready sooner."

The woman shut the door behind them and there she was, alone with her mother.

Dani hesitated. She had been looking forward to the buffer of other people. This . . . Even with the guards outside, they were alone.

She pressed down a relentless wave of emotions: dread, fear, regret, and—the worst, the one she couldn't ever trust—hope.

Her mother looked at Dani finally. "Are you going to sit down or not?" she said.

Dani walked across the linoleum as if it were a plank. She might as well be boarding an enemy captain's ship.

There was a small chair bolted to the floor beside the bed, and Dani took it.

Injured or not, Maria Poissant was as self-contained as ever. She somehow managed to make the baggy scrubs of the inmate uniform fit as if tailored to her—hell, they might have been, by some new sycophant, for all Dani knew. Well, except they clearly had enough information about her ability to manipulate people that she wasn't being allowed to mingle.

Dani examined her more closely.

Whatever she expected, it wasn't this. All these years she'd wondered, obsessed, over what her mother's life in jail had been like. There were two lines, faint, on either side of her mouth. The suggestion of crow's feet. Other than the injuries, no time might have passed. Her hair was still black, any gray hidden, an impeccable bob.

Her mother placed her free hand on top of the cuffed one on the rail, and then Dani noticed another difference. Her nails were bare. No French-tipped manicure.

"You look good, considering," Dani said. And added, "You haven't aged at all."

Her mother stayed quiet for a long moment. Then, "You'd better not be fucking Archer."

Reality stuttered and Dani blinked.

"Nice to see you after all these years too. How have you been, Dani, my long-abandoned daughter? Oh, don't worry about me. I'm making it okay."

Maria pursed her lips. "Well, are you?"

It was ceding ground, but Dani answered. "No. Of course not." She shook her head. "I thought you might be dying when I got the phone call last night, but now I see that's not the case."

Maria rolled her eyes. "Darling, take it down a notch. You of all people know why I'm here."

A punch to the heart. Even though she knew it was coming. "I don't, actually, know why you are here *now*."

Her mother nodded. "Yes, you do. Do you know how much it pained me to have to sweet-talk someone inside on a basic smash and grab into stabbing me so I could come see you? She threw in the scar and black eye without my approval." Maria's lips tightened. "And you'd best be glad I'm here."

Maria reached over to the table beside her bed. It held a plastic water cup and a newspaper, which she picked up. "What did I always say about discretion?"

She unfolded the paper and pointed to the photo accompanying the story below the fold on the right. Dani immediately saw herself behind Rose and beside Brad Hackworth. The headline was, predictably, about the auction.

Shit.

How hadn't she seen this coming?

Her mother tilted her head, birdlike, considering. "Dani, did I really teach you nothing? What is this amateur-hour bullshit?"

Dani didn't bother reaching for the paper. Her mother's statement meant she was mentioned in the story too. *That's* why the woman at the bank recognized her.

Yes, it was sloppy. She was going to have to do better. No one paid attention to the kind of jobs she usually did; that was why she picked those targets. "Look . . ."

"Shhh," Maria said. "I'm here *now* because Archer asked me to help you."

Dani's jaw clenched tight, but she got the words out anyway. She spoke with care to leave her mother's belief intact, that she wouldn't have remembered Archer when they met. "He claims you were partners. Who is he? And why am I stealing a painting of him?"

Maria's lips quirked, something like a smile. "Because I'm not exactly available."

Close to the same phrasing Archer had used.

"You know," Maria said, "I lost everything because of you. Only Rabbit stayed in touch."

"I would have been there." Maria hadn't even let Dani apologize. Dani managed to keep her voice neutral, then realized with horror that her hands were extended to her mother.

Maria looked at them.

Dani hesitated, then pulled her fingers back into her lap. "I'm sorry," she said. "So sorry. For everything. I screwed up." *I was afraid for you, Mom,* she didn't say. *For what Archer might be doing to you.*

"I got the letters," Maria said. "Now's when you prove it. You can't afford mistakes like this." She tucked her chin toward the paper. "I need you to pull this off, so don't fuck it up."

"Did you know Hackworth's secret? What the collection is?"

Maria sniffed. "Of fucking course. I may be trapped in here, but don't underestimate me."

Maria Poissant was all politesse when Dani was growing up. Sure, she could terrify anyone, and no one crossed her unless they were complete fools, but she maintained a sheen of class that she'd adopted, not been born with, no matter what. When they arrested Maria, she had extended her hands and looked—just looked—at Dani, after asking, calm as a flat gray line on canvas, "What did you do?"

She rarely used what she called "vulgarity" and sometimes tsked foulmouthed Rabbit. She was, in fact, the only member of the crew who didn't throw around "shit" and "fuck" and "damn" like a spice. Except Dani, and that was only to keep her mother happy. There had been more changes in Maria; they just weren't visible.

"I wouldn't even try to estimate you," Dani said.

"Good."

"Where is Archer? How do I reach him?"

Her mother's lips tightened, and then, "Where were you, when he came to you?"

"St. Louis. Why?"

"He'll be spent, recovering. You'll see him soon, I'd wager. But remember, he only sought you out because of me."

A weird answer, but maybe it had something to do with his particular power.

Dani had circled what she asked next in her mind, never saying it out loud. "Is he my father?"

Her mother lifted her chin, haughty. "Don't be silly. Though he did encourage me to have you. You should be thankful for him."

That was about the last thing Dani felt. She kept it to herself.

Maria continued, "To help you—to help you help him—I've released them. They can and will work with you. All of them. You're back in, so don't waste it. Call Rabbit."

Dani didn't know whether to thank her or not, after Rabbit's slap. "I'm doing this for you, Mom."

"I know. Be more discreet," Maria said, nodding at the paper. "Don't ruin our family name. We'll talk again."

Maria raised her voice and called, "Ready."

The door opened, and the guard reentered. The escort had waited. She smirked at Dani as if to say, *I knew you wouldn't last long in there.*

A million questions rose to Dani's tongue, but she had to swallow them. Like always.

CHAPTER EIGHT

BACK HOME, IN the smaller upstairs bathroom, Dani peeled off dye-coated gloves and set the timer for her hair. She didn't go as dark as her mother's color, and not quite as dark as her own natural color, but close. A big change from her usual blond by several shades. Brown with a few lowlights. The photograph had made her too recognizable, but that was an easy correction.

She didn't want to draw the eye too much, but she didn't want to stand out in the posh art crowd either, so she had chosen something expected. A shade any of those women might walk into a salon and get talked into by a stylist who knows they say they want a change but really want attention for a few hours and to stay conservative, one of the group.

Sunflower lolled on the hall floor, rolled over on her back, napping with her feet in the air. Trusting. And it mattered more than it should, how completely Dani's dog trusted her and always had. Especially as no one else seemed to. Dogs were good judges of character.

Although having a dog in her line of work was ridiculous. She had explained this to herself when Sunflower showed up and started shadowing her while Dani was shaking down a creep in Tempe. When she took the dog to the local shelter, they'd said, "Her owner died. We can't keep her from escaping. She's a Houdini."

"Is it a kill shelter?" she'd asked—a last-ditch. It had been, so then she had a dog. Yet in the lowest, quietest moments of life, a dog made you feel redeemable. If a dog loved you, you must not be all bad.

Dani carefully stepped past Sunflower so as not to wake her and made her way over to the stairs.

On the night Dani betrayed her mother, they had the whole thing down to . . . well, a fine art. In her mind, she might as well be back in that museum at seventeen. Her mom behind her, and the corridor stretching out in front of her, a dark mouth luring her into its silent scream.

The FBI agent who approached Dani shouldn't have, and she shouldn't have talked to him. But her mother's personality had been getting darker and more erratic. She'd been hearing angry voices, that low thrum of Archer's, as she hid at the top of the stairs. Her mother's beautiful face had dark circles stamped like bruises beneath her eyes. She was hardly sleeping.

And then she'd done something Dani couldn't believe or forgive. Every time Dani asked about Archer, to meet him, who he was, her mother had put her off. Dani finally worked up the courage to make a demand. Her mother was planning their biggest score yet and soon—the hit on the Fortress of Art. They had one smaller target to do first. "You need me," Dani had said, "and you need to tell me the truth. Who is Archer? I want to meet him."

Her mother had peered at Dani, eyes narrowed in annoyance. She took Dani's shoulders and squeezed and forced Dani to look straight at her. In contrast to the rest of her demeanor, her voice was soft, nearly sweet. "You don't care who Archer is, not anymore. Do you hear me? It's none of your business. You'll stop asking about him. Do you understand?"

Dani had seen her mother in action before. Her voice got kinder than usual, her focus more intense. Physical touch helped.

She was trying to work her magic *on Dani*. Make her pliant. Make her forget her worries.

She'd never done this *to Dani* before.

"Do you understand, sweetheart?" she pressed.

She'd probably be as surprised as Dani to find out her ability didn't work on her daughter.

But she wasn't going to.

"Ye-Yes," Dani said. "I'm sorry. I understand."

"You don't care about who Archer is," her mother said.

Dani's stomach churned, but she didn't let it show. She got the words out. "I don't." Then, she laid it on thicker. "Who did you say?"

Her mother nodded, confident that she'd handled Dani the same way she'd handle a stranger. She had chosen Archer—the silent partner who was becoming anything but silent—over her daughter.

Agent Sharpe with the gut feeling had shown up the next day, at exactly the right moment for Dani to see him as a way out. As a good guy. As someone who could stop her mother from getting worse, from disintegrating. Who could maybe allow them to reassess. With their magic—especially Dani's—maybe there was another way to live than this . . . Free from Archer's ever-present shadow.

The whole night, as they broke into the regional museum, Dani was on the verge of confessing, blurting out what she'd done and hoping it wasn't too late. Maria had been entirely focused, of course, not knowing they were due to be interrupted. And Dani wasn't sure when it would come.

In that hallway, dark and quiet, Dani stopped, about to tell her, but just then Maria gave her a brisk wave—the meaning clear: *Come on*. So Dani kept quiet. She was angry. Angry about her mother's attempt to alter her memory, angry at her mother for risking their relationship for someone Dani had never met. She was seventeen, in other words, and she had been mistreated. She didn't know if *this* was right or wrong, but it was a decision. A possibility for change.

And anyway, Maria had always told her right and wrong didn't exist. Only what was right for them.

They made it to the door of the first gallery. Her mother had the keypad code, procured by Rabbit's network of little helpers. The museum had a handful of extremely valuable pieces, but only so-so security.

The next part was a thrill, every time. Even that night.

Having somewhere they weren't supposed to be all to themselves. Taking what they wanted, and no one being the wiser. Not until they wanted them to be.

Rabbit had infected the cameras with a virus, causing them to glitch. Dani's mother had put her flashlight on the floor in the gallery, angling it up at the star painting in the museum's collection. She lifted the antique frame away from the wall, then flipped the painting facedown to remove it.

Dani knelt beside her and unrolled her own painting. Every stroke was perfect. She started training with oils when she was eight and could replicate any master, past or present, by seventeen. Her pieces would stand up to scrutiny by an expert because of the care she took with materials and technique, but for the most part that never happened. Because when someone looked at Dani's painting, they believed they were seeing the original.

Swiftly, her mother removed this original from the frame and rolled it up carefully while Dani set the replacement in its place. Her mom was humming a little. The Beatles' "Here Comes the Sun." Happy. She stapled Dani's canvas to the frame, and together they placed it back on the wall.

A still life of flowers on a table, beginning to wilt. Decay at the edges, their beauty in the dying. The gasp of color they still hung on to. Manet became obsessed with flowers near the end of his career. Dani had always liked painting them too. By now, Dani was praying that the plan had changed and the agent wouldn't show up tonight. She might as well be in that vase, dying slowly.

Her mother stole two other pieces, and didn't replace them with copies. It was *their* theft that was meant to trigger the museum to

call in her mother to consult on a security upgrade and try to find
the missing pieces. The mystery would be why the thieves left the
most valuable piece behind. Why did they switch it out instead of
just fencing Dani's fakes? The exhilaration of obtaining the real object. Her mother's commitment to her craft. The one time Dani
asked outright, Maria said it was what they did. They made double
this way, triple sometimes. Anyway, you couldn't be the best at
something if you stopped doing it. And they *needed* to be the best.

They were back in the hallway, ready to leave. Three minutes
had passed since they'd entered.

Dani noticed the sweep of a light in the hallway behind them
first. And she knew in that moment, with a certainty that burned
through her, that she'd made the wrong choice.

"Mom," she said. "I need to tell you something."

Her mother carried the two paintings in frames by straps over
her shoulder. Dani held the rolled-up Manet. "Not now," her mom
said. "We need to go."

The flashlight got closer.

"Mom, it has to be now. I'm—I didn't mean—"

Her mother's mouth set in a frown. When she turned to see what
Dani meant, there he was, the agent from the Art Crime Team. He
was leading a small group of men and women in jackets and bul-
letproof vests.

"Maria Poissant," Agent Sharpe said. "You're under arrest for . . ."

"What did you do?" she asked as he rattled off Miranda and
started on a list of felony charges. Then more firmly, she told Dani,
"Go!"

Dani understood. She ran off to alert the van that there was trouble. She could at least save the others. She gave two short bursts
with the flashlight at the window at the end of the hall. The agents
were occupied with her mother, only one coming for her. Rabbit
got the crew out of there. Elliott was driving. Mia would be waiting
at home. Rabbit was a survivor and she'd lie low, cover their tracks.
Dani couldn't imagine what they would think of her when they
found out.

The boiling heat of anger inside Dani was gone by then. Dani had broken the rules, and it wasn't Archer who had destroyed their family in the end. *She* had ruined them. Right before her mother was about to carry out her most anticipated score.

Dani had told their secrets. Some of them.

She begged to be forgiven, but her mother didn't speak to her again. Not until today's visit. After a few months—once the sentencing happened, the stone house was put up for auction, and Dani was alone in the basement of a perfectly normal foster family—she had realized that she'd been an idiot to wait for her mother's mind to change. Forgiveness was not coming. Not on any certain timetable.

So she'd have to go for atonement instead. That's when she started forming the idea of running her own cons. And by then, Rabbit and Mia refused to talk to her, instructed by Maria; there was no one to talk her out of leaving. She'd thought Elliott would come with her, but she'd been a fool.

The timer went off and she headed upstairs to rinse the dye off before the team arrived. She refused to chase them down at Rabbit's. Let them come to her.

She needed all the help she could get. And their memories of the stone house should be far less complicated than her own.

CHAPTER NINE

THEY WERE LATE. Dani understood—an attempt to earn back the ground she might have gained from holding the meeting here. Hell, she might have done the same if the circumstances were reversed. Not that they had the time for one-up-womanship and games, but she had plenty to do. She waited by working her way through the remaining materials and building a supplies list.

All the while, she tried not to imagine the crew gathered in this small, much-loved space around her. Rabbit, pacing, cursing: a know-it-all who was annoyingly (nearly) always right. And Mia. Would she come? Dani suspected she would. Then there was Elliott . . .

Thinking about Elliott made her stomach tighten like hands grasped too tight. Even though she had no business thinking about him as anything other than a member of the team.

Still. She wondered if he had a girlfriend now. He must. Maybe she was a horror fan, or maybe she just pretended to be, since Elliott faithfully read every word Stephen King published—or he used to when they were kids. It was all too easy to envision Elliott and this mystery girlfriend cuddled up sweet and normal on some couch they bought new, a scary movie playing on a giant TV and her screaming and grabbing onto his arms and burying her face in his shoulder, and him reassuring her with a laugh that it's okay, the monster isn't real . . .

Dani realized she'd crumpled the sheet of paper she was making the shopping list on and smoothed it out.

The sharp slam of a car door, then another, finally signaled their arrival. Sunflower sprung off the floor nearby, waiting for Dani to tell her whether to bark or not. Dani made a little motion with her hand. Sunflower hesitated—which wasn't like her dog—wanting to stay near Dani, probably understanding Dani's emotional state better than she did. Dani made the gesture again and Sunflower slunk behind the couch, out of sight, the sound of paws sliding as she lay down on the hardwood floor.

Rabbit marched through the front door wearing the mud boots that would never have been allowed by Maria. Dani decided to let that go, but not everything.

"No knock?" Dani said.

"I guess I was raised in a barn." Rabbit raised her shoulders in an exaggerated shrug. "We came, didn't we?"

Mia entered next, offering a sympathetic nod to Dani that was somehow worse than Rabbit's combative greeting. Pity? Dani had never wanted it.

"Hi, Mia." Dani gestured to the couch and the chairs. "Make yourself at home."

Elliott came in next, shutting the door behind him.

Sunflower trotted over to Dani's side again, giving a low disgruntled growl. Dogs and their sixth sense could be inconvenient. In this case, outing her uneasiness at Elliott's arrival. She felt like a fool all over again for thinking he might show up that first night back.

"Sunflower, go lay down," Dani said, a hand on her hip to show she meant it.

The dog gave Dani a baleful look and trotted over to the side of the couch, lowering herself into that border collie sphinx pose, ready to leap into action.

Way to read the room, dog.

The only truly friendly face she saw was Mia's.

"She really is named Sunflower," Mia said, almost smiling.

Dani nodded.

"It's a good name," Elliott said.

A confusingly pleasant observation.

"Much as I like dogs, we're here for a reason." Rabbit crossed her arms and took one of the cushy chairs, crossing one leg over the other too, so she was all elbows and angles.

Dani had to admit, awkward as this was—unsettling as it was—it was also familiar. She noticed then one of the reasons why. They'd all taken up their childhood positions. Mia was on the floor with her legs out in front of her, leaning against the side of her mother's chair. Elliott was on the couch, inches from where Dani had been sitting. Rabbit was barely contained by that chair, and soon enough would be pacing, from kitchen to living room and back to the kitchen. Where there was that one chair at the table.

The one where her mother used to sit, presiding. Planning.

Dani had dreams too much like this over the years, and only one person in them was missing from this room right now. Her eyes pricked with heat, but she'd die before she shed a tear or even look like she might in front of them.

"Thanks for coming," she said. "We can get started."

Dani deliberately walked over to her mother's place and took it. Time to see how they would react to the fact she was in fucking charge, even if they *were* only here because Maria summoned them.

"Well, well," Rabbit said.

Elliott cleared his throat. "Let's get down to it."

She didn't want to thank him, so she ignored it.

"I'd say it's good to see you all, but I'm not sure if it is or not," Dani said and rushed on when Rabbit's mouth opened. Rabbit wasn't expecting pushback, then. But Dani was no longer a child. "I'm sure you feel the same." She threw them a bone. "But I need your help and I'm glad to have it."

Rabbit hesitated then held her hand out palm up, as if ceding Dani the floor.

There were other places to start, but Dani was still hung up on this one piece of the puzzle. "Before we get into it . . . Did any of you ever meet Archer? Do you know anything about him?"

Rabbit's eyebrows arched.

Mia shook her head. "Not this again, Dani."

"Why?" Elliott asked and his look was piercing.

Might as well tell them. They'd have to know. "Because we're doing this job for him."

A moment passed, and Rabbit nodded. "That figures. Maria never could say no to him. And no, I've never met him. But he's not someone to try and fuck over."

"So that's why you came back," Elliott said, as if confirming a theory when he couldn't have a clue. "What's the job?"

He was more talkative these days. Hearing his voice hurt, a little stab. She'd just have to use it as a way to keep her from forgetting he wasn't for her. Not these days.

Focus on the job—the thing that would actually help her finally move on.

"We're stealing a portrait from the Fortress of Art."

"We figured it was something like that, Miss Page One," Rabbit said.

"Save it; I already got it from Mom." The word "Mom" echoed like Dani just fired a gun. She rushed on. "It's fine. I fixed it." She tossed her colored hair. "The portrait is *of* Archer, and he wants it back. Details on it are slim, but I've seen it."

"Because you're the security consultant. Sure you still need a team?" Rabbit asked.

Dani gave up her mother's throne to pace. She needed to move around. Sunflower followed her with her eyes. "Yes, I do. Otherwise, I wouldn't ask. The entire thing, it's like some sort of Rube Goldberg machine of magic. The paintings, all together, arranged just so, they were a power source for Hackworth."

"No shit?" Mia asked.

"You can feel it the second you go in there." All of them except Mia would be able to anyway, but she didn't point that out.

"What do you mean, magic machine?" Rabbit asked. She would, with her gifts for working with everything electronic.

"Not that kind of machine. Wrong word—Hackworth, he built a sort of engine, using the magic in the art. Archer's painting is part of it."

"An engine is part of a machine," Rabbit said.

"I don't think you can hack it," Dani said, more direct. "But you can hack the surveillance system. It's world class."

Rabbit settled. "I've heard rumors about complicated workings, but most aren't so big or flashy. The Fortress is some target. Not even your . . ."

Not even my mother managed to do it . . . and we all know why.

Dani went on. "There are other people interested in Archer's portrait too. And the family will be watching me, of course. But I do have access and we might just be able to pull this off."

"And you want to do this?" Elliott asked. "You seriously want our help?"

"I have to do it. Archer . . . My mother still cares about him. Look around; this is the closest she's ever come to letting me back in. And I owe her."

No one protested that. Elliott's brow furrowed.

"When is this?" Elliott asked. "How long do we have?"

Mia was watching the two of them, her eyes going from Elliott to Dani and back in a speculative way that Dani didn't appreciate.

"The auction is in a week. That'll be our last chance."

"So grab it before?" Elliott asked.

Rabbit's hands cracked together in a smack. "You want us to hit the Fortress of Art—where you're working—inside a week? And it's some kind of magical engine too? That's a yearlong job just for the preparation, even without competition. I don't think Maria would set us up"—unsaid, she might set up Dani—"but she doesn't always have the best judgment where Archer is concerned. And she's been out of the game a long time. She doesn't know how much harder it all is now . . ."

"The family just won this court case, and they're moving at warp speed before anything can derail the auction," Dani said. "This is it. All the time there is. For anyone."

"You're up to it, Mom," Mia said and Rabbit didn't argue but frowned.

"I have to do it." Dani had no choice. They must see that. "And I need you to help."

"I don't like it," Rabbit said. "But Maria kept us out of the, air quotes, 'late unpleasantness of your betrayal,' so we owe her too. What's the plan? You have anything?"

A knot in Dani relaxed a fraction. Maybe, maybe, she could do this impossible job now that she had them. "I'm still working on it. In the meantime, I need supplies. Eighteen-nineties era. Paints, canvas, frame, I have a list."

"I thought you said it was a portrait of Archer," Elliott said. He hadn't shaved this morning, the shadow of stubble on his angular face. Damn, she wished she could switch off noticing things about him.

She'd betrayed her mom, sure, but he'd betrayed her and he'd never said so much as sorry.

You didn't give him the chance.

He also didn't ask for it.

That reminder brought her back to what was important.

"I estimate it's more than a hundred years old," she said.

There was silence as they absorbed that.

"But how is that possible?" Mia asked.

Dani might as well level with them. They were her team. "Your guess is as good as mine. It's the only painting in the collection without an artist or image attached in their private inventory. I don't know if there's someone out there as good as me, or if he's fucking with us, or what. But that's the painting. I'll have to make a copy. The supplies are for that."

She didn't tell them she hadn't touched a paintbrush in a decade. She wasn't worried her magic wouldn't show up; she could feel it stirring in her fingers, even at the promise. Her magic had been waiting a long time to be used again. Tempting her every time she stole documents she could have made.

Rabbit finally got up and started pacing then, and that was when Dani knew they were actually on the job. Dani sat back down.

"I've been working on a way to combine AI and 3D printing to make forgeries that are perfect," Rabbit said.

"Let me guess," Dani said. "It doesn't work because of brush-strokes. A good eye can tell."

Rabbit scoffed. "It doesn't work because despite my best damn efforts, technology still isn't magic. Your magic. Anyway, we have a new person we work with on that stuff. Materials."

"I'll take her to see Roxie," Mia said.

"What am I doing?" Elliott asked.

Dani couldn't believe she was about to go through with this, but it made the most sense.

"You willing to get a haircut?" Dani asked him. His brown hair hit at his chin and she had to stop herself from imagining dragging her fingers through it.

"Yes. Why?"

"You're going to pose as my assistant. You were always the best of us at entries and exits. This way, you can see everything up close. I want to figure out what Brad knows."

"Brad?" Elliott asked immediately.

"Yeah, Hackworth. The heir who's selling it all instead of keeping it for himself."

Elliott frowned.

"He must not know then," Rabbit said. "Who would do that?"

Dani had the same questions, but . . . "He seems decent, the op-posite of his father."

"You *have* been gone awhile. He's the mark. We better hope he has weaknesses," Elliott said. "Will they go for you bringing me in?"

Her hackles rose on instinct, like Sunflower's might, but she swallowed the need to say she thought maybe *she* could be one of Brad's weaknesses. Elliott wasn't saying no. He'd be good at this part.

"They will," Dani said.

Rabbit tsked. "I'll make Elliott a new ID. I don't want his name on the radar. They'll do a background check."

"And you'll make sure it shows exactly what we want it to, as usual," he said.

Rabbit appeared somewhat mollified by this compliment. "You got specs for me?" she asked.

Dani nodded at the binder with the security info. "You can have that."

Rabbit snatched it up. "Okay, let's go."

Dani hated to bring this up, not when the meeting had gone relatively well. But . . .

"There were others there, from our side of things, at the viewing."

She didn't have to explain, not to Rabbit. "Who?" Rabbit asked.

"Brenner and the Evil Twins."

"Well, shit. And of course they knew who you were."

"I was introduced. Anyway . . . what can the twins do? I didn't really know them much."

"I did a gig with them last year. They can make short illusions, together," Elliott said. "He does the sound, and she can make a visual to go with it."

"Distractions," Rabbit said. "That's what they do."

That wasn't good news. "They saw me looking at the portrait."

"But they weren't looking at it first?" Rabbit clutched the binder.

Dani remembered the footage. "No, they were. Before I even came in the room. All three of them. And Hackworth's former curator wants it too."

"Let me see what I can dig up. Damn, girl, you are *still* a liability."

Dani couldn't let that pass. "I'm not. I've been working solo for a long time, and I've never been caught. Not once. And I'm not going to start now. I made a mistake then. I won't make it again."

Rabbit looked her over from head to toe. Elliott and Mia stood and flanked her, preparing to leave. Sunflower had gotten up too and butted against Dani a little, support.

"You better not," Rabbit said.

Mia nodded to Dani. "Tomorrow morning?"

"Works," Dani said. "Elliott and I need to go to the Fortress tomorrow afternoon."

"I guess I'm getting a haircut tonight then," he said.

Mia followed Rabbit out, but Elliott surprised Dani by hanging back. Even when a honk from Rabbit's truck sounded outside.

"I'll have your back," he said.

"That'll be different," she said before she could stop the words.

Elliott shook his head, then leaned in close so his breath whispered against her neck. "I like the color change," he said, ignoring her words. "Now you look like you."

"You don't know anything about me anymore," she said, barely getting it out. "What are you doing?"

"You smell like you too." His breath was almost a kiss against her skin. He smelled the same as well. Like paper, like the stories he was always reading. Like safety and spice, all rolled up in one. What she wouldn't give . . .

But no. And he shouldn't taunt her like this. He'd never been cruel.

Well, until he was.

"You smell too," she said instead. "Like you've been mucking out Rabbit's barn."

Rabbit honked again, this time laying on it.

Elliott hesitated, then said, "Forgot myself there. It won't happen again."

"It's fine," Dani said, though it wasn't. "You better go."

The honking became short bursts, Rabbit's ire growing.

Sunflower stalked him to the door, waiting until he left, then smiling at Dani with her tongue hanging out.

Once he'd gone, she eyeballed her dog. "You're right. He's not for us."

She had to stay focused. The job. The endgame: getting her mother back in her life. She finally had a chance at the amends she'd been trying to make for so long.

She allowed herself to be mad at Elliott for flirting with her, with zero apology. After she gave him room to make one, reminding him of how they left things.

Of how she left.

Alone.

Having him pose as one kind of assistant and actually be another was the right move, but she had a feeling it was going to end up as another of her regrets.

SIX DAYS OUT

CHAPTER TEN

DANI WAS WAITING on the porch when Mia pulled up in a canary Mini Cooper that was both adorable, and so unexpected, and so *her*, Dani couldn't help but laugh.

Mia got out and propped her hands on the top of the car. "Do not laugh at Drogon," she said. "He's very sensitive and classy."

"Apologies. Drogon is another dragon, I take it? And Rabbit approves of this car?"

"When I bought it, she said, and I quote, 'You bought a toy car.' I love it with my entire being."

"Okay, BBC America, got it." Dani hesitated. "Can I bring Sunflower? I can drive or . . ."

Mia rolled her eyes. "I said I loved the car, so of course dogs are allowed in it."

Dani whistled and Sunflower darted from around the side of the house.

"However," Mia said, "Roxie is allergic."

"Oh." Dani let Sunflower back inside with a pat and went to the car.

Once Dani was in the Mini, Mia glanced over at her. "She's not allergic to dogs. She's allergic to . . . structure. And she might want the dog as payment. So better not to put it out there. You'll see."

Absolutely no way anyone was taking Dani's dog, and she didn't know whether this new information intrigued or worried her.

"Oh also, she likes to be called the Curator." Mia said it blandly. "I'm the only one allowed to call her Roxie."

The secret world was filled with extreme personalities. Some exhausting in a good way, others not so much. If Dani was honest, she missed this part: the web between everyone who either had or knew about magic—most of them born poor, a combination that made a certain criminal lifestyle more likely. "Nature gave us an advantage and it's our duty to use it," Maria used to say. By the end of their run, Dani questioned if there wasn't some other, better way to do that. She didn't like everything they were doing, or what her mother seemed to be turning into.

Dani's mother had an expert in paints and materials dating—a former art historian who knew where to get certain things or how to fake them as closely as possible. Baking the paper in the oven. Aging with tea and coffee. Sourcing antique frames. Unearthing information about little-known marks on the back sides of pieces. Tricks of the trade—even though, with Dani, they were simply backups. He was usually their first stop before a new job.

"What happened to the Gentleman?" Dani asked.

"Died of mercury poisoning five years ago."

"What?" He'd always been nice to her, and kind to her mother, who had something like a soft spot for him. A man clearly born to wealth, but who was drawn to the darker side of what his knowledge could show him. He didn't have magic, but he was fascinated by it.

"Might have been an accident, might not. Word is he fooled someone he shouldn't have."

He'd been old, and nearly anything else might have been natural causes. "I heard him tell my mother once that he hoped his death was a mystery."

Mia sniffed. "Got his wish, then."

She drove for a few minutes without talking as Dani watched the passing fields. Colt season, by the looks of it—not that she'd ever picked up much more than bits and pieces about how the whole Thoroughbred business worked. As with so much, her mother's disdain for the people in it colored her own opinions. She had no idea if those frolicking ponies were destined for racetracks or to be broodmares or some snotty rich kid's dressage companions.

Mia tapped her hands on the steering wheel. The car eased Dani's anger at her for sticking around. She was still Mia, and she was living her life on at least some of her own terms. And there was the fact that Dani needed her. Mia was the closest thing to a friend she had who wasn't Sunflower. Still—even after everything.

Mia gave her a sidelong glance. "You finally met the infamous Archer. What was he like?"

They were back in the city and driving into one of its better neighborhoods and then through it, the houses getting bigger, grander.

"He threatened me, and he played me. He made me an offer I couldn't and didn't refuse. Despite common sense." Dani sighed. "So . . . about how I'd figure someone who messed *her* up so much would be. I suspect he's got some kind of persuasive mojo. I think it surprised him that I wasn't charmed."

"Ha!" Mia barked it. "You, charmed. That'll be the day."

"I can be charmed." Dani was offended for reasons she couldn't explain. Maybe because what Mia said was true. Charm was often a first step to gaining trust—a way into a mark's head, often the best way to start a con. She could be charming, but being charmed? That was for normal people. She'd never told Mia about her mom's attempt to whammy her. Never told anyone. She kept her tone playful. "Okay, fine. I can't. But I do wonder what it's like."

"It's great," Mia said.

And when she looked over to find Dani eyeing her, said, "I'm not like the rest of you and you know it."

"But you stuck around."

"Because I think with my heart."

She said it like it was a bad thing. Dani knew that meant to let it lie. Not contradict, not agree.

"It got broken, you know," Mia added.

"By who?" Dani knew her tone said she'd fight them, and she kind of wanted to.

"My ex, Liz. I don't think it's really over over, though. We're still in touch."

"She'd be a fool to let you go."

"That's what I keep trying to convince her. But she's mad I never let her be around a job."

Dani shook her head. "A tourist? You're with a *tourist*?"

"I don't think she would be a tourist. She'd be great at it," Mia said. "Anyway, here we are." Mia turned in to a driveway. She paused and waited until their eyes met. "Trust her, okay? She's the best at what she does. Better than the Gentleman."

"She's one of us?" There was no way she was better than the Gentleman without something extra. She had to have some kind of magic. Her own strand, as unique as a fingerprint.

Mia nodded. "You'll see."

The house was a country mansion inside city limits. High brick walls with wild rosebushes climbing up them sealed off its unkempt, English-style garden in place of a traditional yard. Mia parked at the top of the drive and they climbed out. A cat sprawled in the center of the stone walkway to the front door and didn't even consider moving for them. Mia stopped to pet its fluffy belly.

The door opened just as they reached the porch steps. Dani half expected a butler, but the woman was clearly the mistress of the house. Bangles and sparkles and bright red nails. She sported a multicolored turban over hair that must be silver. Her clothes were goals—silk and flowing, essentially pajamas so nice she could meet the fucking president in them.

"My dragon-tender! Mia!" she said and pulled Mia into a hug, which Mia accepted with good humor. The woman released Dani's friend. "And this must be *her*."

Roxie—no, the Curator—squinted at Dani, who understood immediately this was part of the process. She stood, presenting herself for inspection. "Do I pass?"

"Shh," the Curator said and pressed Mia into the house behind her, lingering on the porch with Dani. She kept moving her focus all around Dani, eyes still squinted, and then at last she nodded and offered her hands. Dani slid hers cautiously into them.

"I'm the Curator. Come on inside."

"I'm Dani."

"Obviously," the woman said with a cheeky smirk.

She closed the door behind them. The house was another surprise. At first, Dani thought, *Hoarder*. But then she began to tease some order from the chaos. She remembered Mia saying that the Curator disliked structure and, wow, was that underselling it.

"Come in, come in," the woman said, effortlessly winding through the cabinets and stacks and bookshelves and curiosities everywhere. This was not a woman who received idle visitors, and Dani recognized her surroundings for what they were; she'd been in so many different ones. This was a collection. Even as it appeared to be mess upon mess, it put her in mind of the Fortress; it had been assembled with purpose.

The Curator. The name fit her.

They entered a room with a long antique oval standing mirror and a table covered with various things. Bottles, branches, papers, brushes. Paintings dotted the walls and they were masterworks. Some of the artists were known to Dani, and others were probably just the talented people whose work never made it in front of the right eyeballs. The Curator had taste.

Dani almost complimented the house, but then she said, "Your collection is magnificent."

The Curator grinned wide at Mia. "You told me I'd like her. I think you might be right."

Mia shrugged and sank onto a red velvet couch with pink arms. "Stop, Roxie, you'll hurt my feelings with all this confirming my instincts."

"I consider you a diamond in this rough world and you know it."

Mia blew on her ragged, grubby nails. "Facts are facts."

"You," the Curator said to Dani, "over here."

Once Dani was close enough, the Curator took her shoulders and steered her toward the floor-length mirror. The feet were gold with clawed toes, as if it were a creature instead of an object.

Dani looked over at Mia, who was watching without alarm. While her own mind screamed to balk, she trusted Mia. She did. And so she let the woman stand behind her, gazing into the mirror at Dani's reflection. She squinted again, then made a disgruntled noise.

"Wait," she said.

Dani tried to circumnavigate whatever this was. "Did Mia already give you the list? I have a copy—we need items from the—"

"Dani, no." Mia cut her off.

The Curator nodded to Mia and then left the room.

"What the hell is this, Mia?"

"You'll see," Mia said. "You're out of practice, Mom says, so we can't be taking chances. It'll be worth it."

Dani didn't quite believe that anymore. The Curator was the kind of woman who could look at you and take something away. Some piece of you, adding it to her collection, then turning up with it at the worst possible moment.

Mia must have sensed Dani's mental wheels grinding. "Besides, I told you the Gentleman is gone and there's no one else this good— and definitely not who will be able to help us in time."

This Dani recognized as truth. Six days. Max.

The Curator returned with a steaming cup of tea on a saucer. The aroma filled the room with the scent of brackish water. Or mold. Brackish water mixed with mold.

Dani opened her mouth to refuse it, but the Curator presented it to Mia, who accepted it gratefully, and not like the garbage water it surely must taste like. "Lots going on, my Mia," the woman said. "This will make you feel better."

Mia sipped it and didn't even make a face.

The Curator turned back to Dani. "Now, let's have a real look."

"I need the items to re-create a painting. What does that have to do with looking at me? I can give you a list."

The Curator put her hands on Dani's shoulders again. "That's not how I work. I will know what you need. Just be still and remember the piece you wish to re-create. Hold it in your mind, clear as you can. Can you do that?"

Dani nodded. The idea of focusing on the painting made her uncomfortable, but she'd have to do it to paint the copy anyway.

"Close your eyes."

Dani did. Two warm, soft hands landed then, one on each side of her face, and the Curator murmured, "Don't lose it. Keep it clear in your mind."

Dani didn't like this, any of this. Her skin itched as if she might shed it, and conjuring the painting of Archer in her mind was worse than unpleasant, but she did it. She centered it in her vision—the detail of the frame, and then the piece itself. The long black coat, the walking stick, and that lean, hungry, haughty face.

Archer's face elongated, his eyes seemed to move, and Dani wanted to block the image, but the Curator said, "No, stay with me. Stay with him. A moment more."

The steel beneath her tone made Dani do it. She hung on, despite the desperate longing to let go.

Archer was leering now, which wasn't his expression in the painting, and she could nearly feel his eyes on her, pinning her into place. Those eyes were black and bottomless . . . and . . .

"Let it go *now*," the Curator ordered and Dani felt the woman's hands shake against her cheeks before she dropped them.

"He saw you," the Curator said. She tilted her head. "But you weren't who he was looking at."

Dani's heart pounded and she had to force herself not to see those eyes staring at her. "What the fuck just happened? Who *was* he looking at?"

Archer couldn't see inside her mind; that was impossible. *How do you know what's impossible? You're impossible too.*

"Sit down, have some tea," the Curator said to Dani. "I'll be back."

Her voice was thinner than it had been, and she rushed from the room. Whatever just happened, it had spooked her too. Dani went over to the couch and Mia offered her the teacup.

"I've never seen her like this before," Mia said. "Are you okay?"

"I am not drinking that."

Mia frowned at her, concerned. "It really will help."

Dani wanted to shake off the feeling of being watched by Archer like a dog shaking off nerves, and since she couldn't do that, she took the damn tea and then a large swallow. *There, that did it.* The taste of swamp chased the rest of the fright away from her mind.

Well, almost.

His eyes came back to her when she blinked, so she shook her head and took another sip.

This time, the image left her. The tea had an undeniable soothing effect. Her heartbeat slowed to normal.

That was when the Curator returned. She carried a large canvas bag and offered it to Dani.

"Everything you need is in here except the frame. I have one that will work with slight modifications. I'll have it brought out by Wednesday."

Dani accepted the bag and opened the top to peek inside. An old palette, tubes of antique paint, brushes, a roll of canvas. "From the eighteen nineties?"

"Yes," the Curator said. "The painting is old, but he's older." She hesitated. "He wasn't looking at you, but he was looking at someone connected to you. And there's something else there . . . something familiar, but I can't place it just yet."

Now, this part, Dani didn't miss. Riddles and the way that magic would give you some of what you needed, but not all of it. Never all of it.

"What does any of that mean? Who's connected to me?"

The Curator seemed regretful. "I couldn't bring myself to find out. But I think you will know before this is all over."

Mia sat up then. "Is she in danger?"

"Mia dragon-keeper, we are all of us always in danger."

"You know what I mean," Mia pressed.

The Curator closed her eyes and Dani almost said, *Please don't say another word. I don't need to hear anything else.*

"Do you know who he was?" she asked instead.

"Who he is," the Curator corrected. Her eyes opened. "*What* he is. I am sorry I couldn't look closer."

Dani absorbed that. She didn't like it, but referring to Archer as a what instead of a who felt right to her, and she sensed the Curator was done sharing. "What do I owe you?"

"Nothing," the Curator said.

This was against Maria's rules. And on this point, Dani agreed. "I don't want to be in your debt."

The Curator shrugged. "You aren't. Mia, you will take the cat."

Mia nodded as if this were a normal transaction. "I hope she likes chickens."

"Don't forget the frame," Dani said and this time she almost successfully ignored the flash of Archer's face through her mind.

"I'll never forget any of it," the Curator said. She picked up the empty teacup and saucer and escorted Mia and Dani to the door. She paused there, and Dani waited for her to say something more, make another troubling pronouncement, but instead she simply opened it to let them out, and closed it behind them without a word.

CHAPTER ELEVEN

AFTER THE CURATOR'S rattling her—intentional or not—Dani decided it was best to have Elliott meet her at the Hackworth estate. That way, she wouldn't have to be confined in a car with him for an hour drive there and back. It also might give her more time to pump Brad and Rose for information, and scrub those flashes of Archer's portrait from her brain. At least until she had to start painting the copy. She needed to bring her best, and that'd be hard enough with Elliott around anyway.

She dressed casually this time in jeans, boots, and T-shirt, so she'd feel like herself. And she brought Sunflower. Her backup–slash–security blanket. When she parked at the house, Brad met her; he'd been waiting on the porch. There was no sign of the Fates and Furies, aka the ex-wives, or his daughter. Sunflower barked, then capered around Dani, happy to run on the manicured lawn.

"You brought your dog?" Brad said and he bent despite being in a well-pressed suit and summoned Sunflower.

Sunflower hesitated, but when Dani nodded, approached him.

Dani had never been that skilled at greeting people and Sunflower was an excellent buffer. Brad grinned up at Dani, an uncomplicated grin that she found she wanted to return. So she did. "How are you?" he asked. He lifted one hand to indicate her hair. "I like the change. It suits you."

She definitely did not hear Elliott's, "You look like you," and feel the ghost of his breath against her neck as he "forgot" himself. *He* could take lessons in charm from Brad. Maybe she'd suggest it.

"I felt like it might be better for the job if I wasn't quite so recognizable as my mother's daughter."

"The paper," he said with chagrin. "I should have thought of that. Sorry."

"Not your fault. I should've been thinking about it more. I told you I'm an odd choice for consultant, but if I'm running your security, I need to fade into the background."

He scruffed Sunflower's neck and then stood, surveying her. "Now that I'm not sure is possible," he said with the trace of a smile.

Dani's cheeks heated. It wasn't that she never flirted, but to her dismay, she liked Brad Hackworth, and she didn't flirt with people she liked. Only with marks or the occasional one-night stand to scratch an itch before she left a town behind.

"Stop," she said in a way that could be interpreted as either *you flatterer* or *please, actually stop*. "I have a colleague joining me today, an assistant. He's meeting me here."

Brad looked taken aback. "We'll need to run a background check."

"Of course. I told him to bring all his documents; he's worked on some of the latest technology. I might do a few quick targeted upgrades, and I trust him to carry them out."

"Upgrades with just a few days left?"

Ah yes, this was the business side of Brad Hackworth. He did say he ran the finances. He wasn't going to let her have carte blanche without an explanation.

"Do you believe I can do this job?" she asked.

He hesitated. "I wouldn't have hired you if I didn't."

"Not even with Archer's recommendation?" *Whoever and* whatever *he is.*

"That's why I hired you. There's too much at stake for too many people I care about."

He'd chosen those words carefully, and she still couldn't tell how much he knew. "Then let me handle the details you hired me to handle."

He finally nodded. "Okay. You're bringing on an assistant. I'm afraid I have something you're probably not going to be too thrilled about to prep you for."

Dani braced, aware any small change could send this job even further sideways.

"The FBI wants to be at the auction. They're sending an agent with a lot of experience over to check out things, make sure we're not selling stolen goods or doing anything illegal." He paused. "As if Rose wouldn't have buried anything like that already."

He didn't sound worried about them coming, which meant there was another reason Dani wouldn't like it, then. She'd managed the last ten years without any further contact from the FBI Art Crime Team. The last thing she said to Agent Sharpe was at eighteen, before she skipped town. He probably remembered the words as well as she did: that she hoped he ended up rotting in hell. He just thanked her for her cooperation.

"Let me guess," Dani said. "Agent Sharpe?"

"They switched on us at the last second."

"The paper."

"The paper," he agreed. "I really should have thought harder about having the press here, but Rose wanted it. After all the fighting, seemed like something to give in on. We only let them take photos outside, but . . ."

Sharpe must have been near retirement. She never changed her name to avoid running into him again, but she knew how to stay off the radar.

Until recently, it seemed.

Suddenly, there she was, on the front page. How could he resist?

Dani was cautious about how much of her reaction she let show. "We have history, obviously. I was a teenager then, but now I'm all grown up. He'll never manipulate me again."

"So you hate him?" Brad said it encouragingly.

"Absolutely."

"How did that even happen anyway? How could they use an underage informant?"

Because he convinced me to set it up so they caught her in the act. "He's good at his job. But I'm better at mine. Don't worry about him."

There was no way he was coming here for any other reason than to spy on her. Another layer of scrutiny to navigate while pulling off the impossible.

A shiny silver Mercedes glided up the driveway, and when it stopped, Dani expected the federal agent to climb out, but the driver was Elliott. He must've borrowed it; a lot of people owed Rabbit favors.

He looked every inch the high-end security assistant. Stylish suit, hair trimmed short but with some texture on the top—enough that she still thought about dragging her hands through it. She put them in her jeans pockets. What was wrong with her?

Sunflower darted away on an antic race for him, and it'd be funny if it didn't embarrass Dani that her dog had apparently decided to like Elliott, after all.

"This your guy?" Brad asked and there was an edge to it.

"Yes, my assistant," Dani said as Elliott strode over to them. Did he have to come across so cocky? It was in every step he took.

"Dani." He extended his hand to Brad. "Emmett Strauss," he said. "Nice to meet you."

If Brad had an edge, Elliott was scissor sharp. Brad picked up on it. "Brad Hackworth. Your boss."

"Dani's my boss," Elliott said with a shit-eating grin.

"Should we go see the collection?" Dani said before this went any further south. "Is Rose meeting us there?"

Brad murmured okay, but he and Elliott were still squaring off like they might challenge each other to a duel. She started walking. Sunflower followed. She looked over her shoulder to see the guys—finally—practically bumping into each other to catch up with her. Jesus. Like she had time for men comparing the size of their egos.

Elliott should know better. The stakes here were huge for her. Her mother. Back in her life. He, maybe alone of everyone, should understand what she'd do for that chance.

Brad moved in front when they approached the holy temple, the Fortress of Art, to check that Rose was already onsite.

"Knock it off," Dani whispered to Elliott.

Elliott rubbed his jaw. Clean-shaven today. "What? You like him? You into rich boys now?"

"I'm not into *boys* at all. So you should stop acting like a child."

Elliott leaned in. "I'm a man."

Dani stepped back. "Then prove it by acting like one."

Elliott's eyes narrowed and she wondered if she just waved a red flag in front of a bullheaded man and encouraged further shows of bravado. Before she could fix it, if she could have, Brad had the guard open the door to summon them in.

Sunflower settled down near the Bourgeois spider, comfortable in its giant metal shadow. Rose was waiting inside the grand foyer, and as they entered, she gave Elliott a smile that said if he was into older women, then she was happy to oblige. He smirked at Dani without letting the others see.

She resisted the urge to scream, or roll her eyes, or turn and leave. To act as childish as he was being.

Brad assumed control of the situation and she truly could have kissed him. "Rose, why don't you show Mr. Strauss around? He'll be helping on the technical aspects, but first we need to do background on him. I'll take Dani wherever she wants to go in the meantime."

Elliott clearly wanted to protest, his jaw tightening a hair, but then he turned on the charm for Rose. It annoyed Dani to see that he had some when he wanted to. "Of course."

Rose was probably still carrying that gun in her handbag, but Elliott could take care of himself. He was a *man,* after all. And Rabbit's paperwork would surely be impeccable. Elliott craned his head back and whistled low and impressed. "Tell me about this glorious place," he said to Rose, and she beamed at the compliment as she led him back outside. To the nearby security headquarters, no doubt.

Dani had noticed there were no offices on the plans, but she'd considered there might be *something* tucked away. But no, she'd confirmed that the Fortress of Art was just for Hackworth. He wouldn't have worked here, except when drawing on the place's magic, and he reportedly didn't allow anyone besides the guards in. And they were based in a separate building over the hill.

Brad was slightly apologetic. "Hope you don't mind me sending your assistant away? I thought we could cover more ground."

No, you didn't. "Good call."

She had three main things she wanted to do today while they were here: try to find out more about Archer, check out the potential weak spots she'd identified in the security and suggest fixing a couple of them to maintain credibility, and identify other potential targets besides Archer's painting someone else might be after. It was too bad she didn't get a chance to brief Elliott on what they needed from Rose—more context for her relationship with the family and why she wanted Archer's portrait—but he'd been doing this a long time. Maybe he could guess.

"Sharpe will be here in half an hour to forty-five," Brad said with a glance at his watch.

And a new fourth objective, to avoid piquing Sharpe's interest any more than it must already be.

"Let's move, then." She hadn't let herself inhale the visual feast so far, but she did as they moved through the galleries. She thought of the Curator and her collection, assembled by magic, no doubt pulling her to the items and objects someone would come to her needing. The supplies she gave Dani were accurate to the period, not fakes. But there was a warmth to her house. Despite the surface chaotic similarities and magic purpose, Hackworth's Collection made a stark contrast. He'd gathered all these artworks and put them into this cold, lonely purgatory for his gain only. *That's* who she needed to know more about. More than what was public.

Only the questions you asked could get answered. She put her hand on Brad's arm, laid on the kind of false charm she was so good at. "This is an odd line of inquiry, but . . ."

Brad waited, face open and expectant. He wanted to please her. She wasn't used to it, and she felt a twinge of guilt at treating him like a mark. *But he is. You're here to steal from him.*

"Tell me about your father," she said.

Something about him altered subtly, a layer of protection sliding into place. But he began to talk as they circulated the galleries. "He made me who I am. He was everything I vowed never to be . . ."

Dani could understand that, since she grew up with the reverse. The desire to win her mother's approval had burned inside her so badly, she'd wanted nothing more than to be as perfectly self-possessed as Maria . . . Until she didn't.

She'd never met someone like Brad Hackworth—slick, wealthy, and seemingly *nice*—before. Certainly, she'd never expected to feel anything in common with someone like him.

"I get that," she said.

Her thoughts returned to Elliott and how she had allowed herself to believe she understood him once. That they were alike. That he felt the things she did. She wouldn't make that mistake twice.

"How'd he get into art? I don't get the impression he was into social graces . . ."

"He was incredibly crass, is what you're trying to say." He held up a hand to silence her protest.

"Did he take you to galleries growing up?"

Brad stopped and glanced at her. "No. He tried to get me to hang out in the Fortress, but I refused once I was old enough."

Now that was interesting. "How old was that?"

"Thirteen."

This was exactly the history she needed to rummage around in. "I don't want to pry, but . . . what were those times like?"

"When he brought me here?"

"You must be the only other person—or one of them—who ever saw it. Before this week."

"I don't like to think about those times, and I never talk about them." He said it smoothly, shutting the door. "Why do you ask?"

Retreating seemed like the safest bet. Would Brad have witnessed his father using the collection? Again, if he had, why would he sell? "I'm nosy, I guess. And you know my relationship with my mom has traditionally been—"

"Strained?"

"Understatement. She's difficult, but she's still my mom."

"My father only cared about building wealth, then passing it on to me so I could do the same thing he did. The rest of his life he spent making the world a worse place and everyone around him miserable. He might be the only multi-billionaire on Earth who never gave a single penny to charity. Was big on everyone pulling themselves up by their bootstraps. Not caring about taking over or preserving his precious collection is my revenge."

She didn't know if she was listening with such intent because he was a mark (or mark-adjacent, at least) or because she was growing curious about *him*—not for gain, and not because she wanted to understand his father. He spoke as if he wasn't hiding anything from her, though he must be. Everyone hid something.

"Did you know it's actually impossible to pull yourself up using bootstraps?" she asked.

He smiled at her. "I did."

"Did he make Rose miserable too?"

"Not until he tried leaving this all to me, and making it untouchable. Not until I refused and told our lawyers to find a way around the will. She still wanted to honor his wishes." He shrugged. "But no one beats a Hackworth in court—that might be the only thing my father and I have in common."

"You beat her, but you also beat him," Dani observed.

His smile widened. "I did. Better stay on my good side."

She put on a false grin. "Noted."

Rose's smile was even wider when she and Elliott rejoined them, and Dani had to give him a slight nod of approval. The woman would obviously divulge anything he asked—or she'd be ready to by the end of the week. He had clearly expanded his non-magical skills in the last ten years.

This was the gallery with Archer's painting and Dani was carefully keeping her back to it. The sense of being seen she'd had earlier, when she'd envisioned it for the Curator, his eyes pinned on her, persisted. Looking into those eyes was not something she wanted to repeat. Not yet.

"Dani, you mentioned some security holes?" Elliott asked.

"Is he cleared?" Brad asked Rose, not hiding his skepticism.

Aha, so he thought Rose would gently reject Elliott's employment. Dani was willing to bet that Emmett Strauss was a Boy Scout on paper, with a faultless history.

"Absolutely," Rose said. "Quite an impressive résumé. We're lucky Dani knew about him."

Brad inclined his head. "We are lucky to have Dani."

"What was it you wanted me to check on today?" Elliott asked.

She let herself stand closer to Brad just in case it rankled him. "Apparently, it's possible to disable all the motion sensors. Mr. Hackworth liked to get close to the art."

"Hmm," he said thoughtfully.

"We just won't do that. Isn't that enough?" Brad asked.

"The plan is to disable them only when the pieces are to be removed after the sale," Rose put in.

Yes, Dani had read that part of the briefing.

"I'd like to install additional motion security on a few individual pieces, as a fail-safe." Dani swept an arm around. "A few obvious big-ticket items, and a handful of smaller ones. Like the painting you said you're interested in, Rose. Just something I can keep an eye on to make sure there's no extra activity near them that might indicate a problem."

"Which piece do you want, Rose?" Brad asked.

She nodded toward Archer's painting. "A sentimental favorite."

It occurred to Dani this might be a dangerous line of conversation. Brad had made his feeling on the will clear. "Unless you're rethinking your stance on gift giving?" she asked him casually. "Save us the trouble of upgrading?"

Brad and Rose exchanged a look. Rose shrugged. "I have to bid just like everyone else—the will. I couldn't go against it now."

Dani kept her relief on the inside.

Elliott steered them back around to Dani's original point. "Just show me the pieces you'd like and I'll oversee it."

The second layer of motion capture they installed would allow Rabbit undetectable access to the entire system. It would also allow Dani the moments she'd need to pluck Archer's portrait off the wall and replace it with the one she'd paint.

That was the broad plan, such as it was. The timing was slightly in flux—a judgment to be made about when was the optimal chance—but this was the first step.

Brad opened his mouth, but Rose said, "Good idea. Can it be done before the gala?"

"The gala?" Elliott asked.

"Yes," Rose says, "a party with all the auction participants. The night before the main event."

Dani frowned. "They'll have access to the gallery during it?"

"Yes," Brad said.

"Sounds like a security risk," Elliott said.

Brad shrugged. "Mom and the other wives want a party."

"The wives?"

"You'll meet them," Rose said as if it were a warning and a curse. Close enough.

"It's a manageable risk," Dani said to shut down Elliott. "Don't worry. Can you do what I asked by then?" *Stop challenging them,* she thought.

"We'll overnight the equipment, and I'll get the security guys to help," he said. "No problem. Show me the pieces." He turned a blinding smile on Brad and Rose. "We won't take up any more of your time."

Brad hesitated, but Rose smiled and nodded. "We'll leave you to your work."

"I'll hold off the shark as long as I can while you finish up. Call if you need anything from me," Brad said to Dani—and pointedly not to Elliott.

"We will," Elliott said.

As soon as Brad left, Dani put the toe of her boot on Elliott's foot. "Ouch," he said.

"Oh, I'm sorry, did I get in your way?"

"Don't trust that guy," Elliott grumbled.

"You're one to talk." Dani didn't want to turn around, but she shoved aside the instinctive part of her that was balking at taking in the image of Archer more fully. Whatever happened with the Curator was weird, but she'd been in Archer's *actual* company before. This was just a painting of him.

"Remember, there are cameras on us," she said under her breath.

"I am your fake tech expert. I know," he said. "The one in the corner?"

He knew, of course. That was Elliott's gift. Give him an objective and he'd find it sooner or later, even if it was hidden at the bottom of the world. He could sense where specific things were, once he was close enough to them. Identifying a painting of Archer, after having it described to him already, was as simple as a sleight-of-hand master producing a card from the center of a deck—as easy for Elliott as breathing.

Nothing for it now but to look. She was grateful, even if she wouldn't say it, that Elliott was with her. He was aware of the stories about Archer, and of what Archer cost Dani. She didn't have to pretend this was simple.

Dani moved to stand right in front of the piece, then sat in the high-backed chair. The old man clearly spent time here, based on the wear and the positioning. The magic network inside the building flowed toward this spot. It must have been where he made his most profitable decisions. Elliott prowled closer to the frame to study the lines, like a tiger stalking prey, which she supposed he was.

Then he backed up and lingered beside the chair. "We can't

spend too long in here with it," she said. "Just in case it comes up later."

"I don't want to. It's creepy as fuck," he said.

Dani allowed herself to look at Archer's portrait directly. She had to if she was going to paint it. She had to allow it all the way in.

Much as she didn't want to.

That was the way her power worked. She had to be able to capture the emotion of what she was copying, the beating heart within the artwork. Then those who viewed the forgery would see the real soul, which made the painting as legitimate as a fake can be. That was Dani's theory anyway. Every piece was a door and Dani somehow made sure hers opened to the right place inside a person.

The heart of this painting was dark and thrumming and she wished she didn't have to hold it inside her.

"Dani?" Elliott said.

She stood on shaky legs, dreaming of breathing in air and folding her arms around Sunflower outside. But they had to select a few more paintings for the extra security treatment. Rose or Brad could be watching.

Anyone could. She hadn't been up to the security building yet. She'd have to do that next. And Agent Sharpe would be arriving at the Hackworth estate any minute.

"The Monet in the next gallery, that's one we should protect. The Rothko."

Elliott shook his head, frustrated. "You don't have to hold out on me. I'm on your team. What's wrong?"

"The Rothko, definitely," she said in answer. "The Kahlo upstairs, and the one in the front hall too. The Warhols. The Vermeer, obviously." She ticked off the others. "You go ahead. I need to do rounds with the rest of the security team." *I need air. I need to get my legs back under me.*

Elliott watched her. "What did he mean about a shark?"

Well, he was going to find out anyway. "Agent Sharpe is coming, and I'll have to meet with him too."

Elliott gaped at her. "You're going to see *him*?"

"I have to. It'll be too suspicious otherwise."

Elliott wouldn't look away from her, so she avoided his eyes. "You don't have to do any of this," he said.

She kept her chin level. "Yes, I do. And I'll be fine. I always have been."

Elliott might be about to call bullshit, but he hesitated and then let her make the call. The cameras *were* watching. He headed off into the labyrinth of the collection.

She turned to look back at Archer's portrait one more time from the door to the gallery, some distance between her and it. She wasn't sure if the sense of the stare being vacant now was her imagination or if the painting was no longer looking back at her.

That wasn't how this worked; it was never how it worked. The thought should be nonsense, but it seemed wholly within the realm of the possible.

The painting might be an abyss on canvas, but it couldn't stare back into Dani . . . Could it?

She left rather than try to discover the answer.

CHAPTER TWELVE

THE FORTRESS'S SECURITY headquarters were clearly the previous director's multimillion-dollar pride and joy. The man Dani replaced had built a playground for paranoiacs and filled it with people Hackworth would respect and whose lack of interest in art was a bonus.

The NSA wished it had this much firepower. The Louvre. The Met. Most heads of state.

There were eyes everywhere in the galleries, cameras on every entrance and exit, and the men and women on duty seemed as well trained as their résumés indicated. And they didn't trust her, not one bit.

So they were smart. But they were also about to be out of work, since with no Fortress of Art to protect, this surveillance haven would no longer have a purpose. A few might be kept on at the estate, but they also might not. She'd considered trying to turn one or two who had arrest records in their pasts . . . until she met them. She asked them what they planned to do next and was informed that Rose was giving everyone a hundred-thousand-dollar bonus and a promise of great recommendations after the auction.

Not worth the risk. Not now that she had allies, a team, even if they were working with her under duress. Her mother's thumb, still right on top of them all. But it was a comforting pressure. Dani had another shot at earning her approval, and then her forgiveness. Eyes on that prize.

She wound her way from top to bottom of the three-story complex, asking questions, and receiving cursory answers. She spotted Elliott on a monitor, doing exactly what he should be. When she reached a guard desk with a view of the gallery with Archer's painting in it, she paused. "I hear this was one of the places Mr. Hackworth visited most often."

The man at the desk shrugged. "We turned off the cameras when he went in."

Interesting.

"You didn't even keep the footage?"

"Erased." He gave her a look. "None of my business what he did in there."

The implication being that it was none of hers either. She suspected the man was reading her meaning as saying Hackworth was a pervert, beating off to priceless artworks. The reasons he would have wanted the cameras off were clear enough to Dani. Not just the working of magic, but allowing people to see the details could make you vulnerable, depending. He wouldn't have wanted anyone in there after he died, because he'd had no intention of sharing his power with anyone—save Brad—even post–mortal coil.

Brad's revelations about his father helped fill in the outlines she'd gathered from the information she already had. A so-called self-made man, cruel and lucky enough to prove to Dani there was no such thing as god or karma out there presiding over people's fates. At best, some forces that didn't give a shit about the result were out there betting on people like horses at the track. She'd also asked Brad when his father started to collect art, but he'd shrugged. Rose might know, was the answer.

"Of course, he was the boss," Dani said. Implying: *And now that's me*. Through the auction, at least.

"Don't worry," the man said, "we'll keep all the footage from this week. No matter who goes in there."

"Excellent." Dani was probably supposed to feel threatened by this. But Rabbit's magic would soon create windows of space she could waft in and out of, a ghost in this machine. And while it still wasn't going to be easy—because there were too many physical guards here running shifts on the collection that she couldn't cancel without raising eyebrows—this guy had never dreamed of what Rabbit could do with tech. She spoke it like a language—into being, into doing what she wanted.

While Dani wasn't watching, Elliott had left the galleries. She knew because she heard the security team greeting him like a long-lost friend as he traveled through the desks and monitors and gleaming white surfaces to join her on the first floor. "Done so soon?" she asked.

"You work with the best," Elliott quipped.

The man who just threatened Dani high-fived Elliott. Nice. Maybe she overestimated her own ability to be charming.

A brusque woman holding a cellphone to her ear came over. "Mr. Hackworth says the FBI is here now and would like to meet the head of security."

She made it clear she hardly viewed Dani as that.

"I'd better get out there, then."

"I'll go with you," Elliott said.

I didn't ask you to. But his new friends were waiting for her to bust him down a notch, and that would only make them like her even less. The hoops women had to go through, and still they'd never be likable enough to earn the high-fives or bragging rights Elliott got after ten minutes of small talk.

"Fine."

Elliott slid her a grin and she did her best to be unaffected by it. She waited until they were outside to elbow him in the ribs. Not too hard, but hard enough to make him wince.

"What was that for?"

"Being part of the patriarchy."

He laughed. "You haven't changed a bit."

Well, that wasn't true.

The Fortress was over a rolling hill from the security outpost, and as soon as they crested the walkway, Dani saw Agent Sharpe. How was she ever taken in by such a walking cliché? The suit, the sunglasses, the central casting of it all. But he was smart, and she wouldn't underestimate him. He had made her feel like he was saving her, saving her mother. Like this was a way out.

And Dani had desperately thought any way out would work.

"I can hear you grinding your teeth," Elliott said.

Dani took a slow breath—the secret to keeping cool—and forced herself to relax. She nodded to Agent Sharpe. There was no reason to make a show of how much she hated this. He'd make a meal of that. Brad rushed forward to meet her, and she appreciated that he stood beside her, showing support. Elliott was on her other side, and for the moment, it wasn't him jockeying for position but a protectiveness she was grateful for. That didn't change that the patriarchy could be damned.

"Hello, there, Danielle, it's good to see you." Sharpe was silver haired, craggier. His smile was still a mask, as was his manner. Seventeen-year-old Dani couldn't see past it.

"I wish I could say the same," she said.

Elliott chuckled.

"And who's this?" Agent Sharpe asked.

"My assistant." Dani glanced at Brad. "I assume you've already shown him around the collection while we were with security? I'm sure Emmett would be happy to introduce you to the rest of the security staff. We stepped in last minute."

"Yes, so I heard," Agent Sharpe said. "A heart attack. Ben had a good rep."

He sounded suspicious about it, like she was out here stopping people's hearts. *But then, Archer might be.* "He left a very well-trained team. A thorough operation. We're just doing some tweaks to make sure everything goes smoothly."

"What have you been up to all these years?" Sharpe asked, as if she'd answer.

Brad put a hand on Dani's arm, which Sharpe obviously made a mental note about. "I don't see how that is any of your business," he said. "Dani reports to me. You can give me your questions about the auction and I'll relay them to her when I have time."

Dani almost snorted. So that was how someone like Brad Hackworth told an FBI agent to fuck right off.

"You go by Dani now?" Agent Sharpe said. And then to Brad, "And how did you come to hire her? I wasn't aware Ms. Poissant had any background in security."

"A mutual friend made the recommendation." Brad left it at that, and if Dani had to guess, the next question Agent Sharpe asked would be met by a card for one of the family's many lawyers. Sharpe was allowed here as a courtesy, and while he could get some judge to sign off on the paperwork to be more aggressive in monitoring the sale, Dani was willing to bet Rose had ensured the collection and the auction were clean enough to make that difficult.

"All right, all right." Agent Sharpe paused and she could tell he was leading up to something. He removed his sunglasses and Dani saw the true toll of age then, around his eyes. "You saw your mother yesterday? Interesting timing. First time in what . . . it must be—"

"The first time since you convinced me to sell her out?" Dani asked and gave a subtle snap of her fingers. Sunflower capered over, right on cue. "She was attacked with a knife; that's why they transferred her to Lexington. I guess she was feeling sentimental."

Sunflower stood on her hind legs, putting her paws on Sharpe— a distraction she was trained to provide. Sharpe wasn't getting anything else from Dani. He'd made quite the professional name out of bagging the notorious Maria Poissant. At this point, Dani might be the only person involved in the arrest who hadn't been in a dozen true crime specials.

Agent Sharpe played sympathetic and pretended not to be annoyed at Sunflower's attention. "I was looking forward to catching up, Dani. I hope you've been well. You did the right thing back then."

As if she needed that from him. "No, I didn't. But you got what you wanted. Those are two different things. I need to get going. Sunny."

Sunflower immediately left him and was at Dani's side. Agent Sharpe extended his hand to her, like there was a chance in hell she was going to shake it. Her dog growled. "Good girl," Dani said.

Agent Sharpe frowned. *Yeah, you got played by a girl and her dog.*

"Come with me, Agent Sharpe," Elliott said. "I'll introduce you to our team." Not Ben's. Theirs.

Agent Sharpe finally dropped his hand.

Dani found some solace in the fact that Agent Sharpe was about to be shown around by someone who got away clean, with him never the wiser.

"I'll check in with you later," Elliott said to her.

Brad ushered Dani away, Sunflower trailing them, and she told herself she wasn't running away—though it felt like it.

"Thanks for doing this," he said. "I didn't realize . . ." She expected him to circle back to the news that she visited her mother, but he didn't. Then again, he had a whole security team who could dig into whatever he wanted.

"Hey," she said, "thanks for the backup. And remember, you're making it worth my while."

Dani was a strange combination of jumpy and exhausted when she returned to the stone house, already listing the things she had to do next. Set up the canvas. Start the painting either tonight or tomorrow. She hadn't examined the items the Curator gave her as closely as she might have, so first up was confirming they were as accurate to 1890s painting materials as possible. Somehow she knew they would be.

Once, when they were kids, Mia asked why Dani didn't just finger paint and then use that as the fake, since people who looked at her work didn't usually examine it much more closely. It was overstating Dani's powers—the pieces had to be good enough to hold up to *some* kind of scrutiny—but Maria overheard the question. To her, it wasn't even the necessity, but the principle. "Sloppiness is what gets people caught," she told them. "Just because we have magic doesn't mean we don't also have to master our craft."

"What craft?" Mia had asked. Her bottom lip had jutted out because she hated being reminded that *she* didn't have magic.

Maria had paused to consider. "The art of getting what we want and not getting caught."

"I can do that art too," Mia had declared. Maria had given her one of those rare approving smiles, and Mia had accepted it with glee.

So Dani would follow their old protocol, painting a copy perfect in every way possible. She'd duplicate the abyss. Besides, while swapping the painting out would be complicated, it was by far the easiest way to pull off this job. Sidestep the others who wanted it. The sooner she completed the forgery, the sooner this could all be in the rearview.

Her skin prickled at Sunflower's rumble of warning as they approached the front door, and that sense of being watched returned. The house looked undisturbed. There was no one in sight, but it was dark around them and lots of things—and worse, people—could hide in the darkness.

She hurried back to her car and retrieved the Taser from the glove box, and then and only then did she unlock the front door.

She walked inside on high alert, clutching the Taser. Sunflower was right next to her, still growling, and then there he was. Archer, in the flesh. He tapped his walking stick on the hardwood floor of the living room. "I'd like a word."

Her mother had said she'd hear from him.

Dani needed a drink for this. She headed to the kitchen, opened the bottle of bourbon on the counter, and took a pull straight off it. She leaned against the counter and let the heady burn of the drink warm her. Sunflower stuck right beside her, ready to take a bite out of Archer at the slightest signal from Dani.

"This should be good," she said. "I thought vampires had to be invited in."

"I'm no bloodsucker," he said, amused.

"Then what are you?"

A cold show of teeth. "You're asking better questions."

Seemed that didn't mean he was going to be supplying better answers. He wore that same old-fashioned getup, a mirror to the painting—a costume, or was it the only clothing he had? Or was there something else at work here? There were certainly plenty of criminals in their world who had a signature look. Like Mr. Hands, the pickpocket who wore a black leather jacket and T-shirt and never got caught despite the visibility of the pseudo rock star clothing. The Hawaiian shirt and pastel suit guy, with his fake tourist act. The Accountant, who always had on thick-framed glasses and sky-high Jimmy Choos.

"Why are you here?" She capped the bourbon. She wasn't inviting him to stay.

"What? You don't want me to sit for the portrait?" he mused. "I've always heard painting from life is what most artists prefer. It was how the original was produced." His devouring eyes narrowed. "But then, you've always just copied. Sad all that talent going to waste."

"Watch it or I'll decide this job isn't worth it."

"No," he said. "I don't think you will."

"Why are you here?" Dani asked again.

"You were asking Brad about the old man, about what interested him in art."

"He told you that?"

Archer ignored the question. "Rose won't know what I do."

Dani longed for another pull of bourbon, but she remained still. "What's that?"

"The first painting Hackworth collected was mine. He had a sense of what it was truly worth, which most people didn't. He won it in a poker game, in the back room of a bar in Atlanta, from someone stupid enough to risk losing it."

"When was this?" If he was divulging information, she might as well get all she could.

"Forty-five years ago."

Dani did the math. "That's when he went into business."

Archer's lips pursed. Then, "That's when he started to become *successful* at business."

Dani pulled in the various bits and pieces, the timeline she'd assembled, the insights into Hackworth. "And when he started building the collection."

"You're sure you don't want me to stay? You're cutting it close. I could keep you company." Archer came a step closer and Dani had to motion to keep Sunflower from attacking him. She was *such* a good girl.

Archer ignored the threat. "Your mother loved me to keep her company on nights like this. It'd be just like old times."

"I'm doing this for her, not you." Dani pointed to the door. "You best head out. I have a painting to start."

Archer twirled the walking stick under his palm as he pivoted to leave. "Such a waste of talent," he said as if he had regrets. She doubted it.

Dani waited until the front door closed behind him before she poured herself a healthy glass of bourbon, fed Sunflower, and retrieved the Curator's bag of supplies. Her mother had implied that traveling to St. Louis would've taken a toll on him, but he'd seemed his regular loathsome self. She should have gone out to see if he had a hidden car parked somewhere. How he got here, how he left.

But she didn't want to follow him into the night. And he wasn't wrong about cutting it close.

FIVE DAYS OUT

CHAPTER THIRTEEN

DANI HAD LAID out and inventoried all the supplies from the Curator and there were only a few other basics she needed to get started. The canvas seemed dead-on period cotton, pre-stretched and primed with white grounds. She'd reopened her old studio, cobwebs and all, the night before—a homespun fallout shelter hidden in the field behind the house. Even back when her mother was busted, no one ever discovered it. So while it wasn't ideal—underground bunkers didn't exactly have the best lighting—it was a safe place for Dani to work.

She didn't start the night before, not with only an electric lantern for company. The light from open doors above would chase away some of her hesitation at painting Archer today, as if she might conjure him back onto the property. The narrow, creaky steps and dark, musty floor were workable in daytime, but she didn't want to be down there at night if she could avoid it.

Sunflower begged to go out early and Dani expected her to be waiting on the porch when she opened the door after her shower. The dog would be ready to hop in and come to the art supply shop with Dani. And Dani would be using a credit card under another name for these purchases; Rabbit left her two untraceable ones for the purpose.

As predicted, Sunflower's tongue lolled hello when she lifted up her head from her sprawl, and then Dani spotted the beat-up leather trunk beside her. She recognized it. Elliott's—the same one he'd dragged out of the barn and cleaned up and made a dresser of when Rabbit realized he wasn't intending to leave and had invited him to stay for good.

"You should have barked and woken me. He's not ours," Dani said.

She undid the latches and pried open the top. Inside, she found the rest of the supplies she was about to go buy. Mia would have known what to tell him to bring.

Then she realized there was something else inside the trunk too. A T-shirt. She didn't like the way a small beam of light seemed to bloom in her chest.

Dani pulled the piece of clothing out. The beam grew into a small sun and she had to make herself think about Archer and everything—everything she'd lost—to discourage it from continuing to grow.

The shirt wasn't Elliott's; that would be too obvious. She did have one of his old T-shirts, somewhere, in the bottom of a suitcase. It didn't smell anything like him anymore, but she kept it anyway.

No, this shirt was *hers*. Or it used to be.

She held it up, the fabric worn soft. The shoulders were a shade smaller than hers now, the faded image of *Starry Night* something that could've been a terrible tourist shirt—except it was the first present Elliott ever gave her.

She left it in his room before she snuck out that last night. She told him to bring it with him, that it was her favorite. But when she showed up at the bus station hours later, he didn't come. She waited, and he still didn't come.

So she left without even her favorite T-shirt on her back. She went into the world and she survived on her own. Brokenhearted— *broken,* period, for a time—and then she called on the things she'd learned from her mother. She could do the craft even without using her magic. She could start to address the mess she'd made, if not directly, at least indirectly. One mark at a time.

Alone. Always.

Until Sunflower herded her way into Dani's life.

What did it mean that he kept it? Not as much, she realized, as his returning it now. The last thing he had of hers.

The shine that Elliott's gift originally gave her dissipated. It was a false sun, a promise made of pyrite. If Elliott meant something other than *here's your shirt back,* he would've explained himself. He would use his words.

"I told you," she said to Sunflower, "don't get attached."

She lugged the trunk across the backyard to the now-closed fall-out shelter, which she reopened so she could drag it down the stairs. She positioned it near the easel holding the canvas.

Dani adorned the antique palette from the Curator with various paints from the period tubes—how? Part of her magic, Dani guessed—that the woman had provided. While there were leftover frames and embellishments propped against the wall toward the back of Dani's studio that would work in a pinch with her power, she hoped the Curator didn't forget to send a frame as she'd promised. A few of Dani's old sable brushes—two from the right period, still soft because her mother always insisted she be meticulous about cleaning them—were in the same concealed hole in the wall as the safe-deposit key. She had them nearby already. Sentiment might overwhelm her if she spent too much time thinking about using her magic for the first time in a decade.

Instead she summoned the image of Archer's portrait into her mind, an invasive darkness.

And she painted. As bleak as this work was, as much as she disliked the abyss flowing through her, the freedom of the brush against the canvas woke something inside her that had been asleep for the past ten years.

She started by adding layers of paint. She worked wet into wet like any good Impressionist, using strong brushstrokes and generous daubs applied with a palette knife. Deep navy became a man's form in a suit, variations creating the long shadow stretched out behind him.

She had always sensed her magic, waiting, since that first day it woke within her. But she found that expressing it today felt different from when she was younger. She didn't know if that was her or the work. She might have been standing in an echo, seeing what the original artist—whoever they were—saw. The darkness of Archer, to be pinned down by paint. An image to allow him to truly be looked at—to be seen, as they say—but not in a way he'd like. There was more truth in what she painted, even in the copy.

Time passed in a rush, flowing around her. Her head swam and she almost saw double when she made the first strokes to outline his face. She should keep going, but she needed a break. She barely had the time, but she couldn't afford to pass out down here either. When she stopped, she didn't look back at what she'd done as she scrubbed her hand across the back of her neck, kneading her tight shoulders.

She cleaned the brushes and then shook out her fingers. She circled the small, subterranean room, still lined with jars of canned food on the shelves. Such shelters were common enough in this area, and she guessed, there were probably lots of new places like this being built by preppers. When this was constructed, it would've seemed sensible. Maybe it was.

Sunflower appeared in the opening above Dani and placed her paws carefully on the old wooden steps. She trundled down them and plopped onto the floor beside Elliott's trunk, her tail thumping. Thud, thud, thud.

Dani eyed the trunk. "All right," she said, "but we're not calling first and he might not be there."

Sunflower bounced to her feet and headed up and out.

Dani wanted to give him a chance to explain what his gesture meant, in case it was different from what she assumed. She wouldn't ask—just give him the opportunity to volunteer it.

She needed a favor from him anyway. That was closer to the way things were done in the secret world. She climbed from her hideaway and relaxed a fraction after she closed the door, trapping her version of Archer and his shadow below in the dark.

When Dani arrived at the Rabbit Hutch, Rabbit's truck was parked in the drive—and so was the silver Mercedes from the day before. Dani realized Mia's Mini wasn't in evidence the other day on her trip to the farm and decided it probably lived in the barn. She would baby it, just like one of her animals.

The chickens were pecking in the yard, and after a cautionary tongue click from Dani, Sunflower just watched them like they were a reality show especially for border collies.

Despite the slap of the other day, the fact they were all on the same team again made Dani comfortable walking in without a call or text or any other signal. Rabbit would likely have seen her coming out the window or on one of her many monitors. And it wasn't like Dani got any warning about the surprise on her front porch that morning either.

She went in through the garage door, the family entrance that went from stairs to kitchen, and closed the door gently. There was an argument taking place inside.

Rabbit and Mia and then a voice she didn't recognize. A man's. Not Elliott. Not Archer either.

"I told you the car would require something in return," the man said. "On top of your other debts."

"We have enough to worry about right now. You know I'll pay it off; it just needs to wait."

"No. I want to talk to her."

"She can't help you," Mia said.

"Correct." Rabbit scoffed. "You just think you want to talk to her. She's been out of the game for years."

Ah, so they were talking about Dani. And they were busy enough that they didn't notice her driving up. But she was too curious about the identity of the mystery man to play it cool and eavesdrop until she had a handle on everything.

"I have and I haven't," she said, striding into the kitchen. The living room beyond it was filled with monitors and consoles. Upgraded by ten years, but otherwise the same. "What's the problem?"

The man was Brenner, the snoop whose magic involved locks. He'd posted up at the kitchen table, red-faced from not getting his way. Rabbit did say she was going to work on him. Dani thought she meant digitally, not personally. So the car was Brenner's. That's where Elliott got it from. Speaking of, he was still nowhere to be seen.

"Since she's right here, surely I can talk to her now?" He looked at Rabbit.

She pulled a face. Her glasses frames were purple rectangles with diamond edges, but she was still sporting her customary around-the-farm gum boots. "Like I can stop either of you from being assholes and not taking my advice." She got up, gave Brenner a hard stare, and shrugged.

Mia hesitated. "Dani, you don't owe him anything," she said. "And I was just putting him off before."

"And here I thought you were all truly working in sync again, one big happy family." He was a slick one, all right. "Maria's team back together. I, ah, did the boy a solid yesterday, and I'm just looking for an edge in return."

Favors: the currency of the moment, and of their entire world. Dani'd come here to ask for one, and instead she'd end up deciding to grant one or not. She remembered hating that, the feeling that you were always running up a tally. Everything you did would result in a payment or in owing someone. Not a great way to go through life—but then, she was old enough now to know most people operated that way. It was certainly not exclusive to the criminal milieu. The risks involved, the possibility of jail, just made for higher stakes. She didn't like the idea that Rabbit was in debt to this guy.

"Of course," he continued, "I could try to contact Maria. See what she says."

"That's not necessary," Dani said. She stood at the table to maintain a physical advantage in the conversation, towering over him. The thing about old tricks was, they were old because they worked.

Mia sighed at Dani agreeing to talk but stayed.

"I'm running this job, not my mother," Dani said. "What did you have in mind?"

"I have a buyer for one of the pieces. Perhaps you could make it easier for me to get it?"

"Which one?" She went through the most likely candidates. She held up a finger before he could respond. "Wait, let me guess. The Rothko."

In 2012, another Rothko, *Orange, Red, Yellow,* sold for almost ninety million at a contemporary art auction. The highest price ever for something from the period to date, and Christie's crowed about it loud enough that even she saw the story. Dani had copied two Rothko paintings in her time and she understood why they were so valuable. Some people might see only large swathes of color and say stupid things like, *I could do that.* Dani's internal response to such claims usually varied from *No, you couldn't* to *But you didn't.* The emotion in a Rothko piece was devastating and complete. Potent as a punch or a kiss.

"Maybe you do have some of your mother in you," he said as if impressed. "Little turncoat."

Dani didn't bother to counter, but Mia surprised her by leaning both elbows onto the table. "You want her to help you, you respect her," she said.

There was that light peeking through Dani's chest again. She couldn't afford to get used to people having her back. Or even acting like they did.

It also made her feel guilty. Everyone here knew precisely what she'd done.

"God save me from thieves so loyal they even hang out with supposedly reformed snitches."

Mia hissed and Brenner hesitated before opening his hands. "Fine," he said. "Sorry for the insult. Will you consider it?"

When he asked so nicely? "I've got plenty to do of my own, and I think the Hackworths will notice if one of their highest valued pieces suddenly goes missing. We're in the process of installing extra security on it."

"I just need to make sure I get the piece. It's out of professional courtesy that I'm asking instead of just pulling it. It's not like we plan to get in your way otherwise, not like the twins."

That confirmed they were also after Archer's portrait. Or he wanted it to seem that way.

He was good with locks and maybe he could outfox the security system. Though she doubted it—even with magic—unless his team was the same caliber as theirs. If they were that good, he wouldn't be here. Would he?

"What can I do to keep you out of our way?" she asked.

"Help. A nudge for things to go my way, that's all."

"And Rabbit's debt would be considered paid, then?"

Mia cleared her throat. "Can I talk to you in the hallway?"

Dani nodded.

Brenner held his hands up again. "I won't move a muscle. I know the Rabbit Hutch rules."

Mia nodded. Rabbit didn't like people poking their noses into her process. No one roamed the Rabbit Hutch unsupervised, except the residents.

Dani followed Mia through the living room and the whirring heat of the computers into a private foyer. "What is it?" Dani asked.

"He's serious. Mom wouldn't like you trying to dig her out with him."

"Do you know who his buyer is?"

Mia shifted from one foot to another. "Not yet. Still looking."

Which implied they would. There were some people you didn't want to cross, and some people you could roll the dice with. Knowing which kind the buyer was would help.

"I'll at least give us some time," Dani said.

Mia's head bobbed as if it were an acceptable answer.

"And, Mia, for before—thanks."

Dani turned away before she could see how that landed. Brenner, true to his word, didn't look like he'd moved a hair while they were gone.

"We'll be figuring out the timeline for the auction today and tomorrow," Dani said. "I'll try to get you something you can use."

His eyes narrowed, but he accepted it. "Try hard. You need to make things easier for me, or they might get harder for you."

Rabbit strolled back in. "I know I did not just hear you threaten one of these girls in my own kitchen. Out!"

Brenner didn't hesitate. He left.

"What are you doing here?" Rabbit asked Dani.

She could admit the truth, that she came to see Elliott. Or she could do the much easier, more explicable thing, and lie. "I wanted to check in with you. How are things? I can help you with him."

Rabbit ignored that. "Elliott left bright and early to install your bugs." She stretched her arms overhead, neck cracking as she moved it side to side, and then filled a mug with the coffee on the burner. "How's the painting?"

"I started." Dani found Mia and caught her eye. "Thanks for the help with the supplies."

Mia shrugged. "That was Elliott's idea."

Rabbit trained a withering glance on them both before seeming to decide this wasn't her business. She started to head to the living room, but hesitated. "Be careful with Brenner. Whatever you want to tell him, pass it through me. Okay?"

Dani didn't like agreeing to undermine her own authority, or the implication that she wasn't allowed to help Rabbit. She didn't know what she'd agree to tell Brenner, if anything.

But . . . Rabbit was her elder. The right thing to do was respect what she was asking. Dani had a lot of trust to earn back. "All right."

"Good," Rabbit said. "It'd be too damn much to ask to have this gig all to ourselves, I guess. Choosers can't refuse beggars, though."

Rabbit was well-known for coming up with opaque sayings that only she could decode. "They can't?" Dani asked.

"Not unless you want a beggar stealing the rug out from under you. On a job like this, we'd better remain standing."

"You check out the twins yet?"

"Elliott's taking point there. Ask him. Now I'm about to go in and see what's what. Give me a few hours and I'll know all there is to know about Hackworth's eyes and ears, the whole system. You want to watch the boot up, my entrée in?"

She didn't wait for an answer, just saluted with her mug and headed into the living room.

It was a gift. Rabbit was offering her a gift.

Because Dani had missed being one of the few people who got to witness Rabbit using her mojo. She cast a shocked glance at Mia and followed.

Rabbit strutted over to one of the tall stacks of vinyl records in the corner, threw her head back as she ran a finger along the edges, then, at last, stopped and extracted one—somehow without toppling the whole tower.

Dani moved to get a better look as Rabbit crossed to the turntable. Just as Rabbit had always done, she kept her eyes closed as she flipped on the power switch, removed the record from the sleeve, and gently settled it, then dropped the needle. She'd let instinct do the choosing, and the rightness of the sound flooded through her. Then, as now. One thing in this world that hadn't changed. The first raucous strains of "Let's Go Crazy" filled the room. Her eyes flicked open. She turned and pushed out a chair at one of the center consoles with her gum-booted foot, sat in it, and adjusted her glasses on her nose.

Rabbit worked to the music of three and only three artists: Dolly Parton, John Prine, and Prince Rogers Nelson. The three Ps, the royal principalities, the purple and the practical.

She leaned her head down, nodding in time as she stroked the keyboard.

Dani could almost hear her cooing to the computers. She realized Mia talked to her chickens the same way, echoing her mama's magic.

Rabbit began typing then, fingers moving at a furious speed, each screen transforming in a rhythm which she clearly controlled and she alone understood. Dani saw schematics, and she saw empty galleries. She saw a view from high above.

"Watch and learn, my pretties," Rabbit said with a low whistle. "Oh, look at you, sexy, sexy surveillance. All the latest fashions."

"Am I supposed to understand this?" Dani whispered to Mia.

"She's taking a look around, imprinting her signature along the code and—"

Rabbit lifted her fingers, cracked the knuckles, and grinned. "And then I'm making it entirely my bitch. Watch and learn."

The screens began to switch again, Rabbit keying in various commands and whispering terms of endearment. "That's right, you're mine now, sweet, sweet cameras. Let's talk to some locks next."

"Can they hear her?" Dani asked. She didn't remember the whispering.

"Everyone likes a lullaby before you put them down for the night, Danielle," Rabbit said, then went back to whispering.

"She's even better now," Mia confirmed.

Rabbit had started to sing along with Prince under her breath, still typing. She stopped and tossed them a look, gestured. "Impressive fight, but who's the big brother now? It's me, that's who. I can make this bad watchdog do whatever I want with just a sweet nothing. Elliott's new sensors are in place. Time to see what I can tease out."

Dani was about to voice her admiration for Rabbit's performance, but before she could, she felt the buzz of a phone call. The number was unknown, but few enough people had the line, so she just said, "Great," and headed out of the din to pick up. Mia came with her.

Once outside, she answered, and Elliott said a lone word: "Help."

Dani was on instant alert. Mia frowned a question as she came with. "What's wrong?" she mouthed.

Then Dani heard them in the background, female voices. Bickering, one over the other. Beverly, Sandi, Diana. The ex-wives.

"Emmett?" one of them called.

She had to laugh. "I'll be there as soon as I can."

"Hurry," Elliott said.

Dani hung up, still laughing. Sunflower loped over, thinking it was time to go. Dani figured the wives would be a lot less sanguine about her dog's presence than Brad. "Can you watch Sunflower for me?"

Mia nodded. "Obviously. We will have so much fun together," she said to Sunflower, who was still watching Dani. "I take it there's nothing too bad going on?" She directed that to Dani.

"Nah," Dani said. "Elliott just needs some help." She would explain, but then she'd lose it again. She was still giddy with Rabbit's show of trust, small as it had been. To Sunflower, she said with a head scruff, "Stay here. I'll be back."

Sunflower whined, but stayed by Mia's side, watching Dani as she headed off to rescue her first love. His suffering could be the karmic payment for confusing the hell out of her with the whole T-shirt business.

CHAPTER FOURTEEN

SURELY ELLIOTT WOULD have managed to free himself by the time she showed up at the main house. Speeding, it was an hour's drive. She texted him when she arrived. The painting that she'd been copying tugged at her from across the grounds, like it wanted her to come. She couldn't decide whether the smart thing was to honor the feeling and go visit the piece, though she'd rather do anything else. A reason to be glad she had to visit the home first and not the collection.

She wasn't sure she wanted to know how they lured Elliott over here in the first place.

Rose emerged from the front to greet her. "You'd better come in," she said. "I tried to help him, but . . . Well, you've met them. They wanted to discuss 'the security for the party.' And then Emma came in."

Oh dear. Dani remembered Elliott being vaguely terrified of children, even when they were children. And, of course, the exes were the exes.

Dani and Rose exchanged grins. "Lead the way," Dani said. "I'm assuming you're actually doing the gala prep?"

"I hired someone, but I'm overseeing it. The three of them chose the menu and consulted on the guest list. That was a battle royale." Rose paused inside the foyer of a house as tacky as it was grand. William Hackworth, flaunting his wealth again. "It's black tie."

Dani didn't miss the scan she received up and down. The subtle implication that however she got this job, she might only own the one pantsuit and jeans. Whatever hint of camaraderie there was evaporated. "I assumed," she said.

In her head, she heard her mother saying: *They will never truly accept us as the same as them. They think they're better. But we know the truth.*

Rose led Dani upstairs and through a hallway. Along the way, Dani noted that, for all the gilded décor and fancy mirrors and cabinets, there wasn't a single piece of art on the walls. The man had kept *everything* in the Fortress, it seemed.

"No one's been living here?" Dani asked Rose as they got close enough to hear voices that were still bickering. And one crying out in delight, identifiable as Brad's little girl, Emma.

"They've been staying here until the auction, but no. How did you guess?"

"There was the clothing disposal the other day," Dani said. "And someone would have redecorated."

Rose nodded. "The house will be the next to go. Not nearly as many stipulations on it."

"Brad isn't keeping it?"

"I doubt it."

She wondered where he and Emma lived normally, and realized she had no cause to wonder. It was none of her business.

"Where will you go from here?" Dani asked. "Or are you staying on?"

"I have a few offers from other collectors, but we'll see. Assembling William's collection was my life's work, and I can't imagine something like that coming along twice. Here we are," Rose said and gestured toward an arch that served as entrance to a room bathed in light. A solarium, Dani saw as she walked in.

Plants dotted the airy, open space, and since they were still alive and healthy, someone had made sure they were well cared for. Which required telling the staff to keep them alive.

Elliott was sitting cross-legged on the floor in a suit, with Emma clapping her hands in delight as she applied red marker to his cheeks.

Perched on the edge of an Edwardian couch nearby were bitch baby Sandi on one side and crone Beverly on the other, both in full makeup and designer dresses. By contrast, Diana was in designer jeans instead, filling a tumbler from a decanter of what appeared to be scotch.

"You're sure I can't tempt you?" Diana asked Elliott.

Elliott looked past her to Dani and she refused to acknowledge the twist of something near the vicinity of her heart when he . . . brightened at the sight of her. That was the only way to describe what happened to his face.

Of course he's happy. You're here to save him.

"The marker's washable," he blurted.

Emma squinted at him as if she couldn't believe what he'd just said. "You're not just going to take this off, are you? This is *my work.*"

"She's been picking up a lot about the art," Elliott said. "And you."

"She eavesdrops," Diana said fondly.

"You can do art," Emma declared and pointed her finger at Dani. "Emmett said so."

Dani suddenly might be in way more trouble than Elliott was. "I can draw a little."

Neutral, cautious, true.

"She was the apprentice to a master thief," Beverly added.

"What thief?" Emma asked.

"Well," Diana started to answer and Elliott stood up.

"We don't need to rehash the past. Maybe Dani could give Emma a quick art lesson." Elliott offered this as if he were helping.

Emma jumped up and down with a screech. "Yes! Show me how to draw something!"

Well, shit. Elliott seemed to understand the misstep from read-ing Dani's reaction. He gave her an apologetic look, which the red circles on his cheeks would make hilarious, if Dani wasn't panick-ing. He didn't think through what it meant for her to draw or paint for someone like this. Her mother had always told Dani to keep her ability secret, and she had. She didn't want to bring even a hint of her fakery into this moment either. But Emma was obviously not going to let it go.

The girl had a large pad of paper on an easel and what must have been a sketch of Elliott. His head looked like a lumpy, misshapen potato.

"Show me something, please?" Emma said.

"What do you like?" Dani asked, when the rapt attention of the other women made it equally clear she wasn't getting out of this.

"Circuses," Emma said after a long consideration.

"Hence," Elliott said and waved at his cheeks.

"I would be happy to help wash that off," Beverly purred.

"Me too!" Sandi said and then dodged Beverly's elbow.

Dani almost threw him to the wolves. But . . . "Have you finished installing the extra sensors?" she asked, even though Rabbit said he had.

Elliott leaped at the excuse. "I got sidetracked. Sorry."

"I see. We'll finish after this. Wait by the door."

Elliott went over to Rose instead. "You know, a friend of a friend is part of a troupe that does aerial performances at parties . . . Cirque du Soleil–style stuff." Dani wondered what on earth he was doing. Probably just making a randomly helpful suggestion. "Could be a nice surprise?" He glanced over to Dani and Emma.

Rose nodded as if she would consider it.

Dani held out her hand to Emma. "I'll show you how to draw a circus tent."

"That's boring," Sandi said.

"Emma asked for a lesson," Dani said.

"Pleaaaaase!" Emma said. "Just a little drawing."

Dani should say no, just so the girl could learn that, even with her wealth, she wouldn't always get what she wanted. But that would only prolong this. She turned the paper with Emma's drawing over to the back of the oversized pad and revealed a blank page, then reached out for the marker. All the sticky situations she'd been in since she left, she'd never felt on display like this. She could feel them all watching—not just the exes, but Rose and Elliott. And, of course, Emma. She tried to focus on the girl.

"First, sketch the shape," Dani said.

The marker flew across the sheet as she made that easy pointed big top and then used the red contrasting with the white paper to make the stripes. When she stopped, Emma gaped at her. "You're so fast!"

Right, it was a lesson.

Dani refused to look at anyone except Emma. "Now I'll do it slower, so you can learn how."

She flipped to a fresh sheet and slowed things down, passing the marker to Emma so she could do some of the stripes. They had that wavy messiness typical of kids' artwork. Something Dani was trained out of so, so early. She said nothing about it, only praised the girl's efforts, not a word of implication that it should be cleaner, better, perfect.

"Great job," Dani told Emma when she finished. She smiled at the praise, but not big enough to sell that she believed it.

"Now we'd better go," Dani said, "finish up that work in the Fortress."

Dani had to turn to the—for lack of a better word—audience. They seemed underwhelmed, which was a relief. Elliott had an apology written all over him, having gathered this was not Dani's favorite moment of the day. She followed his glance to something behind her and looked over her shoulder to see that Emma had returned to the sheet with Dani's flawless big top. The lines weren't perfect, because she wasn't trying that hard. Still, they suggested movement. She could practically feel the breeze ruffling the fabric of the tent.

And so what Emma had learned was that she wasn't as good as a grown woman who used to tag along with a master thief (whatever she'd later be told about that). She'd never know it was because of magic. Dani was incapable of making a piece that didn't draw the eye. Her heart was always there on display.

Whether she wanted it to be or not.

"But we don't want Elliott to leave," Sandi, the baby, pouted.

"What Sandra means is that we were thrilled to have such an interesting guest." Beverly cut Dani a look, then Emma. "We really shouldn't be bothering you, I know."

"You're my employers. What bother could there be?" Dani hesitated. "Is Brad around?"

"No," Emma answered. "He's doing something boring."

Her grandmother sipped her drink. "I'm watching her for him."

Elliott gravitated closer to Dani, the red cheek circles still ridiculously present. Dani had to make a little fist with her right hand to avoid reaching out to touch him. What *had* he meant with the shirt? Anything? Nothing?

"You are coming to the party, though, Emmett?" Rose asked this.

"Of course he is!" It was Diana who answered. "Emma would be beside herself otherwise."

He checked with Dani, who nodded. What else could she say?

"Apparently the answer is yes, then," Elliott said. "I wouldn't want to leave anyone here bereft."

That seemed to mollify everyone in the room. Except Dani—who could only vouch that being left bereft by Elliott was a terrible experience. She didn't recommend it. And the other hell of it was that "bereft" was such an Elliott word. He was usually quiet—or in the old days he was—but there was all that reading. He'd always been full of unusual words when he did talk.

"We'll see you soon," Dani said.

Emma was still studying Dani's sketch when Rose led them from the room. She wanted to go over, tear down the sheet and ball it up, flip to Emma's and point to it as more real. But she didn't.

She smiled and nodded and walked out through the same gilded, artless temple she'd entered through.

. . .

They didn't talk much on their walk over to the Fortress. That it had become a familiar path in a few days was disconcerting to realize. The distant growl of some groundskeeper on a riding lawnmower reached them.

"How'd that happen?" Dani asked to break the silence.

At the same moment, Elliott decided to ask, "Did I bring everything you needed?"

She thought of the shirt again and almost asked him about it. But instead, she said, "I think so. I'm working on the piece."

"Mia thought you might not have that stuff, but I told her, you've been out there doing something to make a living."

Damn Mia for being so perceptive.

"This is the first time I've painted since . . . you know."

Elliott blinked, taken aback, because of course he was. "I can't imagine you not painting."

She shrugged. "I've done other things instead. I get by."

"I never doubted it." He stopped walking. "Back there, I'm so sorry for putting you on the spot. I didn't even think . . ."

"It's all right. Just don't do it again." Then Dani did something rare, something she'd probably regret: She explained herself. "I don't think you ever knew this, but no one was supposed to be aware of what I could do. Outside the team."

"Of course, she would've wanted to keep it secret. Your painting is something to see."

"It's not that. I liked not being put on display."

"Oh." Elliott hesitated. "How does it feel to be working again?"

"Weird," Dani said. She didn't try to describe that sense of being trapped in an echo, the way painting Archer seemed dangerous. She might have once, but she'd already given more of herself than usual. She couldn't make that a habit.

"Now it's your turn to answer," Dani said, smirking. "They got you up there how?"

"Rose let it slip I was out at the collection doing work."

"And chaos ensued."

Elliott sighed. "Calling those women chaos is putting it mildly. Thank god for the little girl."

"Emma. She and Brad definitely seem like the most normal of the bunch. Brad's mother too."

Elliott frowned at her. Almost a pout.

"What?" Dani said. "He's nice."

"Nice and boring," Elliott said. And then sarcastically, *"Brad."*

"Brad is a normal name. And I don't know why you're saying either of those other things like they're bad. Nice is refreshing. Boring is unlikely to end in federal charges."

"Since when are *you* worried about federal charges?"

Ouch. She stood there like he didn't just take a sword and insert it directly through her chest. Like she was still breathing normally. The others really did get away clean. He hadn't been forced to sit in the courtroom, the way she had after her mother's lawyers insisted it would show how young Dani was, how easily manipulated. She'd hoped that her mother might talk to her. She refused to testify, but by then, it didn't matter.

Her mother had ignored her. Every second since she'd been aware of just how badly she'd fucked up and she'd paid the price for it.

He must know that. But then, maybe not. Maybe he didn't know her, if he thought she'd been out there painting forgeries and making her living that way. Maybe he thought she went out and found another family, like he did as a kid. She could say that and it would hurt him the way he just hurt her. A knife in exchange for the knife he lodged in her.

She chose not to. She shook her head and started walking fast, outpacing him up the path.

"Dani," she heard him say. Then, "Danielle . . . Fuck. I'm an idiot."

Oh no, that would be me, out here assuming for one hot second that you meant anything at all by giving me back the damn shirt.

He was probably cleaning out drawer space. Had used it as a cleaning rag.

He caught up. "I'm sorry. Dani, I—"

"Don't be. You just said what you actually think," Dani said and somehow she'd found it, that magic skill she learned from her mother, the best and most useful of them. The ability to keep her emotions hidden, if not in check. She said it lightly, unbothered. "I prefer it when people do that. Then we all know where we stand."

"Dani," Elliott said it one more time. "I was an asshole."

"No argument there."

She bounded up the steps of the Fortress and nodded to the mustached guard—an ex-Marine—stationed at the door. "We need in," she said.

Damned if the guard didn't check over her shoulder to make sure the man he preferred had okayed this visit. And if Elliott didn't nod like it was his right to.

She was still channeling the superpower though, so she acted as if she didn't care. Not one single bit. She breezed around the guard and through the door.

"Hurry up," she said to Elliott over her shoulder, brisk enough to make clear who was in charge. The security guard had no choice but to stand aside so *her* employee could do as ordered.

She almost felt calm at reestablishing control—until she looked ahead and found Archer in the overwhelming grandeur of the entrance gallery, talking with Brad.

Fuck. Like today hadn't been a mess of complications already.

CHAPTER FIFTEEN

BRAD GREETED THEM with a puzzled expression. "I thought you'd gone for the day," he said to Elliott. "And I wasn't sure *you* were coming in." Dani earned a smile. "You know Archer," he said.

Dani kept her "no problem" air in place. "Hi, Archer," she said as if it wasn't a surprise to stumble on him here of all places. "And this is my associate Emmett."

"Emmett, is it?" Archer said, detached. "My greetings."

Elliott didn't respond.

She focused on Archer, not checking Elliott's reaction until she could do it without seeming to. She could still practically sense Archer's portrait on the far side of this obscene, glorious, soon-to-be-empty building. Tugging at her.

Archer caressed the top of the walking stick Dani had only ever seen him use as a threat or weapon.

His look was measuring. No surprise there. She was confident even after just a few encounters that Archer was *always* measuring. Specifically, the distance between people and how to get them to do what he wanted. Was that why he and her mother had such an unbreakable bond? Or did he force her into becoming that person? Force them *all* into leaving aside the morally gray side of stealing and magic and their chosen family, and into the full darkness that trying to control the impossible brought as an inevitable side effect?

But she wasn't going to abandon the chance to glimpse his and Brad's relationship up close, however much she hated being around him. The ways people interacted with others could be a shortcut to understanding their psyches.

"What are you two up to?" she asked. "Emma said it was boring."

She finally spared a glance at Elliott and noticed his mouth was slightly open. She nudged him. He moved forward with her to join the two men. *She* still had to force herself not to gape at the overwhelming beauty displayed on the walls, but Elliott had never quite had that reaction to art. So he must be reacting to Archer, who, if she was right, he'd never met before.

"She thinks everything I do is boring, I'm her dad," Brad said. "Archer wanted to take a peek at the collection before it's gone. He's busy the night of the gala."

"And make sure you were living up to my recommendation," Archer said to Dani. Before Brad could hop in, he added, "I'm assured that you are."

"Of course she is," Brad said.

There was the sound of a fuss behind them and Dani turned to see a golf cart driven by Rose had stopped outside, the three ex-wives and Emma piling out of it. Emma barreled past the guard's weak protest, the other women and Rose waving him off as they followed behind.

"Mom?" Brad asked Diana when she neared, his eyebrows raising.

"Emma wanted to go through the collection with our expert." She gave a shrug and nodded toward Dani. She still had her half-full tumbler of scotch in one hand. "Dani gave her a drawing lesson at the house."

Brad looked to Dani. "You did?"

"She's the best!" Emma declared.

Brad reached over to ruffle her hair. "I take it she did this to you?" he asked Elliott.

Elliott's jaw was tight; he'd plainly forgotten about the art on his face. Rose approached with a makeup wipe in her hand and asked Elliott. "May I?"

"Give us one moment first," Elliott said, and though Rose frowned, the women beamed at him.

Now Elliott was trained on Archer with a man-eating tiger's assessing gaze, checking out someone he wanted to snack on. And Archer was giving it right back to him. Dani felt the situation hanging by a thread. Too many people were involved. Her heart beat too fast, but she held on to her outward calm.

"Nice to finally meet the infamous Archer," Elliott said. His voice had the gravelly tenor Dani recognized from when he was lying. "Where are you based again?"

Archer looked thoroughly amused. "Here and there," he said.

"You look just like the painting in the last gallery." Elliott wasn't backing off, though Dani wanted him to.

Brad sensed the tension, and he tried to offset it with a chuckle. "I've told him the same thing."

"A funny coincidence," Archer said.

Rose was barely holding the group of interlopers at bay. Emma's bottom lip jutted out, and though Dani didn't know much about kids, she could predict a tantrum might not be far off.

"So it seems." Dani let her tone call bullshit for her. She needed to work fast if she was going to learn anything she didn't already know. "How did you two meet? Brad never said."

"William introduced us, of course," Archer said smoothly.

"He would have," Brad said, frowning. "But I don't care to remember."

Archer gestured with his walking stick. "Your audience awaits."

"You should join us," Dani said. "I'm certain you know as much about the pieces here as I do."

Archer's smile was humorless. "Mine is an idle curiosity."

"Anything in particular catch your eye?" Dani wasn't letting him off that easy.

"There was one thing," he said, and that surprised her.

"Show, don't tell," Elliott said. Then, to Brad, "We may as well all go."

Emma broke away from the group and skipped their way, and Archer said, "All right, but then I must take my leave."

Rose came forward to clean Elliott's cheeks with quick strokes.

The rest of the party enlarged the foursome of Brad, Dani, Archer, and Elliott into a chaotic clump. Dani looked over to find Archer watching Elliott and then her speculatively. *Don't ruin our family name.* Her mother's words from the prison hospital room returned to her. She didn't have a chance to ask what it meant. Maria said it as if Dani hadn't already, as if their family name wasn't a public marker of shame itself. A mother captured because her own daughter betrayed her. No one cared—no one knew—that Maria had betrayed Dani first.

Not that it mattered. Not that it would change the nature of Dani's sin.

The only opinion that ever mattered to Maria outside of her own was Archer's. Although she *had* always enjoyed the respect and fear directed at her by their criminal peers. That was when Dani realized it wasn't *their* name her mother meant—Poissant, hers and Dani's—but their family's reputation. All of them. Rabbit, Mia, Elliott.

The clump walked slowly, the women's heels clicking on the marble. Archer showed them all the way and Dani was more than content to let him—he was the only one who knew the destination, after all. Emma attached herself to Dani's side, and Elliott and Brad stayed close too—much to the grumbled complaining of the other women. There were several attempts by Beverly and Sandi to ask Elliott about this piece or that; Diana just sipped her drink.

Elliott brushed off the ex-wives with a genial: "All in good time."

Brad glanced at Dani and leaned in as they traveled the upper hall toward the larger galleries. "I'm glad I caught you today. I'm realizing how much I like your company. You are a quiet point in all this madness. And I haven't seen Emma this excited in forever."

Dani smiled at him before she could help it. Her? The calm in

someone else's storm? Him being happy his little girl liked her? She
didn't feel he was playing games with her. There was no endless
mass of questions to wonder about whether he was interested. It
was refreshing.

She didn't have to check to know that Elliott would be scowling
from whatever misplaced jealousy he harbored. He had no poker
face.

*Well, except for the night he fooled you into thinking you mat-
tered to him. More than the job.*

Archer led them into one of the wide middle galleries. She didn't
expect him to take them to his portrait—she still sensed it nearby, a
lurking shadow—but she also wouldn't have guessed the painting
Archer selected. He stopped and cast his arms out wide, and Emma
dodged his walking stick. Dani and Elliott exchanged a look.

The Rothko. She didn't like or trust it. Especially now that she
knew Brenner was after it for someone.

She should never have engaged with Archer.

Emma squinted at the uneven bands of vivid red and orange and
then cantered closer with her hand out.

"Careful," Dani said, catching her shoulder.

Emma wasn't used to being told no, she remembered a second
too late.

"I just put a sensor on this one, Miss Emma," Elliott said, bending. "If you get too close, it'll trip it. All the guards will come running."

Emma peered from Elliott to the large painting and back to
Dani, and Dani could read her mind: *Sounds like fun.*

"Listen to what they tell you," Brad said.

"Yes," Archer put in. "You wouldn't want to get caught trying to
steal this one. Tell her how much it's worth."

"Yes," Beverly said. "Tell us how much the asshole paid for it."

"Well, he paid less than you'll get at the auction," Dani said and
all three of the ex-wives seemed gratified by that. Rose too.

"It's one I'd buy if I had the funds," Rose said. "What do you
think it'll net?"

"I have a feeling the mood in the room will encourage people to go higher than they would otherwise. So I'm expecting a low of around a hundred million. Might go for way more."

They all gaped at that—Emma included. It seemed even the obscenely wealthy could be wowed by a large enough number.

Sandi, childlike herself, blinked. "We are going to be so—"

"Much richer," Brad said. "And Dad's haven will be gone. Everyone wins."

"Yes, everyone will." Archer raised his hand, the one with the walking stick. "And now I'll be on my way."

"Are you sure you won't stay?" Dani asked—a challenge. She couldn't afford to let him get the better of her by bringing them up here. She wondered if he *knew* Brenner. Or who his buyer was. Their world was small. If Rabbit could find out, then odds were . . .

"You almost sound like you want me to," Archer said, a sinister purr.

Dani tilted her head. Could Archer be the buyer?

Elliott nudged her. He wanted to know what she was doing. He'd have to keep wondering.

Dani waited Archer out.

"I'm afraid I can't." The warning in his eyes for Dani was clear. This wasn't what he wanted from her. "I'll leave you to *your* work."

Which parading children through the gallery isn't.

Something inside Dani refused to allow him the last word. Not today. "There's a painting here that looks *exactly* like Archer. I'll show you," she said to Emma.

Archer was gone by then, but she was certain he heard. And Dani discovered she was still full of questions, as usual.

Brad gave Dani a small frown.

Elliott was crouched, explaining the security precautions on the Rothko to a rapt Emma. Dani turned to the women and Brad. She steered them toward the door.

"The rest of you had really never been into the Fortress?" Dani asked the women. "William didn't want to show his wives his treasures?"

Beverly snorted and pushed up the gold bangles that lined her tanned arm. "No, my dear, he liked to keep his treasures separate. We weren't as valuable to him as all this."

"I noticed there's no art in the house." Dani waved for everyone to come into the hallway. Elliott was still playing perfect backup. Was this what having a partner was like?

Brad chimed in. "There were a few pieces there, but we sold them off. Not officially part of the collection."

"They weren't valuable," Rose said.

At the slight tightening of Brad's lips, Dani wondered how many tens of thousands they'd fetched.

"We picked them out," Diana said and rattled the ice in her now-drained-of-alcohol tumbler. "That's what she means."

Rose conceded. "Touché."

"I just bought what I liked," Sandi said.

The other two women echoed the sentiment. "Just as you should," Dani said, despite it not being what either an art thief or a security consultant should say. It was what she believed, though. Even people who bought all those ugly horses. That was fine if they liked them. Sometimes the art world got it right, recognized true genius, rewarded it, and sometimes other reasons and outcomes prevailed. There were a lot of broke geniuses. A lot of dead, valuable artists. And if they became famous while they were alive and had sold a painting for seventeen dollars when they were younger? The artist didn't see another dime on that piece if it suddenly became worth seventeen million dollars and someone else sold it. That part of what their family did always made sense to Dani. It was an ecosystem they were part of balancing.

No different from any other con. Or business.

"And Dad bought what was most valuable," Brad said.

"It's just, the way you describe him . . ." Dani decided to offer an opening to see if any of the women suspected what this place truly was. But carefully. "The arrangements in here—he wasn't the typical art lover."

"Art lover?" Diana said, laughing. "No. I don't think he loved anything but money."

The rest added noises of assent. Nothing to indicate they thought of this as anything but a selfish hoard.

"I want Dani whose Mom was a master thief to show me around," Emma said from behind them. "That's why we came here."

The rest of them froze, in that way adults did when a child revealed how everyone thought about someone.

Dani was no fool, and she'd have to be to assume they saw her any differently.

Brad shook his head. "That's in the past. We're polite to guests, remember?"

Emma nodded and turned to Dani. "I'm sorry."

"It's all right," Dani said. It was impossible not to find Brad's gentle touch with his daughter—and the way he continued to look out for Dani—appealing.

The group began to move again. Elliott stopped with Emma to chat about a piece she pointed to, and Dani was surprised in a way that made her feel foolish that he was content to leave her walking alongside Brad.

This hallway housed two works featuring the ballerinas Degas fetishized, called "little rats," and painted so beautifully. Beside them, Dani saw the self-portrait of Marie Bashkirtseff that she was initially surprised to find in the list of holdings. Dani noticed it because her mother had covered the history of the Académie Julian with her as a child. It was the Parisian art atelier the young Russian painter attended before dying far too young. Remembered mostly for her diaries and letters, which Dani also read—in the original French—as a kid. Her mother always said they had spiritual ties to France, and that it was the language of art.

Dani didn't believe that art was its own language, but she didn't tell her mother that. She learned French anyway.

"I snuck in here once," Beverly announced. "Into the Fortress."

The others were plainly shocked. "You didn't!" Diana said.

"How?" Sandi asked, skeptical.

"Well, I was *friendly* with one of the guards. And I wanted to know what William did in here all the time."

No one commented on the obvious declaration of cheating. They took it in stride.

"He let me in one night when William was here." Beverly pushed her bracelets up again. A nervous tic.

"What happened?" Brad sounded worried. He checked over his shoulder to make sure Emma was still occupied.

Dani noticed where she had led them, without deciding to. Archer's gallery. That damn painting, pulling at her through the ocean of magic.

"I found him in here, actually," Beverly said and nodded to the seat in the corner, the seat placed directly in front of Archer's portrait.

The image seemed to be watching Dani, the shadow of it confronting her, and she felt abruptly detached. It was as if she were in two places at once—in front of her easel painting it and here in this room and . . . also a third place she didn't recognize. Her head hurt and her heart pounded, but she shook her head so she could listen hard.

"What was he doing?" she asked.

Beverly almost looked like she'd laugh off the question, but when she answered, it was in a whisper. "He was talking to that painting. The one that looks like your friend."

Dani didn't need her to indicate Archer's portrait, but she did. No one commented that the painting was identical to him, the coincidence too strong to be one.

Diana snorted, a little drunk. "What about?"

"He was arguing with it."

"That checks out." Diana rolled her eyes.

"Demanding," Beverly whispered, "something from it."

"That's how he always was," Sandi said and shrugged. She strolled closer to the portrait, screwing her face up to examine it more closely. She reached out a finger like she was going to touch it, but stopped at the last second. Dani wanted to pull her away. Elliott and Emma rejoined the group and then—immediately bored—Emma raced over to Sandi.

"Beverly, are you okay?" Dani asked.

The woman's overly tan cheeks had gone pale and she stopped fiddling with her bracelets. She lifted her hands to her ears.

"Beverly?" Dani tried again.

"What's happening?" Brad asked.

Beverly was standing there with her hands over her ears and then she shook her head violently and dropped to her knees—for all the world like someone was talking to her. Someone they couldn't hear. Screaming at her.

Brad grabbed Emma before the little girl could run to her. He held her fast.

"What's wrong with Beverly?" Sandi shrieked and hugged her arms around herself. "You have to help her!"

Dani took in the group, the portrait, the panic. She gestured to Elliott and Brad. "Have the guards call an ambulance."

Beverly's eyes went wide and she kept shaking her head *no, no, no,* and Dani managed to get hold of her arm and lift her to her feet. Brad was suddenly there on the woman's other side, assisting, while Elliott barked orders into his phone. Emma began to cry. The other wives and Rose surrounded the little girl in a futile attempt to prevent her from witnessing too much of this.

"Make it stop," Beverly pleaded. "You don't hear it? Make it stop."

Dani didn't look at the portrait, but she felt it looking at her. At them. The sensation was as distinct as a touch. She couldn't help the creeping guilt that she'd caused this—provoking Archer, leading them in here.

"I will," Dani said and she hoped like hell it was the truth.

FOUR DAYS OUT

CHAPTER SIXTEEN

THE NEXT MORNING, Dani wished she had told Elliott to rally the troops at seven instead of nine. She should go down into the fallout shelter turned studio and finish painting the piece, but some superstitious part of her didn't want to go down there alone and paint those dark watching eyes on Archer's face. She needed at least the comfort of her dog, who'd spent the night at the Rabbit Hutch.

So she sat on the porch step and turned the small safe-deposit-box key over in her hands. A reverse image search earlier had turned up nothing. No surprise there, other than how many people put pictures of random keys online.

The night before was a riotous blur of activity interspersed with holding her breath. Beverly felt better nearly as soon as they got her outside and put some water into her. When Dani asked what she'd heard, she just said, "Whispers. A voice. And my heart—it felt like it might explode." She seemed confused. "You didn't hear any-thing?" she asked, before letting it drop, obviously embarrassed.

The ambulance and paramedics were on the scene by then, and so the mention of voices merited a mental health screening and the heart pain a trip to the emergency room. Dani felt duty bound to accompany Beverly, despite everyone's objections—except for Elliott. He didn't say a word when Dani simply told him, "I need to be there. Bring everyone to the stone house in the morning. Early. Nine?"

He'd simply nodded. Brad had accompanied Dani, but there hadn't been many words exchanged. "You ever seen anything like that from her?" Dani had asked.

"Never seen anything like it, period."

He'd set his hand over hers, a comforting stroke of his thumb across the top.

She'd left it there for a while, as they waited in plastic chairs in that grim silence hospitals demanded. Coffee spurted from a machine went cold in the paper cups they eventually held to have something else to do with their hands.

Dani didn't know how to feel about any of this. Her emotions pulled her in several different directions, and it'd be a lie not to acknowledge one of them was Brad. Lying to protect herself came as second nature, though. So she did. She was there for Beverly, to atone for her role in what happened.

The doctor had emerged after a few hours with a tired but head-held-high Beverly who refused to stay the night. "Her heart is fine. I suspect a migraine caused the rest," he said and handed off a prescription. Neither Dani nor Brad questioned it, and Beverly had declared, "I'm not filling that."

Dani suspected there was no reason to, but kept it to herself. Whatever Archer's intention, Beverly's meltdown involved him. The portrait. All of it. Why did that lone acquisition—a targeted win in a poker game, if Archer was to be believed—kick off a man's obsession with building a magical collection of art? What did it have to do with her mother? What *was* Archer?

Dani wanted to scream at her lack of ability to arrange the pieces she'd been given into a picture she could understand.

Rabbit's truck pulled in at the stone house five minutes before nine. Early, this time. As soon as the passenger door opened, Sunflower jumped off Elliott's lap and sprinted for Dani.

She met her dog, apologetic, and grateful for the thumping fan of her tail, the enthusiastic greeting, even if it did involve a few less-than-graceful licks to her face. The reaction to coming home told her how badly she'd freaked out her dog. Most creatures, given the choice between Mia and Dani, would go with Mia every time. Or Rabbit. They both possessed that not actually magic, but still somehow magical touch with animals.

But Sunflower was Dani's good girl.

Since Mia, Rabbit, and Elliott were watching, she didn't apologize out loud to her dog for leaving her somewhere else for the night. She'd do that later with a giant treat. Possibly a steak.

"Meeting time," Rabbit said. Rabbit was wearing vibrant yellow glasses frames today and she snapped her fingers. She and Elliott unloaded several wood chairs from the back of her pickup truck. Undoubtedly from the cache of . . . a little of everything in the barn.

Mia accepted the chair handed to her, and then Rabbit and Elliott picked up theirs and they all schlepped inside while Dani held the screen door open. They assumed their places around the kitchen table, Rabbit swinging her chair around backward before she sat. Dani was left with her mother's old seat. It felt more comfortable to take it this time, less a flex and more a reality. Sunflower settled on the floor beside her with a contented groan.

Dani kicked things off by filling them in on the broad strokes of last night.

"Migraine my ass," Elliott said. "Whatever happened to her was . . ."

"Some kind of magic." Dani put her hands on the table. There weren't that many aggressive forms of it, but the world was wide. People were inventive. None more so than those with gifts beyond the normal. "Agree."

"I don't," Rabbit said like they'd both gone soft upstairs. "Rich white ladies freak out all the time. She probably just wanted to get Elliott's attention. I don't see how it has anything to do with us or Archer's portrait."

Mia pursed her lips thoughtfully. "This is Dani's job, Mama."

"It's all *our* job," Rabbit said.

Mia frowned. So did Dani.

"Don't you wonder what it is we're stealing?" Dani asked. She meant it. Rabbit could be a good soldier, but she wasn't usually the rank-and-file kind who didn't question orders. Her curiosity used to drive Dani's mother up the wall.

"A portrait of your mother's partner, soulmate, whatever," Rabbit said. "What else do we need to know?"

And, thing is, maybe Rabbit was right. They didn't *need* to know more to do the gig. Dani did—but for her own reasons. She'd been promised things she thought lost forever. She should be striving to make her mother proud again. She wasn't that good little girl anymore though, so she'd do her best to manage both.

Dani saw Elliott about to disagree and decided to put a stop to it. "Table all that for now. Let's outline the plan. Are we agreed that the best time to do the grab is right before the painting changes hands? Auction day?"

"When they're taking it off the wall to go to its new owner," Rabbit said. She pushed back from the table and began to pace—a sign she was feeling much more comfortable with this turn in the conversation. "The sensors will be down then. Elliott put the gear in place and I've got them set up to disable piece by piece for the biggies, gallery by gallery for the rest."

Dani didn't point out that she'd bet there were a half dozen biggies that didn't even count in this context.

"What if no one buys it?" Mia asked.

"Rose wants it." Dani turned over the possibility. "But worst-case scenario, Elliott can bid." And before they could question the pot size or where it would come from, "That will trigger someone to compete with him. Trust me. It'll sell."

"Smart," Mia said.

"Have you got anything on the Evil Twins?" Dani asked Elliott.

"Haven't had a chance yet—figured we could go see them together."

Made sense. "I assume they'll try to time their move roughly the same," Dani said. "Maybe we can scare them off."

"Doubtful, because they are batshit, but we can give it a shot," Elliott said. "Can you walk us through the whole thing?"

Elliott's magic ability to find something if he was close enough wouldn't come into play at the auction. He'd be the last-ditch bidder, Dani's backup, and, if needed, put his getaway driving skills to use. Oh, and continue doing his cover gig, same as Dani.

"How will you get yours in and it out?" Mia asked.

"I'll take mine in early, in my trunk. There will be all sorts of shipping containers around, and part of our jobs as security will be overseeing their loading. It'll be easy enough to slip the copy into a crate and the original into a different one. I'll take it out the same way it came in. The trunk. Rabbit, you can distract them with a glitch at the right moment?"

"What a question. I can distract them with a glitch anytime I want, upstart." Rabbit's way of saying yes.

"Do I get to help?" Mia interrupted again.

"Sure, baby," Rabbit said. "You'll be manning the comms."

Mia pouted. "So I get to sit at home and do nothing."

"The less of us exposed, the better," Dani said. "I don't trust Archer"—understatement of all time—"and we can't forget Sharpe will be there. He'll be watching."

"Will he be in the Fortress or in the security headquarters?" Rabbit asked.

"I can make sure it's whichever one you want," Elliott said.

"Fortress," Rabbit said at the same time Dani said, "Security."

The two of them looked at each other. Dani nodded for Rabbit to make her case. "The Fortress will be filled with more people and activity. He'll be easier to distract there. What's your argument?"

"The same will be true watching the cameras, only there will be many more of them. He can only be on top of so many places at once and didn't you just admit it's easier for you to manipulate those than what's happening on the floor? If he's onsite, he'll stay on me. No question."

Rabbit's mouth worked, her eyes shining. She was clearly thinking her way through the various approaches. Then she shook her head. "Shit, goddamn it. I hate being wrong. Okay, put him in the HQ."

Dani was surprised at the quick fold, but she did also think she was right, so she wasn't going to fight the win. "Elliott will take care of it."

"Dreaming of putting him in a deep dark hole in the ground the whole time," Elliott said.

"Only you could make that sound charming," Mia said. She hesitated. "I don't know—is this coming across . . . too easy to anyone else?"

Dani stayed as motionless as she could. Until she heard Rabbit's snort-laugh and then glanced across the table to Elliott's face as it broke. She gave in too.

"What?" Mia demanded. "What's so funny?"

"It's just—" Rabbit couldn't rein it in. She threw her head back.

"It's just," Dani said, "I don't think you've seen this place. It *is* a fortress."

"Of art, I'm aware," Mia said.

"No," Dani said. Then, "Well, yes, but it also has the best security of any place I've ever seen. Or heard of. And there will be upward of seventy-five people there, not counting staff. More if one of the ex-wives goes rogue with extra invites. The FBI Art Crime Team— and its member who specifically fucked up my life—is going to be there, trying to ferret out any shady activity. The security team loves Elliott but loathes me."

"'Loathes' is strong," Elliott put in.

"*Loathes* me. Would love nothing more than to turn me over to the feds. And the painting we're stealing might be haunted or some- thing like it. Oh, and Brenner and his team are trying to grab a Rothko and I still don't know what to do about that—"

"Let me handle them," Rabbit said.

"You keep saying that," Dani said. "Why?"

"Your mother owes them too."

There weren't many things that could puncture Dani's sails when they were this full of wind, but that did. "It's being put up thirty-second. If the schedule stays on track—"

Elliott said, "It will."

"The auctioneer will get to it at eleven forty-six A.M., give or take a minute. Is that enough help?" Dani hoped so, because anything else was practically doing the job for them.

Rabbit patted her shoulder. "It'll do, pig."

"You figure the buyer yet?"

"Not yet, they're a tricky one. But I will," Rabbit said.

Dani made a note to circle back on that, and possibly poke into it herself. In her copious spare time. Ha. There was a painting to finish . . . And so much else.

Rabbit nodded at Mia and Elliott and went for the door with a wave, summoning them. "More to do, y'all, let's go."

Dani still had to figure out Archer. No matter how much she shouldn't. "Elliott, can you stay? I need to talk to you about something."

Rabbit made an extravagant show of flapping her hands about. "Keep the chairs. Consider them my wedding present."

"Hilarious," Dani said.

"Mom, enough, let's go," Mia said and pushed back from the table with sympathetic eyes for Dani . . . and Elliott. "Bye, Sunny dog." She lingered one last second. "Do you think the painting is really haunted? Is that possible?"

Dani knew they were both remembering the Curator's strange reaction to her. "I don't know."

"Good lord, you're turning into the Scooby-fucking-Doo gang on me. No, the motherfucking painting is not harboring a ghost." Rabbit practically towed Mia to the door.

Elliott didn't move. He was staying.

Dani didn't let herself show emotion, but Sunflower put her head on Dani's boot.

They waited, quiet, until the rumbling growl of Rabbit's truck pulling away faded.

"So?" Elliott asked.

It'd be better if she followed the rules. Their world's rules. Instead of asking him as if it were personal. "I need a favor. I'll owe you one."

A favor for a favor, that was how it went. Every time. You paid, you were repaid, and then it all happened again endlessly.

"What is it?" Elliott asked.

"Does it matter?" That did make it sound personal. Too late now. She left it out there anyway.

He looked at her. *Why* couldn't he have turned ugly? *Wouldn't matter. You'd still like him too much.*

"No, it doesn't," he said. "You know that."

She didn't until this second, actually. And she wasn't sure she believed it. But she said, "Then come on, let's go. We'll visit the twins, and then I need you to find something for me."

CHAPTER SEVENTEEN

GETTING TO THE Evil Twins' lair took Dani and Elliott to a section of town she wasn't even passingly familiar with. Giant warehouses that had been converted into lofts butted up against cleverly branded craft breweries and shops selling handmade candles and bars with signs for shows by obscurely named bands.

"Was all this here when we were kids?" she asked.

"It was abandoned buildings and some railroad tracks back then," Elliott said from the passenger seat. "The literal wrong side of them. I went to a couple of sketchy keg parties in an abandoned distillery warehouse out here. They set fires in old barrels to warm the place. The rest of this got built up in the past decade."

After you left went unsaid.

"Tell me about the twins, the job you did with them." Dani gave Sunflower a little tsk so she removed her head from between their two seats.

"Turn here." He pointed at an alley ahead and Dani did. She steered along the narrow lane between two tall buildings. "All the way at the end. Small job. Someone stole an emerald ring with sentimental value, and the owner hired the three of us to get it back."

"Were you friends?" She'd gathered they weren't anymore, if so.

"The twins don't have friends, they have each other. Moved back home from Detroit a while ago, no clue why. They made a fast name for themselves. I didn't see any reason not to work with them at the time."

At the time. "The job went that well?"

"They're a little psycho. But the main issue is they're flashier than I prefer."

Dani chose a spot then cast him a sidelong glance. Elliott wore his assurance like a garment, especially when they were at the Hackworth estate. But then, to be fair, he was playing a role there. The hotshot expert. On jobs when they were young, he'd always been serious, quiet, cued into any signal from Rabbit.

She turned off the car outside the last apartment building, reached across Elliott—not breathing in how good he smelled closer up—and popped the glove box for her Taser. She tucked it into the back of her jeans. "I hope they like dogs."

No way she was making Sunflower wait in the car.

"I'm sure it'll be fine," he said in a tone the opposite of reassuring. He closed the glove box and they got out, Sunflower climbing over Dani's seat.

"With me," Dani said to Sunflower.

The dog stayed glued to her left side, Elliott on her right, as they walked toward a towering, moldering apartment building. The rehabilitation of the area hadn't spruced up anything back here. She'd seen it before in many other cities. Gentrification at its most obvious. The displaced had to live somewhere close enough to work in all those new businesses but stay hidden out of sight and mind too.

The question was whether the Evil Twins chose this rental because it was off the beaten path or they weren't flush with cash. The answer might help point to why they were after Archer's painting.

Elliott opened an outer door that admitted them into a dank hallway. A set of stairs that might or might not be safe to use went up. There was also an elevator that looked original to the building, and not in a good way.

Elliott read Dani's skeptical measuring of the two options.

"Lucky for us, I found out they're on the first floor."

"Do they know we're coming?"

"They know I am. I thought the surprise of you might be useful."

Dani nodded, reached down to pat Sunflower's head, and followed Elliott past the steps to a corridor flanked with doors.

Elliott knocked on a unit labeled 1D, and Jer answered, sister Jenn smirking behind him. Their eyes widened at Dani and then Sunflower. A fluffy gray cat wound between Jenn's legs and hissed at Sunflower.

Jenn just laughed. Sunflower liked cats fine, so Dani didn't worry about it.

"Look at the company you're keeping," Jer said, his judgment clear.

"Yeah, right? I thought snitches got stitches, not second chances," Jenn said.

"Nice to see you again," Dani said—though she'd crossed paths with them only a couple of times when they were at school together. But if you knew someone was in the secret world, you kept an eye on them when you intersected. There was a kinship, paired with the knowledge they might mean trouble.

"Nice to see *you* again, Elliott. I guess come on in," Jer said.

Jenn looked like she might disagree, but she shrugged one slim shoulder and moved aside to admit them. The cat raced ahead. Sunflower stayed near Dani.

There were more cats in store, a trio of them, sleeping on the sofa. Jenn picked up a black one and put it in her lap. The others didn't rouse.

"So they allow unlimited pets here?" Dani said.

"Why else would we be in this dump?" Jenn asked.

She had a point. The furnishings were quality, even if the dingy greige walls were stained.

When Dani didn't answer, she said, "To what do we owe the . . . honor . . . of this visit?"

Jer sat down in a stiff chair. The gray cat draped itself across his feet.

Dani made a snap decision to stand. She didn't think they'd be here much longer.

"This is a courtesy call," Dani said. "We think you're after the same target as us, and we thought we might warn you, in case you weren't aware."

The twins exchanged a long look. "Why would we care? May the best thief win," Jenn said.

"Why do you want it?" Elliott asked.

"More valuable than you'd think," Jer said. "Our pop, rest his soul, lost it in a card game with the elder Hackworth, way back. Why do you?"

Ah, the fool Archer had mentioned.

"None of your business," Dani said.

"And yet," Jenn drew the words out slowly, "here you are, acting like you have a right to ours."

"We are the best thieves," Dani said, "and we have better access. Like I said, I'm trying to do you a courtesy, save you some trouble, some risk. You know I could post photos of you both in the guard booth."

"But that would lead to a lot of questions, wouldn't it? And not be very sporting," Jenn said.

"I'd consider it a favor if you looked elsewhere for your next score," Elliott said. "One worth repaying."

Dani cut him a look. Had he lost his mind? Offering a blank future check to these two?

Elliott shrugged at Dani.

The twins exchanged another of those long speaking glances. "Excuse us for a moment," Jer said.

They got up, Jenn depositing the cat, who eyed Sunflower warily, and left the room. Their whispering was audible, but not understandable.

The two returned. Jenn lifted her hands. "We won't fuck with you," she said.

"Your job, hands off," Jer agreed.

That seemed way too easy, but Elliott's gift was rare and exceedingly valuable, and he did not offer its use often.

The sound of Sunflower snarling and snapping—sudden as a lightning strike—jolted through Dani. She watched in shock as Sunflower ripped into the black cat, who cried and screeched and screamed, fur and blood flying.

"What the hell?" Elliott demanded.

Then Dani felt a lick on her hand. Her well-behaved good girl, of course.

Illusions. Elliott had said they could cast them.

She closed her fingers in Sunflower's fur. Flashy and psycho were about right.

"You absolute assholes," she said.

Just like that, the vision went away.

"You must have really been taking a vacay, sister," Jer said, "if you thought this was going to work out. Like I said . . ."

Jenn finished. "May the best thief win."

"We're out of here," Elliott said, a hand on Dani's arm. She was already moving toward the door, Sunflower beside her.

There was nothing to do but the next errand on the list.

Still freaked from the fake audio-visual show of Sunflower attacking the twins' cat, Dani parked outside the first bank on the list she'd made last night of the eight likeliest in town. No way her mother was banking outside city limits. The piece of notebook paper was in Elliott's left hand, and the key in his right, back in the passenger seat. She hoped the elimination round didn't take too long or require going inside—sometimes it used to, depending upon how good a sense of what he was looking for Elliott had.

"Nope," Elliott said. "Nothing here. I'm sorry about that—what happened back there."

"It's okay. I should have expected it. Something like it anyway."

She stole a look at the sheet to see what the next spot on the list was. Then she put the car in drive. They were back among the roads and streets, the ways of Lexington that she knew well, despite so long trying to forget. The curse of having a home, maybe, was that it stuck with you. The blessing too.

They merged back into the moderate traffic that residents loved to complain about. "Does it still feel the same for you?" she asked. "An emptiness when it's no, a ping on the radar when it's yes?"

"Both are sharper now, clearer," Elliott said. "It's more like a quick yes or no, a switch that flips on or off."

"You're never uncertain?" God, what would that be like?

"Are you ever uncertain when you're painting?" he countered.

"About the painting, no. About everything else? That is a 'hell, yes,' of course."

"I don't see you that way. Never have."

She could only have this conversation, only ask, because she had to keep her eyes on the road. Someone cut them off just to prove it and she tapped the brakes. "How do you see me?"

"You always knew your own mind, your gut, more than any of us. What you wanted. We knew we were getting in too deep, but we did it without a second thought. Your mom . . . She *was* different at the end. Worse. You weren't wrong."

"But what I did about it was wrong." Agent Sharpe just happened to catch her right after her mom tried to mess with her mind. And not long after her history teacher did a lesson on looted art that included information Dani's mom had glossed over in their own history lessons. The Nazis stealing Jewish art, and also the ways in which so much cultural wealth had been taken from the places it belonged. Was that what they were doing too? Or were they simply righting the scales against the too-rich, like Dani's mom claimed? It wasn't like they always left their marks with nothing. The lucky ones had Dani's copies.

Somehow that had been the sourest realization.

Elliott didn't argue Dani's point, so she just kept driving.

"This is in no way meant to imply anything like what Jer said about being out of the loop . . . But I can't believe you haven't been painting," he said. "Why?"

"Felt wrong to use it. I guess not doing it was like an apology." And she'd been afraid of where she'd end up if she kept running on magic. She still had the craft. "I chose my marks for a specific brand of . . ." She searched for a word, turned in to the lot at the next bank, and glanced over to see Elliott watching her, rapt. "Douche-baggery." She shook her head. "Don't tell anyone, but I usually split the take with whoever they'd hurt most."

"Dani . . ." Elliott said her name like a wish.

She couldn't believe she admitted her charity to him. Anyone in their world would see it as weakness. But to her, it was necessary. She didn't need the whole pot. She would've been splitting it with them, with her mother, otherwise. And so, she didn't keep it. She didn't use her magic, and she didn't let herself get too comfortable. Atonement.

Maybe there was something else there too, but she wasn't going to pretend at heroics. Even though on the occasional dark night, she might've wished for that.

He held up the key. "It's here."

"You're sure?"

"The switch flipped on."

She reached across for the key, but he closed his fingers around it. "I should go in," he said. Then, with a smirking twist of his lips, "Someone else might have a doll collection."

Dani's cheeks blazed. "You heard about that? How?"

"One of the guards knows one of the Fortress guards. It's a great story. You had to know it would get out."

Dani had hoped it wouldn't. "Fine, you go in. But I want what-ever is in there, okay? No deciding for me if it's too much or not. Whatever it is."

Elliott set down the list and touched her arm. "If I say it's empty, will you believe me?"

She told the truth. "Depends how you say it."

He frowned. "I don't have a tell."

"Then don't worry about it. Go."

"I don't."

He gave her one final look, which she returned impassively, then climbed out of the car.

There was more than a fair chance the box was empty. Elliott would have sensed it anyway. He was locating the box that the key went to—the same way they would sit outside a private house at fifteen and he'd confirm that a particular painting hung inside on the wall after he was showed a picture or had it described to him. Or if money someone had stolen was tucked away in someone's house. Or other loot. Or a stray cat Mia was worrying over, hiding somewhere near the Rabbit Hutch.

Elliott had been used for a lot of favors over the years. And that was before she left.

For a moment she felt like they were karmically even for his volunteering her to draw the other day. Then she realized she might have been the only person Elliott knew who had never asked him to find a thing, before today.

Archer was changing her too. Not the same as her mother—not yet—but using Elliott's gift was a bigger line than she should be crossing without stopping to notice it first.

The bank was boring beige, the bottom floor of a taller building, but it had a retro look. She had checked them all out on Street View, looked up their business registration licenses on her personal machine. They were all in their current locations when her mother was active. She imagined the conversation Elliott was having inside, and how much easier it probably was for him to get access.

Her phone buzzed. It was Brad, so she picked up. "Hey, I'm sorry I'm not in yet, but—"

"We need you here," Brad said. "I know it was a long one yesterday, but the security guys are unloading all the shipping supplies and Emmett isn't around either, so there are some questions."

"I know," she said a little cheekily, because it *was* her job, as far as he was concerned. "I'll take care of it."

"Of course," he said. He sounded frazzled—unusual for him. "You went above and beyond yesterday. Thanks for going with me to the hospital. Bev's attack . . . That threw me off-kilter."

"'Attack'? Don't you mean 'headache'?" She cradled the phone tighter.

"I guess so." He sighed into the phone. "I didn't get much sleep."

"Is she all right today?"

"Telling everyone how she could have died except she's too strong, and that she fought off whatever happened before it could hurt her."

Dani snorted. "How's that going over?"

"Sandi's translation was, 'So you're too bitchy to die, great,' to which Mom said, 'No one is too bitchy to die if William bit the dust.'"

Dani laughed despite herself. "And how's Emma?"

"She's been drawing on her easel all day. I think it might be a portrait of you."

Her heart did something it absolutely should not do. "Oh, how sweet."

"She is the sweetest, and she likes you. I do too, and I hate to be that boss, but—"

Elliott came out, grinning, and holding . . . something. "Hold that thought," she blurted. "I have to go. Don't worry. I'll be there in a bit."

Dani was out of the car and on her way toward Elliott before he reached the car. She snatched a bundle from him. It was wrapped in cloth, and there was a long piece of old rope or leather tied around it. "You drive," she said.

Finally, she possessed one of her mother's secrets. *Please, please let it mean something.*

Elliott got behind the wheel without hesitation. "Nervous?" he asked.

She explored the object. A book, maybe, and something else . . . The cloth was rough but worn—canvas or linen, at a guess. It smelled old. Anyone who thought old didn't have a smell had never been asked to figure out whether something was valuable or not. Not that old things were innately valuable—they weren't—but it was one of those things people tried to fake and mostly couldn't. Dani'd never had to worry about it, but her nose for someone else's fake, or trash, had always been keen.

She was almost afraid of whatever she held.

"Are you going to untie that? Don't you want to know what it is?"

"You didn't peek?"

"Didn't feel right."

She was seventeen again, foolish, in over her head, desperate to find an answer. "I think I should wait until we get it home."

"What if it's got some kind of poisonous pigment?" Elliott asked and backed out of the parking spot. "Also, why am I driving?"

"Stop asking so many questions when I'm on sensory overload." Dani clutched at the object in her hands like it might wriggle free and escape. "Poisonous pigments? How do you know about that?"

"I read books."

Fair enough. "Brad called while you were in the bank. He wants us onsite, but . . ." She peered down at the parcel. Her mother hid this and kept the key. No, no, she *left* the key, where it was likeliest that Dani—and not anyone else—would find it.

"I'll go," Elliott said, and he didn't even bother with a snarky aside about Brad. "Though he really shouldn't be riding you about anything after how late you stayed last night."

"It's almost like you're jealous," Dani said, not looking up from the parcel.

Elliott gripped the steering wheel tighter and sped up. The drive still passed in a fog—taking forever, taking no time. She only realized they were at the stone house when Elliott opened her door and Sunflower hopped out.

"You mind if I borrow your car? I'll bring it back later."

"Of course," Dani said.

She was already walking toward the house.

"Dani," Elliott said, "whatever's in there, I hope it's what you want it to be."

She didn't know how it could be, or what that was. The answer to a prayer she hadn't made . . .

"Be careful," she said.

It was too intimate a thing to say. It was what you told people getting in a car if you were their mother or their lover. She wanted to pull the words back in, tuck them inside. She expected a smart-ass quip in return.

"I will," he said.

She bolted the rest of the way to the house, Sunflower at her side. She instinctively dropped to a seat at the spot in the living room where she had first started painting her fraudulent miracles. The exact place on the earth where her life changed—different before, transformed after.

She breathed, intentionally slowly. Sunflower trotted over in front of her and sank down, head on her paws, watching.

There was nothing to do but open it. She should get gloves—if not conservator's, then gardening would do the trick. She had some in the studio. But she didn't want to wait and her bare fingers were steady. How could they not be, after so many years of training? She worked the old knot loose with care, not allowing herself to rush. Then she put the cord to the side.

She wanted to rip away the cloth to get to the contents, like an overeager kid at Christmas, tearing into a present they either weren't surprised by or wouldn't even remember fifteen minutes later. They had never worked a lot at Christmas, because the big families would be home. Museums would have been a decent target, but Maria Poissant liked getting gifts and giving them. Dani's childhood wasn't all bad memories.

Dani had many good ones that looked much like this. Opening a gift from her mother, only with a special pair of holiday socks on.

She took her time unfolding the cloth and set it aside with the cord.

What lay within was a book, as she'd guessed, but it had the look of something cobbled together by hand, the binding sewn, also probably by hand. The paper feathery, varied.

Her fingers trembled as she opened it. Handwritten. *Secrets Concernant l'Atelier des Arts passage des Panoramas, Académie Julian.*

A year, 1894.

A location, Paris.

And a name Dani had never seen or heard before.

Maeve Poissant.

Secrets Concernant l'Atelier des Arts, passage des Panoramas, Académie Julian

1894, Paris
Maeve Poissant

September 7

We have arrived in Paris, after the long journey from New York that Papa claimed would put me off notions of painting forever. He does not understand that I am a woman with a will as strong as his. I have assured my chaperone—Mama's spy, Gladiola—that this is a book for taking notes on method and technique. And I have styled my name here, in private, as Maeve Poissant, which Mama told me once was part of her name before she met my father, when she lived in France as a little girl. She said that I should always remember the name, but never use it in front of Papa. I claim it now, as I intend to become my true self in Paris.

At any rate, Gladiola is too incurious to turn from the first page to this one after seeing words in French, and so this will be my journal of painting and secrets both.

Our pension is not far from the pont de l'Alma, which we were assured to be a respectable location. The damp abode causes Gladiola to grouse and shiver, despite the sun in the streets, and so I claim to find it perfection itself. Tomorrow, I will make my first visit to the atelier. I insisted on attending Monsieur Julian himself's original location at passage des Panoramas in the second arrondissement, where the competition is said to be fierce.

Finally, I will meet more of my kind: women who need no one's approval but their own. Perhaps I might encounter someone of my other kind, as well.

Gladiola will write Mama to tell her I am no longer harboring ill wishes or intent against others, and perhaps it will even be true.

SEPTEMBER 9

What a whirl the past two days have been! I must set it down here to gather my thoughts.

Our first lesson was of painting from life—a man— a specimen who preened for us like a peacock without its finery in evidence. Some of the others allowed him to compliment their paintings and drawings, and fluttered their hands at him at day's end, cheeks blushing at his seeing their rendering of his naked body.

I chose to indulge in the Impressionist style, particularly as the form of a man is of no interest to me, not since I learned what harm it can do . . . I was quite proud of the result, only to discover the ways of most at the atelier remain stuck in the mud. My piece was singled out to use as a critique of the lack of detail, specificity, and polish in the work of Monet and his cohort. I would counter that it makes its own argument for capturing the form and spirit, the light and shadow. That I am working in the mode of Berthe Morisot or Mary Cassatt, whose talent even Edgar Degas admires. I held my tongue for now, difficult as it was. I do prefer such painting, and the way it resonates within me—but to speak too freely might make me an outcast once more.

I believe that the model knew something of my thoughts, for he alone chose to compliment the contents of my easel. I painted over the image to make it plain I was unmoved by his praise, and he—one of those tomcats who likes to toy with women like a mouse—may have taken a liking to me for it.

I hope it will not last.

September 13

I have gained a confidante. Her name is Charlotte. Imagine my delight at so quickly finding another young woman who thinks as I—she also admires the Impressionist artists and all things modern—and who is a native Parisian. I may have misjudged this place—something I have done before but rarely admit. It seems there are several other students interested in taking expeditions out of doors to work in the newer style, and a small measure of encouragement among certain of the faculty to do so. We women have always been good at making a meal of such small encouragements; they are how we progress. Is it not my own misfortune and how I handled it that made Papa think it wise to send me abroad? But it is here that I shall find my true path forward. When I return, I am determined to make my own decisions.

Charlotte has invited me to a salon this evening where she says the most interesting people in the city will be. She claims to know "une petite" witchcraft, but I did not question if she knows of true magic. It is far too early for such a confidence as that, confidante or not.

Gladiola forbade me from accompanying her, of course, but Charlotte tells me that to skip the salon is fine. It is the midnight salon after that is not to be missed. And so I have prepared a tea for Gladiola, a gentle blend

only, with herbs that Charlotte secured for me, that will
see her sleep well this evening. She complains of the
creakiness of the house keeping her awake, so truly it is a
kindness I offer.

Once she is snoring fit to shake the walls, I shall sneak
out and make my way to the rendezvous with Charlotte
and meet her confederates. She says that they are an artis-
tic bunch. Several are former students of our own school,
and others attend the men's atelier.

I voiced my worry the second will believe themselves our
superiors. However, Charlotte assures me they typically—
if not always—keep their heads out of their derrieres.
Perhaps one day all our paintings will hang together in a
grand display. This is how such allegiances begin, and
then become legend.

I set this down so that if I am abducted by pirates or
murdered by some Edward Hyde on the street, Papa can
say he was right in all his predictions, and that I brought it
on myself. Mama too. It is what they said about Mr. B—'s
unwanted advances and what he did to me. But I will have
my confederates with me this time.

And, of course, I have found my own ways of protecting myself.

SEPTEMBER 20

After Mr. B—'s attack at our house upstate, and its lingering consequences, I should never have thought the night
would hold much appeal for me again. I was excited about
attending Charlotte's midnight salon, but did not admit
even to myself how nervous it made me, venturing out in
the dark.

And yet, Paris at night! It is playground and fantasyland
in one. Charlotte's set are the most interesting people I

have met, to be sure. Most of them are eccentrics of the best sort, who know all manner of obscure facts. One girl, Lili, has the same fascination with Books of Secrets as me, though I do not believe her investment is as intimate. She was quite charmed when I shared that I have disguised my journal as one. But then our conversation was interrupted by . . . who else? The pale gentleman peacock from my first day at the atelier.

Charlotte is besotted with the gentleman, whose name is Archer. He styles himself a scandalous lord, though he only chuckled when I questioned what he is lord of. I am hopeful his appeal to her will wear off soon.

He inquired as to which Books of Secrets we had come across—only those concerned with collecting the secrets of painting techniques (which women like us were not supposed to have access to until recently and some still believe we should be denied), or others that contain darker information. Lord Archer spun tales of books filled with alchemy and witchcraft—at which, of course, Charlotte became intrigued—potions and recipes. Anyone who knows of magic knows it has very little to do with recipes. I thought such books might be instructive at first, and explain to me the qualities of myself I do not understand. I thought they might provide a way to get myself out of the . . . trouble that had been pressed upon me by Mr. B—. That was my initial reason for seeking them out. But failing to find anything useful, I then became interested in the more straightforward facts within them. These seem far more likely to be accurate. (Though I doubt Albertus Magnus's cure for a toothache, which involves squeezing moles slowly to death. Gruesome! I should prefer to let my teeth rot.) As for Archer's claim, I informed him that information is neither dark nor light, it simply is.

He laughed once more, and I realized my mistake. I should never have engaged his conversation at all. Char-

lotte hissed at me later, as if I want to steal his eyes from
her to me, but then when Lord Archer offered to let the
two of us see his private collection of such compendiums,
she agreed on both our behalves. He says he will gladly
give us a guided tour, if I will but paint him a picture.

If he believes I shall risk my friendship with Charlotte
in order to make my first commission, he is a fool. He
simply palmed his nightstick—which seems naught but a
pretension with its ornate headpiece—and said it was my
decision. He said it as if it surprised him.

What he does not know is that I am a Book of Secrets,
all on my own, bound in skin, filled with blood, bone,
and magic.

I let Charlotte choose, and so we will go to Lord Archer's two nights from now. Lili will come too; I confess
the idea of simply talking with her makes my heart
quicken. Yet my dread of the fall of evening has returned,
for that occasion alone. I try not to think on it, but somewhere out in the night, tucked away by Mama, is a girl,
growing by the day. I did not meet her, only heard her cry
and knew I had not given birth to a boy. I was thankful,
for I dreaded that part of him might pass on through me.
Papa might put the blame to me, but it is he who should
choose his friends and associates with greater care. No one
wishes to believe ill of powerful men, however. Not when
a young woman is conveniently available to settle it upon.

My dread at what Archer shall request of my painting is
not so potent, but it is a tangible presence.

SEPTEMBER 23

Last evening was our trip to Lord Archer's private library.
His residence is extravagant enough to support his claims
of holding a title, though there were only a handful of

staff that I saw. It was scandalous for three young, unwed
women such as Charlotte, Lili, and I to visit without a
chaperone, but Charlotte questioned what of an inappro-
priate nature could happen with all of us there? I had put
the decision in her hands, and it was too late to back out.

I fear I have made a fool's mistake. But I run ahead of
myself.

At first, Archer was all things courteous. He offered us
refreshments and bid us follow him down a set of spiral-
ing metal stairs that led to a passage beneath the house.
The stairs had been added by the previous owner, and Archer regaled us with stories of the catacombs—only to reveal, at the bottom, that we were about to enter them. He
lit a torch—and while Charlotte exclaimed with delight,
and Lili laughed nervously, I felt a dread at the skulls
lodged within the walls around us. For I have not only
been near life—been its genesis—I have been near death.
And I have been its cause.

I do not like the idea of the dead looking at me from
their hells. Even Mr. B—. He faded into nothing after Papa
bade me let him sit so I might finish the portrait I had
begun during his first visits, and though I did not know it
would happen when I began, I was glad. He was captured
there, inside the canvas, where he would hurt no one else.
His fury and hatred burned in his eyes, captive as his soul.
The cause was my blood in the paint, from an accidental
cut made to my hand. A palette knife, used through tears,
split my own skin and thus brought forth my power. I
claimed he had left abruptly after the session, and released
his horse, which ran as I would if I had belonged to him.
Papa had the finished painting delivered to his home. The
rumors that he was missing began weeks later. I alone knew
the truth, though Mama suspected. I ended his cruelty.

I do not know why thoughts of him still intrude in this
manner. I wish I could end that as well.

Charlotte saw me peering at the skulls and dared me to touch one—I refused on the grounds that it amounted to desecrating a body. Lord Archer took this as an opportunity to observe that he hadn't expected me to be such a frightened little mouse.

I still did not touch the skull, but I followed where he took us. The catacomb passages vary in size, and this one began narrow—so much that I forced my eyes straight ahead on the back of Charlotte in front of me, rather than accidentally meet the empty eye sockets of one long dead. The crunch underfoot, I imagined, to be small shards of bone. The passage then slowly grew wider, until we progressed into a chamber as large as a room.

This, Lord Archer has styled as his library. A collection of pamphlets and books, several I recognized, were strewn across a large stone that served as a natural table. A library of secrets, hidden among the dead.

The hairs of my neck and arms stood at attention as if they'd been electrified. I wished in that moment I had not read Mary Shelley's book about the modern Prometheus. I felt a kinship with the monster—galvanized, possibly a danger, and also in danger.

Lili and Charlotte, by contrast, were delighted. They immediately began to riffle through the books and read sections aloud.

Lord Archer watched only me, again as if he knew my thoughts. He took my arm and bade me join in. He had a special rare volume he thought would be of interest to me.

Charlotte frowned at me, for his interest, and Lord Archer both saw and ignored her. I could hardly admit it was Lili's attentions I craved.

He found a thick black volume among the lot, the binding sewn with red thread, and passed it to me, standing far too close. I felt I had no choice but to open it, with Lili and Charlotte watching. And him, of course.

I longed for the time when I could not read French. For the name of the volume was Secrets des Ouvriers Magiques. I gasped.

Charlotte came over and took the book from me, to read the secrets of magic workers, not realizing she stood beside such a one. Lord Archer cautioned her that the book was meant for me and she made a rude noise and kept flipping the thin, age-grayed pages.

And then, then a terrible thing happened. She put her hands to her ears and began to whimper and then to scream. To ask us if we did not hear the voice that plagued her. She clutched at her heart as if on the precipice of death. She was pitiful. She only stopped when she dropped the book, and then Lord Archer handed it back to me and bade me borrow it.

I felt I could not say no without revealing myself. When we were outside, I asked Charlotte what had taken her and she said to both Lili and me: Did we truly not hear the whispering? She felt it was coming from the book or the air, a madness that might break her. Her heart pounding a rhythm too fast to sustain.

The source was not me, for that is not within my purview, and though the book may contain evil secrets, I do not believe it is magic. So it must have been Lord Archer.

I have come halfway around the world, only for my past to find me.

Scared little mouse, he called me. It makes me furious that he is correct. I refuse to be intimidated, but that does not mean I am unafraid.

SEPTEMBER 28

Though I did not know its name then, Secrets des Ouvriers Magiques is precisely the type of volume I was seeking when I first began to look for Books of Secrets. How Archer knew—that or about me—remains a mystery. I have managed to avoid him.

Charlotte has been ill, meanwhile. Lili and I visit her each day after class, in her bedroom, where she mumbles and mutters and continues to be plagued by the phantom whispers . . . It troubles me that I wish for it to be madness, and not what I suspect: Lord Archer. Is he punishing Charlotte because I am avoiding him?

In the book are tales of those gifted with magic working in concert, typically on criminal enterprise. There are daring burglaries detailed, people with all sorts of odd powers. A man who can see for miles if he knows what he is searching for. A woman who can speak a lock into opening. Another woman who can cause those around her to lose the ability to hear for brief periods. Dozens and dozens of such people are described. All their abilities are different, and none the same as mine.

None so dangerous as mine.

There is no story of anyone losing their ability, no steps of how to remove it. Not that I am certain I would take such an extreme step, but I admit that a way to not be always on guard against myself, to be able to fully express my talent without fear of my true nature being revealed, is my dearest wish. Mama has warned me that no good comes of bringing such things into the light.

OCTOBER 1

Lord Archer was waiting in the street when I left the atelier. Gladiola was with me, and yet, after he introduced himself and smiled at her, she agreed to let him walk with me. Alone. Gladiola has never taken a shine to anyone. I took it all as confirmation of his powers. I do not understand how his seem variable, larger than those in the book or my own. I am only grateful his honeyed tongue seemingly does not work on me.

He asked how I had enjoyed the book, whether it had enlightened me. He believes we could work together, he and I, and achieve more than any of the exploits within it. That we could hold yet more power between us. The idea made my heart beat faster, and while he holds no appeal to me, I could imagine living a life of complete freedom . . .

Except it would not be that way with him by my side. This much I know of men like him.

Rather than answering his query, I demanded that he reveal if he is the source of Charlotte's misery. I asked him how he manages this.

He laughed, as is his usual way, and told me that surely I had noticed his magic is not like mine, not like any human's.

What can you mean, sir? I asked him.

He took my hand in his and my skin crawled as if with the feet of insects.

I am a demon, he confessed. A stain on this world here to spread corruption and misery.

And perhaps I am mad, but I believed him. Utterly. I told him I am not interested in befriending demons. He told me that I intrigued him, that he knew I must have some magic that enables me to resist him.

He admitted to tormenting Charlotte. He told me in excruciating detail of how he torments many women—any who won't do his bidding, and some who will. That is his demonic charge, and his whispering is but one part of the means: the voice that seems to come from within, but is far crueler. He persists until the women cannot bear it, and then he crushes their weakened hearts. One by one, he chooses and breaks them. He makes of them a meal to nourish his powers.

And that is not all he can do, he says. He claims
he can also answer impossible questions. He can travel
at will and use his persuasion to obtain secrets both
personal and of commerce. He tells me he could bring
me wealth, the kind of power the world recognizes.
He says that to corrupt me—immune to his false
charms—into being his partner would be his greatest
achievement. What misery we could sow, and then reap,
he says.

I did not tell him I have been corrupted many times over
against my will, and that the one who did so regretted it.

Instead I appealed to him with flattery. I bade him let
me paint the portrait he requested at the visit to his library, a means of furthering our relationship so that I am
not in his debt and we will be equals. So that he might see
what I am capable of producing. He accepted my lure as
his due with greedy haste.

I did want to smile then. Who is the cat now, and who
the mouse, I might have said, but I am smart enough to
hold my tongue. I growled my assent and he will sit for me
soon.

I must prepare.

OCTOBER 4

Charlotte is dead. If my path wasn't clear before, it was
once I received the news. Lili arrived at my door, bereft.
Perhaps this is why I have the ability I do, in order to fight
this demon.

I shall once more paint such a portrait as has never
been heard of.

I only hope I shall survive. I am certain I will never be
the same afterward if I do. But it shall be worth it if Archer plagues no one again.

CHAPTER EIGHTEEN

DANI'S FINGERS CONTINUED to shake as she turned each precious, fragile, faded page. A handful of pages had been removed following the entry for October 4—ripped out, the ragged edges left behind. Those that remained were all blank. Maeve Poissant may well have made more entries in her journal, but they weren't there now. She must have survived, though, right? Or Dani wouldn't be here. Or was Dani part of the line of the little girl who she'd given birth to, who she'd had to leave behind when her parents shipped her off to Paris?

Poissant was passed on as a last name, by her or someone else, and given the fact that Maria had this book, then Maeve was an ancestor. Possibly Dani's great-great-grandmother? Dani didn't know anything about her grandparents or great-grandparents, let alone her great-greats. She had never met any of them. Never heard stories about them. Her mother was mute on the topic. Dani had always envisioned their family line as starting with Maria. The two of them, striking out against the world. Mother and daughter—at least until their estrangement.

And then there was Archer. A demon with a special relish for tormenting women and great powers of persuasion, among others.

It should sound too outlandish to be true—but none of the available evidence worked against it as a theory. Maeve believed instantly, and Dani was inclined to do the same. It seemed that Dani—like Maeve—couldn't be manipulated by him. Could her mother?

The biggest question of all: Maeve likely painted this portrait of Archer, but was that all she did? Whatever she intended to do hadn't been fully successful, because he was still here. Still playing his games.

None of this explained why Dani's mother never shared this fragmentary journal with her but did leave her a key to find it. Or why she used to hear her mother whispering back to Archer at night, or how he was able to come track Dani down on the road, unless it had to do with his being a demon. And why was he interested in the portrait if he was still alive, not getting any older, and torturing people at his leisure?

Dani closed the cover and stroked the soft, worn surface. Answers always had a nasty habit of bringing more questions with them. She moved her hand to absently pet Sunflower's head. The dog remained glued to Dani's side.

"I'm sorry I left you overnight," Dani said. "I won't do it again."

Except apparently she'd made a bargain with a demon who had a hold over her mother. At least, she thought that was what she had done. She frowned. She called Mia.

She considered niceties but went for direct instead. "Do you know anything about demons?"

Mia didn't miss a beat. "Not really, but the Curator knows something about everything."

The beep of an interrupting call sounded. Dani checked, saw it was Brad Hackworth, and ignored it. A risky move given her need to keep her position, sure, but she'd smooth it over later. They liked each other. She could fix it.

"Can you pick me up?" Dani asked. "Elliott has my car. I'll be in the studio."

Because if there was one thing Dani was going to do right this second, it wasn't let Brad Hackworth chew her out over sending

Elliott instead of coming herself, or flirt with her, or whyever he was calling. No, no matter how creeped out she was in the fallout shelter studio alone, it was time to finish her copy of that painting.

She had to be ready to make the switch. And the frame hadn't arrived yet, so they needed to go see the Curator anyway.

She had a feeling the woman wouldn't be surprised or happy about them turning up at her door again. Tough.

Another cat, large and black this time, lazed on the path in the wild English garden at the Curator's mansion. Sunflower stopped and let the cat swipe playfully at her, rolling on its back, then touched her nose to its.

"I hope she didn't see that," Mia said.

Mia wanted Dani to leave Sunflower at home, but she wouldn't do that to her girl until she had to go back to the Fortress for the switch. The painting was complete, and all it lacked was a frame of the era that could be altered to match the original. She didn't know if she should be disconcerted that she didn't feel *observed* as she had before when she finished it, or as afraid. She painted the last details filled with anger.

Mia had no reason to worry. There was no danger of the Curator taking Sunflower. Dani would never let that happen.

The door opened before they reached the steps and the Curator swanned out onto the porch in a pair of flowing emerald silk pajamas, a turban in complementary jewel tones on her head, a frown on her red lips. She carried something large and rectangular wrapped in a sheet with her. "Here is the frame," she said, imperious as any queen. "Now go."

Dani glanced at Mia and her friend waved her forward. "I will take the frame," Dani said, "but I'd like to come in. I need to talk to you."

The Curator stared at her. Then she noticed Sunflower. She stepped back inside, widening the door. "You had to bring the dog, didn't you?" She sighed the same way she did everything: with drama. "Come in, even though I'll regret asking you to."

She carried the draped frame as they followed her through the stacks and curio cabinets and paintings, back into the room with the mirror. "I won't look again," she said. "He might see us this time."

"Archer, you mean," Dani said.

Mia settled on the red sofa again.

The Curator set the frame by the wall and held up a hand. "Shh. I don't wish to know his name. Why are you here, besides the frame? And why did you bring her here again, dragon-keeper?"

Dani exchanged a look with Mia, who leaned forward. "You once told me you have the ability to know whatever a person needs."

The Curator nodded and the answer was a preen. "That is my gift, yes."

"We need to know about demons," Mia said. "Are they real?"

It wasn't the way Dani would've brought up the topic. The Curator sealed her lips together, and it was unclear if she'd answer, or even if she was able to.

Dani had never given much thought to the existence of things like demons or angels, or monsters of any kind other than human. Her mother was never one to drag her to church, and once she learned as a child that magic was real, organized religion seemed both more likely and less likely to be true. More likely, because . . . why not? Less likely, because magic's rules were not easily codified. Besides, the world had never felt like good versus evil to Dani, more like those with power at the top and those with power at the bottom trying to even things out and failing again and again. Maybe that was good versus evil, just not so simple as it was usually implied.

"Anything that has been given a name is real," the Curator said finally. "Some of those things may no longer exist, but they did. We think people are creative enough to make these things up, but they aren't. Not really. No, they put a name to what they encounter. That's all."

"So that's a yes?" Dani asked.

Another dramatic sigh. "Yes." She eyeballed Mia. "Would you like some tea?"

Mia bobbed her chin, and Dani couldn't believe it after how disgusting the stuff had tasted last time.

"Some for you too," she said to Dani.

Ugh, no thanks, she wanted to say, but Mia's expression made her keep it to herself. The Curator rose and swished from the room. Sunflower got up and trotted after her. "Sunflower," Dani called with a hint of panic.

"Don't worry, she'll come back. She's guarding you." Mia tugged on a stray curl that had escaped her bandanna.

"Do I need guarding from the Curator?"

Mia scoffed. "Everyone needs guarding from her, except me. We're friends. She has many favors she can call in."

Fabulous, given that Dani was almost guaranteed to need to give her the promise of one to get straight answers. Everything that had been given a name was real? The kind of distracting sentence that set the mind on fire but wasn't actually helpful.

The full-length mirror with the golden clawed frame and feet across the room drew Dani's attention. She was almost visible in it. She started toward it.

Mia's eyes were wide when she whispered, "What are you doing? Dani, no."

"If anyone has a magic mirror, it's this lady. She had me look in it before."

"No, Dani. Roxie does not like people using her stuff without permission."

The aroma announced the Curator's return, eau de summer swamp from a pot on the tea service tray she carried. Sunflower passed the older woman and inserted herself between Dani and the mirror.

The Curator half smiled. "You won't want to mess with the mirror, not unless you want to end up somewhere else. Somewhere it's hard to return from. Even your dog knows better."

She set down the service on top of a roughly level stack of books and magazines on a table and poured Mia a cup of tea, then Dani.

"Drink it," she ordered.

Dani would rather not, but it didn't seem optional. And Sunflower didn't seem to think she needed protecting from it. Besides, Mia was already tasting hers.

The first sip was like swallowing liquid mud. But after, she was tempted to take another. Before she noticed, she had drunk the whole cup.

"Now we have some privacy," the Curator announced.

She might be *better* than the Gentleman, but dealing with him was a helluva lot more straightforward. Dani decided not to ask for an explanation of the comment. She replaced her teacup, obviously a piece of fine bone china, on the tray, and gathered her hands on her lap. She'd taken a seat beside Mia at some point too. She had no memory of doing it.

"Good," the Curator said approvingly. "You're ready to listen."

She gave Dani, then Mia, a good hard look. "You are staying for this?" she asked Mia.

"Would you have given me tea if you thought I wasn't?" Mia countered.

"Fair enough."

The woman relocated a small stack of volumes to the floor, then sat in a red velvet chair across from them. Dani wondered if she had a collection-within-the-collection of Books of Secrets around here somewhere.

"So you've crossed paths with a demon," the Curator said. "That makes sense, given the other day. The darkness I sensed then was . . . deep. Did you discover your connection to the person he was looking at?"

"I think it was my great-great-grandmother. Maeve. In Paris. She was a painter too."

The Curator's eyebrows raised. "You've learned quite a lot."

"But not enough." Dani sat up straighter. "That's why we're here."

"If I had the painting, I could tell you more—but I do *not* want it here," she hurried to add. "I said the feeling was familiar, and I think I now understand why. But first, tell me what else you know."

"How dangerous is he?" Mia interrupted. "This demon?"

"Very," Dani said, thinking of poor dead Charlotte and then remembering Beverly's collapse the other day. "He torments women with his abilities. Feeds on their misery." She thought of the security guard and his heart attack. "Well, mostly women."

"What does he do to them?" Mia asked.

"You know when your brain is being an absolute dick?"

Mia nodded.

"Now imagine it's a demon's voice whispering the worst over and over again to you. And he can do something to their hearts too. People have died."

"Holy shit!" Mia said.

"He's been part of Hackworth's collection. He was the genesis of it. He claimed he had other powers, vast, before—and Hackworth must have found a way to use the ones left to profit. Maeve said he promised her riches, that he could persuade people to give him information to profit from. But she wanted nothing to do with him. Not like that." She would keep the rest of Maeve's secrets, about what had happened to her before she went to France; that pain was private.

"He's connected to your family," the Curator said. "He's chosen you."

"There's one good thing . . . I don't think his powers of persuasion work on me. It didn't seem to work on Maeve either." She wanted to believe they worked on her mother, but a small voice inside her wondered if Maria was simply following his lead. Either way . . . "My mother will do anything he asks." Though she'd hidden the journal.

Dani was unpacking that and what it might mean about their relationship, about her mother's cutting Dani off completely after she screwed up . . . Before all that, she had secreted that journal away, tucked away the key. Even if she *was* susceptible to his powers, the idea of Maria getting involved with him knowing what was in Maeve's journal was not something Dani wanted to think of her mother. Despite her flaws, was she capable of that?

Something else occurred to her then. "I don't think he had any control over William Hackworth. The Fortress, I believe it must have . . . harnessed his powers. Ar—" She didn't say the name after a scolding look from the Curator. "*He* only hired me to get the painting of him because it's about to be sold. I suspect he can't directly do anything with it or to it himself. He can't buy it or steal it. He needs someone else to do it for him. It's the only explanation."

"Mmm." The Curator appeared to roll this over in her mind. "Here is what I know of demons—admittedly, not so much. They may or may not be tied to some great deity. Just as often, it seems they act as free agents. It doesn't much matter, however, given that the stories make them sound very much like those with magic. Each has a specialization. They pursue it and their own survival to any end necessary. They can travel the world at will."

"My ancestor Maeve, she had a book called *Secrets des Ouvriers Magiques*. Do you have it or can you get a copy?"

"Never speak French with your accent."

Dani pulled a face. Her French was excellent. At least, for reading. And for impressing adults when she was a child. But they might have been quietly horrified at her accent too.

Too afraid of my mother to let on.

Mia put a sympathetic hand on Dani's arm. Dani asked again, "The book?"

The Curator went quiet, eyes closed. She shook her head at last. "It doesn't exist anymore."

Unsettling, but definitive. "Can you tell . . . do the pages missing from the journal still exist?"

The Curator took longer this time. She rocked side to side and her eyes opened. "They do. And they seem close by."

Dani hesitated. "Do you know . . . do demons need anything to stay alive?"

The Curator raised her brows. "You are truly asking if they can be killed, aren't you? That, I do not know. Destroyed, banished . . . possibly. And they can be bound. A working involving blood."

Dani's brain went off like fireworks. The chair in the corner in front of the piece; Beverly telling them she saw Hackworth talking to the painting. And then collapsing before she could tell them more. Maeve's mention of the painting of her rapist and her blood in the pigment . . . "She bound him to the painting!"

The Curator blinked. "Entirely possible."

Dani was already on her feet.

"Unwrap the frame," the woman said. "It's not just a frame. I understand why I was moved to give it to you."

Dani looked at the bulky sheet-wrapped rectangle. Mia set down her cup of tea and came forward to help. When the sheet fell away, a man's face stared out at them.

Sunflower growled.

The brushstrokes were recognizable immediately as matching those of Archer's painting. And Dani felt that same tug toward it, the pull from the angry, hateful eyes of the gentleman, who had been painted wearing a tan summer jacket. The lines of his face were hard and savage, cruelty seeming to bleed from his reddened cheeks, simpering angelic curls of blond hair above. Looking at him felt like being haunted by a terrible past.

"Do you know who he is?" the Curator asked.

A dead man, Dani thought.

"His soul is trapped there," the Curator continued. "But he is no demon."

Dani covered the painting again. "Where did you get this?"

"I was moved to accept it as payment once. The frame will work, no?"

"Yes, it's the same period. I can make it work . . . You should know . . . Maeve, my ancestor, she painted this too."

The Curator nodded. "Take it and leave."

Dani stopped, because they should settle up.

The Curator stayed seated, but she must have guessed the reason for Dani's hesitation. "You will leave the dog, of course. As my payment."

Sunflower growled again, sensing Dani's frantic spike of anxiety.

Mia put her hand on Dani's arm. "Roxie, is that really necessary?" Mia asked.

"A painting with a soul inside is no small thing. It requires a serious payment."

Dani put her hand on Sunflower's head and the dog looked up at her with a whine. There was no easy way out of this. Mia had warned her. She should have listened.

"She must choose," Dani said.

"What?" the Curator asked.

"She must choose to stay here. You wouldn't put your will over that of an animal, would you?"

It was a gamble. She was prepared to fight her way out of here, ridiculous as that seemed, impossible as it likely was, considering all the items at the Curator's disposal.

The Curator stood. "Send her across the room."

Dani nodded her head and pointed. Sunflower slunk away.

"I don't like this," Mia said.

Dani's eyes didn't leave her dog. "I'm not thrilled about it either."

The Curator scooted forward to perch on the edge of her chair and made a clicking noise, waving Sunflower forward. "Come here, girl. Come stay with me. You'll have all the treats and sunshine and cats to play with that you could ever dream of."

Another click of her tongue.

Sunflower's head tilted to the side, her ears lifting. Listening.

What if her dog wanted to remain here? Maybe she should allow it, if so. Dani's heart pulled in two directions, and she understood heartbreak in a whole new way.

"Good girl," Dani said, but not calling her, not leaning on the scales.

Sunflower walked forward slowly and—at the last moment— veered toward Dani, licked her hands, and whined. It was her "let's go" whine.

The Curator sat back. "Fair enough. But there still must be a payment."

Dani wanted to bend and hug her dog, but she managed to stand straight and wait. "I agree."

"Should you make it through this, Danielle Poissant, then I will call on you should I ever need a favor. There's a particular painting I used to love that is lost."

That was about the best-case scenario Dani could imagine. A forgery.

"Or maybe I'll ask for something else. But for now, go, be careful. Your dog loves you, so I would hate for anything to happen to you. And you, Mia, stay clear of this, as much as you can."

If Archer was bound to the painting, she had to steal it for an entirely different reason than whatever he was intending. No wonder he didn't want it sold. She would bet it came with some strings attached—the kind that allowed William Hackworth to assemble his magical collection and use it to grow a vast fortune. The same kind of deal Archer offered Maeve way back when. Truth was, Dani knew that her mother had accepted whatever deal Archer offered her. She'd intended to steal the painting. It was only Dani's betrayal that stopped her.

If Dani stole the painting and kept it, then it would be hers. And she could force Archer to answer her, force him to leave her mother alone, force him to do anything she wanted.

Or maybe none of that was true, but it was the best idea she had. And now she had three whole days left to figure out how Archer's existence worked and how to make the devil pay.

THREE DAYS OUT

CHAPTER NINETEEN

DANI LET ELLIOTT drive them to Louisville in her car.

After three missed calls from Brad the night before, and Elliott's grumbled "I handled it" when he came to pick her up that morning, Dani wasn't looking forward to having to put on her most winning face and sell a cover story to Brad about being MIA yesterday. But she had one—of course—a classic for its simplicity: food poisoning. No one wanted to hear more intimate details about a case of food poisoning. And the meds most doctors would prescribe for it knocked you out for hours.

Thus, no phone answering.

Not even a summons from your uber-wealthy, solicitous boss.

Dani didn't feel great about asking Elliott to play with Sunflower while she finished up something and then used his distraction to move the now complete and framed painting of Archer into the trunk of her car. She could and should tell him about its presence, but . . . she was afraid. She had no idea what Mia had shared of their wild visit to the Curator. She'd removed Maeve's other painting and turned it to face the wall in the studio. Dani had no idea what to do with it—but she hadn't wanted the man's rough gaze on her while she painted.

"I take it," Elliott said, "that you're really not going to tell me what was in the safe-deposit box?"

Mia had been vault Mia, it seemed, keeping what she knew to herself. Dani felt surprisingly touched.

"It was a journal from a relative who was a painter. From 1894."

"Like you?"

"She had magic, but different from mine. She knew Archer."

"Really?"

Elliott gave every appearance of rolling with the fact Dani had just confirmed that she believed Archer was more than a hundred years old, despite the fact he appeared to be in his early thirties.

"She painted the portrait."

"That makes sense," Elliott said, nodding.

"How?" Dani truly wanted to know.

Elliott glanced at her, then focused on the interstate.

They were always talking in cars. Of course, it took a while to get from Lexington to Louisville, or even from the stone house to the Rabbit Hutch. And they didn't have to directly face each other. The road had been Dani's default home for years. It made sense to Dani that this was where she and Elliott might be a little bit honest with each other. Assuming honesty was what she wanted.

"There's obviously some connection to your family—Archer is too obsessed with you otherwise. He could have hired anyone, but you? And he's still in touch with your mom?"

Her mother. Dani knew it was time for another visit to Maria, assuming she'd say yes and was still at the medical center.

"Did I tell you that she asked me if I was sleeping with him?"

"What?" Elliott sputtered.

"It was actually the first thing she said to me."

"Dani . . . That's fucked up, even for her. I'm sorry."

There was some comfort in the acknowledgment, although Dani didn't understand her need to share that. Of all things.

"Went about as well as *our* reunion," she said dryly. If Elliott felt sorry for her, she might as well die.

"Dani—"

"Don't worry about it. Rabbit made it clear how she felt about me."

"That's not why I didn't say anything."

Dani shifted in her seat, angling toward him. "Then why?"

Elliott stared straight ahead. "Did you ever sense anyone looking for you out there over the years?"

"I think Agent Sharpe might have. A few times I got that back-of-your-neck feeling and had to pull up stakes early. Even missed a take or two. Or it could've been Archer? He found me somehow when he wanted to."

Elliott kept his eyes on the road. "That was likely me. I kept tabs on you."

Dani didn't understand. "What? Why?"

"I don't know. I just . . . wanted to make sure you were okay. But that's not all . . ."

"What else?"

"Archer found you because of me. I told him where you were." He said it in a rush. "Rabbit didn't know, by the way."

"What do you mean?"

"He came to me two days before you returned and asked me to find you, and of course, I knew I could. At first, I only knew when you were close. Then after you left, a day's drive, not much more. But as I got older, and my power grew . . . I've always been able to find you. I'm sorry for agreeing, Dani. I didn't even tell Rabbit what I was doing. But I thought maybe you'd want to come back—to finish things with him . . . and your mom."

Dani grappled with this information. He'd lied to her. And then he'd lied again and pretended never to have met Archer. This was not the apology she'd expected and longed for all these years. "You should have told me."

"I'm telling you now. I felt guilty . . ." Elliott hesitated, hands taut on the wheel. "Then—and now."

"Let me get this straight—not only did you find me for Archer, you knew where I was before and you never said anything to me? No 'hi, how are you,' no 'heads-up, a bad dude wants to see you'?"

Dani had been made a fool.

Elliott's jaw was as tight as his hands on the wheel. "We both made our choices."

"Wow." It shouldn't hurt this much.

He sighed. "That came out wrong. You left, and you didn't come back. I had no right to barge into your life. Especially after so much time had passed . . . I know I said you're the same, but you've changed. You're a different person than the one I knew when we were kids. I didn't have the right."

Dani couldn't deny it. Being on her own for so long, carrying the guilt over what she'd done, she *was* a different person. That scared little girl had been left behind. Dani could look back on that self and feel sorry for *her*, but she didn't feel sorry for herself.

Especially not when she was so close to finally turning things around. It hurt, that Elliott had given up on the idea of *just talking to her*; he did have the right back then and he let it go. But saying that to him wouldn't change things. Elliott had lied to her, but he'd confessed. She couldn't be mad at Elliott for working for Archer in this capacity, not when he'd been right. She had wanted this chance. She understood the messed-up things carrying around guilt could do to your logic.

"You're different too," Dani said. "You came to find me because you felt guilty?"

"Still do," Elliott said.

"But it's not because you're on Archer's payroll? You're on my team now, right?"

"Of course, I am. That was it. Finding you was the only thing I agreed to."

Dani resisted asking how many times he'd visited her from afar, when he'd started, and the biggest question she still held on to, for that little girl and for who she had become: Why didn't he show up the night she left?

What would her life have turned into if he had?

But she couldn't bring herself to ask.

Instead she told him about Maeve, about the painting with a soul in her studio, and about her suspicions about Archer.

They made it all the way to the Fortress and inside to do a last set of rounds before the gala prep began without running into Brad. Archer's portrait called to her like a siren to a doomed sailor, but she didn't go there immediately. She could almost feel the tension between the copy in her car and the one on the wall. A line between them, and her walking on it with tender-soled feet, taking as much care as possible.

Elliott wanted to show her the packing station set up in a freshly erected tent next to the security HQ. There were extra workers crawling all over the grounds today, awaiting their permission to scope out the Fortress for the exes' party and to begin decorating in earnest.

But Dani couldn't leave the Fortress without visiting Archer's portrait. She'd expected him to turn up in the shelter as she'd finished the framing. Some superstitious impulse made her want to confirm it was still there, the painting he was bound to. And to see if fresh details made themselves known with the new context she had. What she wouldn't give for those missing pages, and the rest of Maeve's story.

Or for that matter, for the stories of all the women he'd tormented. The stories they might have lived if he hadn't crossed paths with them. And what if he'd never sought out her mother? What might Maria and Dani's story have been?

"I'll be right there," she told Elliott, and he apparently realized she wanted to see Archer's piece on her own, so he didn't move to follow when she split off.

She blinked when she crossed the threshold to the small gallery. Emma sat in the chair in front of the portrait, kicking her feet back and forth, not tall enough for them to touch the ground.

"Brad?" Dani called out, her heart doing its best to leap from her chest. He must be nearby if Emma was here.

Elliott and he showed at the same time, and their bumping into each other in a rush to find out why her voice was high and troubled might have been funny if Emma staring at Archer's painting wasn't such a terrifying prospect.

The girl turned and grinned at her.

"Dani! The art thief!" she said. "I found out what that means. You are so cool!"

She ran over and threw her arms around Dani's waist, in that abandoned way children had—particularly well-loved children who weren't used to rejection or admonitions. Brad had done a fine job raising her. William Hackworth's hard nature hadn't tainted his son.

Sometimes parents could be a cautionary tale; Dani knew that as well as anyone. Yet you still wanted them to love you, no matter how imperfect they were. She didn't have it in her to pry the little girl's barnacle grip off.

"What's up?" Brad got the query out first.

Elliott came over and bent to talk to Emma, which had the effect of making her release Dani. Dani sent him a grateful look.

"I was just, uh, startled. I didn't know anyone was in here." True enough.

"You should have called for me," Elliott said. "I was right behind you."

"I wasn't sure whether to expect you today," Brad said neutrally, coming closer. "I had trouble reaching you."

"I told you she had food poisoning," Elliott put in from over Emma's head. "Do you want a full accounting of her day?"

Of course Elliott would guess her cover. Maybe he did still know her, despite what he'd said.

"I hope you feel better," Brad said.

"I do," Dani said and mustered a smile.

"Emma, why were you in here?" Brad asked her. "You were supposed to stay close."

"Auntie Beverly said Grandpa used to talk to that painting."

She said it as if it were obvious. With a shrug.

Brad frowned at her. "You shouldn't be in this gallery alone. If you're going to be in the Fortress, you have to follow my rules."

"Sorry, Dad. I didn't think it was a big deal."

Interesting that Brad was concerned about her being in here specifically.

"Did you talk to the painting?" Dani asked.

Emma scoffed. "No, that would be weird. I think Grandpa was weird."

"Good," Brad said. Then dryly, "We wouldn't want you to be weird."

"Daddy!" The little girl laughed.

Dani couldn't risk following up with a question of whether the painting had talked to her, and she didn't detect any hint of untruth from the girl. Children usually had obvious tells. Fidgeting. Refusing to meet the eyes. Making up altogether wilder tales. So while she wasn't thrilled about Emma fixating on Archer's painting, she hoped the oddity of the other night was all that fueled it. And not that he was somehow . . . targeting the girl.

Dani wanted to get her out of here, just in case. "Can I show you the painting I'd talk to, if I was going to talk to a painting? Even though paintings don't talk back?"

She said the last to see what reaction it got, but Emma only hopped and clapped her hands. An obvious yes. Not an obvious: *But paintings do talk.*

Elliott looked questioningly at her. "Shouldn't we get over to security?"

"That'll wait," Brad said.

Dani wanted to sigh at their continued jockeying for position. Brad had been so worried about her not showing up and now that she was here, she seemingly had carte blanche. The painting wanted to pull her eyes to it, to Archer. But she offered Emma her hand and led her into the hallway.

She skipped around the list in her head, the map of pieces, and tried to decide which one to go to. She decided on a self-portrait by Cecilia Beaux, known as the "female Sargent"—a term that made

Dani and Maria both eye roll when they'd covered her in Dani's studies. Why wasn't it enough for her just to be a brilliant portraitist? Did she have to be compared to a man to get across how good she was?

She'd attended the Académie Julian several years before Maeve, but the painting had been done in 1894, the same time as when Maeve wrote her journal. If paintings did talk, in a non-creepy way, Dani could ask her more about what it was like, and if Cecilia—who painted with a strong Impressionist bent after her time in France— had ever met her ancestor. Why had her mother never mentioned Maeve? Why hide the journal away?

The Beaux was near the Bashkirtseff portrait, in the hallway outside the larger gallery with the Rothko.

She recalled Archer's bringing the entire group to it. She hated that he now had an association with one of her own favorite artists. She didn't believe for a second that Rothko's emotional resonance was why he'd chosen it.

Dani was so focused on stopping at the painting of straw-haired Cecilia in a high-necked gown that she almost missed the shadow of a person in the door of the nearby gallery. She dreaded that it might be Archer.

"Wait here just a sec," she said to Emma.

Elliott and Brad waited with the girl as Dani went to the gallery.

There were two men in it, wearing the kind of blue work coveralls that no one would question with all the new people around today. They were in the process of removing the Rothko from the wall. A large wheeled crate, big as a person, waited beside them. At least Archer wasn't with them.

She couldn't fix on one of their faces. But the other was not on the books as a worker here. And there'd be no reason to mess with the Rothko regardless. Rose would've mentioned it if there was a plan to.

They must have snuck in via the loading dock and the hidden stairs. If they'd moved quickly enough, they could've gotten past the cameras without anyone noticing.

"Stop," she said quietly as she approached them. "Wait five minutes, then leave. Without the painting."

"We don't work for you, snitch, sorry, we're with Brenner," the man closest to her said. He had mean eyes. He must have some kind of magic, but she couldn't tell what it was yet. He seemed to think mentioning Brenner would convince her to back off.

"Don't make me sound the alarm." She wanted to know why it hadn't gone off already. Brenner was supposed to wait until the auction. They had extra security on this painting.

Rabbit could have disabled it. She owes Brenner.

And she said your mom does too.

"I can't let you take that. Not today," she said, seizing on to the cold in her belly at knowing she'd been crossed by one of her own crew. "Come back on the auction day."

The one with the blurry face put down his side of the large canvas. By all appearances, they'd intended to waltz out of here with it in the crate. He advanced on her, and she knew what was about to happen from his body language. She'd spent a lot of years as her own muscle too, and she wasn't that great at it. Especially when she was first on her own. She could call out, probably *should* call out for help, but it would only blow up the situation. She wished for Sunflower or her Taser.

She had that moment to attempt a dodge before he hit her, and the punch clipped her right shoulder hard enough to make her gasp. She drove her fist in his belly and the surprise knocked him farther back than the impact would have.

"Don't do this. You're going to fuck up everything," she said, keeping her voice low, pushing her hair back from her face. Her shoulder throbbed, and she braced for another assault. "See reason."

"What's up?" Elliott asked from the entry to the gallery.

Well, the possibility of handling this discreetly was over. Unless he'd known Rabbit intended to help Brenner and his men today.

The thought of that was an entirely different type of blow, coming on the heels of his revelation—a sucker punch right to her gut.

CHAPTER TWENTY

THEN IT WAS really too late for any chance of damage control, because Brad and Emma were in the doorway. "Get her out of here," Dani shouted to Brad, "and pull whatever alarm is closest!"

Brad did exactly what he was told. Elliott had made it to Dani by then, and though she tried to keep him from getting a look at her expression, he saw her rubbing her shoulder and rage visibly overtook him.

"I want to handle this quietly," she said to him.

"Fuck that," Elliott said and lunged for the guy not holding the painting. He managed to land a fist somewhere in the blur of the guy's face, the crack of it connecting audible, even if Dani couldn't quite see where.

The whoop of the fire alarm began. Sprinklers had to be triggered by smoke or manually so as not to damage the art, so at least it wouldn't ruin the pieces. Saving a Rothko would be worth a lot to Dani, even though she could theoretically copy it.

The man with the mask set down his side of the canvas.

"Get out of here now." Dani pointed to the door. "I assume you were going out the loading dock. Go. Fast." She turned to Elliott and the other man, his hand lost in the blur of his face that she couldn't quite fix on. "Elliott, let him go."

"Fuck that," Elliott said. His vocabulary was much smaller when he was pissed off.

"They're Brenner's men. We have to let them go. There won't be any camera footage."

Elliott wanted to roar his disagreement. She could see it and so did they.

But he also understood what she meant, what Rabbit must have done. Did that mean he *didn't* know?

"I better not see you again," he said to the men and shoved the one loose.

Dani could see the guy with the hard-to-identify magic was about to wave an idiotic red flag like *you can't order me around* in front of Elliott.

"Do you really want to go back to jail?" she asked calmly. Because she'd bet her life they'd both been inside.

That finally got through to them and they took off at a sprint for the door. Dani and Elliott ran after them because anything else would look suspicious.

A security guard joined them in the hallway, catching up quickly, gun unholstered. "Should I clip one of them?" he asked Elliott. "The leg?"

"No," Dani said. "No shooting! We caught them before they got anything. We need to de-escalate. Then question them."

"Do what Dani says," Elliott bit out.

She hoped against hope that the non-blurry guy had a trick up his magical sleeve that would allow them to get away. Questioning them on the record was the last thing she wanted to do. The timing was disastrous enough.

They reached the end of a corridor and hesitated in a clump. It had looked like the thieves were going right, the way Dani expected. But the sound of their feet on the marble went left.

Ah, and there was the magic talent of the second crook. She'd bet anything Brenner had unlocked the back loading-dock exit with his skills and was waiting somewhere nearby in a getaway van. Probably disguised as a caterer or florist vehicle.

She'd made no deal she hadn't honored with him. She'd given him a great piece of intel and instead he'd decided to blow up a grenade of clusterfuck in the middle of *her* operation.

But, well, what choice did she have? "Don't you hear them, come on!"

Following Dani's lead, they all broke off in the wrong direction.

The guard's radio crackled. "Cameras are back up. They're not inside," someone said on it.

Dani grabbed the radio and Elliott gave the guard a warning head shake not to challenge her. "Run it back," she said. "See how they got in."

She knew full well there'd be no record of it. She didn't dare exchange a look with Elliott. He was doing a good job of acting as if this were unexpected, but she didn't want to see if there was guilt there. Not yet. He'd kept quiet about his leading Archer to her, after all. And then divulged it on the way here . . .

Her shoulder ached and she caught herself holding it again.

"We need to get you looked at," Elliott said, coming closer.

Brad showed up then, sans Emma.

"Are you okay?" he demanded, crowding in on Dani too. She could see the adrenaline all over him—the tiny dots of his pupils, the slight sheen of sweat. And excitement. This must be far more interesting than watching numbers dance across a screen, even big ones that could get him whatever he wanted. Brushes with the secret world could be addictive. She'd seen it happen. If he wasn't aware of its existence, she felt moved to protect him from learning more.

He didn't deserve that. Best to keep everything aboveboard. Nothing had happened here today that couldn't be explained, which was the tacit agreement of how their people did things.

"I'll be okay," she said.

"She needs a medic," Elliott said. "One of them hit her."

"I was trying to keep them in place," Dani said. "Nothing I can't handle."

Brad frowned and put a hand up, almost like he was going to touch her cheek before he dropped it. "They were after the Rothko, huh? Any idea who they were?" he asked.

Shit. It hadn't even occurred to her, but of course they would be under suspicion now. Not even they: she. She would be under suspicion now.

Nice play, Mom, she thought. But it wasn't. It ran the risk of messing up the real objective. What on earth did they owe Brenner that was worth this?

"No," Dani said, and also knowing it would make everything that much harder, "we should double security onsite. And you should consider canceling the gala."

"After-action later, medic first," Elliott said.

Brad, for once, agreed with him. "You shouldn't have tried to take them on alone, Dani."

"It's how I do things," she said.

And now she remembered why. A crew could be a help . . . or a liability. What the fuck had Rabbit and Maria been thinking?

Because there was not a goddamn way that Rabbit would have pulled this without the approval of Dani's mother.

The fallout was worse than Dani thought it would be. Way worse.

Agent Sharpe had been alerted by a friend who worked in security—Dani wanted to know who but didn't want to risk pressing the issue—and showed up way too quickly. Dani was still in the middle of the chaos of the security headquarters as they tried their best to figure out what had happened. A paramedic was looking her over, completely unnecessarily, and she'd refused to leave the room.

Not that she could do a thing while he prodded her shoulder and asked if it hurt. Yes, it hurt.

She looked over from the third such question and spotted Sharpe talking with a guard and gesturing for Brad to come over. She brushed away the unnecessary medic's hand and said, "Ice it later; take it easy. I got it."

"You should get an X-ray. There's already a nasty bruise."

"I said I got it." She winced a smile and he shook his head and backed off.

Elliott steered him away, back outside. He was right. They couldn't trust anyone at this point. *She* couldn't.

"What are you doing here?" She took a breath and stopped thinking about the shoulder and butted into Sharpe's convo.

"When an attempt is made on a hundred-million-dollar piece of art, we tend to be interested." He made her sound like a fool.

She loathed it when people she had it in for were right. "You can help us review the footage."

Give him a bone, and maybe it would even satisfy him.

"How kind," he said, the smartass.

"We don't have much," a security tech warned as he waved them over to his console and monitor. A small crowd of security acted like they weren't gathering but made a rough half circle around the monitor in question.

"You okay?" Brad asked Dani, stepping up next to her.

"I'm fine."

"Why's that?" Sharpe asked the tech. "The cameras glitch?"

Dani knew what he was thinking. Maria Poissant had always been aided by Rabbit's help, which meant no video footage. "My mother is in prison."

Agent Sharpe didn't even look at her. "You aren't."

"Are you trying to blame Dani for this?" Brad asked, offended.

"I'd be shocked if he didn't," Dani said. "He loves ruining my life."

"That's ridiculous," Brad said, because he could afford not to fear the FBI. "Dani stopped them."

"Mmm," was all Agent Sharpe said. "Roll the tape."

Dani wondered what Elliott was up to; it'd be nice to have his backup on this. She scanned the room and saw him chatting with a couple of the security team in the background. Was it really possible he hadn't known?

As Dani had expected, there was no useful footage. There were two workmen, hidden behind a transport crate, visible entering through the front—the guard on the door had conveniently left his post for a minute, giving every appearance he'd heard something off to the right.

The one guy's power to throw sound a different direction at work, Dani had no doubt.

Then there was the other guy. The last shot the camera got before it went to a static mess that could only be Rabbit's doing made it look like someone had edited the film to blur his face. Truth was, if Dani had the right of it, he could make himself impossible to describe or focus on.

Not that she would've, but she couldn't give names because she didn't have them. Well, Brenner. She wondered if his buyer now had a name.

"You know either of those men?" Sharpe asked.

"That's enough," Brad said. "She's my head of security, not yours."

Agent Sharpe made the regretful expression he'd used to such good effect on young Dani: the hate-to-ask-this face. She could guess what would be next and a slow panic began to take hold. She needed to get Archer's portrait. More than ever. The Evil Twins might decide to strike early too.

"You can't keep her on, not after this," Agent Sharpe scoffed. "We'll look for those guys, but they got away. It'll be all over the criminal world. You need to let the real professionals handle the auction security for you. Us. We're already familiar with its contents."

Brad wasn't used to being talked to like this and he did not like it. "I'm not firing Dani!"

Agent Sharpe, on the other hand, was a pro at ordering people around, no matter what. "You don't have a choice."

Rose came in then, the hush as she passed a sign of how much all these employees respected her. Of course, she'd engineered huge bonuses for them. They would.

"Agent Sharpe," she said, a crisp hello without one. Elliott joined them then too. "Emmett," Rose said. "I understand we had some excitement."

"Someone tried to steal the Rothko," Dani said.

"So I heard." Rose sighed. "I've prepared a big severance for you, Danielle. And you too, Emmett."

Brad frowned. "We're not letting them go."

"If we don't keep cooperating with the FBI, the auction might not be able to go forward," Rose said. "I talked to our contact there. They're serious."

Rose's contact, the implication was clear, would be far higher up than Agent Sharpe. Probably the director. The rich and their hot-lines to the powerful . . . Dani sometimes saw the appeal of the low road. At least you knew who you were working with, for better or worse.

Or thought you did. What if this was all a setup? Bring Dani home and punish her for what she did at long last.

"This is ludicrous," Elliott said. "If we hadn't happened to be there, they'd have gotten away with it."

"Exactly," Agent Sharpe said. "I find that just as suspicious as if they *had* gotten away with it. We haven't found any works with problems in the provenance yet, but we're not through with our review either."

Dani wanted to reach over to the desk of the tech worker, pick up his mug of coffee, and toss it in Sharpe's face. But it might not even be hot. She settled for letting her fingers become fists, then relaxing them.

"Fine," she said. "A hundred-million-dollar painting, and it's *more* suspicious that we foiled a robbery. We may as well go."

This had always been an impossible job, stealing from the Fortress of Art. Now it was more than impossible. And by whatever magic she had, she would figure out how to do it anyway.

Game on.

"Good," Agent Sharpe said. "Then you won't mind us searching your house and car."

"Of course she—" Elliott started.

The painting in the back of the car would mean much more trouble than any of this.

"Warrant," Brad interrupted. "You need a warrant before you can search anything. I don't appreciate you treating Dani like a suspect."

"She could volunteer access . . ." Agent Sharpe cut a look at Dani. "It would be a good-faith gesture."

She might be fucked, but she would enjoy this moment. "To help you? Never." She looked at Brad with gratitude. "Get a warrant. I'll see you later." Then, to Elliott, "Let's go."

"Dani." Brad caught her arm and pulled her to the side. "I don't think you had anything to do with this, and I have to do damage control here, but I'll find you later. We need to talk."

She couldn't afford to say, *No, don't bother*. And, honestly, she didn't want to. Brad had been helpful and didn't seem to think she was guilty. That was about 90 percent more credit than most people she'd met gave her.

"Okay, then we'll talk. Be careful with the shark," she said, eyeing Sharpe. He had a triumphant air about him as he turned to order the tech to play the video again.

She wished for an easy way to sneak the painting from the trunk into a crate and leave it onsite, closer to where it would need to be. But with their access curtailed, someone might find it.

Too much of a risk. No, they needed to get it to the Rabbit Hutch for safekeeping, and Dani needed to clean out the studio on the off chance the feds finally found it. They didn't have a second to spare, not with that warrant coming.

Archer wanted his painting stolen, so why had her mother okayed this? It was all a mystery, and Dani knew just how dangerous mysteries were. Trying to solve them could ruin your life. But sometimes you had to anyway.

CHAPTER TWENTY-ONE

DANI'S SHOULDER ACHED and Elliott's jaw was strung tight as a bow string. Her car fishtailed as he turned in to the Rabbit Hutch's long dirt and gravel road. He'd only asked her where to go first.

They wouldn't have time for a full autopsy of the dismembered plan that was all they had left. They'd basically have to start over from scratch. Elliott screeched to a stop at the house.

"Keys?" Dani asked and held out her hand. He plunked them into her palm.

She got out and unlocked the trunk, then did a double take as Rabbit raced outside to meet them. Mia was behind her.

"How could you?" Elliott demanded of Rabbit.

Confirmed, then. He didn't have a clue she'd planned to assist Brenner today.

And Dani had never thought she'd see it in her lifetime, but Rabbit's face held an apology.

Rabbit's hands went to something like a prayer pose. "Listen, I did what I had to do and—"

Elliott wasn't receptive. "Dani could have gotten hurt! She did get hurt. But it could've been *bad*."

That was . . . not what Dani thought the problem with Rabbit betraying the crew was—or not the most important one. More that their entire, solid, well-reasoned plan was now a paddle-less boat stranded somewhere up shit creek. She popped the trunk open and lifted her painting out. She had to resist the urge to spit in the facsimile of Archer's face she'd created. He wasn't going to be thrilled about this either.

Somehow, Dani knew she'd get the blame.

"Are you all right, baby girl?" Rabbit asked.

Now she was "baby girl"? Today's wonders would never cease.

"I'll be fine," Dani said. "We don't have time for this right now. You did, however, fuck us all over. I hope it was worth it. I'm fired and Sharpe is getting a warrant to search my—the stone house." Would it still be hers? That seemed unlikely now. "I have to get over there. Hide this painting." She handed it off to Rabbit. "And find out who Brenner's buyer is already."

"I'm going with you," Elliott said.

"No." Dani shook him off. "It's better if you don't."

Mia came forward. "Can I?"

Dani wanted to say yes, but she also didn't want any of them becoming more closely aligned with her publicly. "No, you all stay here. We'll regroup on this shit show of a total clusterfuck later. I don't want the feds getting another look at your faces, not next to mine. Does Emmett have a house on paper?"

Rabbit nodded. "Subdivision off Hamburg."

"Good. Make sure we can use it if we need to."

"Already done." Rabbit often found unoccupied properties to accompany paper trails of identities. They could boost enough furniture or repurpose stuff from the barn to make it seem like a bare-bones gig worker's place. But maybe Sharpe wouldn't be interested in going after Emmett.

"I don't like you going alone," Elliott said.

Her phone buzzed. "Brad's calling. I have to go."

Elliott liked that even less, which he proved by kicking the ground hard and then letting her leave. She glanced in the rearview as she pulled away, and saw him take the painting from Rabbit, handling it gingerly.

"You home yet?" Brad asked.

"Almost."

"Judge granted the warrant, but they're just leaving here now. Rose stalled them nailing down some details."

"I didn't have anything to do with what happened." For once, it was true.

"Dani, I honestly wouldn't care—well, much—if you did. I'm sending a lawyer. Use him. I'll be there as soon as I can."

Dani hung up and her brain spun. Brad didn't much care if she'd tried to steal a hundred-million-dollar painting? The backup was welcome, and if he wasn't cutting ties . . .

She could use that. Cruddy as it felt, she knew she *would* use it.

She'd been fully aware when she agreed to Archer's job that it wasn't just the green fields of home she'd be going back to, but the muck. Dani had been good at moving through the regular world since by going after people dirtier than her. William Hackworth sure as hell had been, with his fingers in every exploitative industry on the planet. And Archer was a fucking demon.

But Brad was a good man as far as Dani could tell. Then again, she didn't know him beyond the surface level.

Justifications could always be found. Another lesson from her mother.

Sunflower trailed Dani nervously as she rushed around the house, making sure the diary was concealed in the wall where the key had been hiding, along with the brush that went with it. There was a sinkhole in the woods where the leftover paint got deposited, and by the time she had closed up the fallout shelter, it was back to being undetectable by the casual eye, far beyond the bounds of the yard proper. Maeve's other painting was still tucked away inside it, but that couldn't be helped. The only way they'd find the studio is if they got serious about infrared or sonar or some other gadget the FBI had. There was no reason to deploy that against someone like Dani.

She'd barely wiped away the sweat from her face and taken a seat on the porch with a beer, Sunflower at her side, when the line of SUVs arrived. Three of them. No TV cameras followed, which told Dani a lot about what Agent Sharpe thought he had. Nothing certain or he'd have tried to gin up the story with the media already.

He emerged first, with other suits following, and a couple of the agents with the branded vests. She nodded and ticked the beer at him. "I'd offer you one, but I'd prefer not to."

"Can't drink on the job anyway." He had the warrant paperwork, and she held out her hand for it. She took her time reading it, though it was standard, granting the search of the contents of home and car.

"Come on," Sharpe said. "I know you don't want to cooperate, but you could stop stalling. It wastes all of our time."

"Give me a minute," she said. They could, of course, barge in, but they weren't. And she was curious when Brad's lawyer would turn up.

Think of an esquire and one appeared. A fourth SUV pulled up in the drive then, but this didn't belong to the feds. A Cadillac, way too nice. And it had a novelty license plate visible on the front that read: ACQU1T. Someone had been watching *The Lincoln Lawyer.*

Dani stood up and handed back the warrant. "I think this is my attorney."

Agent Sharpe turned and sighed a curse under his breath. Dani almost laughed.

There wasn't just one guy in the lawyer's SUV. Four attorneys got out. Three men and one woman. And it seemed everyone knew one another.

"Agent Sharpe," said the oldest of the attorneys, and the most senior. The others hung back, deferring to him. He had lizardish skin, cold eyes, and a thirty-thousand-dollar watch. Exactly what you wanted in a defense attorney. "I would appreciate a moment to confer with my client. Also, please take it easy on the house—it belongs to Bradford Hackworth."

The confirmation that it wasn't hers—and probably never would be now—stung. But she didn't let it show.

Agent Sharpe must have wanted to protest—after all, he'd called Dani on her stalling tactics—but didn't quite have the balls. Particularly after the attorney added: "I'm sure you can see how, given your prior history with my client, this might look like a case of un-fair targeting. Borderline harassment."

"Fine, Carlton," Agent Sharpe said. "Knock yourself out. We'll give you five minutes."

The attorney handed Dani a business card. "Carlton Minton of Minton, Reynolds, and Associates. Can we step inside?"

"Certainly," Dani said and opened the door for him. Agent Sharpe took a step in that direction too and Sunflower growled. He put up his hands and backed down off the porch to wait.

Brad drove up, parked, and got out of his car. He took in the scene and nodded to Dani. But he stayed outside.

"We're so popular today, Sunny-bunny," Dani said as she trailed the attorney in and shut the door behind them.

"I can tell your dog has good instincts," Carlton said. He turned to face her. "So do I. I don't need to know if you tried to steal from my other client; Brad has made it clear I'm to represent you any-way. I will keep you clear, but I need to know . . . Are they going to find anything here?"

Dani appreciated him getting right to the point. "Anything in-criminating, you mean? No. He'll find the materials on the Fortress of Art that Rose and Brad gave me as part of my job for the Hack-worths. Nothing else."

She noted that he hadn't asked if there *were* any such materials, only if they'd be found. Her laptop was in one of the hidden hollow spaces her mother had made. She'd be willing to bet they weren't going to look that deep—they never had. And now this lawyer was present. Even Agent Sharpe must recognize a bigger shark than him.

"Good. We have leverage because they want Brad to continue cooperating with them. All we have to do is keep them busy for the next few days, then they'll move on. Don't worry, I have my marching orders. Nothing is going to happen to you."

"That's sweet and all," Dani said, "but I'm fully aware where your first loyalty is."

The attorney smiled—something she got the impression he rarely did. "Ha. I'm not going to let Maria Poissant's kid go down. I wish she'd let me represent her at the time."

Wait . . . what? "You know my mother?"

"Only from the pitch meeting back then. I could've gotten her off. I don't know why she went with that other guy."

The other guy had owed them a favor, that was why. "I don't know either," Dani said, because she'd have chosen Carlton Minton in a heartbeat.

"Probably because I would've gone after your credibility."

"Doubtful." Dani guessed it was because the guy who owed Maria a favor was part of their world and she'd trusted him more. Enlightening to know that even her mother was capable of making misjudgments—and not just where Archer was concerned.

"You'd know more than me. Okay, we've kept them waiting long enough. Let's go. I'll have my team following the agents around, pissing them off. We won't let them wreck your stuff."

Not that she had much stuff, which went unsaid.

Dani hesitated. "One quick thing first," she said.

She went over to the spread of security materials and picked up her notepad, flipped to a blank page, and wrote: *Fuck you, Agent Sharpe.* Then underlined it.

The lawyer looked at her, amused. "Really?"

"You seem good and what am I going to do? Draw hearts around his name?"

He laughed. "Leave it on top of the pile."

Brad met them outside on the porch. "I'm so sorry about this. I tried to convince them it wasn't necessary."

"Which isn't your job to determine," Agent Sharpe said, climbing the steps. "This is simple due diligence."

Carlton said, "Be our guest," and Dani motioned Sunflower out of the way as the agents went inside, followed by attorneys.

Dani pulled Brad over to the porch rail. "I know how this stuff tends to go." Her mother was still behind bars, after all. "You've gone above and beyond. I don't think I needed this much firepower, but I'll take it. And . . ." It was the truth, so she might as well issue the note for it. "I owe you one."

"Carlton's fun," Brad said. "He will take care of you."

"I want to make sure you know that wasn't me."

Brad nodded. "I know."

As usual, he seemed to be sincere. "How, though? Why are you so sure?"

"Because you would've gotten away with it."

"Flatterer," Dani said. Not that he was wrong. "I am—was—your security manager, though. It shouldn't have happened."

He pitched his voice low. "Dani . . . I told you we needed to talk. I'm not sure we have time to wait for a better moment. Now okay?"

And here came the other shoe. She'd known Brad must have secrets; everyone did.

"Let's walk in the yard," she said. "We won't have to worry about anyone listening then."

Brad's agreement was gently touching her arm and starting to the steps. Once they were clear, he spoke, voice still lowered. "I need to tell you something—I almost did at the hospital. But can I speak freely with you and know it will be kept between us? The rest of the family can't know about this. Neither can Rose."

That he'd even pretend to accept Dani's word on something so obviously important was both touching and—given who she was— foolish. "Okay."

Brad hesitated only to take a deep breath. Then, "I know what

Archer is, and what he was to my father. I still don't know exactly why he wanted only you for this job, but he promised me that Emma would be safe if I said yes. So I did what he asked. Made sure you got hired."

Wow, so Archer had used both Elliott and Brad to manipulate her into place. Dani hated that.

"Have you heard from Archer?" she asked.

He shook his head. "Not since the other day. We don't talk that often."

She fit this new information into her head. "That means you are getting rid of the collection *even though* you understand what it is?"

"Yes," he said. "Like I told my father, I don't want this legacy. My magic, it's to do with numbers. We have plenty of money, so there's no reason for me to risk becoming what he was."

Brad had magic too, but he wasn't part of the secret world. She nearly envied that.

"Do you think Archer could do that?"

"I don't know, but being in league with a demon can't help your soul. Can it?"

Dani thought of her mother. "I guess not." She brushed her foot against his shoe. "What about Emma?"

"Nothing unusual about her yet," he said. "Except her personality . . . It's why I insisted she live with me. I'll be there if she has a gift, to guide it."

Emma would never know how good she had it—a parent who wouldn't immediately want to use her ability, if one emerged. "She's lucky."

"Thank you."

Dani searched her mind to fit this new information. "Does Rose know? What she built?"

Brad snorted. "My father would never have told a woman the truth. None of the wives know either. It's better if they don't." He looked at her. "You obviously have some experience with this kind of thing, though. That's why you're here, isn't it?"

Dani measured what she should say. "You'd be right."

"I don't care why Archer wanted you close, or whatever you might be planning. As long as you're confident it won't hurt Emma or me or the rest of the family," Brad said.

The one thing Dani felt certain about. "It won't."

Brad accepted that. "What Archer did to Beverly the other night—I realized there are other people I care about that he could hurt. I had the distinct feeling you two were not bosom buddies the other day, and then with his attack . . . That felt like a scare tactic aimed at you. Tell me one more thing . . . Are you working for him or against him?"

"Both."

Brad nodded. "Then I still want you around. I don't trust these people as much as I trust you. Do what you have to do—I don't want or need to know the details. Stay, finish it, and we'll call things even. If you get caught, I don't know anything."

She'd expected him to pooh-pooh the idea of her owing him something, but he was human, after all. His protection would only extend so far as it didn't cost him anything, which just made him a real person. In some ways, more relatable than ever. If that stung a little, Dani pretended it didn't. He also wasn't thinking clearly. "I'm good with that, but I don't think the feds are letting me or Emmett anywhere near the collection again."

Brad shrugged with the confidence of someone used to getting exactly what they wanted. "That isn't their call. Besides, Emma made me promise she'd see you both again. I have a solution. Will you come to the gala with me?"

Dani was taken aback at how quickly he'd come up with the perfect solution. The part of her that had been raised to learn the craft—not just her art—knew it was exactly the opportunity they needed. The so-called gift horse that no criminal would look in the mouth. The saying supposedly came from the practice of checking a horse's teeth for its age, which, in fact, seemed like good sense to Dani. If someone presented a so-called colt that looked like it was elderly, checking the teeth made sense. And the people of Troy might see the whole gift-horse thing differently too.

But attending the gala immediately began to amass the weight of a new plan.

Could she trust her crew? And if she couldn't, maybe she'd do it on her own. The way she usually did. She felt relieved Brad hadn't asked about the specifics of what she could do, or what she planned.

She was, however, surprised the show was going on. "You're not canceling it?"

"Please. After today, it's the hottest ticket in town. And I'm making a big announcement about the business there. Well?"

They'd walked back to the porch, and so Brad asked to the soundtrack of the agents rummaging through the house. As predicted, one of them emerged with the materials he had given her as part of her job. She had all those facts down cold by now anyway.

She lifted her voice for anyone who might be eavesdropping. "I'd love to. I'll buy a dress and everything. I could tell Rose was worried I'd show up in consignment."

"Whew." Brad gave her what looked to be a real smile. "I thought you might say no. I'm glad you didn't."

Maybe he honestly didn't care about the Rothko or any of the other art besides Archer's portrait, as long as most of them sold, bad dad Hackworth got a final middle finger, and the demon left the building. Fair enough. She wondered what the announcement concerned.

She had a passing thought she might be able to just say, *Hey, I think that portrait of Archer belonged to a family member, why don't you give it to me?*

But Rose wanting it complicated matters—not to mention, if the estate rules prohibited giving it to Rose, then they would likely apply to Dani too. Beyond that, it wasn't what she'd agreed to with Archer. And her mother was obviously inserting herself into this. So no, she wouldn't be doing that, even with Brad's tacit go-ahead. Besides, a journal that claimed to be from an ancestor and that demons were real—hardly the stuff provenances were made of in the FBI's eyes. As much as Brad thought he knew of Archer, Maeve's history might be too big a bite for him to swallow.

And it's private. I will honor that. Honor her.

She hadn't even divulged the full specifics of Maeve's history to Elliott. Just the parts about Archer's portrait.

Dani needed to speak to her mother. And to Rabbit and Elliott and Mia soon.

"I'll leave you in Carlton's capable hands before you change your mind," Brad said.

The lawyer peeled off and walked Brad to his car, then came back.

"I don't make you for a gold digger," Carlton said genially when he returned. "But if you are, it won't take you long to reel him in."

"Now, now, we both know there are far easier ways to get gold than marriage." She nudged him with her good shoulder. "How many wives?"

The lawyer shook his head. "Number five is a keeper."

Dani laughed.

Agent Sharpe emerged then, disgruntled as usual. "I'm assuming this is your idea of a joke?" He held up the notepad.

She frowned. "Do you know what a joke is? It was more of a welcome mat. Find anything?"

"No."

"Because I didn't do anything."

Carlton cleared his throat. "No talking unless your attorney says to."

The look of frustration on Agent Sharpe's face was a thing of beauty.

She just hoped this farce didn't take too much longer. The party moved up the timeline. And now it made a lot more sense to make the exchange during the party than the auction.

And so tomorrow night was it.

She had to get that painting before anyone else did.

~~TWO DAYS OUT~~

ONE DAY LEFT

CHAPTER TWENTY-TWO

THE SEARCH HAD disordered everything just enough to remind Dani someone else had been in the house. Which, in turn, reminded her that the stone house wasn't hers, not for much longer. When would Brad kick her out? When would it be time to move on?

Although . . . he had come clean to her about his knowledge of the secret world. It was refreshing to meet someone who wanted no part of it. What if he wanted her to stay in contact after the auction?

She'd thought the whole you-can't-go-home-again thing was bullshit, but the joke was on her. She fell asleep on the couch to these musings, and dreamed of the demon who was tied to her family. His face, thin and pale and cruel—and in her dreams, she *could* hear him whispering: about what a failure she was, about how this situation proved it yet again. About how she had no true family, because she didn't deserve it. She couldn't be trusted . . .

The sound of the door woke her, and she didn't panic only because Sunflower's happy tail thump told her it must not be Archer. Must not be a threat.

Oh, but Sunflower did have a weakness dangerous to Dani's heart.

Elliott eased down onto the couch beside her. "You awake?" he asked.

"You picked my lock," Dani said. "I am now."

The room was dark, save the glow from the moon and the security lights through the windows. What should have felt like an intrusion instead felt intimate.

"They didn't wreck the place," Elliott said.

"Brad sent a big-shot lawyer."

"Oh, he did." A little salt on his tongue.

"Why are you here?" Dani wanted to sit up, but she also wanted to close her eyes and go back to sleep.

Elliott rattled something in his hand then: an ice pack. "I knew you wouldn't be doing shit for your shoulder. If you don't ice it, it'll hurt way worse tomorrow."

"Nurse Elliott."

"Just let me put this on your shoulder, smartass. I can sleep on the couch. Switch it out every couple hours."

"That's where *I* sleep, as you can see."

Elliott gave a small shake of his head. "You know, you make it really hard to take care of you."

That's because she took care of herself, she wanted to say. But for some reason—the darkness, how tired she was—she didn't.

Elliott took advantage of the moment to adjust her shirt so he could check the swell, the bruise, from where Brenner's man had punched her. She anticipated the bite of the cold from the ice pack, closing her eyes, but instead came the warm press of Elliott's lips on her bruise. So soft, so gentle, she might have imagined it.

Only the contact might as well have been full body. She felt it everywhere, radiating through her, and she started to panic at the response.

"Sorry," he said.

Don't be, she wanted to say. Which would be madness. He'd known where she was for years, and he hadn't seen fit to even tell her hello. He'd felt guilty, and then he found her for Archer, not because *he* wanted *her*. He might think he did now. He had a jealous streak where Brad was concerned. Maybe he was right to, because thinking of Brad gave her pause.

But . . . Elliott and Dani's chemistry was undeniable. What would the harm be in indulging it?

That's a door you will not want to close. And Brad might deserve a chance, if he still wants one. Now you know he's not too perfect for someone like you anymore.

Dani's skin protested the thought of going with good sense over sensation.

Elliott put the ice against her tender shoulder then and she was grateful. The cool put her back in her body—her right-mind body, not the Elliott-just-kissed-my-shoulder-and-I'm-filled-with-terrible-ideas body.

He stretched out next to her, his head on the opposite end of the couch. They barely fit.

She lay there, staring at the popcorn ceiling in the dark, convinced she'd never be able to sleep with Elliott's body touching hers. She was still thinking it when she drifted off again.

Dani woke before Elliott. Somehow she managed to extricate herself without disturbing him, ending up in a crouch where her head had been and leaping over him to get free of the couch. She thanked whatever god there might be that he didn't stir, because she must have looked ridiculous doing it.

It was early—too early for the first stop on her list: a visit to her mother. Though she could call and put in the request. Somehow, she knew her mother would say yes this time. She had gloating to do, about how hard she'd screwed over Dani.

She made some coffee, as quietly as she could. Elliott had always slept like a vampire in his coffin during daylight, complete and sound.

Sunflower came with her outside, bounding ahead as they made for the studio after Dani hung up with the prison medical center. The morning was quiet, a light fog hanging over the grass that gave it an otherworldly vibe. The lawyers had assured Dani before they left that no bugs or surveillance requests had been made or granted, and also that no devices had been left behind. It truly wasn't fair that good lawyers—thorough, good lawyers—were something only the rich seemed to have ready access to. But it was nice to see how the other side—the side that rarely went to jail—lived.

If Carlton had represented her mother, she might not have gone to prison. Figuring out whether that meant she'd have forgiven Dani sooner—or ever—was too painful to contemplate.

The life you lived was the life you lived. Dani was beginning to understand that in a way she never had before.

In the studio, in the thin light, with a few greasy bare bulbs flipped on, she was drawn to paint with a rare sense of abandon. She stretched and prepped another canvas, and she siphoned the tumble of emotion inside her onto it. More focused, less disconcerted than she had been in her first painting session.

History at large must be—was, in fact—littered with women like Maeve: forgotten, never given their full chance to be known. To make their marks. Dani had never identified as one of those women, but maybe she should. The secret world had always been the only one open to her. The trips into the light, a farce, for show. Demons could take many forms.

Thinking back to the intensity of her mother's transformation, the increasing frequency of Archer's nighttime visits, and her betrayal of Dani . . . She didn't think Archer wanted payback. That would've been too easy; he could have targeted them earlier. Why would he have encouraged Maria to have a child? Maria had been driving toward stealing his painting . . . but what larger possibility had she seen in her association with Archer?

For once, Dani wished Archer would appear. Then she immediately shook her head. No, she'd never wish that.

"Knock, knock," Elliott said from above, a shape silhouetted by the now-bright day. He'd visited the studio only a couple of times when they were younger. The memory of the second visit, the one where they'd been alone, brought a flush to her cheeks and the sensation of his lips on her bruised shoulder the night before. She still didn't know how to feel anything but confused disappointment that he'd watched her over the years, but never said anything . . . never felt he *should*. That he'd never stopped to think she might desperately want to hear from him.

"Come on down," she said. Then, "Wait, what time is it?"

"About nine-thirty. I found something I think you should see."

She'd lost two hours at the canvas. She wondered if he'd turned up one of the not-supposed-to-be-there bugs. "I'm coming—and I'm going to see my mother again this morning."

"I can come."

"No, you can't." She could practically see the wheels turning, him marshaling his arguments as she left the shelter and closed it up. "You're not on her approved visitors list."

"Well . . ." He scrubbed the back of his neck. "Damn it. You're right."

"Besides, we have a lot to do today. We've lost time. You and I are going to that party tomorrow night, and that's where we'll have to do the switch and grab."

"You're going as a guest too?" he asked.

"With Brad. You're with Rose?"

Elliott had an adorable pout. He'd probably pout even harder if she pointed it out.

"Emma invited me."

Dani laughed into her palm.

"She's a sweet little girl," he said. "I had to say yes. And I figured the same thing as you. Any opportunity . . ."

"Don't worry, I'm sure the exes will dance with you."

He took a deep breath and let it out, as if being such a good face man was a burden, not an asset.

"No idea's too out there at this point. You know Sharpe will be all over me, at least. So start thinking."

She walked across the grass and so did he, Sunflower running ahead of them. The sun had burned off the mist long since. Fluffy white clouds hung suspended in a forever of blue sky. It could be so beautiful here. Ugly too, but also beautiful.

"I have been."

"What's this you've found?" Dani asked.

"You'll see." Elliott sounded off, and it took her a moment to identify the wrong note. Worried.

"The way you're acting, it's like you found the paintings from the Gardner."

"Nah. Rabbit told me they had to destroy them."

"What? Really?" Dani had always wondered.

"Too hot to move or hang on to."

"That sucks." What a loss.

Elliott grunted agreement.

When they got inside, he led her over to the kitchen table. She recognized the faintly grayed paper, saw the torn edges. "Where?" she asked, going over and picking them up gingerly. He'd found the missing journal pages.

"I dreamed that I was looking for something in the house—that happens sometimes—but when I woke up, it's like I could feel a thread—the same feeling as the safe-deposit box, connecting two different points."

"The main journal is in the wall over there."

"And those pages were in the wall behind the medicine cabinet in your mother's old bathroom. Did you know she had a hiding place there?"

"No," Dani said. "I only know about the one down here, and one in my room. But I knew she had more. I should read these. Before I go."

She glanced down at the familiar handwriting.

"Dani . . ." Elliott trailed off.

"Yeah?" She looked up at him.

"Don't let her get in your head."

Dani didn't respond. Her mother had been in her head every day of her life. That wouldn't stop now, whether she wanted it to or not.

"Okay, fair, I know that's too much to hope for. You'll be over later?"

Elliott could read her as easily as she could read the pages of this journal. He knew she wanted privacy again.

"Thank you . . . for helping take care of me."

He nodded and left.

Dani pushed out the chair and sat down. Sunflower placed her head firmly on top of Dani's sneakered foot.

OCTOBER 6

I have reserved a studio at the atelier for tomorrow night, after most will be gone, and made my preparations. I would prefer not to have Lord Archer visit our house—Gladiola is too susceptible to his mysterious charms. It turns my stomach, even if she is Mama's spy.

I sent him a note proposing that he come alone for the painting, to seal our pact of association.

Perhaps someone would feel guilt at luring such a beast into a trap, but not I. Not when I think of Charlotte and imagine the others he has tortured for his own gain. Let him believe me ambition incarnate, swayed by the prom-ises of our great deeds from his honeyed tongue, when in fact his magic leaves me utterly unmoved.

I prepared the pigment earlier this evening, using a pair of the scissors Gladiola employs in her embroidery to make a cut on my upper thigh. The bloodletting was quick and purposeful, the mixture of it into the dark shade a simple task. Then I used a paste procured from a shop Lili told me Charlotte frequented to staunch the bleeding. Its sting reminds me of the task ahead.

Tomorrow evening, I shall paint the demon into death with a clear eye and a cold heart. Let the matter be closed.

OCTOBER 8

I write this at speed, for I cannot stay long—not here in
our dreary little house I will miss so much. But let me set
it down, to fix it in my own mind.

At first, all went according to plan. Lord Archer arrived, smiles and gleaming teeth, and I positioned him
just so and took my place at the easel. I had already begun
to paint the backdrop when he arrived. We were alone, it
being a late hour. Paris's charms had lured the others
away, as I had known they would. He sat with patience and
when I flirtatiously scolded him to remain silent so I
might concentrate on the painting, he did.

My hands did not tremble as I did my work. My intention remained steady, the visage of Charlotte occurring
behind my eyelids from time to time. I captured his form
in his tailored coat, and then finished the features of his
face. Just as with Mr. B—, this was the moment when
magic coursed through me, when I felt the working
quicken. Lord Archer sensed it, for he let out a cry. "Foul
bitch, do you think you can best me with your magic?"

But he stumbled over his feet, toward the painting,
clearly struggling against his own movement. I hastily
scrawled my initials and backed away. He became a great
cloud of darkness, drawn into the canvas as I watched.

He was bound to the painting, but he did not die. I
presume his lack of humanity saved him.

Suddenly he was both the image and in front of it. He
tried to lay his hands on the painting. "I will destroy it
and then you," he said.

But he couldn't. Every attempt of his to touch the canvas fell short. He realized as quickly as I that the painting
could not be harmed by him. So he turned on me. I had
been riveted, too foolish to run while he was occupied.

"You think your pitiful blood will hold me—but it will

also release me," he spat and then he fell on me, his hands gripping my shoulders hard enough to bruise. "That is the way of such workings. I will make you bleed, and then I will be released from this cursed image. You think to destroy one such as I? I will not allow it. You could have had greatness, and now you will die like a common whore."

He began to claw at my arms, but my clothing frustrated his efforts to reach skin. He raked a hand across my face, his nails drawing blood, digging into the flesh. He laughed as he forced me toward the painting, red on his pale fingers. I have felt the same terror, the lack of control, once before in my life. My body screamed its protest and I managed to shove him away, kicking and biting. There was a large pot of linseed oil nearby and I ripped free the lid, bore it up, and tossed the contents upon his face and body. And then I ran as he roared behind me.

I hid like the quiet mouse he thought me to be in the alley nearby and watched as he stalked past. I knew he would come here, and so I waited, and waited, until I could be sure he would have come and gone. I thought to attempt to destroy the painting myself—perhaps that would destroy him. But I must be as sure as possible. He will kill me at the first chance and use my blood to free himself.

I have come back for a few of my things and the Book of Secrets, and I will find another place to sleep while I determine how to end Lord Archer for all time. Else, he will end me.

Dani flipped to the next page and her heart caught in her chest, beating hard. Horrified.

OCTOBER 10

My findings are grim. If Charlotte were still here, she would believe me. But Lili accused me of madness. When

I found her last evening, she said the painting has been the subject of great debate in the atelier. That it is an accomplished work—if in the Impressionist style—but that the artist has seemingly disappeared. No one has seen Lord Archer since either.

So far, Lord Archer has not found me, hiding on the filthy streets. I have not seen him visit his home either, in the few times I have spied nearby.

I found my way to a woman Lili told me had sold her charms from time to time. She purports to be a witch. I brought with me all that I have left: the fresh wounds on my cheeks, my torn dress, my journal, and the Book of Secrets from Archer's library.

She gave me a cup of foul tea, and she heard my confession. "You have bound a demon, lessened his powers. He is right, a blood binding can be undone by blood of the same line. As with so many things, fire is the only true means of destroying this creature. It will cleanse the entire earth one day, and it will burn the soul you have trapped as it burns the canvas."

I despaired.

I cannot risk going near the painting. Not even to attempt its destruction. He would not let me escape again, and my blood could free him. No, I cannot remain anywhere on this wide earth drawing breath.
I hope that binding him will lessen the harm he is able to do.

I have left this journal at the little house that Gladiola might read it and either dismiss it as the fanciful nonsense of a girl about to commit herself a grave harm or share it with Mama who will see its truth. I hope if you are out there, daughter, you are cleverer than I. Should your path ever cross Archer's, protect yourself and those you love, above all.

We share blood, and you have my heart. May it burn brightly.

I must go.

Dani sat back, reeling.

Why had her mother hidden these pages separately? Suddenly, it made a terrible kind of sense. The key would lead her to the journal that explained part of Archer's truth, and part of their family's. But these pages—these pages meant something else.

If Maeve had been correct, they were about how to free him *and* destroy him.

Who knew what all these years of twisted contact had done to her mother? She'd changed. Dani had seen it happen.

And with Brenner's men yesterday, she and Rabbit had put Dani on her back foot, scrambled the table. Made doing this job more difficult.

Dani had always known she'd have to fight for the chance to redeem herself in her mother's eyes. Given what she'd learned about Archer, she would be fighting for both herself *and* her mother.

Whether her mother wanted her to or not.

She needed to take a closer look at the portrait by Maeve the Curator had given her, but first, it was time to confront her mother.

CHAPTER TWENTY-THREE

WHAT A DIFFERENCE a few days made. Dani had the same escort as on her first visit to the Federal Medical Center, but the wariness about Dani's mother seemed to have markedly decreased. Maria must have chosen her opportunities well.

"Your mother is quite the entertainer," she said. "So many stories."

"Mm." Dani stopped listening as the woman went on, nodding and mmhmming on autopilot. The woman took her on a different path than before, and then, at last, she scanned a card that opened a door to the outside.

Dani paused and raised her brows.

"Oh," the woman said. "It's such a nice day. Sometimes we let patients use the patio for visitation."

Dani recalled that her mother had gotten the information about "that cute little patio" out of the guard. She didn't bother mentioning all the other people they just left behind in the waiting room, who would surely like to be outside too. She also noted the woman referring to her mother as a patient rather than a prisoner.

The patio turned out to be attached to the other prison camp next door, a place for low-risk inmates. A slab of concrete with heavy concrete benches and tables scattered around, but still there was fresh air and Kentucky sky above. Better than a stale room with a hard metal chair bolted to the floor. Two women sat across from each other at a table, hunched over it playing cards.

Beyond them sat her mother, facing the other direction, looking out at a grassy yard penned in by high, barbed fence. She was in a wheelchair next to a concrete table, so still recovering.

"I'll leave you two alone," the woman said.

Dani spotted two guards who seemed to be minding their own business stationed close to the side of the building.

More changes in protocol.

When Dani got closer, she saw that her mother was having a smoke, which surely wasn't allowed. The other two women in the card game were bickering with each other. The woman with the tattoo of an eye on her eyelid gave Dani a cheeky, stagy wink.

"Looks like we're in for a mother-daughter celebrity reunion," she said.

Dani's mother tossed her cigarette in their direction and the women cackled. Dani stepped on it to put it out, then took a seat at Maria's table.

"I see you've wrangled privileges," Dani said by way of greeting.

Maria smiled, the wound on her cheek accentuated by the movement. "They always get sloppy. I encouraged a guard to take a smoke break, promised to be good. He left the other. Then I got the woman alone. She feels very unappreciated."

The effect wouldn't last; it never did. Eventually, she'd push too hard and the person's will would snap back. There was usually a time limit on how long she could sustain whatever lie her magic was selling—most of the time, it was plenty long enough for Maria's purposes. Dani thought of it as a little like sliding a broken nose back into place. The person might sense the injury, but it didn't hurt so badly.

Dani's magic indirectly altered perceptions, in a way she didn't entirely understand. Whoever pretended magic had simple rules and they understood them all was definitely full of shit. But it wasn't necessarily as if she was making people see what she wanted them to see—more like she allowed them to see what they chose.

Dani pushed aside the chill that came from how casual her mother was about messing with people's minds. She had other business. "I thought you *wanted* me to do Archer's job."

Her mother crossed her arms, defensive. "I do."

"Then why did you tell Rabbit to help with that stunt yesterday? They didn't get the piece they were after, by the way. I had to stop them. It was all for nothing, except to fuck up our plan."

Her mother put her hands on her lap, looked at Dani, and smiled slowly. Satisfied for some reason.

"Oh no, Dani," her mother said. "I simply increased the degree of difficulty."

That phrase was familiar enough from her childhood. If Dani had mastered a certain technique, it was time for another one. A harder one.

"Do you think Archer was respecting you by getting you an all-access pass? This way you have to prove something—that you're a Poissant. Worthy, capable."

"You're sure it wasn't just the chance to screw me over?"

"The job's still young." Her mother laughed with a small wince. Her wound would still be healing. "Plenty of time for that."

Dani had been working through the best way to broach the subject, but she suddenly felt so tired of her mother's game. Or games, plural. It was exhausting trying to anticipate her. Why not try to surprise *her* instead?

"I found the key and then Maeve's journal. I know what Archer is."

Her mother was actively silent for a long moment.

Dani decided to hold on to the fact she had the missing pages too. It was one of the only advantages she had. "Maeve is my great-great-grandmother, then?"

Maria sent a look in the direction of the cigarette she'd discarded. Then, she nodded.

"My mother didn't give the journal to me. I found it, and I took it." Maria's eyes narrowed. "We have a legacy, but she wanted to hide it from me. Claimed I wouldn't know how to handle it. She was projecting."

Dani didn't point out that Maria had hidden it from her too. Maria never talked about her own mother. "What happened to your mom?"

"What eventually happens to all of us."

"Which is?"

"She died, obstinate, just like Maeve. They were both short-sighted. We've all been paying for Maeve's original sin—her rejecting Archer, trying to get one over on him—all this time. I just decided to embrace the chance he gives us."

Maeve killed herself to save others from Archer. To Dani's mind, that made her a hero. "What do you mean?"

"If you're on one side and the universe is on the other, why bother pretending you have a choice? Think of the power Archer has amassed—more now than he had to begin with, after being part of Hackworth's machine for so long. He could be limitless. We could be limitless."

Dani wished she couldn't believe her mother thought this way. She chose her words cautiously. A Maria without limits would be a terror. "I see myself in Maeve."

"You are more like her than you realize. But that's not necessarily going to help you. She didn't have a happy ending."

"Enough riddles. I am stealing Archer's painting tomorrow."

"That is your job," her mother said. "Good."

"Do you know why he wants the painting?"

Maria sat forward and got more intense. "He doesn't want a master any longer. He had to do Hackworth's bidding for all those years—using his precious energy to ferret out information for the man. And the old man took forever to die. I was supposed to give Archer back his agency. It was what I trained for, all those years, all those jobs . . . But you delayed it. He had to wait, but ten years is not so long for a demon. Now, Dani, you must do what I promised. Be a good daughter. Don't think of Maeve. Think of me."

Oh, she was. Because once Dani had the painting, she could end Archer's influence over her mother. So she dropped it. Maria would be safe enough in here, behind bars, while the rest of it played out.

"Is there anything else I should know?" Dani asked.

Maria wagged her chin from side to side after a brief consideration. "I believe I've taught you everything. Don't ice out Rabbit over yesterday. You'll still need her to pull it off."

"Mo—" She stopped herself from using the familiar term daughters had for their mothers. "Have you seen Archer since you've been here?"

"No, but I've heard from him."

"And what have you heard?"

Her mother thought it over too long. Finally she said, "That you better not mess this up."

Maria lifted her hand with a wince, and summoned the escort. Dani's time was over.

Dani had to visit Rabbit's for the regroup to fine-tune the new plan, but first she went back home. Sunflower met her and trotted alongside her to the bomb shelter. The steps creaked under Dani's feet, the thin light seeming to exist only to create more shadows.

Her mother had chosen her words carefully, but the fact she expected Archer to be free—and more powerful than ever—once Dani stole the painting had come into crystalline focus. Dani wanted to believe her mother would choose her first someday. But Archer's hold over her was too strong.

Maria clearly expected that Archer would use Dani's blood for his release, the way he'd tried to with Maeve. Maybe she thought Dani wouldn't even fight him on it, because it was what Maria wanted.

Dani needed to destroy him. She also needed to confirm the truth of what Maeve had written. Much as the last thing she wanted to do was commune with the other painting by her ancestor—the painting of, she shuddered to think, another ancestor.

She slipped aside canvases and old paintings until she found where she'd concealed the Curator's gift. She'd altered the frame size with leftovers and then painted it to appear identical and put it with the copy. This piece waited in a discarded frame she'd quickly pressed it into.

She lifted it onto an easel underneath the bulb.

Maeve's work held the eye despite the discomfiting nature of these particular portraits. Her style and talent were undeniably compelling. Dani mourned that she'd likely never see anything else by her great-great-grandmother, that the world wouldn't ever know her name.

All the more reason to set things right, as much as they could be.

The man might have been handsome, conjured by the hand of someone who hadn't experienced his true nature. Maeve's work, the brushstrokes, pigment rich with blood, the composition, were subtle and beautiful. But Maeve had shown his ugliness. A greedy soul seeping off the canvas. Red cheeked, those hate-filled black eyes that wanted to take . . . that seemed to look back. Trapped.

The sense she'd felt at the Curator's on the first visit, of Archer gazing out at Maeve, flooded through her limbs again. Her skin cooled under the painting's flat regard. No, this was not Archer here. This man had died, Maeve had said so. But the Curator had said his soul remained in the piece.

Perhaps Dani should feel sorry for him, soul trapped all these years—but she didn't. She'd have happily left him there to rot in the canvas, except she needed to know if her blood, as part of Maeve's line, would work to undo the magic.

Sunflower whined when she found her X-Acto and pressed it just under her elbow. The blood came quick under the press of the sharp blade. She dropped the blade on a table and rubbed her palm over the cut. If the journal was correct, Mr. B— would soon be lost to either hell or to nothingness: each a better fate than he deserved.

Dani forced herself to step closer, then closer still, and lift her palm. She stared at the smear of those ruddy cheeks, the deep black of his gaze.

She hesitated before touching the canvas. Her fingertip pressed against the texture of the paint and she didn't *see* anything but the wet gleam on the dark of his jacket. The air charged in a heartbeat, an invisible thunderstorm, a great gush of wind, and the canvas faded until its center was empty, the painting nothing but corners shaded dark.

Dani gasped as a body appeared on the cellar floor in front of her. Those unmistakable blond curls, the face frozen in the same likeness as the painting. She stumbled backward and put her hand over her mouth and wondered if it was bad to feel grateful as the body crumbled to dust in a breath, then two.

The electric feeling went away, replaced by a normalcy that suddenly felt surreal. Dani, her dog, the vacant painting, more dirt on the cellar floor, the safety of the bunker.

She dropped to her knees and petted Sunflower with one hand while she wiped the blood off the other onto her jeans.

Maeve had gotten this right, so Dani had to assume she'd been right about all of it.

CHAPTER TWENTY-FOUR

THE WHIRRING HEAT from the computers in the living room reached all the way into the kitchen at the Rabbit Hutch. Global warming meant that even robust southern air-conditioning didn't always keep up these days. Not when there were so many machines running in the living room, at least. The computers' fans whirred, a constant.

From where she sat, she could see into the Fortress on one of the monitors, into the Rothko gallery, the camera pointed right at the piece in question. The crate had been removed at some point, the painting placed back on the wall. A guard stood next to it. Rabbit hadn't even changed the channel, so to speak.

Dani was sweaty, cranky her shoulder hurt, and disappointed Rabbit was out of bourbon. She'd offered Dani a juice from some sort of cleanse a friend of hers sold. The lowest form of grift in Dani's opinion, the selling of unnecessary stuff.

"She didn't have money to pay, so I took the juice. It's good," Rabbit insisted. "She makes it by hand."

"It tastes like ass," Mia put in. "Here's some iced tea."

Given that Mia had sucked down the Curator's herbal monstrosity, the juice must be truly terrible.

"Okay, fine, it's bad. It's mostly raw kale." Rabbit turned the entire dark green jug upside down and drained it into the sink. "But she has to make a living."

Elliott finally joined them, bounding up the garage steps into the kitchen. "Ooh, look who's back from his tux fitting," Rabbit teased.

Dani felt a jolt of something that couldn't be hurt. "I figured we'd go together tomorrow."

"It's not prom," Rabbit said.

"That's not where I was," Elliott said. "We can go shopping together in the morning."

"I want to come," Mia said.

"God save this entire operation," Rabbit said and made the sign of the cross, though she was not and had never been a Catholic.

"And why is it in jeopardy again?" Dani asked. "Oh yeah."

"We have to move past that," Elliott said.

"Do we actually, though?" Mia leaned her elbows on the table and sighed. "Do we want this painting? Dani's no longer getting the house, right? So why are we still doing this?"

Dani didn't know how honest to be with them. She thought she might still get the house, but saying so would make Elliott pissy, and she'd promised Brad his secrets were safe. Rabbit couldn't be trusted not to tip off her mother about her plans for Archer's portrait. She should be straight with Mia, it was the right thing to do, but . . .

The murderbird rooster crowed somewhere in the distance.

"I still need to do this," Dani said finally.

That seemed to satisfy everyone, except her conscience. She did still have one—buried deep, but alive and kicking. Because she intended to beat Archer at his own game. Her conversation with her mother had convinced her it was the only way *they* would ever be truly free of him. Dani didn't plan on anyone paying off anyone else's debts; she'd pay off hers.

"I might have something," Elliott said. "The Hackworths did end up hiring Liz's troupe to perform at the gala."

"Liz, your ex?" Dani asked Mia.

Mia grinned, a little bashful. "Did I forget to mention that Liz is a circus girl? She does aerial silks."

"Remember how I suggested that Emma might like circus performers at the party?" Elliott shrugged. "It was innocent at the time. I like Liz."

"I thought you didn't want her near a job?" Dani asked Mia.

Rabbit laughed. "Mia is mad she always has to stay here, but she's been trying to get Liz back since they broke up. Elliott, I'm assuming you sent them straight to Liz?"

"I let Mia forward the tip."

"She was happy." Mia shrugged and beamed. "They're paying big."

Obviously. This was the Hackworths.

Dani might still feel a little like an outsider looking in, not knowing *all* the backstory, but the conversation itself made her feel like part of this family again. She was missing something, though.

"How does this help us other than as a potential distraction?"

"We have to get the piece in somehow, right?" Elliott asked.

"They have a lot of equipment," Mia said. "Aerial hoops, rigging, I've got a portable rig in the barn, if you want a look."

"I get the idea," Dani said. "Well, if we can matchmake *and* figure out how to make this job work on such short notice, sounds good to me. Although I'm not convinced they should bring it in *and* get it out . . . And we still need to manage Brenner too."

"Right," Rabbit said. "The buyer."

She produced a folded piece of paper and passed it over to Dani. Dani took a look, anticipation tingling in her fingers. *Huh.*

"I can't say I'm surprised," Dani said. "Can you call Brenner? I have a thought. He'll still get paid."

"Yes," Rabbit said.

"And our Evil Twins?"

Rabbit clapped her hands together. "The twins are on the list for the auction, not the gala, so we should be clear there."

"You're sure?" Elliott asked.

Rabbit nodded. "And I've got next-gen earpieces for everyone, and they're so tiny no one will notice . . ."

They went from there. Brad didn't want to know any of these details, they would be a liability, and so she wouldn't share them. That left twenty-four hours and Agent Sharpe breathing down their collective neck—but mostly Dani's. It wasn't ideal, but Dani *would* get that painting.

There was no other option.

Dani had lots to do back home. She longed to complete the second painting she'd started earlier, but there were documents to create and finish too now, and she should get back home to Sunflower, get a few hours of sleep. Tomorrow, there'd be more left to do and last-minute meetings to attend. Rabbit and Brenner had proposed using Brenner's team to help, and Dani had said yes, but she wasn't proceeding until she met with them. Or Liz.

She was running this operation. They had to understand that.

But the back-of-the-neck feeling returned, and this time it definitely wasn't Elliott. He'd been tasked with sketching out the party timeline and layout for Rabbit and Mia. He knew many more intimate details of the gala, courtesy of his minor abduction by the exes. Dani swept her gaze around to make sure her mind wasn't just tired and tricking her.

No. Archer stood in the yard near the barn. She checked over her shoulder to ensure no one had followed her. They hadn't. She was on her own with Archer.

So she went to see what he wanted.

He'd gone inside the barn by the time she reached it. The chickens were in their coop, the rooster separated in a new small pen. All of them settled for the night. The country chorus of chirping and croaking, from the crickets in the night and the frogs at the nearby pond, filled her ears.

The faded red barn door hung slightly crooked, in need of a new coat of paint. She flipped on the soft overhead lights. It was tall and spacious, as most barns originally built to house tobacco were. Inside was a mishmash of different goods—furniture, some boxed-up electronics, others discarded or waiting around to be stripped for parts, an old car or two, a tractor, and Mia's baby, the Mini, with its own spot and exit at the back corner. Beside it, a large metal tripod about twenty feet tall with a bundle of fabric tied up in the middle that had to be—she was still getting used to the idea—an aerial rig of some kind. And near the barn's center, on an easel, covered by a sheet, was what Dani presumed was her painting.

Archer stood in front of it, his back to her, walking stick gripped in his palm.

There seemed only one thing to do. Unveil it. She walked over and did, with as little drama as possible. She carefully lifted away the sheet.

The man who was not a man at all, but a demon pretending, stared at the facsimile of himself—the shadow in the painting mimicking the one behind him in the barn's low overhead lights.

"Ah, a masterpiece," Archer said. "I can barely tell the difference."

You're not bound to this one.

"Hopefully you're the only one who can."

"Oh, I'm confident in your power." Archer continued to stare at the painting. "You know that your surname is a corrupted form of a word meaning 'great power or influence'? It's a shame but not a surprise that you ended up showing off your work in a barnyard."

"Some would say it's your fault."

"Do you mean Maeve? She was a smart one, like all of you, but she was not as smart as she thought. Not nearly as smart as your mother." He turned to her, the planes of his face sharp and pale enough to remind her of a skeleton, even though a casual observer would likely find him handsome. "Do not cross me, Danielle Poissant. I began the games I play before your mother's mother's mother's mother was born. Before her mother fled with the first man who would take her, bringing what she considered a curse: her magic."

"I'm not convinced she was wrong." Dani hesitated. "Yes, I've read Maeve's diary."

Archer waited a long moment. "So I've heard from my sweet Maria."

Her mother had never been described that way by anyone except a mark.

He went on. "Only I didn't need to read it. I was there. She thought I'd die. The man she'd painted before did, but he was only human. My kind is hardier."

Dani's skin chilled despite the humid night.

"Yes, instead you're only—mostly—trapped. And once she got away from you, how did you manage to make your way after that?"

"I still possessed my persuasive gifts." Archer grinned. "That was the easy part, at first. I assure you that being bound to the mortal world, for one such as I, who could go and do and be whatever took my fancy . . . It was a worse cage than a human could imagine. I might take my old form for a time, but I had always to return to her paint, her blood. Inescapable."

"Until you became William Hackworth's pet demon, locked up safe, the heart of his power."

Archer spat. "Hackworth was wise enough to understand what he possessed, to build a way to use my power. I may have hated him by the end, but I admired his ability to take, and take, and take. There was nothing he wanted that he wouldn't ask me how to get . . . But soon, I will once more follow my own desires. I did learn one crucial lesson from Maeve, since she did away with herself before I could—I needed you, the Poissant women, if I was to ever escape."

The way he mentioned Maeve's suicide, offhand, made Dani seethe. Then he'd turned to grooming her mother, making her into the perfect thief. The logic even explained why he'd encouraged her to have Dani, another member of the only bloodline that could free him. A backup plan.

And then Dani had put her mother away, where he couldn't use her anymore. He'd had to stay trapped in Hackworth's engine, the man's prize. Archer must think himself lucky that Dani still wanted to give her mother a chance, lucky that Brad had no interest in the spoils of tainted magic.

Like all her line, Dani was immune to Archer's whispers of persuasion, but he had leveraged her into position anyway. Had it been the same with her mother? He'd had to wait so long for this opportunity to be freed. He couldn't get untethered on his own, so he expected Dani to do it, for her mother. The one he'd promised to give her back.

But Archer wasn't the only one who could lay a trap.

"Now that you know, you also know there's only one way out of this," Archer said. "Maeve was shortsighted. Your mother sees clearly—that's why her own mother tried to prevent her from learning the truth." He took a step closer. "I understand the guilt you bear toward Maria. I understand she has refused you forgiveness. But I promised you I could reunite you, and I meant it. Do your job, and I'll even make sure Brad sentimentally gives you the stone house. You will get everything you want, Dani, my girl."

But she wouldn't. She'd never get back the years she'd lost. She'd never truly be equal with her family. It was impossible to imagine how her mother could or would change with Archer still in the picture . . . Even a demon's powers had limits. Clearly.

He was a liar.

"Just do as you've promised," Archer said, "and you get it all."

Then he was gone.

Dani refused to keep living in the hell of her own making. She thought of all Maeve had endured, of her lost potential. Of revenge. Of why Maria's mother would have held the diary back from her own daughter—Maria's capacity for sympathy to such a devil. Dani shrank from the most obvious reason why Maria had torn that last section of the journal out, hidden it separately—it detailed the means of Archer's destruction.

The Poissant name meant power. She *would* finally exercise it, in a way that would make Maeve proud. Archer's wishes be damned.

She still owed her mother. She still owed everyone from back then.

And some debts had to be paid.

But no one could tell her how to do it. She wouldn't just be stealing Archer's painting. She'd be figuring out how to keep him at bay long enough to watch him burn.

THE DAY OF

CHAPTER TWENTY-FIVE

DANI'S RIGHT HAND, cramping into a claw, woke her up. All the painting and documents she'd stayed up late working on were catching up with her. At least, she assumed that was what had roused her—until a bang sounded at the front door. Sunflower barked an alert.

She had her Taser inside with her, more cautious with so many elements in the mix, and so her first move was to get up from the couch, staying low, and grab it off the coffee table. She crouch-walked carefully to the edge of the curtain and peeked outside. A black delivery van was parked in the drive, exhaust clouding the early morning. No markings to speak of, so it could be anyone . . .

Dani had saved her shiny new defense attorney Carlton's number in her phone, and for once she followed orders. He'd told her if anything strange happened to get in touch immediately. Not that she thought he meant *all* kinds of strange, but this counted. She texted him that someone was at her house unexpectedly and she'd report back on who it was. He immediately replied not to let anyone in without talking to him first.

Sunflower continued to bark. Another knock sounded, this time in triplicate.

Dani had a couple of messages and missed calls from while she'd been asleep, but those weren't her main concern. She slid her phone into the pocket of her pajama bottoms and held the Taser at the ready as she crept toward the door. Sunflower continued to hold court at the front door, letting whoever was on the other side know they were uninvited.

Dani joined her. Only now did she realize there was no dead bolt. No peephole.

They hadn't had a lot of unannounced visitors when she was a kid. People let you know they were showing up in the secret world.

She gave Sunflower a quick "watch me" command and the dog went silent and sat, riveted on her. Only then did Dani call out, "Who's there?"

"Delivery for Danielle Poissant," the man said, pronouncing her name as "Daniel Piss-ant" in a thick Eastern Kentucky accent, which was almost endearing. If only the answer clued her in on why he was here.

"Delivery from who?" she asked.

"Brad Hackworth."

That name the guy got right. No surprise, given the family's prominence in the state. It seemed unlikely anyone would risk throwing it around illegitimately.

Curious, Dani unlocked the door and opened it, keeping the Taser behind her thigh.

The guy nodded to her and said, "Wait here."

As if there was anywhere else for her to wait. Why not have the delivery on the porch already? She took the opportunity to text Carlton back: *False alarm. It's something from Brad.*

He responded with the smiley face emoji that had money symbol eyes and tongue: *See you at the gala.*

How he knew she was going to be there was a mystery she didn't bother with. She should've assumed he'd be going.

The delivery guy opened the back of the van, set up a ramp, and removed a rolling rack full of clothing, all in black garment bags. He wheeled the rack along the sidewalk and hefted it onto the porch, muscling it up the few steps and inside the door. Then he presented her with a pad for electronic signature.

Dani had seen enough movies to get the gist of what was going on here. She was being *Pretty Woman*–ed. Or makeover-montaged. Whatever you wanted to call it. This was way beyond any gesture she'd expect after he'd come clean and the arrangement they'd made. Was he feeling guilty about basically calling in a favor? She'd had enough of guilt—hers and others'—to last a lifetime.

She signed for the delivery because she wasn't going to throw a fit, not for the moment. There *was* something thoughtful about it. Thoughtful, and a little insulting. She couldn't manage to find her own dress? She'd said she would.

The delivery guy saluted and jogged back to his van. He drove away, leaving her with what would surely prove to be an extravagant selection of outfits for the evening.

Her phone buzzed. Brad calling.

She took a deep breath and then answered.

"Don't be mad," he said by way of greeting. "Rose called a personal shopper friend—she told me she has an eye for sizes, so hopefully they'll fit. Consider it a thank-you gift."

"I wouldn't have shown up barefoot in overalls. I was going to go shopping." With Elliott, she didn't say.

"I never thought you would," Brad protested.

"Rose did."

"That's just Rose. And also, she didn't think *that*. Just that you might lack her favorite designers." He said it with irony. "Anyway, now you can go shopping in your living room. Oh, and you don't have to worry about sending anything back."

She frowned at the rack. "There must be ten dresses here."

"Good eye," he said. "Keep them. Consider me hoping this isn't the only gala we attend together."

"Brad . . ." Dani didn't know what to say. He'd trusted her with his biggest secret, and now this . . .

"Even if it is," he said, "they're still yours. eBay anything you don't like or need. Is that still what people do?"

"I honestly couldn't tell you," she said.

"Goodwill, then. I've said too much. I'm sending a car for you and Emmett later. Should it pick you both up at your place?"

She didn't point out that Goodwill didn't usually have a strong need for ball gowns and that actually her house belonged to him. "That'll work."

"I was kind of hoping it wouldn't, but I'll see you tonight. That's good enough for me. Good luck with . . . whatever you have going on today." He hesitated. "Oh, you'll be glad to know that Agent Sharpe is appalled I'm bringing you."

She couldn't help smiling then. "That is excellent news."

They hung up, laughing. For a moment, she considered it idly, what her life would look like if she was in a position to date Brad Hackworth. In truth, she hadn't thought much beyond today and tonight, getting the painting, and whether she could pull it all off. It was safer not to game out tomorrow when there was no guarantee of it. Or that it wouldn't come with her life on metaphorical fire, her back on the road, and on the run permanently.

That was always a possibility. In fact . . . She went upstairs and dug out her laptop, then checked her accounts under different names. The system was untraceable, just in case Carlton's people were wrong about how closely the FBI was keeping tabs on her (though she doubted Carlton hired people who made those kinds of mistakes). She *could* leave if she had to. There was enough from the last job to finance a retreat.

But the idea of her old life suddenly exhausted her.

So she'd stay in the moment, focused on the job.

She did know one person who'd be truly excited about the wardrobe. She snapped a photo of the over-the-top clothing rack and texted it to Mia, then called her. "You want to help me pick an outfit for the party?"

She held the phone away to prevent Mia's shriek from ice-picking her eardrum.

Sunflower's tail wagged and she tilted her head at the phone in a way that was so adorable it flipped Dani's heart over twice.

"I know, right?" Dani said to Sunflower as she hung up, laughing again, and texted Mia a time later in the afternoon—both for meeting this Liz so much of their hopes were pinned on and for help dressing—and a reminder to bring her one of those sticky ice packs for her still achy, purple and yellow shoulder. She texted Elliott that he should go shopping solo; she still had a few more things to do to prepare for the evening.

She shook out her hands, flexing and unflexing them. Her magic was ready to get to work.

Dani finished barely in time to await the arrival of the circus ex, suddenly a linchpin of the entire plan. Mia, eager for any excuse to see her, hadn't even balked at arranging the meeting that afternoon, prior to outfit selection.

Before she went to the studio, Dani had gone through the rack quickly and slipped on the most likely candidate over her street clothes. Damn if Rose *didn't* have an eye for measurements. Dani'd bet everything on it fit with the same near-perfect lines. It'd just be down to Mia's taste.

Mia and Liz arrived in separate cars, but at the same time. Mia in her Mini, and Liz in a beat-up van. Mia had said the troupe used a lot of equipment for onsite gigs.

Dani had intended to do some open interrogation about Liz's intentions toward her friend *if* Mia was running her usual ten minutes late. That she was on time further confirmed how into this woman she was.

Whatever Dani had expected of Liz, this wasn't it. The woman who exited the van was tall, close to six feet. She towered over Mia. She was slim except for her hips, and had her hair pulled back in a severe ponytail.

Her entire air wasn't that of an ethereal aerialist, but a sensible accountant. Okay, maybe a sensible accountant on vacation, but still. Part of Dani's line was knowing how to size people up.

And at first glance, Liz did not quite make sense.

Mia's boundless smile for her—a golden retriever of a smile—
did, though. And to Dani's relief—so she didn't have to hate her—
Liz answered with a genuine smile of her own. Mia held out her
hand, an offering. Liz clasped it, swung their knitted palms overhead, then turned Mia in a dramatic spin. She finished with a low
dip and a brief kiss to Mia's lips. It was very Gomez tangoing with
Morticia on date night.

Mia practically had stars and hearts radiating from her eyeballs
when Liz set her upright.

"I didn't know you could dance like that," Dani said to Mia.
There was skill in the way she'd immediately partnered Liz.

"There are volumes you don't know about me," Mia said, bragging. "Libraries."

"Like how she's a touch prone to exaggeration," Liz said, but af-
fectionately. "I'm Liz."

"It's exaggeration to make a point," Mia said. "This is Dani."

"I figured."

Sunflower came out and nosed at Mia's hand for a scratch, sniffed
Liz, and looked at Dani with a sly smile, as if to prove that the
stranger had passed the background check.

"You know what we're asking you to do?" Dani asked.

Liz straightened and seemed to gain yet another inch. "Be the
distraction?"

"Of sorts. You'll be helping cover the switch. It's crucial we make
it." Dani wanted to resist being so explicit, but Mia insisted she'd
just tell Liz everything anyway. Dani trusted her instincts—much
more after seeing them together. "Think you can handle it?"

Liz looked down at Mia, and then at Dani.

"While also performing for a crowd of drunken art apprecia-
tors?" She held up a finger before Dani could answer. "I can do it. I
could do more."

"You don't need to do more," Dani said.

"I accept," Liz declared.

"Then the job's yours." Dani was relieved, because it wasn't like
there were that many other options.

"I can't believe you're doing it, going on a job. And I'm stuck working the phones," Mia groused while also beaming at her ex. "You don't have magic either."

This took Dani aback. "She knows about . . ."

"I know about everything," Liz said. "I'm good at taking things in stride."

The calm to counter Mia's enthusiast. Well, cool was good in a pinch. In this case apparently opposites did attract.

"You're in," Dani said. And then to Mia, "And you're not just 'working the phones'—you're backing up your mom and helping make sure we don't miss anything. We need all the eyes we can get. It's important."

"Fine," Mia said. "As long as it's *important*."

Mia escorted Liz to her van for goodbye until later. Then turned tail to come help Dani pick out what to wear.

Elliott arrived just as Mia was about to leave. Dani had walked her out to the Mini and handed over a folder stuffed with documents.

"You look incredible," Mia said to Dani, not for the first time, and air-kissed both her cheeks. Elliott came over to join them. "You too, obviously," Mia told Elliott.

Elliott's blue eyes lingered on Dani and she had trouble not staring back at him in his perfectly fitted tux. He was a beautiful man. His jaw cut an angle over the bow tie that her hand wanted to cup.

She and Mia had chosen a red one-shoulder dress from a label that made Mia cover her eyes and fall back onto the bed in a fake swoon. The ice pack meant to do double duty was tucked under the fabric on Dani's injured shoulder, wrapped to prevent seepage and stuck on with adhesive. Mia said it was blasphemy, and that was all right with Dani. The gown had a high slit so she could walk easily, and the cut wasn't so low that she'd be constantly wanting to tell any ogling men her eyes were on her face, not her chest. Shoes had been included—black glittery heels that managed to be almost the right size, close enough to work with some Kleenex stuffed in the toes anyway. There had been a couple of garments that gaped hideously too, in the end. It was nice to know that Rose wasn't perfect.

"See you soon, brother," Mia said to Elliott with a sock on the shoulder. She didn't say anything about his gawking at Dani, but Dani knew she noticed from her wink.

"See you soon, sis," he said and touched her cheek with affection.

They always said "see you soon" before heading off to a job. It was their version of "break a leg"—it meant everyone would be together again afterward.

Mia would be working with Rabbit, helping to woman—because there were no men involved in that part—the control centers for the cameras and tech portion of the evening. Mia was holding down the home base at the Rabbit Hutch, but Rabbit would be stationed closer, in a tricked-out vehicle they had borrowed, the forged painting waiting there for transport to the Fortress to make the switch.

Between the two women, they'd have a bird-of-prey's-eye view of everything in the Fortress and the security building. Whatever the FBI had done to tighten up the system, Rabbit could still talk to it just fine—though they had to be less ostentatious in terms of using her signature glitch that wiped out everything on the cameras tonight, as the feds had already seen that one. They'd be going much more subtle, if things went right.

After Mia drove away, Sunflower joined Dani and Elliott on the porch. Elliott gave the dog a good scratch, and she rolled over to give him easy access to her belly. "Who's a pretty girl?" he said.

"Should I be insulted?" Dani said. "After all this? Mia did my makeup."

Elliott's hand stilled for a second. When Sunflower protested, he picked back up on his scritches, but his eyes stayed on Dani. "You do look incredible, like something from a dream. And I hate it."

Well.

"Why do you hate it?" Dani asked, despite a neon sign flickering in her mind that announced, *Danger ahead. Proceed with caution*.

"Because it's not for me."

"It's not *not* for you. You have eyes."

"He sent you clothes." Elliott studied his hands. "I'd rather see you in your shirt."

Dani swallowed.

He went on. "Have you worn it yet? Since I brought it back?"

"Why did you? I've been wondering."

"You've been wondering?" He looked at her then, like she was missing the obvious.

"You never said anything about it," she reminded him.

He was gaping at her. Then, "Because it's yours. Because . . ."

Dani threw up her hands. "I don't understand you, Elliott. You didn't come that night. You said you found me, more than once . . . But you never said anything." She could remember that night at the bus station like it was yesterday, like it was two minutes ago. "You let me go. Which would have been fine, except I really thought you would be there."

Elliott scraped a hand through his brown hair, messing it up, and yet somehow that only made him more appealing. "I meant to. I wanted to. But Rabbit . . . I was young, Dani. She was my mother. Not my real mom, but the mom who chose me. The only person who had."

He put up a hand when Dani started to protest.

"She caught me packing my duffel. And she told me that I only thought I was doing what was best for you. She said that if I *didn't* go with you, that you'd come back. That your mother would come around and everything would be okay. She convinced me." Elliott walked forward on the porch, an arm on either side of her, bracketing her so she'd look at him. They were close enough that she could feel his breath. "I fucked up. I knew I should've gone as soon as midnight passed, but Rabbit kept me occupied until it was too late. You were too far gone."

Dani had wanted this answer for so long. Rabbit's logic made sense, but she couldn't have understood how much guilt Dani carried with her when she left. How determined she was to be gone. None of it changed what had happened.

"Would you do the same thing?" Dani asked.

"Now? No." Elliott hesitated. "Back then? Probably. I didn't know enough to make the decision back then. I should never have encouraged you to run."

"I had to." Dani thought back over the last ten years. "I don't think I could've done anything else, other than what I did."

"I tried searching for you right after you left—several times—but you were too far out of range. And by the time you were close enough to show up on my radar again, too many years had passed, and I didn't feel like I had the right to barge in on your life. But I couldn't stop myself from checking, from time to time. And then I found you for Archer, and that was selfish too. I knew you didn't come back for me . . . That's the only reason I've kept my distance. It's been so hard, Dani. I know I've slipped up. And I know I don't have what Brad Hackworth has to offer."

Dani hadn't thought about Brad once during this conversation. Her heart knew what that meant.

"I only wanted you," Dani said.

Elliott looked at her so hard he seemed to see *inside* her. She didn't want to hide anything from him, not anymore, not if this was real.

"I don't want to let you go again, and I won't . . ." he said. "Not unless you ask me to."

Dani could hardly breathe, but she collected herself. "I can't see tomorrow yet, but if we get through tonight . . ."

"We will," Elliott said. "I promise."

"You know what my mother always said about promises you can't necessarily keep?"

"Make them anyway?" Elliott said, guessing wrong.

"I like that better, but no." Dani pressed a kiss to Elliott's lips. She could feel the tension of him holding still instead of moving into it, waiting for her cue.

They couldn't do this, not right now. There was too much at stake. She owed Brad this evening, and an explanation.

She moved far enough back to talk. "She always said promises you can't keep are the prettiest lies."

"You deserve to be able to think past tomorrow. That's the truth."

Maybe so, but she wouldn't. Not yet.

The car arrived then. A limo.

"Let's get through tonight," she said.

Elliott stepped to a safe distance, but their eyes held for a long moment.

The driver got out and approached the porch with a small bow. "Miss Poissant? Mr. Strauss?"

"Just a second," Dani said.

She went back in for her purse. She'd chosen a black one of her own, not the tiny clutch included in the garment bag. If questioned, she'd say it was because she needed something large enough to hold a replacement ice pack for her shoulder. If anyone asked why she hadn't gone with something slimmer, like a lidocaine patch, she'd just say the store had been out.

She paused and kneeled in front of Sunflower, who'd followed her inside. She put her hands on either side of her fuzzy head and rubbed her soft ears. Sunflower's brown eyes watched her, still alert even as she pressed one ear into Dani's palm.

"I love you, my good girl. See you soon."

She hesitated when she stood and then decided to leave Sunflower outside rather than in—a last-second decision based on intuition. She hoped it was the right one. Her dog wouldn't go far, but she'd be happier roaming in a field than waiting by the door. Dani didn't expect anyone to be breaking and entering, but she didn't want Sunflower trapped on her own inside in case.

All this thinking revealed to Dani the extent of her nerves about the evening ahead.

"It's going to be fine," Elliott said, sensing it. "We've got this."

She wanted to believe him, so she told herself she did. *There's no other option. You take down Archer. That's it.*

She made a little "come on" noise for Sunflower, who capered out behind her and then ran around back as soon as Dani made the hand signal that dismissed her.

Elliott put his hand at the small of Dani's back on the walk to the car, but when the driver—waiting at the open rear door now— noticed and looked away, he removed it. Dani felt it clench into a fist just before.

They sat opposite each other, and Dani was both grateful for the distance and devastated by the electricity that crackled between her and Elliott. Facing him didn't make it easier to stay put. The driver raised the partition to give them privacy.

Elliott swung over to sit beside her and offered her his hand. She slid hers into it, and it was a quiet kind of promise. Her mother had never said anything about those.

CHAPTER TWENTY-SIX

THE GALA HAD already spun to life when they arrived.

Apparently no one wanted to be late for an exclusive night at an art collection that had never been seen before this week, and would exist only in legend after tomorrow's auction. A handful of pre-cleared, hired photographers acted as paparazzi on a staged red carpet that poured down the steps of the de facto temple that was the Fortress of Art. Lit up at night, surrounded with glam, it smacked of some fantasy hybrid of the Colosseum crossed with Carnival, set down in a gently rolling field. People were taking selfies below the hulking Bourgeois spider.

"I am supposed to inform Mr. Hackworth that you're here. Wait, please, ma'am, sir," the driver said to them over an intercom. Their car joined a queue dropping off other extravagantly dressed guests at the carpet and looping along a makeshift drive that went to parking behind the security building. Roughly next to where the purchases would be prepared for shipping or other highway transport the next day.

Elliott cracked the window. "Some Enchanted Evening" drifted out of the building's open doors, from a band that was clearly playing old-school crowd-pleasers. No doubt they'd be hearing the big band version of "Happy" or "I Gotta Feeling" eventually.

According to Elliott, the day the exes summoned him to the house, they had argued about bringing in a last-minute multimillion-dollar headliner for the gig (Springsteen's name had been bandied about, as was Lana Del Rey's), but Elliott had pointed out—rightly—that the art was the star of this event. He'd known that any such talent would bring in extra private security—the last thing they needed in the mix. And now the circus performers would add a little extra pizzazz—and usefully.

The gala was for charity, but the cause hadn't been announced yet that she'd seen. Dani would never be comfortable in the kind of place where invites came with a $30,000 to $100,000 price tag. It all seemed a far more elaborate con than needed when a check could be written quietly at home.

Even more amazingly, in the wake of Brenner's attempted theft, not only had the party not been canceled, but—from what Dani could tell—not a single part of the protocols had changed. She took the tiny speck of an earpiece out of her purse and pressed it into her right ear, as deep as it would comfortably go.

"Didn't want me along for the whole ride?" Rabbit said into their ears. The low croon of a John Prine song was just audible in the background.

"Mom, settle," Mia said.

Dani murmured a question. "Everything and everyone where it and they should be?"

"Locked and loaded," Rabbit said. "Except you know I hate guns."

"That's good, because we're not talking about guns," Mia said.

"Please remember that we're about to be surrounded by other people and keep the cross talk to a minimum," Elliott said. "Meant with love."

"Hmph." Rabbit. "You're on in about ten seconds." Oh right; Dani had forgotten there were outside cameras in addition to the drones, and the security system also gave Rabbit access to them. "See you soon," Rabbit said.

"See you soon," Dani and Elliott echoed, and he tightened his hold on Dani's hand in his for a moment, pulling it up to his lips for a quick kiss. He let go before the driver knocked on the window then opened the door.

They were a car behind where the red carpet started, and Brad and Emma stood waiting for them. The little girl might as well have been a princess and she twirled in her dress, which had a circus tent skirt pattern and a harlequin sequin design. Custom, no doubt.

"Hello!" she shouted.

"Why, hello to you, milady," Elliott said, all charm as he stepped out and bowed low to her. "Am I your escort to this ball?"

Emma giggled. She said to Dani, "We match!"

"We do," Dani said and had to remind herself she probably shouldn't crouch so her head was at the girl's level in whatever couture designer this was.

Brad stood and shook his head and gaped at Dani.

"I clean up okay?" she asked. She was flattered, even if she kept the feeling at a distance.

"That's not it." He shook his head again. "Okay, it's a little bit it. Everyone here will be jealous of me tonight."

"Like they aren't already," Dani said and carefully did not look at Elliott. "Shall we?"

She was eager to get inside, scope out the onsite security. She'd planned to have a couple of guards stationed in each gallery. Maybe the outside protocol not having changed was a good sign for what they'd find in there. Agent Sharpe would be on alert for her, but she hoped he wouldn't be on high *enough* alert otherwise. No one would expect them to make a move with a crowd like this. As long as they made the switch tonight, the Evil Twins could steal the fake or Rose could purchase it. Either way worked fine.

Brad stepped up to take her arm and they started their red carpet journey, while Elliott let Emma race ahead—until she came back to his side and shouted, "Say cheese!" for the cameras.

"You look like a billion dollars," Brad said lower, as they smiled the fake smiles that were expected.

"What would that look like? Lotta zeroes on a screen, I bet."

"Fair." He nodded. Point to her. "I've seen both, and you look way better."

"You really have done a good job with her," she said, redirecting to Emma. That the girl could still be relatively normal in the middle of all this luxury, charming instead of entitled and obnoxious. It was a feat.

"Despite appearances—and yes, I *do* mean the stress drinking this week—Mom has been a big help to me too."

"You turned out good, so I'm not surprised."

"She has always had her shit together. She thought she could change Dad, but mostly she thought she could make sure we had everything she didn't as a kid." He shrugged. "She was right."

"Lot for a mother to sacrifice . . ." And an outright stated scheme of gaining money and security through marriage. Women had been forced into, and trained into, the pattern through recorded history. She thought of Maeve trying to find a way free of the constraints on her. Dani certainly wouldn't judge anyone.

Everyone had their con, and she appreciated the people who knew what it was and why they did it.

She liked Brad more for the fact his mom trusted him enough to let him in on hers. She wouldn't examine the fact he was willing to let Dani in too. She got the feeling that he was naturally inclined to be open. He shouldn't be, but he was.

When Dani was young, she remembered Maria saying similar things as his mom about making a living. That she wanted to earn the comfort to be who she was, to never bow to anyone who might think of her as lesser. They needed to be the best at it all, not just their magic but the craft of the con and experts on art.

Dani had needed to please her mother, and never could—never did. She thought of Dani as a disappointment.

Archer. It all came back to Archer.

He'd brought her—all of them—to this moment.

Brad was thoughtful. "When I started to worry, Mom always said she'd be happy later, when he was really gone. Even after the divorce."

"How did he die?" Heart failure could cover a multitude of sins.

Brad shrugged. "Too slowly."

So not Archer's doing, then. He probably couldn't injure the man who spun the magic web.

A flash meant the camera had caught Brad's somber moment amid the revels with his ex–security consultant on his arm. But there'd be no risk of a solemn picture leaking. Or of one with Dani. Not if any of these photogs wanted to work this scene again.

He didn't even seem to notice them. "I hope she can be, now that we're almost done with this. We are, right?"

"If I have anything to do with it. And it still freaks me out that you can offhandedly refer to selling the collection as 'this.'"

"I have a plan for what comes next. You'll see."

They reached the entrance stairs. Dani didn't miss the exchanged glances from the security guys on the doors and, ahead of them, neither did Elliott. She saw him stop to chat and exchange a one-armed bro hug with one of them. Emma had already darted inside, ahead of him. Then she returned to drag him with her. He shrugged to the guards.

Dani didn't get the same kind of warm reception. Instead, there were mocking faces and raised eyebrows. She waited for one of them to produce a screening wand to humiliate her.

Brad noticed before that happened, though. She hadn't expected him to.

"You remember Dani." He directed it to all of them.

They didn't know quite how to react. The line of people backed up gradually behind them, the guard closest uncomfortably shifting, but Brad gave no sign of caring.

It's his party. And they're his employees.

Rose breezed out, dressed like a billion dollars herself. *No, wait, maybe it's* her *party*.

The guards certainly went immediately from awkward to relieved at her presence.

"Dani, can I steal Brad for a second?" She took in Dani's dress. "Good choice," she said.

"I could say the same to you," Dani said. And then, refusing to be convenient, "I'll come with."

She wanted to keep an eye on where Rose was. She needed to talk to her. Not yet, but soon.

Rose squinted at her. "Did they forget the bag?"

"No," Dani said and hung on to the strap of her purse. "Just needed some extra supplies for my shoulder."

Rose shrugged and somehow made it judgmental.

The three of them were given a wide berth into the party that had invaded the formerly quiet, abandoned, lonely Fortress of Art. Dani could feel the energy change. She didn't know if art had feelings or just the emotions of the people who made it, reflecting out to the viewer. But she did think art liked being seen. It liked people looking at it. No matter how they judged it.

Here, now, people gushed at one another and talked, the occasional person bothering to point and gawk at an individual piece of art. There were also a fair number of curators and collectors she expected to be bidding tomorrow, who were coldly dissecting the pieces, one-upping one another. And fans cooing. One woman with reading glasses on a beaded chain over her evening gown was quietly crying to indicate how moved she was at Frida's work. Amid all that, there were also three sexy acrobats in slinky Cubist print leotards, hanging on suspended lyras, which Dani knew from Mia were what the big round aerial hoops were called. There would be more performers scattered throughout the galleries using silks and static trapezes, others doing contortion.

This was pure spectacle. And it *was* spectacular.

With a jolt, Dani realized something. She felt absolutely alive. Lit up. On fire. Among this crowd, among this art, among all of it—

most of all, doing the job. She wasn't just here. She wasn't just doing what she had to do this time. She enjoyed this.

Being here in plain sight, intent on taking what she wanted, with no one being the wiser. Not until she wanted them to be.

She never felt like this on her usual gigs. Survival, and even atonement, turned out to be second-best motivations. Tonight wasn't just about stealing Archer's portrait; it was about stealing their lives back. How could her every nerve ending not be on high alert?

Open bars were stationed at random intervals. Champagne flowed, waiters making sure no one's glass stayed empty for long. She plucked a full flute from a tray and dodged another server holding an assortment of undoubtedly perfect amuse-bouches.

Holding court at the bottom of the stairs up to the galleries were the trio of ex-wives. Dani presumed they all had dates, somewhere among the throng.

Rose steered Brad and Dani in their direction.

This should be fun, Dani thought dryly, and sipped.

Elliott caught her eye from the top of the stairs, on the landing above, and she lifted her glass the slightest fraction. He grinned at her before turning away.

"What's happening?" Rabbit in her ear. Did she sound nervous? That wasn't like Rabbit, or rather, it *was* like Rabbit before or after a theft. Not during.

"I'm assuming they're at the party, saying their hellos," Mia said shortly, picking up on the weirdness of her mother's question too.

"Danielle!" Beverly, who'd been attacked by Archer, cried her name in what sounded like actual delight.

Brad gave Dani an amused shrug and she quietly muttered "shhh" into her glass.

"Beverly! And Diana and Sandi, congratulations," Dani said and gestured. "What a soiree."

"Not too shabby, is it?" Diana said, and took a healthy gulp of champagne. Dani could see what Brad meant there.

"Rose, are we in trouble?" Sandi asked.

Because Rose definitely had her censorious face on. Seemingly not on purpose, because she visibly smoothed it off at the mention. "Of course not," she said. "I just wanted to make sure you and Brad were agreed on the schedule for tonight. I'm getting some push-back from . . ."

"Hello, everyone," Agent Sharpe cut in. He was dressed in an FBI vest instead of a suit, which had to be intentional.

The guests gossiped into their flutes at his appearance. If everyone hadn't known about Dani's past, or about her firing, they would soon.

"Pushback from Agent Sharpe here," Rose finished.

"I didn't actually think you'd show," he said to Dani, ignoring Rose.

"I love a good party as much as the next person who hates you," Dani said.

Brad coughed a laugh. Once he recovered, he said, "I don't see how our guest list is any of your business."

"So I've been informed."

"Can we interest you in a drink?" Beverly asked, lifting a hand for a waiter.

"Oh no, he's on the job," Dani said.

"Is he?" Brad mused. "Because he seems to be here when anyone could be doing anything in the other galleries."

"I have guards posted. Everyone is on duty."

"So, you *are* unnecessary," Dani said. "Thought so."

"You're not helping," Rose said to Brad and Dani.

"I can't seem to care," Brad said.

Dani liked Brad a lot then, sharing her enemy, engaging in some light pettiness. "Me either."

As if on cue, Carlton arrived and joined them. He still looked like a lawyer, even in tails. He had a nearly age-appropriate, predictably gorgeous blonde on his arm. Wife number five, Dani presumed. "You aren't trying to talk to my clients without me, are you?" he asked.

"Okay." Agent Sharpe raised his hands. "I get it. I just came to say that so far everything seems to be going fine. You have a few crashers, but none of *them* with records so far as we can tell. I did wonder if any of you were going to be saying a few words, and when and where?"

In Dani's ear, Rabbit said, "Shit, checking on the crashers."

"That's what I wanted to talk to you about," Rose said.

The exes looked at one another.

Diana blew out a breath. "Speeches are so boring."

Beverly and Sandi nodded. "No one listens," Beverly said.

"I always use that time to go to the bathroom," Sandi said.

Carlton's wife nodded her agreement.

But Dani needed Brad to be occupied talking. It was the crew's agreed-upon cue. The idea they'd skip it had never occurred to her. She tried to figure a way to gently encourage it, but Rose beat her to the punch.

Rose cleared her throat. "Brad told me he has something he intends to announce tonight. I wanted to firm up the timing." When the exes looked like they might argue, she added, "I'm sure he'll do it briefly," which seemed to mollify them.

"I do. But I'm not telling you when," he said to Agent Sharpe, sending Dani a flirtatious glance. "It'll be a surprise."

That wasn't great for Dani either, but she did enjoy how Agent Sharpe looked like his blood had just gone from a simmer to a boil.

He couldn't do much about any of it. "I'm not the enemy. And, Dani, I wish you didn't hold a grudge. I helped you back then."

He seemed to believe all this, and given all she'd learned, maybe there was some truth in it. Dani almost softened toward him. Almost.

But manipulating a teenager to roll on her mother was not a means that justified an end. Even if Dani was beginning to understand that she might have delayed something that needed to be. She might've saved her mother heartache, and the rest of them worse. Much worse.

Rose took the agent's arm, apologetic. "I'll walk you back over."

"I didn't know you had it in you," Dani said to Brad.

"I know," he said. "I had the sense you needed the proof. Let the games begin."

Carlton gave Dani a speculative eyebrow raise.

Dani had thought of her past as a mistake for so long. It was difficult to wrap her mind around the idea that it might have been a good thing, ultimately, betraying her mother. That it alone had brought her to this moment, right now, when she could finally counteract Archer.

She could use her magic, her craft—all of it—to put things right in a way she could never have understood without Maeve's journal.

Or go down in flames trying . . .

Archer would never have hired her if he thought she was a risk to him. Everything needed to go off without a hitch or she'd lose the slight upper hand she had.

"About those crashers, we know them . . ." Rabbit said, and she definitely sounded nervous now.

Dani looked out into the crowd and spotted the Evil Twins schmoozing an older couple. The brother, Jer, nodded to her, and the sister, Jenn, smirked.

"Into the fray," Dani said to Brad and pulled him forward.

CHAPTER TWENTY-SEVEN

DANI HAD BEEN worried Brad might pay too much attention to her. Some was good, as in alibi good, but overkill or fawning would make executing the plan more difficult . . . Particularly with the Evil Twins unexpectedly on the scene.

But she needn't have worried. Brad Hackworth at a party like this? He must've known he needed to leave her some room to maneuver after their talk yesterday. He accomplished it in a number of unobtrusive ways. He pressed the flesh in endless handshakes. Chatted with every other person. He made probably-would-never-happen plans for golf games and meetings, for doing lunch, soon, real soon. It took fifteen minutes even to get up the grand stairs to the hall with the other galleries. And another fifteen to circulate through the first of them.

The few times Brad introduced Dani, the reactions went two ways: glazed and not caring, or *innnteresting, the Poison Angel's progeny is your date* but too timid to say anything.

Elliott and Rabbit were tag-teaming to keep tabs on the twins; him subtly steering Emma wherever Rabbit reported they were. So far, they hadn't ventured near Archer's gallery. Their team just had to get there first—in case the twins planned to do their grab tonight instead of at the next day's auction too. Dani didn't want to follow them closely herself; it would be too conspicuous. And she feared they'd enjoy the attention.

She and Brad finally entered the second gallery. There were two performers in here, one draping herself in contortionist shapes on a lyra, another flipping and climbing and dropping from two ribbons of silk hanging on a rig like the one she'd seen in the barn at Rabbit's. Enough of the crowd watched the aerialists instead of looking at the masterworks around them that Dani wanted to scream.

But then, she reasoned, it was good if the crowd didn't actively care too much about the art. Good for her and her crew anyway.

"It's exhausting being you," Dani said in a brief interlude between the approach of suck-ups and glad-handers.

"Sometimes," Brad agreed. He gave her a significant look. "I know you probably want to soak in the art one last time. Take a turn, I'll find you."

And Brad went on to his next conversation partner.

Emma had ditched Elliott to befriend the hoop performer, gaping up at her tricks, and he stood leaning against a wall beside one of the security guards halfway across the gallery from Dani. Diana had left the bottom of the stairs at some point and was attempting to chat him up. He was keeping the conversation going with an occasional response.

Elliott met Dani's eyes and she followed his across the room to where the Evil Twins were appreciating a Vermeer. He put a hand on Diana's arm before excusing himself. She, seemingly not offended at being abandoned, asked the nearest server for another drink and went to join her granddaughter.

Elliott didn't walk toward Dani, but as he meandered toward the door he murmured and the question came through on the earpiece. "On schedule?"

There had been another unwelcome revelation in the first of the upstairs galleries, repeated in the one she now stood in. More guards than expected were posted. Possibly a few plainclothes FBI among them, though how Sharpe had gotten Rose to agree to that, Dani couldn't imagine.

Dani hadn't been to Archer's gallery yet either, because it would be too suspicious if she visited it repeatedly. Not to mention that she felt his dark eyes keenly enough without looking into them. He was the person—entity?—she *truly* hoped had no idea of her intention. Not that the rest of the group knew either. She was stealing him, all right. For reasons of her own.

She smiled and nodded to the next person she passed. "How many with the target?" she asked quietly.

"Um, three guards, two in the room, one outside," Mia said after a brief hesitation. "And Liz's there . . ."

"Strays in position?" Dani asked. The other extras, also on board just for the evening—the part that made her most nervous. But Rabbit, Elliott, and Mia swore they were trustworthy—at least while stealing. The irony.

"Picked up on schedule," Rabbit said. "Just do your part."

Dani's part was technically all of it, as the mastermind, but she kept that to herself. She watched the rainbow girl in the metal hoop spin, spin, spin, like dice or a coin in the air, full of possibility. The embodiment of the night's real enemy: chance.

She pivoted and left the twins under Rabbit's watchful camera eyes, then moved with confidence along the hall to enter the third gallery, killing time, counting down. But she also had a particular trip of homage to make in here. Something she'd put off.

She stopped in front of the Velázquez portrait, lost for centuries, of Donna Olimpia Maidalchini Pamphilj. The woman had been known in her time as "the female pope," and not in a loving way—at least not by the Vatican. The doughy-faced woman staring out looked unremarkable.

But talk about a legend. Magic circles held that she'd had a power of coercion little seen. She held weekly card games to divest those seeking favors from the contents of their wallets, and heisted the entire Vatican gold treasury from under her dying brother-in-law's—the actual pope's—bed. The Vatican did its best to disappear most traces of her, including this portrait, but the secret world remembered her daring. Hackworth had gotten hold of the portrait, no doubt hoping her scheming self would be tied to it the way Archer was to his.

Dani had made note of it in the list, but hadn't felt like she deserved to tip a glass to her—until now. Donna Olimpia had done miracles of theft, been celebrated and reviled, and ultimately died alone, abandoned by her staff and her family.

Dani and Maria were Maeve's descendants, but they were the infamous *papessa*'s too, if only in spirit. Dani imagined Maria and Donna Olimpia would've loved or hated each other. She nodded in deference and sipped her champagne.

"We've got a problem," Elliott said in her ear.

"The twins or something else?" Dani gazed at the painting, but she was no longer seeing it.

"No. And we do not," Mia said. "Stay in position."

"You need to see this," Elliott said and there was an odd echo. "Target gallery."

"Rabbit?" Dani tried.

Rabbit said nothing.

Dani turned and then entered the hallway, her heart striking up a faster rhythm. She spotted Brad back the way they'd come, at the top of the main stairs, peering down. The band stopped playing. Rose was with him, along with the ex-wives, so this was presumably the moment of his speech. He spotted Dani and waved a summons. She gave a slight shake of her head and his disappointment was unmistakable, but he turned away.

The crowd had quieted and most everyone else stayed where they were. Someone handed Brad a mic and he welcomed everyone, the sound both booming and scratchy.

Which meant it was time to begin anyway—though she wasn't supposed to be headed in this direction. Not yet. She was meant for the Rothko. But plans changed . . . she'd have to take a quick detour.

"On my way," Dani said.

"Shit." That was Mia.

What the hell was going on?

Dani did her best not to seem hurried, passing stray people heading to listen to the speech. There were still people scattered in the last few galleries, though she passed one empty of patrons, where the circus performers were taking the opportunity for a break. One of them rested against the curved slope inside her apparatus, like a human half-moon, and the other sat on a knot of the silk fabric as if it were a glamorous swing.

"You don't need to come," Mia said.

"He just started speaking," Dani said.

That curtailed the cross talk.

"Rabbit, ETA of the B-team?" Dani asked, low. "Location of the twins?"

Rabbit still didn't answer.

Maybe Rabbit had stepped out of the van for a rare smoke or a usual pace. Dani prayed she was in contact with the reinforcement ground crew and the Evil Twins weren't about to blow this up. Rabbit's break timing was abysmal.

Dani made her way down the second stairwell without rushing and then toward the gallery at the end of the hall on the right. The gallery with Archer's painting inside.

She forced herself to go slow, threading through the crowd lingering too far from the speechmaking to know they were missing it. Not that many of them seemed to care. These were the people here to party. She nodded at the security guard at the door, just as a serious Elliott appeared in the frame and jerked his head in her direction.

No job ever panned out exactly the way she wanted, but this, tonight, she couldn't fail.

Whatever she was about to learn, she wouldn't like it. But she would deal with it.

Resolved, she shifted past the guard with a smile and an "Emmett, hi," trying to keep it sounding casual.

The guard let her pass, because he had no real choice to do otherwise.

Dani took in the gallery. No sight of Jer or Jenn, much to her relief. She half anticipated that Archer would be there, but she didn't see him either—except for his portrait in the corner, of course. Liz dangled from two long ribbons. She was meant to be the lone performer in this gallery, and the sight of another brought Dani up short.

Elliott met her eyes. "I didn't know."

Mia, dressed in one of the Cubist leotards, swung herself into a perch on a lyra. Damn it. She'd known way too much about all the circus stuff, the rig in the barn. What was she doing here?

"Rabbit?" Dani asked again. "Where are you?"

Still nothing.

Elliott clearly understood the magnitude of the problem.

"Where the hell is Rabbit?" Dani asked, and her voice was fraying. She knew it was.

Mia, meanwhile, flipped herself around on the circle, and if Dani hadn't wanted to strangle her friend, she'd have gawked, impressed.

"I don't know," Elliott said with a frown.

The last thing they'd heard from her was that the others had done the pickup and were en route. She prayed it was the truth, since so much of the rest of what she expected transformed with every breath.

Dani stalked toward Mia and Liz, to a point in between them, acting as if she were merely interested in their aerial routines. She and Elliott knew each other, so their conversation wouldn't raise any eyebrows. He moved to chat with one of the guards, then the other inside the room migrated over to talk with them. He was buying her a second to find out what had possessed Mia to fuck with the plan.

They don't know everything about how important this is. Be calm. You need them. You care about them . . .

The reminder to herself didn't calm her at all. Her pulse thundered, her heart a storm. This could blow the whole thing.

She pasted an admiring smile on her face.

Liz winced. She was high up on her twin silks and she took that moment to drop, nearly to the floor. "It was my idea," she said. "It only seemed fair."

Fair. That was a concept for babies and rubes. For the people they conned. It wasn't anything Mia would ever believe existed on a job. Or it shouldn't have been.

Liz's forehead gathered, like her ponytail was too tight, but she had to keep up appearances, so she did. She climbed back up the emerald silks, hand over hand, with focused grace.

Dani turned her back on the woman she sure hoped was Mia's girlfriend again, after this stunt, and waited, even though there was scarcely time. Mia knew that. She dangled backward, her head coming level with Dani's, if upside down.

Dani leaned in, slightly. The other people in the gallery were busy laughing and drinking.

"I'm sorry," Mia said without sounding it. And then, far less defensive, more worried. "I don't know where Mom is."

The blare of an alarm sounding upstairs, and then echoing through the speaker system, interrupted. A sharp, earsplitting wail, then silence, wail, then silence. Nothing was happening the way they'd talked it out.

She paused for a fraction of a second and met the dark eyes of Archer's portrait. The shadows of it seemed to vibrate, a warning.

But Dani was going to have to make it work. "Be ready," she said and turned away from Mia.

The guards were evidently confused as well, barking into their own earpieces. Elliott invaded their space, asking what was going on.

"An attempted theft upstairs," the guard on the left answered before the other guard shushed him. Elliott might be their bro, but he was no longer part of the security team. They'd almost forgotten. The guard on the door tried to stop Dani from leaving, holding out a hand and grabbing her arm. She elbowed him hard and kept going as he doubled over.

She headed back up the stairs, trusting Elliott to smooth it over and run interference for her. He might be the only person exactly where and when he was supposed to be tonight.

The continued blaring scream of the alarm sure sounded like the rest of their crew had shown up, a few minutes early.

"Rabbit?" Dani tried one more time as she rushed up the stairs to the gallery where the alarm better have been triggered—if there was any hope of getting this situation back on track.

Still nothing from Rabbit. Fucking fabulous. Rabbit must not have known about Mia's plans to abandon her post—or maybe she just didn't give a shit about tossing Dani out the window and hoping she could fly. Maybe it was more punishment for the past. For all she knew, Rabbit decided to work with the twins too. Regardless, the crew on the ground was currently navigating without their sixth sense, the all-seeing eye of surveillance. The cameras and guards could look at them; the crew couldn't get in front of them now, couldn't circumvent the view. She had no idea where the Evil Twins were . . .

One problem at a time. Dani sped up the hall, weaving between confused, whispering guests.

Shit. There they were.

The snickering twins passed her and they were headed toward Archer's gallery.

"Heads up, incoming duo," she murmured to Elliott and Mia. She had her own part to play right now.

The rest of the guards were trying to decide whether to keep everyone in place or evacuate them, so Dani benefited from the chaos. The alarm finally died, switched off, but the state of upset continued. No band played on.

Archer stepped out of the door of an upstairs gallery, tall, pale, glowering. "You only get one shot at this," he said. "Your mother's approach would be far more disciplined."

Like she didn't know that.

He vanished before she could respond.

CHAPTER TWENTY-EIGHT

THE GALLERY WITH the Rothko had been emptied, except for the people she expected to find there. Brad, Rose, Agent Sharpe, two security guards . . . and the thief who was no longer technically stealing. And his assistant. Finally, a piece of luck, something going roughly as planned—or so she thought until she got a closer look at the man with her paperwork in his hands.

It wasn't Brenner, like it was supposed to be, like they'd *agreed* upon, but instead his muscle, the man with the blurry face who'd punched her. She touched her shoulder in reflex. His face, now static, resembled Brenner's enough to pass, she guessed. His hair grayed, a few wrinkles. They were roughly the same height. And he did appear to have the documents Dani had provided.

He stood next to the painting he'd managed to remove from the wall with the help of a woman with a buzz cut she didn't recognize. That better mean Brenner or their third man was due to show up soon . . . especially if Rabbit stayed MIA . . .

The standoff was tense, a time bomb, since Dani hadn't gotten to prep Rose. Since everything had begun sliding out of shape. She needed to hurry, but this had to go perfectly.

"You're not needed here," Agent Sharpe said when he spotted

Dani. He moved to herd her from the room. The guards had their weapons out and pointed at the would-be thieves.

She sidestepped him. "Brad?"

"She's welcome to stay. Maybe she can explain what's going on?" he asked.

"What *is* going on?" Dani kept her voice neutral and didn't risk looking at the man in the suit or the woman with him.

"He claims to be the rightful owner of this painting," Agent Sharpe said. "Which is ridiculous. We're about to arrest them both."

Dani nodded, taking it in stride. She had to play this just right. "Can you hold that thought for me, Agent Sharpe?" She pivoted to Rose before he could answer. "Rose, can I talk to you for a second?"

Rose frowned, then nodded.

"We're not waiting on you," Agent Sharpe said.

"Yes, we are." Brad's tone brooked no argument. Then he asked Dani, "Should I join you?"

"I think you should stay here," Dani said and looked at Agent Sharpe.

Brad nodded. He had nothing to prove. And he would be invested in this not turning into a bigger uproar for the partygoers to gossip about.

As soon as they got into the crowded hallway, Dani pulled Rose away from the nearest clump of people for a tiny measure of privacy.

"What is this?" Rose demanded in that no-nonsense way of hers.

"I know you want the Rothko," Dani said. "They're stealing it for you. The new provenance will support the ownership claim of that man. He'll quietly complete the job for you, at your agreed-upon price, then get you the piece later."

Rose's mouth opened, closed. "The provenance is impeccable."

"The new one will check out," Dani continued. "Obviously, I was removed as consultant and my records were seized. But they'll find some convincing notes that I had questions about its history." She'd made them to set up a switch like this before Rabbit even identified Rose as the buyer.

"Is this blackmail?"

She weighed the need for finesse against resolving this quickly. Why not both? This was something she could do. Dani had spent ten years confronting people with truths they'd rather keep hidden. Rose was smart. She'd be fast on the uptake. "I asked myself how someone like you, so committed to keeping up with the Joneses, appearances, loyal to a fault, willing to fight in court, was so comfortable around firearms."

That first day she'd showed up at the stone house and Rose had met her with a handgun. Those were the kind of threads Dani had learned to keep track of, to pull on . . . People often gave away so much without ever realizing. Even those who had every reason to be careful. When Rabbit gave her the piece of paper with Rose's name, it had fallen into place. Why shouldn't Rose get a souvenir of her choosing? As long as it wasn't Archer's portrait.

Rose blinked, but she was too strong to cave right away. "I took a class. Are you done? I don't have time for this."

Dani had her. "You'll make time. I know Rose isn't your real name, and that you schemed your way into Hackworth's employ because it was the perfect job for you. And I'll hand it to you, that was one hell of a fake résumé. A regular old background check looked perfect."

Rose said nothing.

"You have a good thing going, *Rose,* and I think you'd like to keep it on track. I just need you to keep Sharpe out of my way tonight. Okay?"

"Damn," Rose said. "I knew hiring you was a bad idea. What do you want?"

"A simple favor. Go over the provenance, and keep everyone busy."

Rose sniffed. "It's not a favor if you blackmail me into it."

Dani shrugged. "Maybe not. But assuming we're good here, your secrets are safe."

Rose breathed out a long sigh. "Fine. But the paperwork better be good enough to fool Agent Sharpe."

Dani actually smiled then. Her magic ensured that much. "Oh, it's practically the real deal."

Rose motioned for Dani to lead the way back in.

"One last thing," Dani said, "the other painting? Why buy it?"

"Because it'll go cheap," Rose said. "This is the one I wanted, and I'm smart enough to keep it hidden. But it would look strange if I bought nothing."

Fair enough. Brad had been right about her not knowing Hackworth's secret. She deserved a prize for working for that man for so many years.

"Well?" Brad prompted when they rejoined the groups, who were still in a hostile standoff.

"Dani informed me that there were some . . . irregularities she noticed about the Rothko's original paperwork. She thought the provenance we were given might have been faked. The artist wasn't fond of selling to the wealthy during the period it was painted. He even took some paintings back from people they were originally promised to. So it's entirely possible it got taken from its intended owner by the sellers and we bought it unaware . . . We'd better take a look at what he has."

The man stepped forward and Dani didn't mind if she stayed out of his way. "This doesn't mean the party's over, does it?" she asked Brad and she tried not to show what a disaster that would be. She needed to get out of here. She trusted Elliott, but the twins' abilities were nothing to play around with.

Agent Sharpe cut a look at her, then Rose, but he had to examine the documents. His job demanded it.

"We should close things down," Agent Sharpe said, "while we review this paperwork."

Brad stepped up to mediate. "Why don't we just close this one gallery? I'd rather not advertise this, or we'll have people coming out of the woodwork, saying the art is theirs. And it's not."

Agent Sharpe took the paperwork the man offered, and she could tell by how he deflated that he knew it would check out. But he gave his crusade a last airing. "Do you have issues with more pieces?"

"I didn't see any," Dani put in before Rose could answer. "This was the only one I had any questions about."

"This is a special case," Rose said, throwing her weight behind Dani's opinion.

Outside the room, the band struck back up—and just as she'd expected earlier they trotted out "Happy." A strange choice, but the alarm was off and she could just imagine one of the ex-wives ordering them to play something to lift the mood.

Agent Sharpe grumbled, but he had no reason to doubt Rose, even if he didn't like Dani. He probably thought he *did* like Dani, but she suspected she made him feel guilty. Somewhere inside of him, he must be aware of the sketchy ethics he'd employed with her.

"We'll cooperate," Brad said. "Fully. Let's just not be too loud about it."

Ha. Agent Sharpe liked attention. But she wasn't going to point out that he'd inevitably leak it. He would be busy for a while checking out her documentation.

In the meantime, they would steal the other painting. Hopefully right out from under *everyone's* noses.

Sharpe conferred with the guards and one of them spoke into his earpiece, requesting a barrier for the door. Dani exchanged a pointed look with the man who Brenner had sent in his stead. She didn't like him, because she didn't like people who'd punched her. Simple enough life rule.

He'd better play his role to perfection. He nodded to her, as if he understood.

Brad caught her arm and pulled her a little to the side, out of earshot of the others. "I wanted you to hear the announcement— I'm donating my portion of the auction to start a foundation, Gates style. It's going to do good."

"I want to hear all about it later," she said.

"Not now?" he tried. "I thought you might be a part of it. After this."

Shit. This isn't how I wanted to do this.

"I'm sorry," she said.

"Me too," he said.

"Brad, we should get everyone in a conference room," Rose spoke up then. "There's an HVAC station and stairs in the corner over there. You can use them to get out of the building and over to security headquarters without making a dramatic exit." She spoke to the supposed owner. "I'll have the painting packaged up for you. If everything checks out, you can take it with you tonight."

A member of the security team arrived then to seal off the gallery. Dani caught Brad's eye one last time, and then slipped out.

"Rabbit?" she asked under her breath. "You back?"

"Nothing from her," Elliott said. His voice was low and tight. "And they're in here. What should we do?"

"Hope for the best," Dani said. Silently adding, *And anticipate the worst.*

At this point, she could envision Rabbit passed out, a heart attack or a stroke or any number of terrible things that their magic couldn't protect them from. She couldn't afford to think that way, but it was impossible not to.

The job was the most important thing in the world—until it wasn't.

She moved through the crowd while second-guessing every decision she'd made. She should have worked harder on a way to get the painting here in advance. Brenner's stunt had screwed that up, but there would've been some way. What if Rabbit and the second vehicle didn't show?

Then Dani might have to improvise and simply take the portrait, implicating herself and gambling on Brad and Carlton the lawyer bailing her out. Brad might like her, might even want her to finish this—but she didn't think that it extended to letting her walk off the grounds with the painting, no questions asked, while the FBI watched. Actually, she did know. They'd met a little over a week ago. Her intuition told her half his interest in her came from the confirmation she knew about magic and the triangle of competition he and Elliott fell into whenever the three of them were in close quarters. The rest was the bond of having an extremely tortured relationship with a parent over the secret world. Now that she'd gently discouraged him, he definitely wouldn't be taking risks for her.

Dani kept her focus ahead of her, bracing in case Archer put in another told-you-so appearance. The first part of the plan was done, at least—Rabbit's debt to Brenner, whatever it was—and her mother's—were both more than paid now. Agent Sharpe would be busy for a while reviewing her ironclad, completely manufactured provenance.

Elliott met her in the hall. "We're going ahead?"

"What choice do we have?"

"Wait and see if the twins take it? Steal it from them?"

"No," she said.

They had some idea what it was. And who knew if they were the only ones? There were no indications that Hackworth had talked about Archer's role in his accumulation of wealth, but that didn't mean he'd never gotten drunk and told the story. She couldn't be certain.

"We have to try." Dani could trust her gut, if nothing else. Even if no one else—save Elliott—had followed the blueprints for the night.

"All right," he said. "See you soon."

She nodded. Found her spine, found the thinnest filament of confidence, a hope it would all work out anyway, and entered the gallery.

She went over and stared at Archer's portrait, ignoring the performance, the buzz of conversation, the security guard who moved to watch her. Elliott wouldn't have followed her back in; he was meant to put some distance between them. Say his goodbyes.

Archer's face gazed out at her, a faint contempt on it. She found she could read all the details more finely after having understood them from the inside out. The shadows. The way Maeve had drawn his features with a measure of contempt. With hatred boiling inside her. And fear. She saw his overconfidence.

"Here we go," she whispered to herself, to the crew, to anyone who was listening. To him.

The Evil Twins were positioned on opposite sides of the small gallery. If Dani's crew had any fortune in its favor, they were on a scouting expedition and would stay out of the way. She wasn't counting on it.

"Danielle! A word please!"

Dani looked over her shoulder to find Rose walking toward her, seemingly on a mission. And absolutely not where she was supposed to be.

Well, shit.

Dani stepped toward her. "Rose, what are you—"

"NO!" This shriek came from across the gallery, where Jenn gripped her ears, shaking her head. Jer staggered in her direction, holding his hands up over his ears too. "No, no, no!" he repeated.

Both of them screamed in pain, collapsing.

The figure of Rose dissipated, there one second, gone the next.

They'd meant to distract Dani with the illusion of Rose, but Archer had interceded. They had no chance. He *wanted* Dani to steal him. Whoever in their family had owned him, he hadn't been a fan.

She didn't have time to worry about the Evil Twins; like Beverly, she had to assume they'd be fine.

"Now," she murmured as the guards went to assist the two uninvited party guests.

She looked at Archer's portrait again, imagining him newly smug, and closed her eyes for a second when the gasp sounded behind her. Then she turned toward the new fussing over the fallen aerialist.

Only it was not Liz as they'd planned, but Mia. Her right leg was twisted at a strange angle that wasn't anything natural, anything good. One look at Liz confirmed Dani's suspicion that Mia had decided to cast herself as the distraction instead.

Which meant she might truly be hurt.

Elliott rushed back in from the hallway. "What happened in here?" He looked at one of the guards, who was torn between whether to assist Mia or the twins. "Radio the ambulance. There should be one on standby."

And here it went. They'd know one way or another, once the emergency responders showed up. Assuming the radios were set to go to the ambulance they'd borrowed, the vehicle Rabbit had tricked out, where Dani's replacement painting waited. Everything hinged on what happened next.

"Let's give her some air." Elliott took charge of the response to Mia's fall and everyone let him. He had that commanding air about him, and for the moment, Dani couldn't hate it.

The Evil Twins were already straightening, Archer's attack receding. They both had wide eyes as a guard tried to get them to remain still. They'd all gotten an unwelcome reminder of what Archer was capable of, even confined—and he'd barely done anything.

"We should call Mr. Hackworth," that security guard said. "And wasn't Rose just here?"

Dani stepped up. "They're busy with the FBI right now. It's okay; we can help out."

The guard's jaw tightened, but Elliott clapped him on the back. A man's authority, prevailing again.

"Ambulance is on the way, I told them to come to the nearest entrance," the other guard said. "I'll meet them."

The Evil Twins were making their way toward the door, regrouping. Dani moved over, feigning concern, took Jenn's arm, and spoke low in her ear. "Get out of here, both of you. Back to the party. You're lucky he didn't kill you."

Jer had his arm hooked through her other one. Their hatred as they directed it toward Dani was potent. But they left the room without a word, a guard trailing behind them.

Dani finally rushed to kneel by Liz, at Mia's side. Liz clasped Mia's hand tight. The two of them were having a silent conversation in stares. Mia flinched when she saw Dani.

"I'm sorry. I don't—"

Dani shushed her before she said too much with a few more pairs of ears around. "This is what insurance policies are for. Don't worry, whatever you need, we'll see to it."

Mia's brown eyes managed to be brave and scared, the kind of description that only made sense to an artist, trained at looking past the surface. "You're going to be fine," Dani said.

"But . . ."

But where is my mother? Dani could hear her question. And she counted the seconds, hoping for an answer.

And that's when it entered the room.

Two people carted a stretcher with them. Two people Dani didn't recognize.

Shit. She might actually just have to grab the painting and run for it.

But then one of them brushed her out of the way and said, "Rabbit sent us."

They set down the stretcher alongside Mia.

"Let's give them some room to check her out," she said, recovering.

None of this answered where Rabbit was. Where Brenner was. But maybe all wasn't lost.

The guards turned their attention to clearing the room and Dani felt beneath the stretcher. Her fingertips hit a surface rough with paint.

"We need to get anyone who shouldn't be here out of the gallery, give her some breathing space," the other fake responder said.

Elliott helped to usher people out and then posted the guards outside the door like he was in charge. There were plenty of times when all it took to be in control of a situation was to take control. Turned out Elliott was good at that.

As the room emptied, Dani found Liz and nodded to her. Liz, to her credit, moved in an instant, and made a show of trying to get her wide ribbons of green silk down, out of the way. But instead, they billowed wide, hiding a large portion of the wall. She kept it going, ballooning them out with a dismayed noise of apology, and Dani could have kissed her.

Dani plucked out the still-cold bandage on her shoulder and pressed it against the sensor on the wall under Archer's painting. She prayed Rabbit had programmed the system to deactivate the motion alarm for sixty seconds at the cold temperature, as she'd claimed to have.

The man who'd spoken to Dani lifted the stretcher and she moved to slip the replacement painting carefully out from beneath it, handing off the bandage to him. By the time she turned, he'd already removed the one on the wall, wrapped it in a sheet. As they swapped places, he stuck the real painting under the stretcher and applied the cold pack to Mia's leg. Dani hung her identical piece in its place on the wall, making like she was straightening the portrait, just in case anyone looked in on them. The silks had been positioned to block the surveillance camera's view too.

"I'm so sorry," Liz said, at last clearing the fabric out of the way.

"I think we need to take her in," one of the men said to Mia, but also louder, presumably for the guards in the hall. "We'll want to get X-rays."

They hefted the stretcher.

Dani couldn't stay behind, not when she didn't know these men. Not when she didn't know where Rabbit was. The Evil Twins might be smart enough to back off permanently, but she couldn't bank on it. She would not be parted from Archer's painting, not when it held the keys to her future. To her mother's.

"I'll ride with you," she said.

If the men thought to argue, Elliott's expression told them not to even make the attempt. But then, out of seeming nowhere, Brad appeared.

"Me too," Brad said and trailed them toward the hallway with the emergency exit to the outdoors. "I need to ask you about something."

"No, you have to stay here," Dani said, night air rushing in as they carried Mia and Archer's painting through. "There's too much going on. All the people here." She gestured at the hallway, back toward the main party.

Outside, the decommissioned but repainted to look good as new ambulance sat waiting, lights flashing. The back doors were open and the inside was as tricked out as any medical show's set. It might mainly be an illusion, but the equipment looked convincing.

"I'll go with her, Dani, you can stay," Elliott said, and he squeezed Dani's hand, even though Brad was there, watching.

Dani searched her heart and found that she trusted Elliott. Despite everything. She didn't have time to tell him Brad knew they weren't legit. She only had to wonder why he was getting in her way at this, the worst possible moment.

"Okay," Dani said.

"Let us know how it goes," Brad said.

Elliott would know she'd find a way out of here and follow as quickly as possible.

Brad turned her back to the door and she let him, not wanting him to see too much of the emergency workers or Mia. The painting should be tucked safely into the pocket fashioned precisely to hold it without damage. He probably wouldn't say boo. But there was no reason to tempt fate. He'd asked to be kept in the dark.

He should have stayed away.

Elliott squeezed in alongside the stretcher and the man who'd done the talking slammed the doors and then took his spot behind the wheel.

Dani itched to turn, bolt, and go with the painting. But the crunch of the tires on the access road's asphalt reached her ears. They were already leaving.

"I just wanted to make sure you were okay," Brad said.

Dani forced a smile. "How sweet," she said. "Agent Sharpe think it all looks good so far, the paperwork?"

She led him inside and farther up the hall, away from the room with the replacement painting.

"I don't know how Rose missed this, honestly," he said. He frowned. "It's not you?"

Ah, so what he really wanted was to know if Rose had played him for a fool.

"She was paid to get the things your father wanted," Dani said. "What choice would she have had?"

Brad conceded the point.

"You should go on back," Dani said.

"Dani—maybe I'm a fool, but . . ." He'd decided to take his shot, leaned in for a kiss. She kept it brief.

Part of her wished she felt something at the contact. But she didn't.

"You'd better get back," she said.

Brad studied her for another moment. "Thank you. I can tell . . . the air is clear."

He headed toward the party.

She knew what he meant as she went to the gallery to meet Liz. No darkness emanated from the corner with her portrait. She knew—she felt—the truth of it. What wasn't there. The invisible net of magic that had suffused the Fortress simply wasn't there any longer.

Though no one without magic would know.

Thinking of the painting driving away, the inside of Dani howled, keened like a wolf separated from her pack. Like a predator from her prey.

"Mia said you were . . . that you could . . . but . . . it's uncanny," Liz said of the portrait. Then, "You want me to drive?"

"Yes," Dani said. "You're forgiven."

CHAPTER TWENTY-NINE

LIZ BEING A performer meant her van had scored a parking spot not far away, hidden from sight of the guests, behind the loading-dock entry. No one seemed to notice Dani leaving with her, which was well and good.

Dani watched out for it, but the ambulance had already gotten clear. They must have thrown on the sirens and gone hell-for-leather. Another saying originally tied to horses, as they sped through horse country.

Liz wasn't afraid to drive her minivan like a getaway car.

"What the hell is going on with Rabbit?" Dani asked for the benefit of the crew who should still be listening on their respective earpieces. "And should we be worried I don't know the men driving you?"

"I've met them before," Elliott said in her earpiece.

Liz shot Dani a prompting look and she asked the question she was going to anyway. "Mia, are you all right?"

"You mean you're still talking to me?" Mia asked.

"How's your leg?"

Liz glanced over. "Her leg's fine. I would never have let her get hurt. I just wanted her to know you're not mad."

Just as Mia said, "Oh yeah, leg's fine. I have a joint thing. It's why I don't do aerials more."

Well, that also explained why Liz hadn't insisted on going in the ambulance.

"It would've been good to know," Dani grumbled. "But at least you showed up. Any idea where your mom is?"

Elliott spoke. "They say Rabbit's fine. She must be if she sent them."

They reached the main road and Liz sped up. The van shook and rattled, but the engine sounded in fine health.

"What is this, then—some more freezing me out?" Dani asked.

Mia sighed. "I honestly don't know. You know I wouldn't have come if I'd thought it would put anyone in danger. I . . ."

"Expected her to be there. I believe you." Dani considered telling them that she intended to burn Archer's actual portrait as soon as they rendezvoused.

But she kept that fact to herself for now. She would conscript Elliott to help her when the time came.

"I should text Brad," she said, almost absentmindedly, pulling out her phone. "In case he looks for me again."

Though she didn't think he would. Elliott might have ground his teeth—she'd never know—but he didn't register an audible protest. Dani fired off a message that she'd left and Brad returned a thumbs-up.

"The twins left?" Elliott asked.

"They have a history with the painting. I think they'll leave it be now," Dani said. Her more important question was about the ambulance drivers. "Who are the drivers?"

"Associates of Brenner's," Mia said.

"He wasn't there either," Dani said.

"Huh," Mia said.

"Yeah, I'm not loving it," Dani said.

When you were dealing with professional thieves, a hundred-million-dollar score when there were several more orders of that magnitude available . . . It might not have been enough.

"You have any idea what our mothers owed him for?" Dani asked. She'd given up on keeping their business secret from Liz, who was focused on the road and yet still soaking all this in.

"I don't," Mia said.

Elliott said, "The only thing I've ever gotten out of him was borrowing a car."

"Maybe it was something from a long time ago." Except Dani remembered her mother not liking Brenner. She'd detested him.

There was a Mia-esque sniffle on the earpiece.

"Mia, you really okay?" Dani asked, afraid Mia was emotional.

She realized the sniffle wasn't hiding a sob only when it escaped. Mia giggled.

"I did good, didn't I?" Mia asked through her laughter.

"Not the point," Dani said. And then, "Yes."

"I've been saying all along, I'm part of the team."

"And I never thought you weren't," Dani said. Mia's joy in her performance was hard to resist.

They had the painting. Everything would be all right.

Dani had rolled with the evening's surprises and they'd still managed the job. She threw her head back and laughed too, and Liz joined in. Elliott was probably shaking his head at all of them, thinking they'd gone mad.

Her phone buzzed and she saw Brad's name and almost didn't check it. But that wouldn't be fair to him. At that precise moment, Dani felt incredibly at peace with the universe. She was on her way to putting things right.

On her own terms.

So she unlocked the phone and looked at the message.

Dani, have you seen the news? Brad asked. *Where are you?*

She responded. *On the road, like I said. Hospital, then headed home. What news?*

Her fingers clutched the phone against her will while she waited for him to respond. What if Rabbit *had* been hurt? But he had no idea who Rabbit even was. That couldn't be it.

He sent a link to a breaking news story. She clicked through.

The headline read, "Infamous Art Thief Escapes from Federal Hospital."

Holy fuck! She skimmed the brief two-paragraph story that confirmed her mother had broken out of the Federal Medical Center sometime in the last two hours. She was considered armed and dangerous, and possibly being aided in her escape.

She hadn't broken out, then. She'd *been* broken out.

"Elliott," Dani said, "change of plans. Make them go to the stone house. Fight them and toss them out if you have to. Keep the painting safe . . . There's an easel and some supplies in my studio for displaying it. Take a look."

"Dani, what's wrong?"

"Check the news," she said. "I think I know where Rabbit's been all evening." And Brenner, with his special ability for opening locks.

They hadn't owed him for the past. They'd owed him for this.

The escape.

If her mother got to Archer's painting before she could manage to destroy it, she *would* release him.

Dani threw her head against the seat and emitted a sound of frustration that apparently needed no translation. Liz put her foot down, and the van heaved forward, accelerating.

Dani ignored a couple of calls from Carlton, the lawyer she didn't need. He was probably interested in representing her mother.

She took out her earpiece too. There was no point in talking more to the crew either. That only meant risking Rabbit tuning back in to them. Maybe she'd given them the privacy of not snooping to see how the rest of the job went.

The main thing they had going for them there was that she'd been busy too. And Archer had been paying attention to what happened at the Fortress, enough to scare off the twins.

Dani spun out a dozen or more scenarios they could encounter upon arriving, as she directed Liz back to the stone house in the dark. They'd arrive first and Elliott and the ambulance—and more important, the portrait—would be MIA. They'd arrive and Archer would be there waiting. They'd arrive and Archer *and* her mother would be there waiting.

They'd arrive and it would turn out everyone had been playing dumb and in on the real plan except for Dani.

That version hurt the most. The plausibility of it. She'd been gone a long time, her penance invisible to them, and the last thing they understood was the why of her betrayal. Not just of her mother. She'd endangered the whole crew. Could she really be angry if the crew twisted the knife in her gut now? Wouldn't that be simply what she deserved?

None of us deserve this. Maeve didn't.

She hung on to that as Liz's headlights lit up the two-lane highway out of Lexington. They were almost to the house, the trees zipping past, the canopy inviting some meandering tourist and not a van driving way too fast.

"Before we get there," Liz said, "you have to know, Mia really didn't know about any of this other stuff. About Rabbit or . . ."

"Or her helping break my mom out of jail while we did the heist? I believe you."

She almost meant it. She *wanted* to believe. She'd filled Liz in on the general situation after she'd collected herself.

"Dani, you should know—she was afraid of your mom back then. She told me you were right. That what you did, she understood it."

Mia might never have been able to tell her the same. Liz had done Dani a kindness.

"Thanks," Dani said and meant it. "Archer—he changed her. She might not have been the most conventional mom before, no mother-of-the-year contender, but she chose him."

Liz kept quiet, listening and squinting at the road. The stone house came into view up ahead, dark, only noticeable because she was looking for it. *Home,* her heart said, even if she didn't want it to.

Dani shook off the need to explain. "Pull over here."

Liz raised her brows at avoiding the drive she'd used earlier, but she slowed and pulled off to the roadside as instructed.

As soon as they'd stopped, Dani opened her door. Quietly. From this side of the house, she couldn't tell if they were the first ones here or not. Which had its advantages and disadvantages. No one would know for sure about her presence, not from the back. Elliott and Mia should have gotten to the house first, since they had a head start.

"Listen, I know you aren't the type who likes to take orders," Dani said, hesitating.

"You're right," Liz said and turned off the van.

Dani reached over and put her hand on Liz's. "Please stay here. I'll send Mia to you and then you two get out of here. Whatever happens here tonight, I want her safe. And you. This is going to be between me and my mother—and Archer."

"That's one thing she didn't tell me," Liz said. "And after what you've said . . . Who *is* Archer?"

A demon. The worst kind you can imagine.

"You don't want to know. Promise me you'll wait here?"

"For at least five minutes."

Dani would have to accept it.

She slung her purse strap over her shoulder, then got out of the van, softly shutting the door. She slipped off her heels and jogged across the yard, alert for any sound or motion. When none came, she let out a low whistle, expecting it to bring Sunflower. When it didn't, she sank into the real sense of dread she'd avoided so far.

She's a smart girl, she's just hiding.

Dani sped up, flicking on the flashlight app on her phone. It occurred to her that if anyone else *was* here, they'd be expecting her. No reason to trip trying to be sneaky.

When she rounded the house, she spotted an unfamiliar painter's van and Rabbit's pickup truck in the drive ahead. No ambulance. Her spirits plunged further into the mire. She turned off the light and crept forward as if she fought against mud for each step. She'd never actually considered that Elliott might not follow her order to come here.

But there were people spread out, talking to one another ahead, in the field just past the yard, not far from the cellar studio. Under the only one of the old security lights that still worked. Dani hurried in the direction of several figures in silhouette, unable to identify them all at this distance.

She passed a shaggy bush and nearly tripped as something grabbed at her ankle. How she kept quiet, she didn't know, but somehow she swallowed her yelp of surprise.

Sunflower tugged her down by the fabric of her dress, pulling her out of sight. Back behind the old, overgrown landscaping border.

Tears stung Dani's eyes. Whatever else happened, Sunflower was all right. Her dog licked her face. Then she loped forward a few steps, turning to wait for Dani.

Dani's throat grew tight. She was ridiculous. She knew that.

She knew it was cosmically sad to hang on to the fact that her dog thought she could handle whatever was going on up ahead. That her dog stood there, waiting on her to save a day that might not be salvageable.

"Good girl," Dani said, low.

Two swipes of a white-tipped tail in the darkness.

Dani followed her dog, pausing when they neared the group. Turned out the gang was all here, except for her.

The ambulance guys must have dropped Elliott and Mia and the painting. She could still hope Elliott had arrived first.

The fallout shelter door lay open, the glow of the light on downstairs visible. The easel she'd mentioned to Elliott was set up in the long grass with Archer's portrait on it. She didn't see the demon himself anywhere. The sheet the stolen painting had been wrapped in to hide it lay on the ground nearby.

She'd have to get closer to be sure of anything.

Rabbit and Mia clutched at each other to one side, while Elliott faced off with her mother. Maria stood in a pair of black jeans and a black long-sleeved top—no hospital scrubs for her. She was maybe a half dozen steps away from the portrait, but Elliott blocked her access to it.

Dani considered how best to announce her presence, walking faster. Archer stepped from the shadows just as Sunflower growled to alert her.

"Finally, Danielle, you join us," he said. "It didn't seem right to start without you."

CHAPTER THIRTY

EVERYONE TURNED TO watch Dani's approach.

Elliott had shed his tuxedo jacket somewhere between here and the gala. The sleeves of his white shirt were rolled up, his hands clenched into fists. "He means we've been waiting for you to tell us what to do."

He stared at her across the lit-up ground and Dani wished her magic involved telepathy. Maybe then she'd be up to giving orders.

"Dani," her mother purred. "You did good tonight, honey."

Dani had heard those exact words before. As soon as she'd turned fifteen and begun asking more questions. By the time she kept demanding to know who Archer was, and her mother tried to erase her memories, it was a standard end to any job.

Even seeing the lies, understanding what her mother had done to her, those words had been the sweetest of rewards. She'd longed and waited for them. That they rang false, finally, came with as much shock as anything else tonight.

Even moments ago, Dani would have sworn she still needed to hear those words. That she still needed to believe them. That accepting a pittance would be enough for her.

She shrugged. "I was at something of a disadvantage, given some of my team didn't show. And some unexpected people did." She glanced at Rabbit, wearing dark coveralls, and then Mia, who stood straight, on an obviously fine leg, just as Liz had assured her.

"I did what I could to make sure you were taken care of," Rabbit said. She held tight to Mia's arm, looking at the work of art Elliott partially blocked, and then at Archer.

Dani could sympathize. The eerie resemblance, the sense of being off that radiated from both the painting and the man, they could be hard to turn away from. It felt too much like leaving your back to a threat.

"I'm sorry," Mia said.

"You didn't know." Dani believed both Liz and Mia. *Liz.* Shit, Liz wouldn't wait much longer. "Liz's waiting for you—you should get out of here."

"I knew something was wrong," Mia said. "I should have told you."

"Go," Dani said.

Rabbit nodded. "Go home, baby."

"I'm not leaving you all here with . . ."

"Who? Me?" Maria scoffed.

"Him," Mia said. "We should have stayed together. All of us."

"Whose fault was that?" Maria said.

"Yours as much as Dani's," Mia said, even as Rabbit shook her head and shushed her. Mia shrugged her off.

"Later, girls," Maria said. "The time to do this is later."

The night breeze swayed the long grass around them.

Dani wondered if Liz had the sense to stay out of this. No, that wasn't the question, was it? What she'd do depended on how much she cared about Mia. Dani suspected that meant she would definitely insert herself, sooner than later.

"Anyway, tonight was fine," Dani said to her mother. "As you reminded me the other day, I'm a Poissant. I managed."

"So you did," Maria said. "We better get on with it, then."

Dismissive. She didn't like Dani claiming their name here, now.

"If you say so." Dani felt Sunflower nudge her knee. She should have taken her Taser from her bag before she joined this party.

Archer lifted his walking stick and thumped it against the ground. But it was the crack of his voice that drew her attention. "Enough. I am owed my freedom."

"Mom." The term passed Dani's lips before she could stop it. "You can't mean to go through with this."

Dani moved closer to her—and to the painting. Sunflower stuck to her side. She paused and clicked her tongue. "Go hide," she said.

Sunflower resisted, which Sunflower never did. Dani clicked her tongue once more and jerked her head. Sunflower slunk off into the yard, back toward the house. She might be able to keep Liz at bay.

"Impressive," Archer said dryly. "I know how difficult it can be to get a bitch to follow orders."

Maria threw her head back and laughed.

Dani had never quite been able to understand her mother's relationship with Archer. Because the more she remembered, the more she thought back, it hadn't just been Archer whispering to her in the dark downstairs. No, Dani had heard conversations. They'd been talking together back then. How had she not understood before? Her mother's loyalties rested with him above all.

Not with Dani or even the rest of Maria's old crew. Her supposed family. She was completely in his thrall, the same way Rabbit was to Maria, ever loyal. But the Poissant women weren't susceptible to his power. No, Maria had *chosen* Archer.

And if tonight went how Maria wanted, she would get her dream of being limitless—after all, she'd undoubtedly produce an endless supply of misery for Archer's delectation. Dani shuddered to think of the two of them together. The bitterest of ends to what had begun a century plus ago. Of that Dani had no doubt whatsoever.

Maria finally sobered, though she continued to smirk. Her lips were classic red, the angry scar-to-be fainter—of course she'd do her makeup for her escape act. She put her hands on her hips, and likely only Dani noticed the tilt to one side to accommodate her knife wound. "Elliott, move it."

Tidy, commanding, it was almost like no time had passed, the ten years gone in a blink, and Dani trying to remember she wasn't a girl anymore. Trying not to regress, to hold on to who she was now. Who she'd grown into.

"Chop, chop, pretty boy," Maria said with a wink.

"Do as she says." Archer's command was frosty.

Elliott continued to look to Dani. "What do you want?"

"She wants to finish this and let me run off into the sunset," Maria said. "Don't you, honey? That's best for both of us."

Sunflower barked her high-pitched "pay attention" bark and Dani looked over to see Liz running across the yard toward them. Mia met her halfway and they argued. Liz no doubt trying to convince Mia to leave with her, and Mia trying to convince Liz to leave without her.

The authorities would arrive, sooner or later. They didn't have long. If Dani held her mother off until then . . .

Archer must have sensed her thoughts.

"You agreed to do a job for me," he said.

"And so I did it," Dani said. "There's your portrait. I didn't agree to anything else."

"I explained to her that we owe you," Maria said. "But don't worry, I'm the only one you need now."

Archer took a few steps closer to Dani. "You have no idea how she worried about you, Danielle."

Part of Dani wanted to say, *Really?* in all sincerity. But she knew the answer. Did he think she was that weak, that easily fooled? Did her mother? Instead she shook her head.

"Mom, how could you do this? All of this? For him?" Her mother had let Archer get close. She'd welcomed him, plotted with him.

To willingly join forces with a demon?

It had taken Dani a lifetime to see that her mother was not the titan of her childhood. Humans were simple, she'd taught Dani that.

Somehow Dani had never seen her mother as one before. Never seen how simple she was, what she craved, even when she'd said it.

She would have used her ability on Dani, and still Dani hadn't recognized what her mother *was*.

Of course her grandmother hid the diary from Maria. She must have known what would happen. And then Maria had hidden part from Dani to protect Archer. Every generation of Poissant women had wanted to guard against or get rid of Archer, except for Dani's mother. She saw him as the partner of her dreams.

"I have my charms," Archer said with the ghost of a smile.

"He's the only one of you who can give me what I want. What I deserve."

She wanted power. No limits.

"And then, you fucked it all up. And you left me alone in the dark, all of you, and he was still there. Waiting." She pinned Dani in place with a steady gaze, her eyes gleaming under the security light. "Being caged is a terrible thing. You wouldn't know."

The words hit their mark. She'd caged up her mother. Just as Maeve had trapped Archer.

But Archer was a demon. Not only that, Maria had traded her loyalty away to him long before Dani's betrayal.

Her mother extended her hand to Archer, an invitation.

In long strides, Archer crossed the ground, pausing to shove Dani out of the way to go to her mother. Elliott flew to Dani's side and caught her. Mia and Liz rejoined the group and Liz said, "Someone should call the cops."

"No," Rabbit said. "They have no place in this."

Dani could see Liz calculating how the art thief on the lam didn't square with that. Mia's girlfriend wore her worry and fear openly. But to her credit, she stayed, holding Mia's hand tightly in her own.

Just as Elliott held Dani. They watched together as the teeth in the monstrous creature's head on top of Archer's walking stick grew, longer, sharper. A flash of gold. He lifted it, his grip on the polished wood tight beneath the adornment.

Maria still held her hand out, waiting.

Archer lowered the walking stick in a slash to her palm, a clean slice. Blood seeped from the wound and Maria smiled at him, calculating, victorious.

"What do we do?" Elliott asked Dani, low.

It was too late. Dani couldn't speak. The air around them thickened. Her nostrils almost clogged with it. She shook her head again.

Her mother bared her neck, laughing, and held out her arm. Archer linked his through it, as if they were on some sort of promenade together. As if her hand wasn't stained red with her own blood. Poissant blood. He escorted her to the painting.

The darkness rushed through Dani—the same shadows that threatened when she made her forgery, when she looked too closely at Archer, when she opened herself to him.

She had to fight to keep it out.

With each step the strange couple took, shadows swirled and pooled like dark flame around their feet, licking through the air. Her mother reached out to the painting with her bloody palm and dragged it down the image of Archer's pale features.

Archer gasped, as if in pain.

For just a second, Dani thought she'd freed him. Reality seemed to glitch, the air filled with electricity as it had been in the studio, and then there was deep, slow silence.

Archer shoved Maria aside, even as the slick of blood shone on her palm. Her mouth dropped open.

He peered into the painting, into the smear over his face. He narrowed his black eyes. His frustration became rage, evident in the way his loose confidence seemed to coil, in preparation for him to strike like a snake. Shadows gathered around him, the same way Maeve had painted him, had seen him.

"Where is it?" he demanded. "What is this?"

Maria stumbled in front of Dani, grabbed her bare arms.

"What did you do?" Maria asked as she bled on Dani. "What did you do now?"

Dani grinned fiercely. "Exactly what I meant to."

CHAPTER THIRTY-ONE

WHAT DANI HAD done was make a painting. A copy. A second forgery. A second frame, faked up to look close to the original's. She'd left the extra copy in the fallout shelter. Her intention had been to lure Archer here, have Elliott burn the real painting while she made a show of freeing Archer from the fake. Finishing what Maeve had begun so long ago. She'd counted on Rabbit's loyalty to her mother and kept the whole plan to herself. She'd been right.

But Elliott had placed Dani's forgery on the easel, just as she'd hoped and hinted for him to.

Her plan obviously hadn't worked out as a whole. But the upper hand was still hers.

And Archer knew it. As he roared, the air stayed thick with shadows.

Dani watched as his eyes found her. "You shouldn't have done that," he said. "There will be consequences."

"You think?" Dani asked.

"I do not think you understand," Archer said. "You won't be the one who bears them."

Maria released Dani's arms then, and did something Dani had

never imagined, not once. She didn't just choose Archer. She went to stand by his side *against* Dani.

"Don't be a fool, Dani," her mother said.

Archer and her mother were a united force.

"Where is *my* portrait, Dani? Produce it."

"Tell him. *You* owe *me* this," her mother said.

The two of them began to creep closer to Dani, the overhead light at their backs making their tandem shadows reach out toward her. And then to Elliott.

As Elliott tried to block their access to Dani. "Stay back," he said.

"You can end this," Archer said to Dani.

"End what?" Dani asked. "I will never free you."

"Have it your way," Archer said. And with a cold smile, he fixed his attention on Elliott. He held out his arm and grabbed Elliott by the throat. "Tell me where it is, lover boy," he said.

"Tell him," Dani's mother echoed. She'd try to manipulate Dani into it if there weren't so many people around, Dani would bet on it. And if Archer was free, she might even be able to.

Elliott did his best to fight off Archer.

"Let him go," Dani said, ripping at Archer's arm.

"You can stop this at any time," he said.

"Don't," Elliott forced out. His eyes were shut, his face twisted.

Rabbit was crying, and she started toward Elliott and Dani.

Maria aimed her plea at Rabbit, and Mia and Liz. "Help me finish this," she said. "Rabbit, I need you to make her see . . ."

"What can we do?" Mia grabbed at her mother's arm. "Wait."

"I have to help him," Rabbit said and shook off Mia's hand.

"His death will be your fault, Danielle," Archer said. "And for what? I will prevail."

Elliott's face purpled and he kept his eyes screwed shut, struggling. Rabbit joined Dani in tearing at Archer's arm. He finally dropped his grip on Elliott's throat, but shadows swarmed around Elliott instead.

"Maria, make him stop," Rabbit said. "Please. I've never asked you for anything."

"Only Dani can stop this," Maria said, self-satisfied.

Rabbit looked at her in horror. Dani wished both that it hadn't taken Rabbit so long to see the truth of Maria, and that she'd never been forced to.

Dani tried to reestablish some veneer of being in control. She had to find some way to save Elliott without dooming all of them. Without letting her mother—or worse, Archer—win.

"Mom . . . did you ever love me? Care at all? If you did . . ." It was weak, but she had to try.

Elliott continued to moan and shake, Rabbit attempting and failing to comfort him with reassuring murmurs.

Archer's smile was icy. "She wanted a powerful ally. You were a fail-safe for me. Another source of Poissant blood. That's all."

"Mom," Dani said and sidestepped him to look directly at her, "is that true?"

Her mother stayed cool. "Make it stop, Dani. Give him what he wants."

Rabbit held Elliott, reached for Dani. "Dani, do what she says. You know it's the only way. Hers is always the only way."

"I don't," Dani said. "It's not."

She suddenly needed Rabbit to know. Needed all of them to. If this was where it ended, they deserved that.

Dani lifted her voice. "Do you know why I flipped all those years ago?" She pointed at Archer's grinning death's-head. "She tried to steal my memories—for him. Because I asked about him."

Rabbit blinked at her. "What in the devil's hell do you mean?"

"She's lying, Rabbit." Maria sounded spooked. *Good.*

"The police or the feds have got to be headed here by now," Mia said. Liz still hung on to her hand like it was life itself.

"You should go," Dani said to them. "Let us finish this."

Rabbit let go of Elliott. She came over and grabbed Dani's arm. Dani had never seen this particular expression on her face. Stricken. "What do you mean she . . . she tried to take your memories?"

"She thought she used her magic on me," Dani said. "She didn't want me to know who Archer was. But it didn't work on me—I hid that from her. I wasn't the only one who broke the rules."

It was very bad form to apply your magic to your allies in the secret world, and all the more if they didn't invite it. You certainly didn't do it without asking permission first.

Archer had been distracted enough that Elliott's eyes were open and he was on his feet. He moved closer to Archer and Dani wanted to scream at him to run instead.

Rabbit blinked again, rapidly. She paced through the grass and then she threw her arms up in the air. She paced back and forth one more time, agitated, then she stalked over and grabbed Maria's arm.

"You've done it to me too, haven't you?" Rabbit's voice was sad. "Stolen things . . . Made me do them . . ."

"Oh no," Mia said. "Oh, Mom . . ."

Rabbit nodded, fast bobs of her chin up and down. "I never felt right about the way we froze out Dani. But I was so *certain*. So certain I had to do what you said. Now I know why. Maria, how could you? I would've done anything for you."

Maria lacked the grace—or the ability—to even pretend guilt about it. "I did what I needed. It worked out fine for you."

"Dani, what are we going to do with *her*?" Elliott said, hoarse but recovering, pointing to Maria. "Are we handing her over?"

"I have to get rid of the painting," Dani said. "Before anything else. Where'd you put it?"

"No," Archer said. "It's mine!"

Archer moved toward the open fallout shelter. Of course he'd be able to find the painting, given a moment. He was tied to it.

Elliott gave a grim nod of confirmation in the opening's direction.

"It's ready," Elliott said. "Waiting for you."

"Slow him down if you can," she said.

Elliott leaped into action, grabbing on to the back of Archer's coat. Archer roared his disapproval and they began to grapple.

"What should we do?" Mia called out.

Rabbit and Mia were waiting for her order, for her cue. They weren't running. They knew the truth now. None of them were running.

"I got this," Dani said, and she bolted for the fallout shelter's opening. "Help Elliott."

"No," Archer said. And then, with satisfaction, "Maria, stop her. Kill her if you must."

Maria transformed to a vengeful wraith. "Honey, this is your chance *not* to be a disappointment," she said.

Dani looked from the cellar opening to her mother. Dani bolted toward it as Elliott and the others grappled with Archer and his shadows.

Her mother followed, just as she'd been ordered.

Dani fought off her mother's attempted grab. She just had to get down there.

She dropped down onto the ladder, descending quickly. The gas can and the old-fashioned silver lighter sat next to the other easel.

And there was Sunflower, guarding the painting and her supplies.

Her dog had eventually hidden, all right. After alerting them to Liz's presence, she'd made her way into Dani's studio.

Dani grabbed the gas can and soaked Maeve's portrait of Archer as quickly as she could, the fumes splashing and stinging her nose. She set down the empty can and seized the lighter.

Maria pounded down the steps, catching up to her. The two of them were alone—well, except for Sunflower. Dani had to be careful, get Sunflower over to the steps before she set the painting on fire. She clicked her tongue and motioned with her head.

Sunflower growled as Maria stepped off the ladder.

The small studio that surrounded them wasn't exactly the safest place for a blaze, but there was no better option.

"Sunflower, go," Dani said, but the dog lingered, bucking her order again.

"You named her Sunflower?" Maria said. Blood from her wound streaked her injured cheek, as she reached up to push her hair out of her face. "Sentimental, but you always were. Weak. Tender."

"I wasn't," Dani said. And Dani knew it for the truth it was. She had never been weak.

"You were," Maria said softly. "I have always done the hard parts. I'm the only one of us with the stomach for greatness."

Maria moved closer.

"Sunflower, go," Dani said. She needed to set the painting on fire.

"You'll listen to what I tell you to do. You'll be a good girl, honey."

Dani realized with horror that her mother was trying to manipulate her again.

"Sunflower, out," she ordered.

Sunflower slunk to the stairs and waited, tail down.

"Now," Dani said.

Her dog turned and put two paws on the stairs, then began to climb.

"Stop what you're doing," Maria said. She sounded desperate, even to Dani's ears. "We can be a family again."

Sunflower was safe. It was time to finish this.

"Mom, listen to me," Dani said, voice shaking. "Your shit doesn't work on me. It never has."

"It was worth a shot," Maria said, but Dani heard the surprise under it.

Dani wished, desperate too, that she could change her mother's mind. Her heart. "Do you really think you can trust a demon's word? But you can fix this. All of it. The past. Right now."

Maria had paused and Dani wondered if she was listening. Finally. Or if she was too far gone, incapable of it.

"You can do the right thing. This one time. Help me destroy him."

Maria hesitated. "What will I have left then?"

Dani's throat tightened. She couldn't promise anything, except: "Me. I'll still be left. I'll always be your daughter."

"Dani?" Elliott called from above. "He's coming."

"Help me. We have to be quick," Dani said, holding up the lighter.

Archer appeared in front of them, in that sudden way he always showed up. "Excellent job, Maria," he said.

Now or never. Dani had to give her mother one last chance. She'd never be able to forgive herself otherwise. Even if it meant her story ended here too.

"Mom," Dani said as Archer advanced on her, murder in his eyes. He reached his thin white fingers toward Dani.

Dani flicked the lighter to life, and Maria lunged, trying to stop her. But Dani kicked her away, like the fighter she knew she was. She'd given Maria a chance, but she was done. Her mother had chosen, and so had she.

Dani touched the licking flame to the painting, and Archer and Maria froze.

For a second, it was as if the makeshift studio had the kind of fancy security system in place that protected galleries. Something that would suck all the air from the room, keep the art from being destroyed. But the gas soaked the painting and when it caught, the air crackled and roared. Black fingers of smoke and shadow surrounded them as Archer cried out in unmistakable pain.

Dani's skin heated and she heard Elliott screaming for her from above, heard Sunflower barking. Her mother stumbled toward her as Archer careened to the painting and returned to the canvas. Once it absorbed him and his shadows, it flared with new heat. His body burst back out of the flames, and her mother clawed her way toward him as Dani backed away.

His face was immobile before he exploded into a cloud of dust— just as Maeve's first tormentor had. Her mother's hands caught nothing but a memory.

The fire spread quickly to Dani's art supplies. It was time to go.

"Come on," Dani said. "Come on." She encouraged Maria when her mother faltered, pulling her to the stairs before they caught. She might no longer anticipate a reunion, but she couldn't leave Maria to die.

The rungs' heat scorched Dani's fingers, but they had to get out. Her mother's self-preservation instinct must have kicked in because she clawed her way up behind Dani.

Her small, unusual family met them both, pulling them clear of the fallout shelter.

Dani collapsed in the grass and Sunflower licked her face. Elliott leaned over her, making a quick check of her exposed skin. "I think she's okay," he said. "Some minor burns."

"Archer's gone," Dani said, pushing up to her elbows, coughing. "Throw in the other painting. Let it all burn."

"Maria seems to be okay too," Rabbit said. She and Mia crouched beside Maria's prone body. She didn't sound thrilled about it.

Liz took care of the painting, her grace evident in every motion of tossing it in, then dancing away from the heat radiating from the fallout shelter.

Dani heard a sob tear from her mother. She mourned Archer. Still. Her ambition was a darkness that consumed her, left room for nothing else. It had taken Dani so long to see it.

The wail of sirens sounded in the distance, growing closer. This tableau would take some explaining.

"Dani?" a voice she recognized asked.

Elliott answered instead of her. "Brad, what are you doing here?"

"I wanted to make sure Dani was okay. She wasn't answering her phone . . . The authorities are behind me."

Elliott put an arm around Dani, helping her sit. She coughed but protested at Brad's rushing over to her other side. "I'm fine," she said. "I'm okay."

"We need to get you to a doctor," Brad said.

"Stop your fussing," Mia said.

Dani wanted to laugh. And then she heard Rabbit say, "Maria?" She raised her voice. "Maria?"

Dani sat up and saw Rabbit had called it. Maria was nowhere to be seen. She'd taken off on foot.

"Where do you think she'd go?" Rabbit put her hands on her hips.

The sirens had stopped, but flashing lights punctured the darkness around the house. New voices were audible in the distance.

Dani took off, running for her memories, and for her mother. She didn't know what Maria had planned next or what her state of mind was. The rest of them joined her, all breathing hard by the time they reached the house.

The authorities were calling out, men and women in FBI vests. Brad waved toward them. "I'll talk to them. Get your stories straight."

Dani nodded, grateful for the intercession. She went for the door, but Elliott ushered her back.

"She won't go home," he said.

Dani understood the truth of it. Her feelings for the stone house? They weren't her mother's. She'd still be bent on escape.

Dani faced the rest of their crew, her family, and Liz, who she thought just might be their newest member. "You remember what she always told us—when you get in the weeds, the plan completely off the rails, never forget the power of a good distraction. Which all this now is for her," she said. "Stay here."

Sunflower nudged her leg and Dani followed her lead. They looped around the yard on the house's far side, which no one had bothered with yet. Dani might have spent years separated from Maria, but she knew her enough. She had a suspicion Sunflower was herding her in exactly the right direction. The police and FBI agents were busy shouting about getting a fire engine in the field before the woods went up. Others were heading toward the house for a search.

If Dani hadn't been looking, even she would have missed the petite figure limping toward the two vehicles parked alongside the road. Liz's van and Brad's shiny black sports car behind it. The cars were just far enough from the responders to avoid being a priority.

As if she felt Dani's eyes land on her, her mother stopped and turned to face her. Dark tension hovered between them.

Dani could raise the alarm. She could send her mother back to prison, where some would argue she belonged. But she'd done that once before, and she'd regretted it.

She lifted her hand and nodded, not sure if she'd regret this or not.

Her mother got into Brad's car—and either hot-wired it or he'd left the keys in—did a three-point with the headlights off and drove away.

No one noticed. Sunflower stayed beside Dani, not shying away from the noise of the various responders behind them.

"I won't ever leave you, my good girl," Dani said.

They walked back to rejoin the party that was nothing like the gala that had begun the evening.

She reached Brad, separating off from an agent to meet her. "I owe you an explanation if you want one," she started, and he held up a hand and then glanced over at Elliott.

Elliott stared at them from a clump with Rabbit, Mia, and Liz. They were watching the chaos around them.

"It's all right," Brad said. "I was going to give you the house anyway. But just to be sure . . . You're going with him, right? Emmett?"

"Keep it under your hat, but his name is Elliott," Dani said it low. "You should know, Bradford Hackworth, especially to be so loaded, you're a good guy."

"That must be why I finished last."

"Somehow, I think you'll muddle through," Dani said and gave him a kiss on the cheek.

"I will," he said with irony.

"What you're doing, the foundation, that's good."

"You could be part of that good."

"It's not my way," Dani said. "Although, admittedly, I'm still fig-uring out what my way looks like." She peered up at the stone house and then back to Brad. "Sell this place. I don't need it anymore."

It was time to move forward, to make new memories. To let go of the idea that she and her mother would ever reunite in a real way.

Brad gave her a small smile. Genuine. "If you ever change your mind about any of it, look me up."

An SUV screeched to a stop and Agent Sharpe jumped out. He scanned the crowd and then headed straight for Dani, two men behind him who looked intent on an arrest.

Brad cut them off. "Leave her be. You can question her later."

And so Dani went to Elliott, who met her halfway. She put one hand, still raw from the fire's heat to Elliott's cheek.

"Are you ready to think about tomorrow?" he asked.

Archer had tortured him, and he was still here. He'd threatened Elliott because he knew, just as Dani did, that he was her weakness. No—she corrected—he was part of her strength. People you loved shouldn't be considered liabilities. She'd have to unlearn that from her mother.

"I am," she said.

And she kissed him slow and soft ready to make up for all the time they'd lost.

After, they joined the rest of the family and Elliott tucked her against his side. She felt comfortable there, and here with these people. A different kind of home than the stone house. She stood with them and said a quiet goodbye to the parts of the past she couldn't keep.

Dani didn't have to explain to the others that she'd let her mother go. She simply said, for the crew's ears only, "She'll probably land on her feet."

To which Rabbit grimaced and said, "She always does."

When the flames were finally smothered, and everyone's whereabouts accounted for, only then did anyone else realize that Maria had left in Brad Hackworth's car. The police found it abandoned in a grocery store parking lot the following day, but there wasn't any trace of her mother, despite her landing on the Most Wanted list.

Dani had lost a dream too, same as Maria had been forced to give up Archer. But, when it was truly over, she couldn't and didn't regret what had happened.

Rabbit, Mia, and even Elliott kept asking if Dani expected her to come back.

Dani didn't.

Dani had given her every last chance, and there was nothing left for her here.

SIX MONTHS LATER

CHAPTER THIRTY-TWO

"Ready?" Dani asked.

Elliott and Liz wore ski masks, as did she. Sunflower lay happily beside her. They were in the back of a van filled with paintings that Dani had spent the past few months on—some framed, and all completed with the Curator's help at sourcing materials. She'd been amused at the request.

"We could rethink this," Rabbit said, and the miracle of her work meant no static echo in their earpieces, despite her only being up in the driver's seat.

"Mom," Mia said from the passenger side. "Think how cool it's going to be."

"Minds will definitely be blown," Liz said.

"You all gang up on me," Rabbit said. "But as your elder, I deserve respect."

"And you have it," Elliott said.

Rabbit sucked her teeth.

"Three minutes," Dani said.

"Three minutes," said Rabbit, "because you are just as crazy as your mother, if less of a sociopath. We have nothing to prove."

Dani didn't argue. "Count it."

The sounds of "Jolene" started on the sound system. Then Mia began the countdown—"One, two, and go"—and Liz opened the back doors for their exit. Dani gave Sunflower a pat and told her, "Stay."

The Isabella Stewart Gardner Museum's security system was second to none these days, even as it awaited the return of thirteen missing artworks from the 1990 burglary that had been Maria Poissant's entry on the scene. And Rabbit's. The paintings had all been destroyed for safety's sake, after the endless publicity.

But Dani's magic made the impossible possible. Vermeer, Rembrandt, Manet, Degas . . . Those were Dani's work. It had turned out Rabbit had kept the bronze eagle flag finial and Shang dynasty gu beaker that were among the take, out of sentimentality. They were priceless, but far less valuable than the rest, and had been in a trunk in the barn the whole time. Tonight, eleven paintings and those two other pieces would be returned.

No one would see who or how, due to Rabbit's talents and apt timing. Carlton had been primed on negotiating for the ten-million-dollar reward after the thieves—returning rather than stealing, for once—had left the building. After all, weren't the pieces themselves worth more than information leading to their recovery? Yes, it was showy to do it this way, but the idea had proved irresistible.

Dani met Elliott's eyes, and then they leaped down onto the pavement, unloading their cargo. Bags were slung over their shoulders. The door opened with a sigh for them, the lock electronic—no match for Rabbit's mojo. The guards were dealing with a disturbance in the courtyard. A fake insert to a camera, also the work of Mia and Rabbit. The sensors were disabled. Three minutes.

Liz peeled off on the first floor, while Dani and Elliott headed up the stairs and to the Dutch Room. Here were several of the five empty gold frames left behind by the Poison Angel and her crew when they'd cut the paintings out of them. They showcased only the patterned green walls—a hopeful sign of anticipation of their former occupants' return.

Dani went to the first one, the Rembrandt's empty frame. They'd gotten the exact dimensions from the impeccable documentation of the thefts. The edges of Dani's replacement were beyond convincingly cut; Rabbit had given them the necessary guidance. Elliott assisted Dani with placing her painting carefully into the empty spot on the wall with museum putty. Identical to any viewer, Rembrandt's *Christ in the Storm on the Sea of Galilee* was her masterpiece and one of his. The ocean fairly roared as it tossed the ship in angry waves.

She and Elliott didn't have time to stop and admire their work, though Elliott did drop a quick kiss on her lips. She'd claim a lingering one in private later.

"It's beautiful," he said.

As they moved on to the next piece, Dani smiled.

"Two minutes," Mia said in her earpiece.

"We got this," Dani said.

The news of the paintings' return would spread fast. With Maria still in the wind, there were those who might theorize she'd changed her ways and returned them, but it was Dani who finally got to put things right. Beating Archer, destroying a demon, had convinced her that a life of crime could be a gift too, used on her own terms.

Because Dani's terms were making art *and* making magic. As if there were a difference.

ACKNOWLEDGMENTS

I'M NOT SURE which I believe is harder now, pulling off a heist or pulling off a heist book. Both require an impeccably talented crew. Thank you to my amazing writing group, the Moonscribers—Lee Mandelo, Alix Harrow, Ashley Blooms, Sam Milligan, Elizabeth Kilcoyne, Alex Head, Z Jackson, Christopher Rowe, and Olivia Saylor—for letting me babble about this idea, helping me brainstorm, and telling me, *Yes, write it.* To the Lexington Writer's Room, place of my heart, and the writers and board: You inspire me every day. To board member and friend Alison Kerr, thanks for your Frenchpertise. To Mur Lafferty for a retreat at the exact right time, and to Ursula Vernon, Good Kevin, and Andrea Phillips for also being there, and saving a murderbird. Kami Garcia and Sam Humphries, thank you for always being excited. And to the Friday Salon Zoom gang for being a continual highlight every week.

I'm so grateful to my agent, Kate McKean, who both helped shape the direction of this story and sold it to my dream editor and publisher. Anne Lesley Groell, you are just incredible to work with, as is everyone at Del Rey. Thanks to Ayesha Shibli, to

Madeline Hopkins for a great copyedit, and Jill De Haan for the gorgeous cover. Any errors are my own. And, last but never least, to you, dear reader, thank you for letting me steal your time and attention.

ABOUT THE TYPE

This book was set in Caledonia, a typeface designed in 1939 by W. A. Dwiggins (1880–1956) for the Mergenthaler Linotype Company. Its name is the ancient Roman term for Scotland, because the face was intended to have a Scottish-Roman flavor. Caledonia is considered to be a well-proportioned, businesslike face with little contrast between its thick and thin lines.